Retribution

Retribution

Paul Henke

To Iain,

All the best on

Father's Day!

Paul Henke.

METHUEN

First published in 2018

1

Methuen & Co
Orchard House
Railway Street
York
YO62 4AN
www.methuen.co.uk

A CIP catalogue record for this book is available from the British Library.

ISBN: 978-0-413-77778-2

Typeset by SX Composing DTP, Rayleigh, Essex.
Printed and bound in Great Britain by Clays Ltd, St Ives plc

Retribution

Prologue

The super yacht was 110 metres long, with a beam of 14 metres and a draft of 4.4 metres. She carried a crew of 28 and could accommodate 30 guests in 20 luxurious cabins. She had been built in Japan in 2012 as the toy of a very wealthy man.

She had a cruising speed of 22 knots and a top speed of 28 knots. Her fuel tanks held 563,000 litres of diesel giving her a safe range of 6,300 nautical miles with enough in her tanks for a further 500 nautical miles. She boasted an ultra-modern stabilisation system that ensured the minimum rolling motion and made cruising more enjoyable. Which was just as well as the owner was not a good sailor when it came to seasickness.

On the stern sat a military H135M helicopter painted in the owner's colours, appearing to be for civilian use only. However, in less than ten minutes hardware of a military kind could be added turning the helo into a formidable killing machine. In its civilian configuration the craft carried a pilot, navigator and six passengers. When in military mode there was only room for four passengers.

Onboard the yacht the passengers' accommodation was on two decks, the third deck was reserved for the owner and special guests. All the crew's quarters, apart from a few privileged officers, were below the waterline. The difference in opulence between the two was stark. The owner had never been below decks.

The chef was a three star accredited Michelin chef who could have had a job anywhere in the world. However, he chose to be on the yacht for two reasons. One was the money, two was the opportunity to fulfil his depraved sexual appetite, sometimes with the owner either watching or involved. Although the latter was becoming more rare as the owner's lifestyle was beginning to take its toll.

The yacht was 50 miles off the coast of Somalia, a well-known haunt of particularly vicious pirates. However, she sailed the area with perfect impunity for a number of reasons. One was due to the name of the owner and the other was what would happen to anyone stupid enough to attack the yacht. Families would die horrible and painful deaths. The pirates knew this. They had seen it happen twice.

The owner sat at his desk in his stateroom using a sat-nav telephone incorporating the latest encryption technology known to man. Anyone trying to listen to his conversations would be unable to pick up anything other than white noise. With him was his secretary, an Englishman who had been at Eton and Oxford University with him.

In both establishments they had been close friends. The owner had been small and weedy as a child and had been picked on a number of times. The bullying stopped when Geoffrey Carstairs stepped in and protected him. Carstairs had joined the British Foreign Office and was doing well until he met the owner at a reception in Riyadh, Saudi Arabia. The job Carstairs was offered was far too tempting to resist. He left the Foreign Office a month later and now, five years later, had no regrets whatsoever.

He was now rich beyond his wildest dreams and there was still more to come. His one regret was that he had never married but it was not too late. He had often read about famous people fathering a child when in their sixties. Although one prerequisite was the woman be in her thirties. Still, with his money that could be arranged.

The telephone was on loudspeaker.

'Tadeas my friend, how is it in Mecca?'

'Very well, your Excellency. As usual all is operating smoothly. I have forwarded you the latest figures. You can see that the number of slaves sold has increased by 8% year on year while actual immigrant numbers have increased by 16.7% over the same period. You will see the increase in revenue and although there has been a slight increase in operating costs this has been more than offset by the increase in gross turnover.'

'Very good. Try and keep the expenses to a minimum. We need every riyal for the war on the infidels and to further our great cause.' He knew the man he was talking to was a fanatic but it never hurt to remind people.

'I know, your Excellency, and be assured I have already informed people in the chain of command what is expected of them.'

'Good. In that case I shall enjoy reading your report.'

There were no pleasantries as the call was ended. Men like the owner did not indulge in small talk unless others initiated it, which was rarely.

'What do you think Geoff? Is he cheating me?'

Carstairs frowned, shrugged and then shook his head. 'No. It is someone else down the pipeline. I suggest the issue is left alone. You are making a great deal of money, everyone working for you is content, don't upset the apple cart for a few dollars more.'

'Huh! It's more like millions, not a few dollars.'

'That may be but it is still not worth it.'

There was a pause in the conversation for a few seconds. 'But you are right as always.'

'Thank you,' Carstairs nodded in acknowledgement of the compliment.

A female servant entered the huge room with a tray of coffee and pastries freshly baked in the kitchens.

As she leant forward to place the tray on the desk the yacht rolled a few degrees more than usual, due to a sudden squall. The coffee spilt onto the tray and a few drops splashed the owner's hand.

The young woman began to shake. The owner glowered at her, stood up and walked around the desk. She was in her late teens, a Nigerian by birth, comely and beautiful, as were all the servants on the yacht. She was also a Christian and therefore of no consequence - less than nothing beneath his feet. The owner held out his hand and the girl licked the few drops of coffee from it. Tears welled in

3

her eyes. She knew what was coming next. She had heard the stories.

'Bend over.'

'Please, your Excellency. Please. I couldn't avoid it. The ship . . .'

'Shut up, whore and bend over.'

The girl leant on the desk on her elbows. The owner was only 5ft 3ins tall with a girth to match. He was in his early fifties but looked older. He was clean-shaven, with black hair and grey sideburns. His face was round, his eyes half hidden beneath fat cheeks and drooping eyelids. He had a double chin, the fat wobbling when he spoke. A third chin was beginning to develop. He was dressed in tan slacks and a bright yellow, short-sleeved, loose shirt.

The girl was trembling uncontrollably. She wore a short smock that covered her body as far as her thighs but was not wearing any undergarments. The owner took down a cane from the bulkhead, lifted the girl's smock up to her waist and stared at her. He brought the cane down hard and the girl screamed. He did it a dozen times, hitting the girl across the buttocks and the backs of her legs. She knew that if she collapsed the beating would continue so she stayed upright.

Blood was trickling down the girl's legs and she was now sobbing, tears running down her cheeks. Carstairs looked on in complete indifference. He had seen it all before, many times in fact.

The owner sent for his head steward and waved a hand at the girl.

'She is of no further use. Share her amongst the crew and then dispose of her.'

'Yes, your Excellency.' The man inclined his head deferentially.

Carstairs knew one thing about the owner that nobody else did. He had grown impotent over the years caused by drug abuse as well as incredible sexual excesses. No amount of the little blue pill helped. So the man took his pleasure in a different form. He enjoyed inflicting pain. It was an enjoyment now shared with Carstairs though he was far from impotent.

The owner logged onto his website that he used to monitor his net wealth and nodded with satisfaction.

4

'Total assets now amount to over 15 billion dollars, the people and drug smuggling operation having added a further eight million in the last eight months. Excellent.'

He may have been 21st in line to the throne but he was wealthier than many of the princes ranked above him. Furthermore, thanks to the unique arrangement he had with the king of Saudi Arabia not only did he live a privileged and charmed life but one that was cleverly protected. He had the title of Roving Ambassador and his yacht had been given the same designation as any embassy in the world. Ludicrous as well as meaningless of course but it did help to serve his purpose. In reality it was Arabic oil coupled with the vast spending power of the Saudi royal household that kept him free from prying eyes and any foreign authority. His crew all carried diplomatic passports, which also helped should any of them be arrested.

Ibn-Mohammed Saud was a contented man. He had four wives, six children - three boys and three girls, and a dynastic family that would last for centuries. It wouldn't happen in his lifetime, he knew that, but his family would see the world turn into an Islamic idyll, where Sharia Law ruled and Islam was the only religion.

In the meantime he was arranging to have his body cryogenically frozen with strict instructions that he was to be brought back to life when his dreams had been fulfilled. Those dreams were laid down explicitly in orders registered at the palace in Saudi. It was amongst a number of such orders.

1

Commander Nick Hunter, Mine Warfare and Clearance Diving Officer (MCDO), Royal Navy, was taking a break from his duties breathing in the ancient culture of Siracusa on the south-eastern edge of Sicily. Unfortunately he had quickly become bored. So he found a dive shack and flashed his diver's log at the shop's owner and tried to hire the necessary equipment to at least get a look at the seabed. It didn't do much good. Only a PADI recognised diver could hire the gear. Hunter showed the man that he had more dives under his belt in everything from pure oxygen to mixed gases than twenty PADI diving instructors but it was of no use. The man went on about his insurance and how Hunter needed to be checked out for his diving skills. To say Hunter was as mad as hell was putting it mildly. So he hired a car, drove across the island to Palermo, bought a diving jacket, fins, bottles charged with air and a half-face mask. He also purchased a webbing belt with a dive knife plus weights.

He made three dives and after the third decided the fish weren't swimming when they waggled their tails, they were waving at him having seen him so often. The kind of diving he was doing suited most if not all sports divers. Hunter got wet in order to carry out a job - usually a dangerous one. Looking at fish and marine life did very little for him.

Hunter was 6ft 2ins tall, slim, wide shouldered and narrow hipped. He was as fit as any athlete competing in the Olympics and kept that way with regular and tough exercise. He also spent hours a week on the firing range, hours examining the mechanisms that were employed when exploding improvised explosive devices (IEDs) and many more hours pouring over intelligence reports that swept across his desk on a daily basis. But those activities were only when he was on the base. Most of the time he was on an operation usually somewhere in Europe, North Africa or the Middle East. In the last six months his hobby, if it could be called that, was learning to speak Arabic at which he was now proficient.

On the evening of his fourth day on the island, he was sitting on the terrace of the Grand Hotel Minareto enjoying the sunset and a cold beer. He had been contemplating cutting back on his leave and heading home to Scotland or maybe going parasailing or sky diving in Switzerland. He'd parasailed there before at a place near Interlaken. But a couple of hours earlier he had received a text from General Macnair, the CO of TIFAT. It had been brief and to the point. *Wait for package arriving asap.*

He took a sip of his bottled beer and wondered what that could possibly be. That took his thoughts down the track of how he had ended up doing the job he now had. To become an MCDO you had to get through one of the toughest courses open to officers in the armed forces. Two years earlier he had been offered a posting to TIFAT – The International Force Against Terrorism. He had accepted with alacrity. The navy was contracting; the number of ships in commission was ridiculously low when the demands on the service had never been greater and the chances of promotion had been significantly reduced. He may have been one of the youngest commanders in the RN but he knew he would never make Admiral. He had chosen the wrong specialisation to even be considered for such an exalted rank. Besides which, his buccaneering spirit could not be assuaged anywhere else other than with TIFAT.

TIFAT had been the result of a paper written by Colonel Malcolm Macnair, now a General and Hunter's CO, some five years earlier. He had written it whilst at a staff college for military officers in America. Some of the best brains to be found in the military attended the event. They had been there to debate and strategise how to effectively deal with the greatest scourge to affect mankind in living memory. Outright warfare, in many respects, could be dealt with. Overwhelming force on one side attacks the other and wins. Hunter knew that if the outcome suits the west then nothing is done. If it doesn't diplomatic efforts are used to conceal the iron fist in the velvet glove. Usually that meant the USA, Britain and other mainly NATO countries becoming militarily involved. But under these circumstances the enemy can be recognised. As was being shown time and again, the problem the west was facing was terrorism – Islamic terrorism perpetrated by people who were not afraid of death and also often embraced it. One statistic was truly frightening. Islamic attacks of one kind or another had occurred in 50 countries. Tens of thousands had been killed, many more thousands injured and millions displaced from their homes, most of them Muslims.

Hunter signalled a waiter for another beer, then thought about the cryptic message he had received from Rosyth.

Not for the first time Hunter pondered that the Middle East was going to hell in a basket while the west sat like rabbits caught in the headlights of a speeding train. Western democracies were paralysed. They had the might, the wherewithal to attack the enemy but first they needed to identify who that was. Even then the biggest problem of the lot raised its ugly head. Political correctness prevented reasonable steps being taken against known perpetrators of crimes such as mass bombings and people trafficking. There were those in society who claimed that using terror tactics against the terrorists was to put the west on the same level of barbarism as those who had declared war on western civilisation.

The problem was, for all their pious words, they had no solution to offer. How did you fight someone who hid in the shadows, struck when they chose the time was right and then hid behind a wall of legal rights?

Macnair argued that it was time to get down amongst the rats in the sewers and clear them out. In his paper he did not use such euphemisms as "neutralise" or "terminate with extreme prejudice" but called it for what it was. Kill the enemy before they did any further damage to the lives of people in the west as well as their own countries.

The idea was too radical for the politicians of Europe and the USA to even contemplate never mind countenance. So the military and security services indulged in a few days of make believe before re-entering the real world of dealing with terrorism with both hands and feet tied.

That state of affairs lasted for three years. Finally, one of the second term USA Presidents declared enough was enough. He had nothing to lose and on being shown Macnair's paper decided to implement his findings.

The first hurdle that had to be overcome was where to put such an organisation. It was agreed that the USA was too far from the frontline action to be of any use. Hence it had to be Europe. When approached, the European countries ran and hid like children under a blanket. The theory was all right; action was something else entirely. Just as many European politicians squawked in public about there being nuclear weapons based on European soil, so in private the majority of them agreed the weapons had been necessary to keep the peace. Mutually Assured Destruction, or MAD, had been and, to a lesser extent still was, a great deterrent to war in Europe. Forgetting of course the little sidelines such as the former Yugoslavia and the horrendous genocide committed there. After all, there had been no direct effect on the European Union.

Basing TIFAT in the UK was the logical choice. Fewer problems from the politicians at home and abroad meant they could get on with the job they were formed to do. It took a further year of negotiating, in secret, TIFAT's terms of reference. In order to succeed The International Force Against Terrorism needed to be given a free reign to get on with things. This was fine as long as few people knew what they really got up to. Macnair had already explained all this in his paper.

He proposed that TIFAT should be the military arm required to fight terrorism while working closely with the American National

Security Agency (NSA). It would also help in the collection, collation and use of information.

The NSA had created a global spy network, codename ECHELON, which captured and analysed virtually every phone call, fax, email, text and telex message sent anywhere in the world. Though controlled by the NSA, the system operated in conjunction with the UK's Government Communications Head Quarters (GCHQ), the Australian Defence Security Directorate (DSD), the Communications Security Establishment (CSE) of Canada, and the General Communications Security Bureau (GCSB) of New Zealand. These organisations were bound together under a 1948 agreement, the contents of which were still secret.

The system controlled intercept stations established across the world. They captured all satellite, microwave, fibre-optic and cellular communications traffic. This information, amounting to billions of intercepts every day, was processed through the massive computer capabilities of the NSA. These included advanced voice recognition and optical character recognition programs and looked for code words or phrases (known as the ECHELON Dictionary) that prompted the computers to flag the message for recording and transcribing for future investigation. Due to the dozens of languages and different forms of writing, the task was enormous. Macnair's paper suggested that when it came to information assessing and disseminating, TIFAT would concentrate on the Middle East, North Africa and Mediterranean areas.

That was TIFAT's cover. Their real task was to track down and kill any and all terrorists that had been identified by the Security Services worldwide. Their successes and achievements were legendary but that of itself created its own problems.

There had been one massive problem that had been ignored by Europe's politicians. It was a fact that made Hunter's blood boil. The people who had wanted the UK to remain in the EU argued that the country would be safer. That fighting terrorism would be easier within the confines of the legislative body in Brussels. The truth, as acknowledged in private by the west's security services, was that the opposite was true. This was thanks to a ruling by the European Court of Justice. It had ruled that any and all intercepts of European citizens could only be kept for a total of 36 hours and then had to be removed and destroyed. Everyone involved in the war on terrorism knew this to be not only ludicrous but self-defeating. Information gleaned needed to be kept for many months if not years. There was no statutory limit on when an attack would take place. The UK had been threatened with daily fines if it did not comply. Leaving the European Union was the solution. Cooperation between the security services would continue at the same high level already in force. Politicians would be sidelined as much as possible. This was in spite of the fact they were forever interfering where they were not wanted and causing a great deal of damage.

Hunter took another drink of his beer and grinned. Politicians weren't much of a match when up against someone as formidable as his boss, General Malcolm Macnair. He was still wondering about the package when he heard a familiar voice.

'Hi boss, no bird in tow?'

Hunter looked over his shoulder. Although he didn't show it, he was surprised to see the three men walking towards him. They were tough looking, fit, and had an alertness about them, looking around as they walked across the patio, carrying their holdall bags in their left hands. They were the sort of men you wouldn't want to pick an argument with. It was Badonovitch who had called out to him.

Hunter grinned. Their presence could only mean one thing – an operation was about to kick-off somewhere nearby. Unless they were also on leave and had decided to get away together. Hunting in packs was the inelegant way that Hughes put it.

'The General said to expect a package but I didn't expect to see you three ugly mugs. A job?'

'Yes, boss,' replied Masters, technically the most senior of the three men but rank meant little in TIFAT, except when it came to General Macnair.

Sgt Don Masters was a REME, a Royal Electrical and Mechanical Engineer. He was of average height and build and a legend in the Regiment when it came to handling all types and makes of explosives.

Jan Badonovitch was ex-Russian Spetsnaz and an ex-NCO. At 5ft 6ins and wide shouldered he was one of the toughest men Hunter had ever known.

Sgt David Hughes, SAS was 5ft 10ins tall and wiry. He could run a marathon and keep going. His stamina was well known, as was his success with the ladies. He was also one of the finest shots with a rifle or handgun anywhere in any armed forces.

A waiter approached the table as they pulled out chairs and sat down. They ordered beers all round. The terrace was wide and broad and there was nobody in earshot but even so they lowered their voices.

'So what's up?' asked Hunter.

'We had a call from the Eyeties,' said Badonovitch. 'One of their ships intercepted a boatload of illegals. One of them said that a gang of smugglers is operating in Tripoli, using a beach about ten kilometres to the west.'

Just then the waiter reappeared and placed beers in front of the three men along with a bowl of pistachio nuts.

'Cheers,' said Hughes, picking up his glass, condensation trickling down its side. The others repeated the toast and took long and appreciative gulps of their drinks.

'What are we expected to do about it?' Hunter asked reasonably. 'I thought all this area was covered by the Italians and the French with a bit of help from the RN.'

'It is,' said Master, 'but according to the information we've been sent this is a particularly nasty gang who are in effect members of ISIL.'

Nodding, Hunter said, 'So what?'

'As you know, Nick,' said Don Master, 'that they are the Islamic State of Iraq and the Levant – Libya Province.'

'Yeah. Formed by Abu Mohammed al-Baghdadi in 2014, I think it was. One man who needs a bullet in the head.'

'He has to be one of the vilest people on the planet,' said Hughes.

'He is,' replied Hunter, 'and he seems to revel in the title.'

'There are three branches, I suppose we can call them,' went on Masters, 'one in Cyrenaica in the east of Libya, Fezzan in the southern desert and Tripolitania in the west.'

'I didn't know that,' said the Commander, 'but we've never been directly involved with the smugglers. Too much pussy-footing around as far as I'm concerned.'

'We're with you there, boss,' said Badonovitch, 'but it seems this guy al-Baghdadi runs the smuggling from Tripolitania and sometimes takes a very personal interest in what's going on. According to our Intel that's what he'll be doing in thirty-six hours or so from now.' He glanced at his watch. 'Maybe forty hours.'

'And we're going to do something about it?'

'That's the general idea,' said Masters.

'When Jan said al-Baghdadi takes a personal interest in smuggling the refugees he means just that,' said Hughes. 'It seems he travels where he likes when he likes.'

'You've got to be kidding me. How is that possible?'

'Ever seen a photo of the man?' Hughes asked. He signalled to a waiter, waved his finger around the table and held up his hand indicating four beers. He also picked up the empty bowl of nuts as a gesture for a refill.

Hunter frowned, thinking about it. 'Yeah, once. One of the dozens of photographs we were shown of wanted terrorists and smugglers. But I don't remember him being in the top ten or even top twenty of the most wanted. It was also a lousy photo but most of them are.'

'A year ago,' said Masters, 'he was barely acknowledged. Didn't even make the top hundred.'

'I remember now,' said Hunter. 'We had a report a couple of months ago about the smugglers and his name was in it somewhere.'

'Well, he appears to have gone up in the rankings and is now in the top ten of most wanted by the Yanks and by us.'

The beers arrived and the men drank deeply. This time the bowl placed on the table contained salted peanuts.

13

'So where is he?'

'Here, according to our info.'

'On the island?'

Masters nodded.

'How sure are we?'

The team exchanged shrugs. 'Boss,' said Badonovitch, 'you know what it's like. The Intel comes via the Cousins from the Eyeties. The NSA is pretty good at sorting the wheat from the chaff. They've said that the info the Italians have supplied ties in with electronic messages that have been clogging up the ether.'

'Why doesn't somebody just arrest him?'

Masters answered. 'If he's here and not caught red handed committing a crime then what do we do about him? Arrest him? Try him where? What witnesses are there? Punish him how? Hell Nick, you know all this.'

'Of course. What I'm getting at is when it comes to this particular man. Don't we have enough proof to go down the legal route?'

'The question never arose,' said Hughes.

'Why not?'

'The Italians have told us that the man is here to instill discipline in the route they are using. And we know what that means.'

Hunter knew all too well. A few beatings if the recipient was lucky, a couple of hands cut off if they weren't but that was also usually followed by the victims' heads. ISIL was a truly vicious and evil organisation the likes of which was last seen in Germany in the 1930s when people were gassed to death because of their religion.

'What are the Italians saying and how did they come by the information?'

'When they stopped a boat two nights ago,' said Masters, 'it was the usual. Twenty-five illegals in an inflatable built for ten. Six were kids under the age of six, four were young teens and the rest were men in their twenties. Oh, and two women also in their twenties. They were Nigerians and Sudanese and had no papers.'

Hunter nodded, raising his glass and taking an appreciative drink.

'One of the men admitted immediately that he was one of the smugglers,' said Badonovitch, 'and asked to be given asylum. It seems he'd been a part of the smuggling crew for three months. He claims to have been coerced, with his parents and sisters threatened with torture and death.'

'What can you tell me about him?'

'He has a knack for languages. He speaks Arabic, English and Italian. His name is Ahmad Samara and he is a university graduate from the Al-Manar University of Tripoli and, listen to this, is also a trained architect.'

'Sounds like the kind of person we could use in Europe,' said Hunter, 'but I don't get it. If his family is being threatened why did he come with the refugees?'

'It seems that in spite of what he was doing ISIL killed his family. He was told it had been an error, an overzealous local commander exercising his control in the area. Samara decided to come across and tell us about al-Baghdadi. It seems he also helped on the boat. He sneaked a dozen lifejackets onboard as well as some bailers. He organised the men to work in watches, continuously bailing out the boat. Even using their clothes to swab the bottom of the boat, just to give it that bit more buoyancy. They ran out of petrol about halfway across and he again organised them. There were six oars on board and he got them rowing, three a side, half an hour each shift.'

'Sounds quite a guy,' said Hunter. 'Is it true?'

'According to the Eyeties it is. All confirmed by the others.'

'And he's the one with the information about Abu Mohammed al-Baghdadi?'

'He is, only there's a snag,' said Masters.

Hunter sighed. 'There usually is. What is it?'

'He wants to come with us.'

Hunter sat silently for a few seconds while he took a sip of his beer before shaking his head. 'No chance. We don't take passengers.'

Masters said, 'We told the General you'd say that.'

'And what did he say?'

'Basically, tough. Samara won't tell us where to find al-Baghdadi but will take us to him.'

'Why does he want to be there?'

'Apparently he wants to be the one to put a bullet in the man's head.'

'I guess I can understand that, but it endangers the operation. You know that and so does the General.'

'Nick,' said Hughes, 'the guy is adamant. And from what we've heard we don't blame him.'

'What do you mean?'

'We got some of the details about what happened to his family. It was pretty gruesome even by ISIL's standards.'

Hunter nodded. 'Then it must have been horrific.' He paused, frowned and then nodded. 'Okay, here's what we'll do.'

The team had arrived at the airport only a few hours earlier. The sort of equipment they wanted couldn't be brought in on civilian flights and so they had flown in a Lockheed Martin C-130J Hercules C5 to Naval Air Station Sigonella, near Catania, on the eastern edge of the island. The base was a US NATO installation as well as an Italian Airforce Base. The base existed to support the activities of the American Sixth Fleet that operated in the Mediterranean and had done so since 1950.

Hunter collected his gear from his room and thought about the challenge ahead of them. He was looking forward to it.

The area was under threat. An invasion was taking place but one that the west seemed powerless to do anything about. The army of invaders came without guns, many demanding safety and a better life. Some were coming to attack and kill people they classed as non-believers, in other words, non-Islamic, and if Muslims were caught in the crossfire then that was too bad. Hunter knew that to the Islamists any collateral damage was acceptable. If the invaders had been coming with weapons then the west could have retaliated, but nobody wanted or was prepared to kill unarmed civilians – women, children and innocent men even if their activities in trying to get to Europe were illegal.

The conundrum of what to do was taxing the west to breaking point with no solution in sight. The team knew all this but what else could they do? Far better placed individuals than they were working on the problem. But as they all cynically agreed politicians and civil servants could not be trusted to do anything right.

Stopping the traffickers was a start but achieving anything of significance was virtually impossible. However, the problem couldn't just be ignored. Something needed to be done, but what? That was the question the world in general and the west in particular was grappling with.

In the meantime the team had a job to do.

Prior to leaving, Hunter went to the dive shack with his diving equipment. The shop was locked but he could see the owner through the plate glass window. He attracted the man's attention.

Opening the door, Hunter was greeted with, 'What do you want?'

'I'm giving you this.' He indicated the pile of diving gear on the pavement and added, 'Don't bother thanking me.' He walked away without looking back.

Seconds later he heard a stuttered, 'Th . . . Thanks. Thanks very much.'

The others were waiting for him in an American Wrangler Freedom. The vehicle was robust, comfortable and roomy. Half an hour later they arrived at the base. They showed their ID cards and were waved through. Badonovitch drove them to a corner of the airfield where there was a low building made of white painted breeze blocks.

They parked-up outside the front entrance. Hunter looked around. There were a couple of fighter jets landing on the distant runway just as a C130 was taxiing for take-off. It was a busy place but then so was the Mediterranean Sea. The sun finally sank beneath the horizon and darkness began to crowd in. In spite of the aircraft, noisy in the background, there was a tranquility to the place that Hunter always associated with the countries around the northern Mediterranean.

Following the others through the door, Hunter saw it was reinforced on the inside with a thin layer of steel and that the windows were barred.

An American marine Sergeant sat behind a desk directly in front of them. 'Gentlemen, I know you three but who's this?' He nodded in Hunter's direction.

'Our boss,' answered Badonovitch, 'Commander Hunter, Royal Navy.'

The man leapt to his feet and saluted.

'Take it easy, sergeant,' Hunter looked at the man's name tag, 'Stewart, we don't salute much where we come from.'

'Yes, sir. Right, sir.'

The man looked to be in his mid to late twenties, putting on weight around his midriff but with a chestful of medal ribbons. Most of them were inconsequential, the US army seeming to enjoy handing out medals that were of no value. However, Hunter did recognise a campaign medal for Afghanistan so the sergeant had probably seen action at some point.

'We're here to see Ahmad Samara,' said Masters.

The sergeant nodded. 'Yeah, I know. I've been expecting you.' He smiled. 'It's okay, I was briefed earlier by the major.'

'The major?' Hunter queried.

'Yes, sir. Major Meadows is in charge of this facility. He was here about an hour ago. Really had a burr up his jacksie. Told me to expect you and that I was to give you whatever you asked for. And that included any guests.'

'Guests?' Hunter repeated.

'Sounds better than prisoners, sir. Truth is, we have a pile of men here we don't know what to do with. They've been picked up after being identified as people smugglers but what then? Where and how do we try them?'

'It's an interesting question, sergeant and no one has an answer,' said Hunter.

18

'I'm training to be a lawyer,' the sergeant added, 'and wanted to go into corporate law but now I'm going to get involved with human rights. I'm doing a part time course courtesy of the army, it's interesting stuff.'

'If you find any answers let us know,' said Hunter. 'Now, can we get to your, em, guest?'

'Sure, sir. Just follow me.

Taking a keycard from a top right hand desk drawer he led the way towards the back. They passed through a heavily reinforced door and into a long corridor. There were doors on either side, about five paces apart, stretching into the distance.

'How many people can you house here?' Masters asked, walking alongside the marine.

'We've got single cells for a hundred and double bunk cells for a further hundred.'

'And how many guests do you have?' Badonovitch asked.

'At the last count, a hundred and forty-seven.'

'What on God's earth are you going to do with them all?' Hunter asked.

Shrugging, the sergeant replied, 'No idea. All that's way above my pay grade. I just do as I'm told.'

'Well, it's above mine as well,' said Hunter. 'Like you, I get on with what I'm told.'

He ignored the looks that passed between Badonovitch and Hughes who were walking in front of him. The looks said aye, in a pig's ear.

'Here we are.' Unlocking the door the Sergeant stood back. 'This is Ahmad Samara.'

2

He looked young but it turned out Samara was twenty-seven. He was of slight build, black hair, regular features, a straight nose and brown wary eyes. He looked suspiciously at the men standing in the doorway.

'My name is Don Masters.' Masters stretched out his hand as he stepped into the cell, 'and these are my colleagues. We've come to take you away from here.'

Samara was suddenly frightened and shrank back. He was sitting on a bunk to the left of the door. There was a small table under a barred window and a hard backed chair in front of it, both fixed to the concrete floor. There was a stainless steel sink in a corner with a toilet alongside. A narrow closet to the left of the window completed the furnishings. The cell was as barren as it could be without actually infringing any of the guests' human rights. At least that was how Hunter figured it.

'Ahmad, don't look so scared. My name is Nick Hunter and we've come to take you away. You have a little job for us and you've made it clear you want to be a part of it. We don't like the idea but we'll go along with it. We know what happened to your family.'

The young man nodded his head and then looked down, hiding his features. When he looked up there were tears in his eyes. 'Al-Baghdadi is an inhuman pig. He needs wiping from the face of the earth,' he paused before adding, 'and I want to be the one to do it.'

'You shall be. You have my word. Now come on. Collect your gear and let's go.'

'I have nothing. Only the clothes I am wearing.'

Hunter could see that Samara had been given a clean shirt and trousers, both army green. Back at the reception desk Hunter nodded his thanks to the marine and they left.

'Okay, what's next?' Hunter asked.

Masters replied. 'There are a number of meeting rooms over in the main building. We've been allocated one and told to report there as soon as we collected Ahmad.'

They piled into the car and Masters drove them the three kilometres to the main building. To one side was the air traffic control tower, dim lights visible behind the green, anti-glare glass surrounding the top of the structure.

In front of them was a substantial orange tinted building with dark orange tiles. The sign just under the eaves read WELCOME TO NAS SIGONELLA.

They entered the building where they found a female corporal sitting at a desk. 'Can I help you?'

Hunter took out his ID. 'My name is Hunter and I believe you have a meeting room available for us?'

'Yes, sir. Through that door and third on the right. They're waiting for you.'

Hunter frowned and the others exchanged looks. Who were they? They went as directed but there was nobody in the room. Instead a woman and a man were projected onto a large screen on the far side of the room.

'There you are,' the woman greeted them.

'Hi Isobel, Leo,' Hunter nodded at the screen while the other three gave small waves.

The room was set out more as a classroom than a meeting room with four rows of single occupancy desks six wide. Another person spoke on screen. It was General Macnair who greeted Hunter with the words, 'Sorry to disturb your well earned break, Nick.'

Hunter smiled. 'Think nothing of it, sir. I was already bored and thinking of coming home or at least heading out somewhere else.'

Macnair smiled. 'I figured you would be. Good day to you Mr Samara.'

The man nodded nervously.

The team grabbed seats and sat facing the screen. Along the top were three cameras giving a 3D effect as though the Operations/ Intelligence room at Rosyth was an extension of the room they were occupying.

At the outset the intelligence department had started with three people. Isobel headed up the team with Leo and Gareth as her assistants. All three, as far as Hunter was concerned, were geniuses when it came to computers. They were particularly adept at computer hacking and lifting unauthorised information. The property of criminals and terrorists was redirected to good causes as well as helping to fund the continuing fight against the enemy. Not having to keep asking governments for more funding was a great asset as far as Macnair was concerned. It meant less scrutiny of operations and reduced accountability to elected officials. People who, in his opinion interfered in security matters without a single notion of what it took to keep the general population safe. Besides which, why leave the proceeds of crime and terrorists in the banks and hands of people who often supported the perpetrators? And if they or their families didn't get the assets the lawyers certainly did. No, Macnair's policy was simple. Take everything the enemy had and then some. Hunter and his colleagues liked that idea very much.

It also meant the charitable foundation the General had set up did a lot of good, from helping to build schools in third world countries to giving support to injured service personnel. The acknowledgement and diagnosis of Post Traumatic Stress Disorder had been a huge step in the right direction. SSAFA - The Soldiers, Sailors, Airmen and Families Association - the oldest charity for serving and ex-military personnel in the UK if not the world, did sterling work but there was never enough money and he knew there never would be. Which was why the charitable foundation was badly needed.

'Nick,' said the General, 'we've had a chance to check out Mr Samara. What he's told us about his background appears to be true.'

Samara looked at them and finally said, 'I am not lying.'

Hunter looked at him. 'I don't think you are either. We're just being careful.'

The Libyan nodded and replied, 'I understand.'

'Isobel,' said Macnair, 'tell them what we know about al-Baghdadi.'

'Yes, sir.' Isobel nodded and began. 'He was low level until about three years ago. The usual foot soldier in many respects. Then he connected to the third ISIL organisation in the west of Libya known as Tripolitania. We thought he was also Libyan but according to Mr Samara he is in fact a Saudi Arabian.'

'You sure?' Hunter looked at the man.

'Yes, of course. He comes from one of the many branches of the Saudi Royal family.'

The men exchanged cynical glances. The population of Saudi Arabia was 30 million; the ruling family was the House of Saud, consisting of about 16,000 members although the wealth and power was in the hands of about 2,000 Saudi Arabians. Just about every member of the House had the title of prince or princess, which was meaningless as only a few direct descendents of Ibn Saud had any chance of becoming king.

Hunter knew that the biggest problem facing the Saudi people wasn't the fact there was no democracy in the country or an autocratic system of government but the existence of Wahhabism, a religious branch of Sunni Islam. It was a perversion of Islam founded by an eighteenth century scholar and preacher by the name of Mohammed ibn Abd al-Wahabb, born in 1703, died 1792. The religion was described variously as puritanical, fundamentalist and ultraconservative. What that meant in reality was intolerance of all other religions and ways of life. They had a deep rooted hatred for the rights of women and reinforcing that hatred were religious police who patrolled Saudi Arabia with the power to beat up any woman not wearing the burka, or even driving a car without a male escort. Wearing the burka meant a black cloth covered the head, face and body of all women in spite of the horrendous heat to be found in Saudi Arabia and other Middle Eastern countries. The men wore white, light robes, much more comfortable under the circumstances. Their hypocrisy never ceased to amaze people in the west.

The sect was also recognised and acknowledged as the main advocates and supporters of worldwide terrorism. Hunter had been told that they had two objectives. The first was to spread Islam throughout the world by any means possible while the second was to turn back the world to the days of Muhammad. If the first objective took a thousand years then so be it, while the second would never happen, as progress couldn't be stopped. However, their sect intended trying and it spread their idea of Islam throughout the western world in the guise of charities and mosques. The House of Saud had already contributed tens of millions of dollars to achieving their aims. The hate-mongering supreme leader of Wahhabism the Saudi imam and Friday preacher at the Grand Mosque in Mecca ruled with a fist of iron and intolerance unsurpassed in the modern world.

'We don't think he's a fundamentalist, as such,' Isobel continued.

Hunter interrupted her, 'He's not? Then why is he doing it?'

'Simply,' she replied, 'for the money. He isn't one of the wealthy Saudis, he's one of the poor ones.'

'That's true,' said Samara. 'I heard him boast that a life of luxury awaits him and his followers once they have moved thousands of immigrants into Europe.'

'I would have thought,' said Masters, 'that saying so in earshot of others is a pretty dangerous thing to do.'

'He didn't know I was listening. Please, let me tell you. I have been working to get near him for many months. I wanted to find out more about what he was doing and give the information to the authorities. To stop him. But all that changed when he killed my family.' Samara teared up and wiped his eyes with the back of his right hand. 'I want to kill him more than anything in the world, which is why I came with the last boatload of immigrants.'

The team looked at the young Libyan with stony faces. His story was all well and good but an opportunity to kill the Infidels could be what he was planning. They needed to hear more.

'Mr Samara,' said Isobel, 'we have done a great deal of checking. We know from your university records that you are who you claim to be. We know about your family. It was horrendous what ISIL did to them and we understand your desire for revenge. However, we need to tread carefully. We still have a long way to go to trust you.'

There was a pause and then Samara said, 'I understand. I am not stupid. I would feel the same if I were you.' He shrugged, 'I don't know what I can do to convince you of my sincerity.'

The General spoke. 'Tell us where we can find al-Baghdadi.'

The silence deepened and then Hunter said, 'Ahmad, I give you my word we will take you with us. There are certain things you will need to do but we can deal with them later. If we are to find and kill al-Baghdadi we need to be told where he is.'

Samara bowed his head in thought.

Badonovitch became impatient while the other two sat stoically silent, waiting for the information. 'Come on, Ahmad, tell us. We haven't got all night.'

Samara nodded. 'Actually, we have. He arrives tomorrow night on the island.' 'Do you know where?' Hunter asked.

Samara looked down at his hands that were tightly clasped together on the desk before shaking his head slowly.

'You don't know?' Hunter looked angrily at the man. 'What do you mean you don't know? What's this all been about?'

'I mean, I don't know where he's going. What I do know is that he will be arriving by Alitalia from London via Rome to Palermo. It is supposed to arrive at about 22.30.'

'How do you know all this?' Masters asked.

'I listened to them talking.'

'You seem to have had a lot of luck listening to his plans,' said Hunter.

'I have been thinking about how to answer that question.'

'You expected it?' Hunter asked.

'Yes, of course.'

'And?' Hunter prompted.

25

'He is a very arrogant man. He has killed his way to the top of Tripolitania and he thinks he is, how do you say . . . invincible?'

Nodding, Hunter asked, 'Why didn't you kill him in Libya?'

'A number of reasons.'

'So tell us,' said Masters.

'Okay. First he is well guarded. Armed guards and armoured cars and moving all the time. We all know about the drones and it's the one thing we are all fearful of.' Unmanned drones, once a target had been identified, could take out the enemy with devastating effect, usually using controlled bombs that could flatten a half block of buildings. 'So I want to kill him and watch him die. I want him to know it is me who is doing it and why and I want him to suffer. If I try this in Libya the chances of escaping are not good. I would suffer a fate worse than death, I think you English call it.'

The men nodded.

'But I also want to live. A week ago I wanted to die and join my family. Now I don't want that. Now I want to help my people. I cannot explain to you but I know it is the right thing to do. Very many people need help and if people like me don't give it then what hope is there for all?' He answered his own question by shaking his head and saying, 'None. I speak fluent Arabic, English and Italian. I can be a lot of use. I am an architect. Perhaps I can help to plan and build shelters for the people around the coast of Europe. I don't know. All I do know is that I can do much to help.' He straightened his shoulders and looked at the screen, seeming to breathe in courage and dignity at the same time, 'At least I can try.'

It was an impressive performance but it still didn't mean he could be fully trusted. But as Hunter had often said in the past, a reasonable amount of paranoia helped to keep you alive.

'Why come over with the immigrants?' Masters asked.

Samara stared at the REME Sergeant for a few seconds before replying. 'It was the only method I had to get away. In the confusion I sneaked onboard and came with them.'

'Some of them must have known you were one of the smugglers,' said Hughes, speaking for the first time.

Samara shook his head. 'No, they didn't. They are kept well away from the point of leaving. They are brought to the beach and searched. Their papers and passports are taken from them, any money and valuables are also taken and they are herded into the boat. If anybody protests at what is happening they are either beaten or killed there and then. Usually with a dagger in the heart.'

'They're barbarians,' said Hunter.

'Worse,' said Samara. 'The women, especially the young ones, are often raped. Two, sometimes three men will take them.'

'Are these girls travelling alone?' Hunter asked.

'Sometimes but also with families. That is sometimes worse. Imagine listening to your daughter or sister being abused in that way.'

Isobel spoke. 'When that happens the girls are often abandoned when the refugees reach Europe. The perceived shame of the family is too much for them to bear.'

'That's disgusting,' said Badonovitch.

'Maybe,' Isobel replied, 'but that's the way they think in their culture. Particularly amongst the Somalis and Nigerians.'

Samara spoke up. 'Please believe me when I say that the Sudanese and many Libyans are no better. There is something I also wish to say. I came forward and told the authorities who I am and that I am volunteering my services for a reason. I wanted to show my good intentions and to let you know who I am. I don't want to be one of the millions arriving in Europe for if that had happened I wouldn't get an opportunity to help the refugees. I hope you can understand that.'

'Nick,' said the General, 'as always, it's your call. We've done a deep background trace on al-Baghdadi and everything Samara says checks out. What we would like to know is what is he doing on Sicily?'

'How can he travel around so freely?' asked Hughes.

'We don't know what he looks like,' said Leo. 'The photograph we do have of him is grainy and at least two years old.' He flashed a photo up on the screen. 'This is what we've got. I've tidied it up as best I can but it's still not good enough for a positive ID. For that you need Samara.'

The photograph was in colour but the resolution was poor. Like Leo said, it was not good enough for identification purposes.

'He's no doubt in possession of a suitable passport,' said Macnair, 'whether Libyan or Saudi, it doesn't matter. If he can show a reason for visiting Europe he can come and go as he likes.'

'He won't be asked,' said Samara, 'he travels first class. What border control officer asks people questions when they are travelling first class and wearing Armani suits?'

3

They were given rooms in the complex. After ditching their gear Hunter went along to Samara's room where he found him sitting on a bunk, his head hanging down, deep sorrow etched in his face when he looked up.

'Come with me.'

'Where to?'

'To buy you some clothes. You can't walk around like that. Not here. You'll stick out a mile.'

'I don't have any money.'

'Don't worry about it.'

'And I don't have a pass to leave this place.'

'Yeah, I know. Just come with me.'

Wearily Samara stood up and followed Hunter along the corridor and across to another block of offices. At a reception desk sat a young, Italian, female soldier. She looked up and smiled at the two men.

'Can I help you?' She asked in English with a slight accent that was appealing and under different circumstances would have had Hunter turning on his considerable charm.

'My name is Cmdr Hunter.' He took out his ID card and showed it to the woman who looked closely at it. She nodded as though satisfied and handed it back.

'Thank you, sir. I received a call. I can sort it for you. Would you like to follow me, please?'

She stood up, pushed down on her skirt to straighten it out and led the way to a security door situated to the left of the foyer. She used a swipe card to unlock the door and switched on the lights. There was a camera set in the middle of the room aimed at a blank wall. She positioned Samara and took a photograph of him looking straight-faced into the camera. Her fingers tapped across a keyboard, she looked closely at the screen, typed in Ahmad Samara, pressed a button and watched as an identity card unrolled from a printer next to the computer. She slipped the card into a plastic folder, placed it onto another piece of equipment, closed a lid over it and waited a few seconds. When she lifted the lid a sealed ID card was ready for use. It was a NATO temporary pass with restricted access but all that was needed under the circumstances.

'That'll get you in and out of the base,' she said, handing over the card to Samara.

'Grazie molto.'

There then followed a brief conversation in Italian before Hunter managed to get him away.

'What was that all about?'

Samara shrugged. 'She asked me where I was staying.'

Looking down at him Hunter grinned. 'Once this op is over come back and talk to her.'

'She is not for the likes of me.'

'Why not? She's about your age, beautiful and obviously interested in you.'

'I have too much to do. Besides I am Libyan and a Muslim.'

'Is your faith important to you?'

Samara appeared to think about it before he replied. 'I used to believe so but now I am not so sure.'

He left it at that and Hunter didn't try and pursue the matter. However, he was slightly perturbed. There were many stories about men willing to fight the terrorists suddenly finding their way back to the path of the One True God. Usually at completely the wrong moment.

They left the airport and walked into town. Although it was nearly 20.15 businesses were still open. The bars and restaurants were busy while the boutique shops were empty of customers but inhabited by hopeful salespeople.

Hunter found a fair sized store selling clothes and they went in. It didn't take long to outfit Samara from inside out, with spare trousers and a lightweight jacket. A pair of sturdy trainers completed the package. The clothes he had been wearing were dumped in a rubbish bin. A supermarket yielded washing gear, toothpaste and a toothbrush. Their final purchase was a holdall to carry the spare shirts, socks and underpants.

Throughout the process Samara had barely said a word. When they were finished and heading back towards the base, he said, 'Thanks.'

'You're welcome. At least you look reasonably presentable now.'

Back on the base they made their way to the bar and restaurant that was for the use of military personnel. It was long, low, could hold at least a few hundred visitors but was only a quarter full. A bar ran the length of the room and at the far end was a small stage. Round wooden tables sat in serried ranks; some with four hard backed chairs, others with six. Badonovitch, Masters and Hughes were sitting in a far corner at one of the bigger tables with six chairs. It was where Hunter had expected them to be. A good view of the entrance and bar, near the back door and with no chance of being taken by surprise. Not that anything like that was even likely to happen, it was merely instinct. It was an attribute that could keep you alive when you weren't thinking too clearly.

As they sat down Badonovitch shoved a menu across the table to each of them. 'Need to order at the bar. Just give them the table number.'

'Thanks, Jan.' A quick glance down the packed menu and Hunter said, 'Sirloin, baked potato and salad. You guys ordered?'

'Not yet. We were waiting for you,' said Masters.

'Ahmad?' Hunter looked at the young Libyan, 'What do you want?'

Samara sat staring at the menu for a few moments. 'It is all too much,' he said in a quiet voice.

'What do you mean?' Hunter asked.

'All those goods in the shops. The restaurants and bars. All those people enjoying themselves and yet . . . and yet just across the water there is nothing, only death and destruction.'

The four men exchanged looks. They had all heard it before.

'Whose fault is that?' Masters asked.

'I am not blaming anyone, I am just saying. It is so unfair. Unjust.'

Badonovitch said, 'I'm Russian. I remember the stories of what it had been like under communism. How we screamed about how unfair and unjust it all was. We ignored the fact that Europe had been destroyed twice in thirty years and rebuilt from the bottom up. The people of Western Europe didn't sit around complaining about their lives and how bad it was. They got on with the re-building. And what do we have in Africa and the Middle East and let's add Afghanistan to the mix as well? Africa is a basket case. The wealthiest piece of land on earth and it's wrecked. Nigeria has as much if not more oil than Saudi. Zimbabwe when it was Rhodesia fed most of Africa with beef, wheat and maize and now it can't even feed its own people. And what do they all do? Shove their hands out and demand that the west take care of them. At the same time the people of the Middle East blame the west for everything and demand Islam rules the world. It's hard not to feel angry.'

His three team mates looked at Badonovitch in amazement. It was the first time they had ever heard him sound off like that. He looked at them and shrugged sheepishly. 'I guess I'm fed up with dealing with all this crap.' He raised his glass and drained it.

Masters spoke for them all. 'You have some valid points. But right now there's no option other than to do what we're doing.'

Hunter said, 'Right you guys, these are on me.' He picked up a pad and pen standing in a plastic condiment container along with salt, pepper, mustard, tomato sauce and salad cream. An Italian salad dressing was to one side in an ornate glass bottle with a long spout. He took their orders. It was medium rare steaks, baked potatoes and salad for the team while Samara chose a beef burger, fries and onion rings. They stuck with bottled beer and Samara asked for Coca-Cola.

The food was pretty good, the beers cold and the chat the sort that filled in time prior to going on an operation. The morning would bring the equipment check and the weapons overhaul.

Hunter hit his pit just a few minutes after 23.00 and slept like a log. At 06.00 he was in running kit and hitting the perimeter fence around the base. He spent 40 minutes running followed by a series of push-ups and sit-ups. Becoming fit was one thing. All it took was focus. Staying fit was something else. That took dedication and determination. Or, as Hunter usually put it, bloody-mindedness, which came to the same thing in the end.

Dressed in khaki trousers with pockets in the legs, a short-sleeved white shirt and lightweight faded green waistcoat covered in pockets he quit his room. There was a cafeteria next to the bar where he caught up with the others just before 08.00. 'Good run, boss?' Badonovitch asked.

'Yeah. Blew away a few cobwebs. What did you guys do?'

'They've got a pretty good gym,' replied Master, 'including a sauna and swimming pool.'

Samara appeared and joined them. They made their way across to the serving counter grabbing trays, plates and cutlery before helping themselves to food.

There was American unhealthy – fried eggs, bacon, sausages, hash browns, mushrooms, baked beans, waffles, maple syrup or Continental healthy – yogurts, fruit, muesli, croissants. They all settled for the American. The food was military good, the orange juice freshly squeezed and the coffee a local brand and excellent.

They ate and drank and then refilled their coffee mugs before talking about the operation. They spent an hour going over their options. They talked weapons, clothes and transport. Ahmad Samara sat silently through it all until the end.

'I want a gun,' Samara announced, 'so that I can kill al-Baghdadi.'

Hunter said, 'You will when the time comes and not before.'

'You don't trust me, is that it?'

'It's not a question of trust,' replied Masters, 'it's a question of ability.'

'What's that supposed to mean?' Samara asked in a low, angry voice.

Hunter said, 'We don't know how useful you are with a gun. Be that a handgun or a rifle. My betting is you're used to spraying an AK74 around the place shooting all and sundry who get in the way. You've not had formal training, you've not spent hours on a firing range using all sorts of guns, honing your skills, in fact, you lot aren't even trained soldiers. Now, I'll say this only once. We need you for this operation. We'll give you the opportunity to kill al-Baghdadi but that will be after we've secured the position whatever that may be. Your job is to identify him. So tell us something of the man. What does he look like?'

Samara shrugged. 'A metre eighty tall, very thin, a close shaven beard that follows his jaw line. His hair is grey while his beard is light brown and streaked grey. When he is travelling he looks like a successful businessman, in Libya he looks and acts like a warrior leader.'

'You sound as though you admire him' said Hunter.

'Nothing can be further from the truth. I have seen the man up close. He is a murderer, a sadist and a coward. It is easy to be brave when surrounded by fanatics who think you are a great leader and an advocate for Islam.' Samara shook his head. 'I want to kill him more than I wish to continue living. I will do as you order but please let me have the satisfaction of killing him in my way.'

'If you do,' said Hunter, 'depending how you do it, you will probably never be the same again.'

'What do you mean?'

'The boss means,' said Hughes, 'that a quick kill of the enemy is one thing. Torturing a man to death is another.'

'Have you ever tortured anyone?'

The team exchanged looks but it was Hunter who answered.

'Some. We use the excuse that we need information. That the greater good justifies what we do. I can tell you that we've saved many lives because of the actions we've taken. Under international law those actions have been illegal but we've deemed them necessary. It's a call we make when in the field.'

'Can you live with it?' the Libyan asked.

'Easily,' Hunter replied while the others nodded. 'I for one sleep like a baby. I have no compunction in getting rid of the scum that exist in the sewers of what we call mankind. The American President summed it up when he visited Turkey, the first one ever to do so when he said that the west has not declared war on Islam, Muslims have declared war on the west. Yet we don't behave as though we are at war.'

'What about the fighting that's going on all across Libya, Syria, Iraq and much of Afghanistan?' Samara asked.

'I'm talking about war in Europe,' said Hunter. 'We are being infiltrated by jihadists who individually are trying to hurt the people of Europe. But what will happen if they organised and attacked as one?'

Masters said, 'We play war games. The enemy isn't stupid. They will become organised and attack in large numbers. Not in large groups but many isolated attacks. They'll use explosives, weapons, and vehicles to mow down people as we saw in France and Germany. Even something as simple as a load of bricks thrown onto a busy road such as a motorway at rush hour will cause huge damage with many deaths and injuries. Think what would happen if there were a dozen co-ordinated attacks like that? The security forces of the west have a huge job in front of them and we're only helping to scratch the surface.'

It was a glum note on which to leave the cafeteria but they had things to do.

They needed to observe without being observed, which was easier said than done. However, there was a factor in their favour. Al-Baghdadi would be feeling safe on Italian ground. Nobody knew him and nobody would recognise him, or so he thought. Hence he would not be expecting any form of surveillance.

4

According to the Arrivals board the plane was on time and due to land at 22.40. It was an internal flight so passengers would be coming into the concourse about 20 minutes later.

Hunter was dressed casually but behind his right ear was a tiny transmitter/receiver hidden by his hair. It worked using the vibrations created in the skull when speaking or listening. It meant there was no need to put your hand to your mouth to transmit like somebody in an action movie where every move was exaggerated and was often laughed at by the professionals.

He was standing on level one looking down at the concourse and the door through which the passengers would be arriving. Isobel had hacked into Alitalia's computer and checked the bookings. The plane was carrying 99 passengers, which was enough of a crowd to get lost in for a few moments, but not one in which to stay hidden. Samara was standing a few metres away, dressed in blue jeans and a black shirt, ignoring Hunter. He was now clean shaven with short hair and wore tinted glasses. They were small changes to his appearance but were highly effective. He looked nothing like the man he had been and as al-Baghdadi wouldn't be expecting him the chances of being recognised were remote. Except maybe by any bodyguards who arrived to meet their boss. Which happened a few minutes later.

Samara had been leaning on a wooden railing looking down when he suddenly stood up and pointed downwards. Hunter was alongside him in a flash and pulled him behind a pillar.

'What the hell do you think you're doing?' Hunter hissed at him and then stepped back, giving Samara some space. Luckily, at that time of the night, there were few people walking around to notice them. They were too busy looking out for family and friends who were arriving at the airport.

Samara looked down at the floor. 'Sorry.'

'Pay attention Ahmad. That sort of thing can get us all killed.'

'Yes, yes, I know. Sorry.'

'What were you pointing at?'

'Those two men who are near the door.'

Hunter looked down and saw two swarthy looking men standing near the arrivals doorway. 'The ones wearing dark suits that are buttoned up?'

The two men were of medium build, clean shaven and nondescript. To Hunter's trained eye he was sure they were armed but probably unnoticeable to the lay person. He watched as two armed policemen walked past. One looked at the two men then looked away.

'Those are the ones. They are two of al-Baghdadi's men. The one on the left is his head of security while the other is one of his fighters. I have seen what they do to the people trying to cross into Europe. It is not nice.'

'Did you catch that?' Hunter asked.

The other three acknowledged. Only Masters could see who they were talking about. He was sitting at a table with a coffee in front of him, relaxed and looking as though he had all the time in the world even if it was late at night. He was dressed in black trousers, a black open necked shirt and an open black jacket. His Glock 19 was in a special holster in the middle of his back. It was uncomfortable to lean against but a comfort to know it was there. It was his favourite handgun. Only 6ins sight to sight, 855 grams in weight when fully loaded with 15 rounds of ammo, it was one hell of a weapon and favoured by many of the armed services across the world.

The others were similarly armed and carried the necessary papers to show that they were allowed to be so anywhere in Europe. The problem was, TIFAT was very much a secret organisation although their existence was becoming better known due to their operational successes. If they were caught carrying then either the people doing the arresting would know and appreciate who they were or they would end up in jail until a more senior officer could have them released. That was always assuming the person doing the arresting didn't panic and try and shoot them. It was a tricky balancing act.

'They're a pair of clowns,' Masters growled. His voice vibrated in his head and transmitted to the others.

David Hughes' voice came over their earpieces. 'There are two cars out here, white Fiats, each with a driver, the second one has two passengers, the other has a single passenger. I would say from what I can see of them that they are Middle Eastern or North African, whatever, they look like they could be trouble if anything kicks off.'

'Roger that,' said Hunter. 'Let's hope nothing does. Looks like we'll be in play any minute now.'

The words were barely out of his mouth when the doors swung open and a man fitting the target's description appeared.

'That's him!' Samara said, ducking back behind the pillar.

'Take it easy, Ahmad. Sudden moves attract attention.' At that moment the advice was superfluous as the two men were looking only at al-Baghdadi but it was advice that could be useful in different circumstances. Reinforcing advice was a good way for a novice to remember what he should or shouldn't do. It could sometimes mean the difference between life and death. A melodramatic thought Hunter knew, but an accurate one for all that.

Al-Baghdadi was pushing a luggage trolley stacked with leather suitcases.

'Let's go,' said Hunter, picking up a brown coloured handbag, big enough to carry a change of clothes. 'Remember, don't look at him, not even a glance. Just walk alongside me as naturally as you would if the circumstances were normal.'

Hunter stood on a downward moving escalator and looked around like any tourist in an airport. Samara was two steps behind also looking about him. Don Masters was striding towards the rotating glass doors and looked as though he was now in a hurry to get somewhere. He reinforced the illusion by looking at his watch.

The three men they were following didn't so much as look behind. Al-Baghdadi was no longer pushing the trolley; he'd handed the task to one of his minions. Hunter was pleased to see that they were so lax, probably unable to believe anything could happen on a peaceful Italian island. It wasn't that unusual for people in their position to think that way. It helped to make life easier for TIFAT's teams. Let the targets have a feeling of safety and comfort and anything was possible. Even so, the team never took anything for granted. People who did rarely lived long enough to collect their pension.

Outside were the two cars as reported by David Hughes. Hunter's car was in the car park on the opposite side of the road. The three targets climbed into the cars, al-Baghdadi in the back seat of the front car along with his head of security. The second man piled the luggage into the boot of the second car and got into the front passenger's seat.

Hunter and Samara didn't look at the cars as they headed for the pedestrian crossing and their own vehicle. The two cars pulled away from the curb and headed out of the airport.

'Jan, they're on their way,' Hunter transmitted.

'Got them, boss,' said Badonovitch two minutes later. He was sitting on a motorbike about half a kilometre away, engine running, ready to go.

'So have I,' said Hughes, also astride a powerful motorbike.

There was one slight difference between the bikes and that was their ages. Badonovitch's was new, the LED headlight brighter than Hughes' older light which had a yellow cast to it. It meant that they could interchange and reduce the likelihood of anyone wondering if they were being followed.

Regular reports of their progress were transmitted to Hunter driving a Fiat about two kilometres behind with Masters in a Renault a further one kilometre back.

They were travelling along the E90, the coast road, heading east from Palermo. They passed through the villages of Villabate, Bagheria and Termini Imerese with no sign of stopping. At 23.38 there was hardly another vehicle to be seen.

The Renault was now in front and Hunter heard Masters say, 'He's turned off the coast road. Gone right onto the E19.'

The road was a well-maintained two-lane motorway. Courtesy of the European Union taxpayer, thought Hunter cynically. But what was a hundred million euros or so plus ten million in bribes and back handers to local officials and European bureaucrats? After all, it wasn't their money.

'Don,' said Hunter, 'drop back and let Jan take the lead. Isobel, you getting all this?'

Hunter was connected to TIFAT by mobile phone. They were being tracked in real time and so their whereabouts were known at all times.

'Yes, thanks, Nick.'

'Any way he can get off this road?'

'Not for another ten minutes or so when they get to a village called Scillato.'

The General's voice came over the ether. 'Nick, I don't think he's going to stop until he gets to the coast or at least near it. There's no sense being holed up in the middle of the island.'

'I agree, sir. If he had to make a run for it he'd have nowhere to go. Much better to be near the coast where there are more roads as well as the sea.'

'There's a large town ahead,' said Isobel, 'called Enna. 'It's the capital of the province. Has a university. You should be there around midnight. It's Friday so there may be people around. Students having a night out, letting off steam, after a hard week of doing nothing.'

'Such cynicism,' said Hunter.

'It seems the older I get the more cynical I become,' she quipped. 'The A19 bypasses the town and heads straight east.'

'Okay, Jan, drop back when I get behind you.' A few seconds later Hunter said, 'Okay, I'm a hundred metres away. Slow down and let me pass. I bet my bottom dollar he's going to Catania. We'll wait for him there.'

Hunter put his foot down and drove past the two cars.

'Nick, you're about fifty minutes away from Catania. On the outskirts of the city is the A18 that crosses at right angles. It runs the whole length of the coast, north to south. I suggest you get off somewhere near the junction and watch for him.'

'He'll be heading south,' said Hunter confidently.

'Why do you say that?' Isobel asked.

'It's closer to Africa.'

They arrived at the crossroads and Hunter pulled off to the right.

After a few minutes David Hughes said, 'I'm behind them and we're coming up to the A18.' A few seconds later he said, 'You're wrong Nick, they're heading north.'

Hunter cursed, started the engine and headed towards the interchange. Seconds later they were on the A18 heading north. The cat and mouse operation continued past Acireale, Giarre and then Taormina. Just beyond the tourist village was a campsite, Lido Camping Paradise and a few hundred metres further was where the cars slowed down, indicated right and pulled off the road. The cars stopped while Hunter and Masters drove past. Badonovitch pulled off the road by turning into the campsite and David Hughes followed a minute later.

There were no streetlights but it was a cloudless night with a half moon. The bikers watched as two gates opened and the cars went through. The gates then closed.

'Do you see where we are?' Hunter asked Isobel.

'Yes. We're pulling what information we can even as we speak. Got it. Give us a few minutes and we'll get back to you.'

'We're not stopping. There may be cameras covering the walls. Jan, Dave, can you stay where you are?'

'I don't think so,' said Badonovitch. 'If anyone comes we'll stick out like sore thumbs.'

'Okay, then get on your bikes and roar away at high-speed back towards Catania. With a bit of luck if anyone is watching they'll think it's an assignation gone wrong or you're a pair of clowns out joyriding.'

Badonovitch and Hughes drove their bikes away from the entrance to Camping Paradise and stopped at the lay-by where the two cars were parked.

The gates to the grounds were about half a kilometre away. Each side of the gates was a wall about 3m high, extending about 40 metres in both directions. The ground undulated by at least 10 degrees and Hunter could see the glistening shards of glass embedded into the top of the wall. A second similar wall at right angles stretched down to the shore. Over the wall they could see a roof and what appeared to be the second floor of a house. The building was large and imposing.

Masters climbed out of his car, stretched cramped arms and legs and joined Hunter who was sitting with his window open.

'What do you think, boss?'

'There is no way that this place has been built legally. Never in a million years. It's too close to the water.'

Isobel came back on the phone. 'We've got a live feed. Leo has also been into the local town authority's computer system.'

'Surely,' said Hunter, 'this house is illegal.'

'Funnily enough, Leo said the same thing. It is and it isn't.'

'How come?' Hunter asked.

'According to town planning guidelines the house should not be built so close to the water and should not impact on a public beach which that house does.'

'So how did al-Baghdadi get away with building the place?'

'He didn't,' was the stark answer. 'He bought it from an ex-Mafia boss, one Guiseppe Pacelli.'

'Never heard of him.'

'Hardly surprising, he's been dead for two years. He wasn't what you'd call top of the organisation, but pretty high up. It appears that his specialty was European Union fraud.' She hesitated, then added, 'It looks to have been on a massive scale. So maybe he was higher up the totem pole than he first appeared.'

'What sort of fraud?'

'According to this he specialised in the big stuff. Like new roads, one harbour installation on the north of the island, oh, and a railway tunnel in southern Italy near a place called Catanzaro. That's about a hundred and sixty kilometres north. So he ran a fair sized area though nothing like some sections. He wasn't main board but probably secondary.'

'What's that supposed to mean?' Hunter asked.

'The Mafia has a senior and middle management structure just like an international company and runs its businesses on the same lines. Hence a main board and a secondary board with a chairman reporting to the main board. All very neat, efficient and businesslike. As you know Nick, many of their operations are legal which is a good way to hide their illegal businesses. The problem they have is the Eastern European gangs muscling in. They are more vicious and vile than anything the Mafia has ever done. Add in ISIL and their control over the trade in illegal immigrants and we have a real nasty mix that could explode at any second.'

'How long has the house been here?' Hunter asked.

'Ten years according to the records. We're sending you copies of the architect's drawings right now. Is Don with you?'

'Here Isobel.'

'Thanks for the photographs. They're pretty good. He won't be going anywhere fast even if he does get away.'

'He won't,' said Masters. The sergeant had taken a series of photographs of al-Baghdadi when he was at the airport using a pen that was in reality a digital camera with a long-range lens.

'We have also identified the other two men with him. They are on America's most wanted list so if you take them out as well we'll earn some brownie points with our cousins.'

Hunter grinned. He knew Isobel and the General couldn't care less about brownie points with anybody, never mind the cousins.

Reaching behind him, Hunter dragged a bag onto his lap, opened it and took out an iPad. He switched it on, pressed various buttons and said, 'I've got the drawings.'

'Good. What they don't show but the overhead photographs do is that there is a jetty sticking out into the sea for ten metres with a boat at the end. Leo has identified it as a Viking 50ft Flybridge Sport Cruiser, probably fifteen or so years old.'

'Nice piece of kit if it's been looked after. Probably the best part of a million dollars today.'

Leo broke in. 'Nick, we've been running the face recognition software on the computers of half the airports in Europe. We've identified al-Baghdadi four times, each time travelling under an assumed name. We can't tell which is his, only that they're different each time. So it means he has access to a number of identities, which in turn means some serious support from officials somewhere in the world.'

'The Saudis?'

'Probably.'

'What name is he travelling under?'

'Mohammed Alfarsi.' Isobel spelt it.

5

They knew where to find al-Baghdadi and so they returned to base. They were 65kms north and made the journey in 40 minutes. Hunter slept like a log, skipped round his morning workout and had the healthy Mediterranean breakfast.

He was on his second coffee when the others arrived and a third cup when a young female tentatively approached their tables.

'Excuse me, gentlemen, is one of you, erm, Commander Hunter?'

'I am.'

She threw him a quick salute and said, 'Sir, the Colonel wants to see you.'

'The Colonel? What Colonel?'

'Sir, sorry sir, I was told to say merely the Colonel. No names.'

No names probably meant only one thing. Members of Special Forces didn't like to advertise who they were, especially if you were British SAS or American SEALS. Even so, it was pretty unusual under the circumstances not to give a name.

'Now?'

'When you've finished breakfast, sir.'

'Thanks. I'm finished. Care to lead the way?'

'Yes, sir. My pleasure.' She turned smartly and marched away.

The team exchanged glances and shrugs and Hunter followed quickly catching her up. She led him across to a corner of the base, away from prying eyes. There was an airport hangar with its doors wide open. Inside were six helicopters. Hunter recognised them as a Black Hawk, a Pave Hawk, two Eurocopters and two Apaches.

The men he saw around the place were dressed mainly in shorts and green tee shirts. None of them carried any fat. All of them looked what they were – tough sons-of-bitches. In other words, SEALS.

The marine pointed at a corner. 'In there, sir.'

'Thank you.'

She saluted smartly and marched away. Hunter watched her go.

'Down boy,' said a voice behind him.

Hunter spun round with a wide grin on his face. 'Hiram, by all that's holy!' Holding out his hand Hunter walked towards his old friend and boss, Hiram B. Walsh who had been second-in-command under General Macnair at Rosyth holding the rank of colonel. 'What are you doing here?'

Walsh was in his early 50s, average height, slim without an ounce of fat. He had short, thinning fair hair, a high forehead and brown eyes that always seemed to Hunter to be laughing at some joke or other. He was dressed in army fatigues, tropical style – a lightweight short sleeved shirt and trousers with no insignia of rank. The SEALS weren't big on displaying rank - they knew who gave the orders.

Their handshakes were warm and their smiles wide. 'Come in for a coffee and we'll chew the fat.'

Walsh led the way into a corner office. There were two desks, one for him and one for another tough looking guy with hair over his ears, a broken nose and wary brown eyes. He looked Hispanic.

'Captain Rodriguez Perez, Commander Nick Hunter.'

The men shook hands.

'Do you want me to leave, sir?'

'Naw, stay where you are. You're up to speed on everything and we've got no secrets.'

Walsh crossed to the coffee machine, lifted the pot and waved it at Hunter. 'If I remember, white, strong, no sugar?'

Hunter nodded. 'You got it.'

The SEAL poured three mugs, added milk to all three and sugar to two of them. He stirred, handed over the mugs and sat behind his desk.

'Grab a seat, Nick.'

'Thanks. The last time I saw you was at your leaving do when you were getting ready to take over at Virginia Beach. I seem to remember a promotion to bird colonel.'

The rank's insignia was an eagle, hence the title and one level below that of a brigadier general or a one star. In the world of the navy it was equivalent to a four-ring captain.

Hunter was referring to Walsh's new job as boss of Seal Team Six, headquartered at NAS Oceana in Virginia. The Naval Air Station was home to a fighting force that considered themselves the toughest, meanest and most professional organisation of its type in the world. The British SAS begged to differ.

'That's where I'm stationed. I'm here for a few days, maybe a week or two, looking things over.

Hunter stared at Walsh for a few seconds and then shook his head. 'No, you're not. That may be what you're telling all and sundry but I figure you're here to report back to the powers what a complete dog's dinner Europe is making of the refugee crisis and the problem in particular of jihadists being smuggled into the west.'

Walsh prompted. 'Go on.'

'You know as well as I do that these people can wait for years, even a decade or two to further their ends. They get into Europe, settle down, get citizenship, get a passport and now the whole of the western world is open to them to attack.'

Walsh glanced at Perez, 'I told you this was one smart cookie.'

'So how come you're here now? When we have a job?'

Shaking his head Walsh said, 'It's a coincidence Nick, really it is. This is a sort of government paid vacation with a job thrown in for good measure. The men have plenty of time off, called out if required, a few interceptions,' Walsh shrugged. 'You know how it is.'

Hunter sipped his coffee. It was excellent. 'And you're full of it.'

The colonel looked across the room at Perez who was sitting behind his desk, 'I also told you he wouldn't believe a word of it.'

'I wouldn't either.' Perez grinned. 'The colonel's told me a few things about TIFAT and what you guys get up to.' His tone held a longing for something similar. 'Unfortunately our politicians seem unable to face reality. We're at war like no other and we're not being allowed to fight it.'

'We've talked long and hard and late into the night over a few malt whiskies in our time on the same subject,' said Hunter, 'but there's little we can do about it.'

'Apart from put our fingers into the dyke,' said Walsh.

'I take it you're carrying out seek and destroy ops?'

'Yeah, across the board. We have to be very careful so we don't do as many as we'd like. Think of the outcry if we were caught slitting the throats of the traffickers no matter how much they deserve it.'

'Tell me about it. Are you targeting specific people?'

'No. We've got a few of our men in North Africa who are quietly but effectively dealing with some of the scum as and when. This is more like a live-firing training exercise. We do five days in bandit country and have fifteen off for fun and sports.'

'Like drinking, womanising and then wasting the rest of the down time.'

Walsh grinned. 'You got it. We've got everything from skydiving to sub aqua. Also we have lessons in various languages such as Arabic and Urdu. Speaking of which, how's your Arabic?'

Hunter replied using the language. 'I've been studying it for six months, listening to tapes and taking lessons using the Internet.'

'Pretty good. Give it twenty years and you'll be fluent.' The colonel spoke fluent Arabic as well as Urdu.

Grinning, Hunter nodded. He knew Walsh was joking with him. His Arabic was good and his accent good enough for him to pass off as a Libyan in Iraq or vice-versa. If asked about his accent he'd point out that he had been educated in England, like the children of most of the regimes in the Middle East and North Africa. His black hair and complexion also helped.

'Ex-filtration?' Hunter asked.

'Large fishing boats carrying raiders just on the horizon. Launch and in within fifteen minutes tops.' Walsh was referring to the rigid raider inflatable craft used by various amphibious forces around the world. The boats could carry eight fully kitted troops plus three crew and with their reinforced plastic hulls could be driven onto a beach without any difficulty. 'We've modified them to run at 65mph although it means their range is down to a hundred miles.'

'Are you doing any good?' Hunter asked.

'We like to think so but the answer is nope. For every trafficker we get rid of two appear. Each vying for supremacy.'

'We've known that for the last few years.'

'Which makes your op about as useful as ours.'

'So you know why we're here?'

'Sure. Malcolm called. Put us in the picture and asked us for a few items to help out. That is,' he added hastily, 'if you want our help.'

'Hiram, you know we're always glad of help wherever we can get it from though right now I'm not sure what we do need.'

'Isobel told us about the house. We've also seen the architect's drawings. I figured it would be better and easier if we looked at them on a big screen, like the one we've got in the main briefing room.'

'That'll be a great help.'

'If there is anything in the way of gear you need let Rod know,' Walsh nodded towards the captain, 'he'll get you what you want. It'll all be off the books so don't worry about accounting for any of it.'

'Thanks for that.'

'Nick, al-Baghdadi is one of the worst. His list of crimes is getting longer by the day. He runs his area with utter ruthlessness and a total disregard for the rights of any of the immigrants, be they men, women or children.'

Perez spoke up. 'He's also a pervert.'

'How so?'

The captain shrugged and grimaced. 'Little girls, mainly. Pre-pubescent.'

'How do you know?'

'We had a report two day ago from one of our men. You were

almost too late. We had him in our sights when he left Libya for Europe. We lost him immediately thanks to his connections, his various identities and his wealth. And make no mistake Nick, the guy is already rich.'

Walsh smiled. 'But not for long if Isobel has anything to do with it.'

'You're right there,' said Hunter.

'What do you mean?' asked Perez.

'Whenever we can,' answered Hunter, 'we relieve the enemy of their assets and wealth.'

'How do you manage that?'

'God alone knows. We do the donkey work while Isobel and her team do their magic with their computers.'

'What's the donkey work?'

Walsh answered. 'Identifying banks, names, accounts sometimes. Isobel and her lot have become pretty adept at it. Do you remember last year?' There followed a few minutes of reminiscences to which Perez sat listening in awe.

When they'd finished, Perez said, 'Why don't we do that in all cases?'

'The law gets in the way,' was Walsh's stark answer.

The marine who had brought Hunter across to the hangar was passing the window and Walsh called to her.

'Rima, fetch the other members of Commander Hunter's team, will you? In meeting room alpha.'

'Yes, sir,' she saluted.

'Does she always salute?' Hunter asked.

'She'll get over it. She only arrived two months ago from basic training and all this is new to her. Basic training fed her the spit and polish end of the marines, which we now need to cleanse her of.'

'You don't normally take new entrants.'

'You're right. We have her for her language skills. She speaks seven languages fluently and another three better than a Bronx native speaks English. She's here as a teacher and interpreter and so far she's proven to be very useful. She also isn't squeamish.'

'Where's she from originally?'

'Syria. She saw a lot and hates a lot. When it comes to dealing with certain types such as the people smugglers she's as ruthless as any of us.'

'Family tortured and killed?'

'You got it in one. Her family was Jewish. Her family name is Kameo. She was training to be a doctor. Now she's a marine grunt.'

'Can't you get her to continue her studies?'

'Not according to her file. It's been suggested to her but she's not interested. It appears she said revenge doesn't come from being a doctor and left it at that.'

'Revenge is a corrosive emotion,' said the RN commander.

'But a powerful one,' said Perez.

'Okay Nick, let's go to the briefing room.'

The three men crossed the massive hangar to a further corner. There were a few men about but not many.

'What's your contingent?'

'Sixty-six plus ancillaries. Fourteen are in action while the rest are taking it easy.'

'Bleepers?'

'At all times. New ones in fact, incorporated into dive watches. They never take them off.'

If a bleeper sounded you dropped what you were doing and headed back to base immediately. It wasn't even 'asap', but instantly. The rumour had it that there had been more than one embarrassing incident, but that was more folklore than fact. It made for a good laugh over a few beers.

The room was big enough to seat 50 people in five ranks of ten using uncomfortable canvas chairs. On one wall was a screen four by four metres and in front of it stood a collapsable table. There was a computer console to the left alongside which lay an infrared pointer. In a corner stood the usual coffee machine, fired up and ready to go.

The rest of the team arrived. There were a few minutes of pleasant reunion as well as introductions to Perez and Samara.

Badonovitch, Masters and Hughes may have been enlisted men but they were senior NCOs, and Walsh may have been a colonel but in the world they inhabited rank was earned not given. And they each had enormous respect for the other. After all, they had been in enough scrapes together.

Walsh pressed a button on the console. The screen on the wall lit up with a lined drawing of a building.

'This is the architect's plan of the ground floor.' He used the infrared pointer. 'The house is five hundred square metres, two hundred and fifty each floor. That makes it just over five thousand three hundred square feet in total.'

'Is there a basement?' Masters asked.

'No. In the original drawings there had been but that wasn't allowed to go ahead for various reasons. I'll come back to that. Let me change to a front of house plan.'

The picture changed to show an elevated drawing of the front of the house. He used the pointer again. 'These are large 'I' beams buried deep into the ground. According to the construction specifications in the plans you could support a skyscraper on them.'

'The place must have cost a fortune,' said Hunter.

'It did. However, al-Baghdadi bought it with a hefty discount.'

'How did he manage that?' Masters asked.

'We're not sure but we think it was part of a business deal with the Mafia for the supply of drugs and slaves at a discounted price.'

Badonovitch said, 'You have to admit it's a pretty good place to have a house. Escape routes by road and sea.'

'As well as an ideal smuggling route into the country,' said Walsh.

'Is that a jetty?' Hughes asked.

The colonel changed the aspect of the drawings to a birds eye view and pointed. 'Yes. It comes out from under the house and sticks out into the sea for ten metres. From the drawings it appears to have been well built and can take a pretty substantial vessel hidden under the house.'

'What about dredging?' Masters asked.

'There's no need,' replied Walsh. 'There's very little sand in that area. It's mainly rocks. There's a gradual beach in the last few metres of shoreline but then it drops away at least three metres and probably more.' He changed the drawing again. 'There are two very large lounges, a massive kitchen and dining area and another slightly smaller room. Maybe a games room or some sort of office. This is a toilet and here's a utility room. Any questions?'

Masters asked, 'Is there a way into the house from the jetty?'

'Yes. A set of stone steps leading to a door at the back of the house. Now the upstairs.' The picture on the wall changed again. 'You can see that there are six bedrooms.' He pointed at each one. 'All are en-suite. There's also a separate bathroom with a large tub with a Jacuzzi, steam room and shower. It's decorated to the highest standard and apparently kept immaculate by a cleaning team that appear only after al-Baghdadi has been and gone.'

'That's a great deal of information,' said Hunter, 'in such a short time.'

The colonel looked steadily at Hunter as though daring him to work it out, which is what he did. 'This is your operation and we've been called in to finish the job.'

6

Abu Muhammad al-Baghdadi was pleased with himself. He mentally sneered at the immigration controls all across Europe as there were none that could keep him out. He knew his Armani suits, fitted shirts and Louis Vuitton leather luggage separated him from the herd. They all screamed out that he was rich and important and not to be trifled with. He travelled on a Saudi passport, which also helped. A rich Saudi could go just about anywhere thanks to petrodollars and an insatiable appetite for oil in the rest of the world. The Saudis were known for being thin skinned and quick to take offence so nobody dared try.

He was sitting at his desk in the house he had bought only months earlier. The money was now rolling in and he was hard pressed to spend it all. He had been brought up with nothing and was used to being careful with his wealth. The lessons were ingrained and so difficult to ignore. On one level his prudence could be mistaken for meanness on another it was the right thing to do. The money could stop at any time, or so he told himself, but it was highly unlikely ever to happen.

Standing up he crossed to his well stocked bar and poured himself a rum and coke with plenty of ice. Since becoming rich he had discovered a liking for alcohol, Cuban cigars and young boys. Sometimes he also included young women in his games of debauchery though that was becoming less frequent. The place was proving to be a good investment. He'd bought it for half its value in cash plus a scheduled payment in drugs and people that added a further 30% to the cost. Thanks to its location, it was already proving to be a good deal.

He looked out of the window. The view was spectacular if you enjoyed watching the never-ending undulation of the sea, sometimes made more exciting when an occasional storm blew up. Otherwise it was as boring as a desert, and al-Baghdadi had seen enough sand to last a lifetime.

In his late twenties, he was ruthless, aggressive, greedy and completely amoral. There was no such thing as right or wrong in his book. It was only what was good for him or bad for him. That was all he cared about.

He had embraced jihad with a passion. That passion had nothing to do with Islam, Muhammad, Sharia or anything else connected to the ludicrous religion as he saw it. His views he kept to himself. He had dared to utter them once and nearly died a very painful death. He had told another man he considered a close friend. Luckily he overheard this friend talking to his mother about it. She in turn advised her son to go to the authorities. He said he would. Al-Baghdadi stepped into the room and shot them both without a second thought. They were the first people he had killed and he found he had a taste for it. Since then he liked to boast that he had killed many people all in the name of jihad. It wasn't true, as most of the killings had been for his personal pleasure.

He logged onto his secure website and started checking his investments. After 20 minutes he was finished and satisfied. His net worth was five million US dollars plus change. The next shipment of goods would be arriving soon and according to his calculations should be worth at least $35,000 from his fees and what he skimmed off the top.

He switched off his computer and turned to the huge screen on the far wall. He played with the controls until he had the porn channel he liked to watch. He found what he wanted and then sent for one of his assistants. He told him which boy and girl he wanted to be sent up.

Walsh grinned and looked at Perez. 'What did I tell you, Rod? It didn't take him long.'

'So you're not denying it?'

'Come on, Nick. What's to deny? It was our operation. Ahmad doesn't know it but we actually helped him get away. We knew he was planning to take one of the boats and escape. We made it seem like it was all his idea. He was about to be shot when one of my lot took care of it.'

The others looked at Samara who in turn was looking shocked. 'I thought I was being so careful. How do you know they knew what I was going to do?'

'One of my guys overheard two of them talking. They were going to kill you. He got to them first.'

'I . . . I would like to thank them.'

Walsh waved a hand. 'All part of the service. We knew that you could identify al-Baghdadi.' The Colonel stared at Samara before adding, 'You came out voluntarily just before we brought you out.'

The implications of the statement appeared lost on the Libyan but the others understood only too well.

'How long have you been working the area?' Hunter asked.

'Coming up to four months.'

'I was about to ask why don't you follow up the job but I get it,' said Hunter.

'You do?'

'Politics,' was the angry reply.

'Yep, Nick. You got it in one. We can do what we do in North Africa and if anyone finds out and points the finger we'd have a number of options.'

'Starting with deny, deny, deny,' said Hunter, 'followed by prove it.'

'Precisely. There it'll be easy enough, here it could be more problematical.'

'Hence us.'

'Hence you. Performing in the way you were commissioned and meant to do.'

'What does he mean?' Samara asked.

Looking at the young man, Hunter replied, 'If the Americans were caught killing someone in Europe, no matter what the provocation, the fallout would be considerable. Every left-leaning, politically correct, anal-retentive will scream blue murder. God alone knows where that would lead.'

'So what happens if we are caught?' Samara asked.

'Our mandate allows us to operate against terrorists and others just about anywhere in the world. There would definitely be some screaming but nothing we couldn't handle. At least for now. We have to see what the future brings.'

'You know something we don't Nick?' Walsh asked.

'Brexit and the Europeans.'

'We wondered about that. Britain being out of the European Union makes Britain safer and what happens in Europe should be sorted by the EU.'

'We're all agreed on that except for one tiny thing,' said Hunter.

'What's that?'

'The Europeans don't like it. At the operational level nothing has changed. Europe's security services still speak to each other. The problem is the politicians and the bureaucrats think they should be controlling events. So without us in the EU they may argue that TIFAT should cease to exist.'

'What if they do? TIFAT is worldwide, not European,' said Walsh.

'We could lose our mandate to operate in Europe.'

Walsh shrugged. 'That'll be Europe's problem. Okay let's get back to the op. Assuming this is a delivery point, we can expect the landing of illegal immigrants and drugs.'

Hunter said, 'Once we start my instructions are not to stop.'

Walsh nodded. 'We want him and his pipeline. That will mean action in Europe. That's why you've been brought in now.'

'We'll roll it up, from Sicily to wherever,' Hunter replied, 'without stopping.'

'I only want al-Baghdadi. That is why I am here,' said Samara.

'That's fair enough,' said Hunter. 'Once we're done with him you can go on your way.'

Tactics and options were discussed, discarded and agreed. The bare bones of a plan of sorts was laid out. As always when on an operation there were too many unknowns to have anything set in stone. Decisions would be made on the hoof, changed and even ignored if and when. It was the way they liked to operate. In the past soldiers going into battle manœuvred in set pieces. This happened right up until the Second World War when things began to change. Now there were no set pieces. Decisions about deployment and action were taken as and when necessary. It meant the people doing the fighting had a better chance of survival. Naturally, those ordering the troops into battle were never in any danger – they were politicians. Hunter often wished he could put a gun in their hands and put them in harm's way.

At 10.35 they broke for coffee and doughnuts.

'How's Malcolm these days?' Walsh asked Hunter as they stood next to the coffee pot getting refills.

'On the whole pretty good.'

'Still battling on all fronts?'

'Yeah, you know how it is. If it wasn't for the support of your President I'm not sure we'd still be in business. We had one battle with a group of MPs just a few months ago and it seems another is looming.'

'Like I said before, come to the States. Operate from there without the political hassle.'

'Sounds good but that's not where the war is. Your National Security Agency is doing a pretty good job. Hiram, you guys have an alphabetical soup of organisations to keep its citizens safe mostly aimed at domestic terrorism. Here in Europe there are far fewer organisations but you know as well as I do this is where the war is happening. Europe is under siege and leaking like a sieve. So we need to be here. The commute to work's bad enough as it is. Another ten hours on a plane would be far beyond the call.'

'I guess you're right. How's the old dog enjoying being married?'

'It suits him. I think it's given him a new lease of life. He has a home to go to instead of sitting in the base all the time.'

A year earlier General Macnair had married Christine Woolford, an ex-Member of the European Parliament. As far as Hunter and the rest of TIFAT was concerned she had shown herself to be a great asset to the organisation. She helped with welfare issues for the families and organised events and outings when the men were away. Knowing your family was in good hands helped when on an operation in an inhospitable land which as far as the teams were concerned was just about anywhere in the Middle East, Africa and now in Europe.

They continued refining their ideas and, most importantly, their equipment requirements. They had brought weapons with them but due to the plan they had devised there was some ancillary gear they needed.

Walsh said, 'Okay guys, we've gone from terminate with extreme prejudice to a far bigger op if we're to roll up the pipeline.'

'We?' Hunter queried.

'Sure. We. If you think you're going to have all the fun you're very much mistaken.'

'What about upsetting our European, I was going to say friends,' said Hunter, 'but you know who I mean.'

'Who are you thinking of using?' Masters asked.

Walsh nodded in the direction of Captain Perez. 'Rod and of course me. Any objections, sergeant?' There was an emphasis on the rank, but it was taken in good humour. After all the man speaking was a bird colonel and outranked everyone in the room.

Master grinned. 'That's what I figured, sir.'

'We also need Rima,' said Hunter.

'Yeah, I agree,' said Walsh. 'We can't hang around off the coast playing at tourists without some female company.' He frowned and stroked his chin, 'I guess we'll invite Lance Corporal Wendy Black as well. She's tough, smart and very pleasing on the eye.'

'I look forward to meeting her,' said Hughes.

Walsh took a mobile phone out of his pocket and pressed a speed dial button. 'Rima, will you come here and bring Wendy with you, please?'

A few minutes later the two women entered the room. Rima was 5ft 5ins tall with a dark complexion and black hair. Wendy was closer to 6ft with short blonde hair and a light suntanned skin. Both women were middle to late twenties and were equally attractive.

The two women came to a halt a few feet away from the colonel and Rima saluted while Wendy stood at ease. After five years in the Corps she knew when to salute and when not to.

'Wendy, Rima, meet these reprobates. That's Commander Hunter, Don Masters, David Hughes and Jan Badonovitch. They're from an organisation known as TIFAT based in Scotland and are here on a job. I want you to take part. We could use your help. Will you do it?'

The women exchanged glances and Wendy shrugged. 'I guess so, sir. But if we're volunteering I'd like to know what we're getting into.'

'That's simple. A couple of days boating, water skiing and parasailing.'

'You're kidding, right?' Wendy said, then added, 'sir,' like it was an afterthought.

'No. We have a surveillance job and we need some camouflage. You'll be playing at tourists a hundred metres or so off a certain beach keeping an eye on a house and its occupants. We'll be covering the road as well but we think if anything goes down it will be from seawards.'

'Are we going to be there all day, sir?' Rima asked.

'Is that a problem?'

'Not for me. But the sun gets high and hot. We'll need shade, a ton of sun block and plenty of cold drinks.'

'Yeah, we've thought of that. Commander Hunter here will arrange a suitable boat, you can arrange the sun cream, food and drinks while these guys sort out the rest of the gear.'

Masters took a credit card out of his pocket and handed it over to Hunter.

'Thanks, Don.'

When on an operation, two credit cards were issued for use by the team allowing them to withdraw money as well as buy items on credit. A one-off account automatically cleared the cards a month later.

They next held a conference call with Isobel and the General and briefed them on their intentions.

'Do we know there al-Baghdadi is now?' Macnair asked.

'At the house,' replied Walsh. 'I have a couple of good men watching the road.'

'What about from seawards?'

'I've had a couple of boats driving back and forth, keeping an eye on the place. According to my guys there's no boat under the house or tied to the jetty. Which means any boat will be coming in from offshore so we've stayed pretty much out of the way. My guys are parasailing and water skiing and keeping an eye on things from far enough away to be unobtrusive.'

'That all sounds as though you have everything under control,' Macnair said. 'All that's left is for me to wish you all good luck.' The connection was broken.

Hunter turned to Samara and said, 'Ahmad, one thing I'd like clarifying. You told us that there's a ship load of immigrants being brought in sometime in the next few days.'

Samara nodded. 'That is correct.'

'Yet you came across in an inflatable boat even if you did only get halfway.'

'It's very simple, Nick. The boat I was on was full of immigrants who would be allowed to escape into Europe and head for any country they chose. That was up to them. The ship I know is coming carries the people who will be sold into slavery, either as workers in the fields, domestics or sex slaves. That is the difference.'

There was very little to be said after such a declaration so they all kept silent.

Hunter and Badonovitch left the base and drove into Catania. They parked at the inner harbour and walked alongside the water. The weather was warm and sunny, there were people strolling aimlessly while others were standing and admiring the large number of boats tied up to the wall and wooden jetties. At the outer wall were a number of Italian warships, one a frigate, the other a destroyer and two patrol craft. From the look of them all four were preparing for sea.

'I guess they're going to hunt for boats of refugees,' said Badonovitch, nodding in the direction of the grey-hulled ships.

'It looks like it. It's a lousy job.'

'Did you ever do it?'

'No. But I came across a ship stuffed with immigrants a couple of years ago.'

'What were you doing?'

'I was sailing around the Greek islands with a friend.' Hunter caught Badonovitch's look and said, 'A woman friend to whom I was very close. We came across a boat that was sinking and had a hold full of men, women and children. The hatch to the hold was also locked.' He paused in his tale, the memories coming back more powerfully than ever.

'So what happened, boss?'

'To cut a long story short we got them out, rescued them and took them ashore. I felt sorry for them. It can't be easy to give up everything you know, face the dangers you do and come to a place where you may not even speak the language. What you go through to get here, physically and mentally, would tax the strength of the toughest people.'

'I suppose desperation makes you tough.'

The two men stopped and looked out across the harbour. A ship's siren sounded three short blasts and the frigate with the number F299 painted on its side slowly made a sternboard away from the wall. They could see the sailors running in the berthing hawsers and then standing to attention in two rows, one in the stern the other in the bows.

It only took minutes for the ship to reach open water and steam majestically away. The Russian looked at his boss and asked, 'Don't you miss it? With your rank you'd probably have command of one of them.'

Hunter shook his head. 'No, I wouldn't. I'd probably have command of a squadron of minehunters, go to sea for maybe a year and then end up in some desk job. The fact is there are far too few ships and too many officers. God alone, plus the Admiralty, knows the exact figure but the RN has more admirals than ships. Nelson, Cunningham, Jellicoe and the rest of the Admirals must be turning in their graves. At least they had fleets to command. I'm better off where I am.'

Smiling, Badonovitch said, 'Glad to hear it, boss.' Then he added as an afterthought, 'Better the devil etcetera.'

'There's somewhere we can get a drink and something to eat.' They approached a bar named Caffe del Porto and went inside. The place was packed but they managed to find a table. There were some patrons who were obviously tourists but most of the clientele were locals. Hunter guessed the majority of them were fishermen who had been out for their early morning catch and were now back for food, a few drinks and a siesta.

'The indoor smoking ban doesn't seem to have reached as far south as Sicily,' observed Hunter.

Most of the men were smoking, there was a clatter of dishes and cutlery and a good deal of loud talk accompanied by hand gestures and arm waving. Neither man understood a word of what was being said. A waitress appeared to take their order of fish soup and a couple of cold beers.

'See anything we can use?' Badonovitch asked.

'I fancied that converted trawler. At least that's what it looks like.'

'With the green hull and awnings?'

'Yeah, that's the one. Something like that will be ideal. We'll need a speedboat as well.'

The waitress appeared and Hunter paid her there and then. He added a generous tip and asked if there was a yacht broker anywhere nearby. She gave them directions and left them to their meal.

'This is very good,' said Badonovitch.

'It is. When we've finished let's carry on around the harbour and then find the broker.'

'What if we can't find anything suitable to hire?'

'We will. It's guaranteed. All it comes down to is price.'

After they had finished eating they escaped into the fresh air and continued their perambulation. Finally they arrived at the office of the yacht broker. A sign in the window said it was closed until 5pm.

'It's 15.25,' said Hunter, 'we can come back later.'

They looked through the window at the number of boats and yachts for sale. The display filled the window and was packed with offers.

'Nothing to hire,' said Badonovitch.

'You're wrong. They're all for hire. Like I said, we just have to offer enough money. Do you keep a wasting asset tied up alongside or rent it out for a few days for a premium? Probably even earning a couple of months' berthing fees for a few days of hire. It's a no-brainer.'

'You're right. Hang on boss, there's somebody there.'

Badonovitch rapped the glass door with his knuckles. A man approached and waved them to go away.

'Open the door,' Hunter called, 'we want to hire a boat.' He lifted up his right hand and rubbed his fingers with his thumb using the international sign for money.

The man hesitated for a moment, shrugged and then opened the door.

Hunter greeted him with, 'Do you speak English?'

He looked to be in his forties, thickset with a bald head compensated for with a bushy moustache. He was dressed in an open-necked white shirt and black trousers and looked like a salesman.

'Of course. We are closed. Would you care to come back at five o'clock?'

'No we wouldn't,' said Hunter. 'What we will do is discuss with you right now the possibility of hiring a reasonably sized boat plus a speedboat. Can we come in?

7

They settled in two chairs opposite the man. The room was typical of its type, with walls covered in photographs of boats for sale, only a few with a red sign of VENDUTO across them. Buying and selling boats and yachts wasn't a booming business in any of the Mediterranean countries. Their economies were too bad and amongst other necessities buying boats came way down a long list. There were three desks, three telephones and three computer terminals. From the dust on two of the desks Hunter guessed they'd been unoccupied for quite a while.

'I am sorry gentlemen, but we only sell yachts.'

'No you don't,' said Hunter.

'I beg your pardon signore, but I know my business.'

Holding up both his hands, palm outwards in a gesture of apology, Hunter said, 'What I meant to say was yes, we realise that but we would still like to arrange to hire two boats. I don't know if you can help. In the window you have a picture of the green hulled boat that's in the harbour. We would like to look it over and rent it for a week.'

'It's for sale,' he shrugged, 'not for hire.'

'Can't you approach the owner and ask him?'

'Sorry, signore, I cannot. He lives in Canada. His instructions are to sell it and wire him the money. The asking price is only one hundred and twenty thousand euros and is not open to any sort of offer. At that price it is a bargain.'

The man swivelled the screen around for the other two to look at. He flicked through a series of photographs. It was as he had said. The boat looked to be immaculate as well as bordering on the luxurious.

'Some boat,' said Hunter, impressed in spite of himself.

'As you say, it is some boat. So the price is well below its value.'

'I'll pay you ten thousand euros for a one week hire.'

The man looked a little surprised but still hesitated.

Hunter wanted to get on with the job in hand and said, 'Okay, the money in cash plus three thousand brokerage fee.'

Still the man hesitated and then licked his lips. 'That's a lot of money.'

'It is.'

'Why do you want it so badly?' He seemed to have a sudden thought. 'You don't want it for smuggling do you? People or drugs?'

'No, of course not.' Hunter sighed and said, 'We want to impress a couple of ladies and we want to do it where we won't be seen. That's all. You know how it is.' He shrugged, 'Somewhere the wives can't follow us, if you get my meaning.'

The man smiled broadly, leant back in his swivel chair and stroked his moustache. 'Si, I understand all too well. We are all men of the world. It is an advantage I have owning such a business. The stories I could tell you.' Then the broker suddenly said, 'This is all well and good and you may be paying handsomely but are you able to drive one of these? You need experience. A great deal of it.'

So Hunter showed him his Identity Card with the rank of Commander, Royal Navy on it and explained his qualifications.

The broker smiled. 'Good. Excellent. Now, you said something about a speedboat.' A boat was identified, that carried six and had a top speed of 45 knots. A hire price was agreed, identities by way of passports proven and contracts signed.

Badonovitch stayed in the office while Hunter went around the corner to the nearest bank where he withdrew twenty thousand euros in cash. Returning to the office he was given keys to both boats and instructions where to find them.

'I'd come with you and show you around but I know nothing about boats.'

'You're kidding,' said Hunter.

'No. It is true. I get seasick in harbour. I can sell them but don't ask me to go onboard. So I leave it to you gentlemen.'

'What about diesel, water, oil and most importantly battery charge?'

'The water tanks are empty but the diesel tanks are full. The engines have been run up once a month for one hour,' he glanced at his computer screen, 'the last time nearly a month ago. So the batteries should be fully charged. They are new and maintain a charge for a long time. Near to where she's berthed you will see a petrol and a diesel pump. Next to it is water and a hose. The filling points are aft under the seats.' He grinned, 'I suggest you don't get them mixed up.'

'Thanks,' said Hunter leading the way out of the office.

'Gone to spend some of that cash more like.'

'Jan, that's what I like about you, your cynicism.'

Badonovitch grinned. 'I was never a cynic in the past boss.'

'So what happened?'

'I met you lot.' He chuckled and Hunter joined in the mirth.

The two men went to the trawler that was named *Il Bel Fiore* – 'The Beautiful Flower'. She had been built in Canada in 1992 and was 60ft bow to stern while her beam was 12ft at the midpoint of the deck. She had oak frames and keel while her planking was cedar. She was clinker built, which meant the planks of the hull overlapped adding to the boat's strength.

Hunter and Badonovitch stood on the jetty and looked her over.

'Nice,' said the ex-Spetsnaz after nearly a minute of appreciative examination. Her wheelhouse was a third of the length of the boat and situated in the centre. In her bows were two anchors and two windlasses. In the middle of the open deck was a raised skylight, 1ft high, 6ft long and 4ft wide. The guardrails were silver painted vertical iron stanchions with horizontal bars and a polished wooden rail around the top.

The stern had a similar skylight set slightly forward leaving a bigger stern area. The surround was solid wood and 2ft high. There were lockers doubling as seats around the stern and a table able to seat at least six fixed to the middle of the deck.

Each side of the wheelhouse had 2ft of deck enabling room to walk the length of the boat on either side. The top half of the wheelhouse was glass windows while the bottom half was wood. On the roof was a 3ft long radio mast through which came satnav information as well as allowing connection to the Internet.

There were three doors, two forward and either side of the wheelhouse and one centre aft. The two men stepped onto the deck and Hunter used one of the keys to unlock the port side door.

It opened outwards against the bulkhead and was fixed in position by a brass hook. The hook had a light patination showing it hadn't been handled for sometime. There was a muskiness to the air and Hunter stepped across the deck and unlocked the other door, pinning it back while Badonovitch did the same to the door at the stern.

The windows were the old-fashioned type that slid up and down. A leather strap with holes in it enabled the windows to be opened from a few inches to the full height of 3ft. They opened all the windows to get fresh air blowing through the boat.

There was a light breeze from the west and the air began to stir, taking away the heavy feel of a stale atmosphere.

The console in the front had the dials and warning lights associated with a twin-engined vessel. Those down the left-hand side were replicated down the right in the middle of which was an 18ins diameter wooden wheel with spokes - the helm. The captain's chair was fixed to the deck by a chain and could be moved a couple of feet in any direction. A hatchway protruded 2ft into the wheelhouse with waist high wooden doors and a sliding hatch. Hunter opened both to let in the air.

There was a large table in the middle of the saloon with white leather cushioned bench seats running the length of the saloon on both sides. At the back, on the port side, was a chart table with shallow drawers underneath. A quick glance showed they contained charts of the area but they obviously hadn't been used in a long while. Electronic navigation ruled the waves, not sextants, a pair of dividers, a roller ruler and pencils.

'This is pretty nice, boss,' Badonovitch looked around appreciatively. 'I could fancy a few weeks of cruising around the Med. Just for
fun for a change.'

'Jan, you'll be bored in less than a week and climbing the bulkheads
in a fortnight.'

'Maybe. Still, with the right company . . .' he left the thought
dangling in the air.

'Jan, you take a look around the rest of the boat while I check the
diesel and water situation.'

Standing at the console, Hunter identified the keys for the engines,
separated them from the bunch and inserted them into the two igni-
tions. He half turned them watching as dials flickered into life and
various lights came on. Both diesel tanks indicated full. The battery
dial flickered to the fully charged position so he pressed the button to
start the port engine. It immediately burst into life. The starboard one
started just as smoothly. He stood there for a few minutes looking at
the dials. The oil pressure for both engines showed in the correct
zones. He flicked a couple of switches and put his head out the port
door and looked down at the seawater. Three thin jets of water were
dribbling out of the hull near the waterline. She was a sound vessel but
even the best wooden boat took on some water over a period of time.

Hunter took hold of the helm and spun it clockwise and then anti-
clockwise, gratified to see the rudder indicator following the
movement.

Badonovitch stuck his head up through the hatchway and said,
'Pretty nice boss. Four cabins, one en-suite, a shower, a head and a
galley better equipped than my place.' Which didn't mean a great deal
as he either ate on the base at Rosyth or bought ready made meals
from one of the supermarkets.

'The dining area will seat eight and there's everything we need in
cutlery, glasses and crockery. There's no food and I've switched on
the fridge.'

'Okay, in that case let's move and get the water tanks filled then
we'd better do some shopping.'

They removed the numerous ropes securing the boat alongside until all that was left was a bow rope and a sternrope.'

'Okay Jan, take off the sternrope.'

Badonovitch removed the rope from the bollard and threw it onboard. He walked along the jetty, picked up the bow rope and pulled the bows closer. He stepped onboard while Hunter spun the helm to starboard and put the starboard engine into astern. The boat moved away majestically from the wall. Once clear, Hunter moved the throttle to the neutral position, waited a second and then moved it into slow ahead. He engaged the port engine and *Il Bel Fiore* began to inch forward, picking up speed.

A few minutes later they secured alongside the fuelling jetty and began to fill the water tanks. It would be a long job with just a single hosepipe.

'There's no point in wasting time,' said Hunter, 'one of us needs to go shopping for supplies.'

'I'll go, if you like. There's a microwave in the galley as well as a Calor gas cooker. There are two bottles, one attached and one spare. Both show full.'

Hunter handed over a wad of euros. 'We passed a supermarket at the edge of town. Better buy enough for dinner and breakfast for seven. Get some steaks or something. Easy to cook with garlic. Also a few beers, wine and a bottle or two of the good stuff.' Then he added, 'Not Indian whisky like last time.'

Badonovitch grinned. 'It was pretty rough. The equivalent of Polish vodka rather than the real Russian stuff.'

'Whatever. I'll leave it to you. I'll also fetch the speedboat and top up her tanks.'

The boat held a lot of water and the hose hadn't much pressure behind it so he left the tap running and went to find the speedboat. The boat was a Starcraft, with two large outboard Evinrude engines. He saw that the boat had an English name – *The Mercury*. It had white leather bench seats plus a seat behind the helm for the driver. There was a tripod 6ft high above the engines to which a towrope could be fastened for water skiing or parasailing. Hunter quickly established the fact there was no petrol in the tanks but an empty can was hidden in the bows. He took it with him, returned to *Il Bel Fiore*, checked the water gauge, which was showing half full, filled up the can with petrol and returned to *The Mercury*.

It took a few minutes to transfer the petrol, prime the engines, flash them up and drive across to the trawler. He tied up alongside *Il Bel Fiore* and clambered onboard. The water was just beginning to spill over onto the deck. He swapped the hose to the second tank and left it to fill. Next, he filled the petrol tanks on the speedboat and also topped off the spare can. The water had been free; the petrol required his credit card. The price per litre made him wince.

Onboard the trawler he checked under the seats. Beneath the leather cushions were lockers mainly empty but a few contained pillows. The locker on the starboard side was a revelation. When the cushion was removed and the lid raised there was a gas-fired barbecue that extended upwards on four stainless steel legs.

By now it was 19.45 and sunset was an hour away. He leant back against the stern seat and let the sun shine on his face while he used his mobile phone.

'Hiram? Nick. I thought I'd bring you up to date.' When he had finished he asked, 'Anything your end?'

'All quiet. Al-Baghdadi is still in the house. We've seen a couple of men arrive and leave again. We used one of the small drones to do an infrared check of the place and as near as we can tell there are eleven people in the house.'

'That's a crowd.'

'Presumably armed guards as well as staff.'

'Could be. But even if there are staff they'll also be a part of al-Baghdadi's entourage.'

'A room of enemies,' said the Colonel.

'Cockroaches more like. They need annihilation. It's just a case of when.'

'Like the General said, watch for forty-eight or even seventy-two

71

hours and then move. If anything happens all well and good, if not, the main objective will be to kill him and anyone with him and get out.'

One of the many things Hunter liked about the American colonel was that he never resorted to ludicrous euphemisms. Kill al-Baghdadi and anyone with him and get out after, of course, they had lifted any and all information dealing with Tripolitania and ISIL. More specifically, assets financial and human as well as any intelligence about potential attacks in Europe.

'What's next, Nick?'

'I think it'll be a good idea if the others join us. We can sit around the deck, be seen and generally act like holidaymakers.'

'Do you think it's likely al-Baghdadi has anyone watching the port?'

'Probably not. But you know me Hiram. Better safe than sorry.'

'Is the boat big enough to accommodate everyone?'

'Yeah. Four cabins, a dining saloon that has a bench seat that folds down into a bunk and another bunk in the wheelhouse.'

'Okay. They'll be with you in an hour or so. There's a load of kit to bring but it's all packed and ready.' Walsh chuckled. 'I hope you all have a pleasant evening.'

When Badonovitch returned they moved the trawler back to her berth and tied the speedboat alongside. The good stuff was a couple of bottles of Glenfiddich malt whisky, while the wine was Italian red and the beer German.

The others arrived half an hour later in two SUVs they'd borrowed from the SEALS. They carried a load of gear onboard and stowed it in appropriate places with special care being taken with their various weapons.

The para-sail they placed in the forepeak of the speedboat along with two pairs of waterskis.

Once they'd claimed their bunks, Hunter flashed up the barbecue and started grilling steaks while Wendy went below to prepare a salad. Into the oven they emptied a large bag of oven-ready French fries and then settled down to enjoy an evening around the table in the wheelhouse.

Walsh and Hunter had discussed the merits of there being such a large party but it was obvious really. Nobody expected a surveillance team of eight people playing at water sports to be watching anybody. The idea was ludicrous.

Although they sat around until nearly midnight they were, on the whole, abstemious when it came to alcohol. A whisky apiece and a couple of glasses of wine with their food was about all they had.

The men from TIFAT never talked in public about their exploits or any of the operations they had ever conducted but Wendy Black brought up the subject after they had eaten and the dishes had been cleared away.

'I asked the Colonel about you lot,' she began, looking around the table at them, 'and he was most enlightening.'

'Huh,' said Badonovitch, 'I doubt that. He'd never tell anyone anything about what we get up to.'

Wendy smiled and said, 'Exactly.'

'What do you mean,' asked Masters, 'exactly?'

'He talked a lot, said nothing and obviously has the highest regard for you all. He told me you were an intelligence gathering organisation based in a town called Rosyth in Scotland.'

'So?' Hughes said.

'So there is no way that Colonel Hiram B. Walsh would spend nearly two years with an outfit collecting and analysing information. We have the NSA to do that. He's an active soldier and one of the best. So you know what I did?'

Hunter said, 'Tell us.'

'I phoned my brother. He works at the Pentagon and is an analyst and that was a very enlightening conversation.'

'You shouldn't have done that,' said Hunter.

'Why not?'

The team looked at each other and Masters said, 'You could have asked us. We'd have told you.'

'No you wouldn't have. You said the weapons were for defence yet you've brought explosives as well. You said we're a surveillance

73

team but that doesn't really stack up. And I know you're not. You're proactive, not reactive. You take the fight to the enemy not wait to be attacked and that means there are no arrests and no trials. Am I right?'

Hunter shrugged and the team exchanged looks. 'Do you have a problem with any of that? If you do you'd better leave now and head back to base.' What he didn't add was that she would be on the next plane back to the States and given some crummy job until she decided to quit the marines.

Wendy laughed. 'My brother confirmed, in his roundabout way, what I thought.' She shook her head. 'I love it and I love to be a part of it. I don't know about any of you but I hate the swine. I was on patrol a month ago when we found a capsized boat built to hold maybe twenty passengers at a push with fifty onboard. Half of them were dead, nearly all children. I helped get the bodies onto the ship to take them to shore for a proper burial. The memory of that day will stay with me for the rest of my life. And it's something we're coming across on a daily basis. The people traffickers have to be stopped and I know no way other that what you're planning to do. So yes, you can count me in and believe me, if and when it comes to pulling the trigger I will do so without a single qualm.'

'Good. Then you're more than welcome,' said Hunter, raising his glass.

A short while later they turned in. Hunter was using the turndown bunk in the wheelhouse.

He slept like a log. Sunrise was at 05.45 and he woke with it. He changed into running gear and hit the pavement, working up a sweat over the next 45 minutes. He followed that with a swim along the seashore, covering the best part of a mile in 22 minutes. Not his best, but not bad, he figured.

When he returned to the *Il Bel Fiore* he had a surprise. Sitting at the table on the aft deck was Hiram Walsh and a very attractive woman. According to the carton in front of them they were drinking glasses of freshly squeezed orange juice.

8

'Hi Hiram.'

'Nick! Good workout?'

'Yes, thanks.' He had recovered his breath and stood on the jetty with his hands on his hips. 'The others are out there somewhere,' he waved a hand nonchalantly. 'Who are you, ma'am?'

'Sorry, I'm forgetting my manners. This is Captain Elizabeth Montgomery. Lizzie to her friends.'

Hunter nodded at her and smiled. 'Okay. Sure. If you want.'

'What's that supposed to mean?' She frowned.

Walsh laughed. 'Nick knows why we're here. Okay means he's okay with it. Sure means, yes, come and if you want means just that. Which is what we do want. I figured ten was even better than eight in the party.'

Hunter didn't tell him of his misgivings. The problem was, Walsh was a senior officer, Rima and Wendy were very junior by comparison. It could make things awkward.

'You sure you don't mind?'

Hunter grinned. 'Of course not. Sitting back at base all day would drive anyone nuts. So you want in. Honestly, that's fine by me.'

'I also have some info. A boat arrived there last night. Just one occupant.'

'What sort of boat?'

'We don't know the make but it's an open speedboat probably capable of holding eight even more passengers. A real substantial piece of kit according to my guys.'

75

'Okay. Thanks, Hiram. Now, if you'll excuse me. I've come for a towel and a change of clothes.' He stepped aboard, grabbed his bag and went back ashore. Across the harbour was a low blockhouse of toilets and showers for visiting yachtsmen. He used one of the showers and, dressed in a short-sleeved white shirt and cut-off shorts and trainers, headed back towards the boat. The others had returned and stopped on their way to the showers.

Masters asked, 'What's with the colonel?'

'He wants in.'

The REME sergeant raised his brows but before he could say anything Hunter spoke.

'Yeah, I know. It shouldn't take him long to realise it.'

'I hope you're right, boss,' said Badonovitch.

Hunter arrived back at *Il Bel Fiore*. The table in the stern had been laid; a fresh pot of coffee awaited them along with glasses of orange juice.

'You okay?' Hunter addressed Walsh and Elizabeth.

The Colonel stood up, said something to the Captain and stepped ashore. 'Come with me, Nick, will you?'

The two men strolled along the jetty.'I guess this wasn't a good idea.'

Hunter kept quiet.

'But you knew that didn't you?'

'Hiram, there are a couple of young and junior members of your outfit here and no matter how relaxed we are there's a limit and from private to colonel is too far a stretch.'

'You're right, I see that now. I just wanted in. It's damned difficult to be standing back, directing operations and not taking part.'

'You had pretty much the same job with us.'

'No. I did a few ops in my time.'

'Yes, you did.'

'Okay, do me a favour. Tell them I was called back on urgent business.'

'Of course. What about the captain?'

76

'Divorced eighteen months ago, thirty-three years old, no boyfriend that I know about and a thoroughly nice woman. And no, nothing to do with me. Never sleep with the staff. It causes far too many problems and ruins far too many careers. Besides which, you know full well that I am happily married. So long Nick, see you later.' Walsh took a few paces, stopped and looked over his shoulder, 'She's also too good for you!' He carried on, chuckling.

Hunter returned to the boat, sat down at the table and helped himself to juice and coffee.

'Where's the colonel going?'

Hunter took a closer look at Elizabeth Montgomery. She had black, straight hair that reached her lobes, clear brown eyes, a straight nose and a wide mouth. Now that he was looking more closely he could see that she was very attractive.

'Do I pass muster?' She smiled.

'Oh, sorry. I was thinking about something. Not paying any attention. What did you say?'

'Where's the colonel going?'

'RTB. Something's come up with one of his men in Libya.'

'Nice try, Nick. Return to base my foot but we'll leave it at that.'

So she's no fool either, thought Hunter. 'What do you do? I take it you work for Hiram.'

'Yes. Where Rod deals with operations I deal with administration.'

'From the look of your tan you've been here a while.'

'Just a month. Here come the others.'

The team arrived and clambered onboard.

Hughes said, 'I'll go below and see how breakfast is doing. Where's the colonel?'

'RTB,' Hunter replied.

Breakfast was a mixture of cold meats, hard-boiled eggs, cheeses and fruit with freshly baked bread from a local specialist bread shop.

When they'd finished eating and had fresh coffees or teas in front of them Hunter said, 'Okay, we'll cast off in ninety minutes. Two and a half hours to get there, and then the sport begins. Remember, weapons available but out of sight. If we make enough of a nuisance of ourselves I suspect somebody will come to investigate. That may give us a chance to assess how professional they are.'

'What are we doing at night?' Elizabeth Montgomery asked.

'Anchoring offshore and keeping an eye on things only closer than your guys are right now.'

'In that case,' said Rima, 'we need more provisions.'

'Dave, take this. He handed over the credit card. 'Rima would you mind helping him? Get what you think we'll need. Also buy plenty of bottled water while you're at it. The water in the tanks is good enough for showering but we'd better not risk drinking it unless it's boiled first.'

Hunter went into the wheelhouse and took out a folio of charts that covered the area. He found the one he wanted and examined it closely. It was deep water to within 100 metres of the coast. Hence anchoring would mean pretty close proximity to the house. Interesting was his reaction.

It was well over an hour before Hughes and Rima returned with the provisions. The boat was ready for sea and minutes later Hunter was at the helm and they were heading out of the marina. Badonovitch and Wendy Black followed in the speedboat. Once the boats were clear of the harbour they tied *The Mercury* to the stern of *Il Bel Fiore* and headed north.

The sky was cloudless, the sun was hot and the slight breeze did little to cool the temperature. In the forward hold was a pile of aluminium stanchions and canvas awnings that they erected in the bows and the stern. It was a relief to get out of the sun. Inside the boat there was a highly efficient air-conditioning system that kept the atmosphere to a pleasant temperature.

The team checked their weapons; every gun was fitted with a silencer and secreted in suitable places around the boat.

After ten minutes at the helm Hunter engaged the autopilot, stood watching it operating for a few minutes and then went out on deck. David Hughes was in the bows sitting on a comfortable canvas chair, with binoculars, keeping watch.

By now the minor chores that had claimed their attention were finished and they were lolling around, enjoying the peace and tranquility of their surroundings. The engines were well insulated and were a soporific murmur in the background. Like Special Forces the world over the team was taking advantage of the downtime and dozing, storing sleep was how they saw it. Originally dismissed as a myth, the Sleep Council had done an investigation into sleep storage to be sure that it worked. For the military it had a name – combat sleep.

Combat sleep wasn't helping the women or Samara. They were seated at the table reading. Hunter was amused to see all four had Kindles, while on the other hand he read books. Usually paperback thrillers. He enjoyed the escapism and the triumph of the good guys over the bad. Sometimes not the case in real life.

He was standing on the starboard side, looking out to sea, when he sensed a presence next to him. He turned his head to look into the brown and captivating eyes of Captain Elizabeth Montgomery.

'This is wonderful' she said in a low voice.

'Yes, it is. Pity about what we're going to do. At times like this it seems so unreal.'

'Do you know Reginald Heber's poem, From Greenland's Icy Mountain?'

'One of my favourites.'

She looked at him in surprise.

Smiling, he recited the first verse. Then he said, 'It's the second stanza that sums it all up.'

When he started Lizzie joined in.

> *'What tho' the spicy breezes*
> *Blow soft o'er Ceylon's isle;*
> *Though every prospect pleases,*
> *And only man is vile?'*

'Apt, don't you think?' she asked softly.

'Yes. It's a ludicrous world when all's said and done but it's the only one we've got.'

'Do you like poetry or just that poem in particular?'

'I like poetry of all sorts. Kipling, Walter de la Mare, you name them.'

'You're quite a contradiction aren't you, commander?'

Hunter looked uncomfortable for a moment. 'Not really.'

'A lover of poetry, from what I've learnt about you a man with a soft heart, probably a romantic, yet you kill people for a living.'

'No, I don't,' he said softly.

'What's all this then?' She waved her hand around her.

'I don't need to do this for a living. There are plenty of other jobs I could do.' What he didn't say was that by anyone's standards he was wealthy. His great-great-grandfather Evan Griffiths had laid the foundations for the family fortune and that had been expanded many times over by his great-grandfather Sir David Griffiths. Now the family business, though a listed company on the stock exchange, was a worldwide conglomerate. It controlled businesses in banking, insurance, the offshore oil industry, mobile phones and a lot more besides. Even though his was only a small percentage of shares it still meant he had more money than he could spend in half-a-dozen lifetimes and probably longer as their value was increasing annually. He never mentioned his financial situation, especially to members of the opposite sex. He wanted a woman to like him for himself, not for his money.

She nodded. 'Yes, I guess so. So why do this?'

'For the most contrite reason in the world.'

'Which is?'

'Someone has to. We can't let evil win and there's a hell of a lot of it about in the world today.'

'There always has been.'

Hunter nodded. 'I'm afraid that's true but this enemy is nothing like anything we've faced before. Then it was army against army. This is something else entirely. It's insidious, yes and vile, and deadly.'

There was silence for a few seconds before she said, 'Please call me Lizzie. All my friends do.'

Hunter smiled and looked into her eyes. There was warmth there and possibly something else. If that were the case, whatever it was, it would have to wait. 'Okay Lizzie, and I'm Nick.'

'Hiram told me something about you.'

'Oh? Nothing good I hope.'

Lizzie smiled. 'Nothing bad at any rate. It seems you're something of a legend in the world of Special Ops. He told me about some of the exploits you and TIFAT have been involved in. It's quite a record.'

Hunter shifted his shoulders uneasily. Praise never sat well with him. 'Yeah, he shouldn't have.'

'We inhabit the same world, Nick. And anyway, before I joined this party I wanted to know what I was letting myself in for. It's one thing to be with my own lot, it's another to team up with a bunch of strangers.'

'I guess you're right. I hadn't thought of that.'

'Boss,' Hughes called, 'there's a ferry coming in on the starboard bow. About four miles away.'

'I see it. I'd better check if we need to alter course.'

He stepped into the cool air of the wheelhouse and stood at the helm. According to the radar the ferry was now about three miles away and on a steady bearing. He twisted the autopilot dial 90 degrees to starboard to make his intentions obvious. When it was evident that the vessel would pass well clear he changed their course again to port and watched as the ferry sailed away. There was nothing else around to cause any concern and he returned to where he'd been standing. Lizzie was sitting down again reading her e-book, so their tête-à-tête was over. She glanced up, caught his eye and gave a small smile.

It was near enough lunchtime when they approached the area where the house was situated. Hunter and Masters stood in the wheelhouse examining the place through their binoculars.

Badonovitch had the helm, Perez was in the bows and the others were standing under the aft awning watching proceedings. The boat slowed and its forward movement stopped by putting the engines into reverse. 'Let go!' ordered Hunter.

Perez tapped the shackle holding the anchor with a hammer. The anchor dropped and the chain paid out. According to the echo sounder the seabed was 20 metres down, the anchor hit the bottom, the chain went slack then tightened as it took the weight, it paid out a few more metres and then Perez stopped the windlass. In naval terms the boat had her anchor.

Rima and Wendy went below to fix lunch. They appeared within minutes carrying cold meats, mixed salad, and avocados with prawns and fresh crusty bread. The food had barely been laid out on the table when Masters called out.

'Here they come. Right on cue.'

They all looked to port and watched as the speedboat that had been berthed underneath the house came rapidly in their direction.

9

The boat stopped a few metres away. Hunter stood leaning nonchalantly on the guardrail. He looked as though he hadn't a care in the world.

The boat had three men. They looked to be in their twenties, black haired, unshaven wearing scowls, short sleeved shirts and jeans.

'You cannot stop here,' said the man standing in the bows. In the stern the man at the wheel looked nervous while the third man was sitting in the middle of the boat with his hands out of sight. It was obvious what he was doing but if he tried anything he would be dead in less than a second. Masters was armed and watching things from the bows, seated in a canvas chair with a canvas screen around the guardrails. If the man in the boat tried to lift a gun to threaten them Masters would merely shoot him through the canvas. The other two would be dead about two seconds later.

The boat could hold at least ten passengers plus a driver. It was immaculate, had two massive outboard engines and was probably capable of a speed far greater than *The Mercury*. A playboy's toy or a working boat, Hunter wondered?

Hunter merely looked at them. He knew how disconcerting that could be. Say nothing and see what they did. Probably threats and a lot of yelling.

There wasn't long to wait.

The man yelled. 'Do you understand?'

They all stood still, said nothing and stared at the other boat.

'Do any of you speak English? Listen you swine, go away. You are not allowed to stop here.' He pointed out to sea. 'Go!'

He looked over his shoulder at the man in the middle and in Arabic asked, 'What shall we do?'

'Shoot them,' said the man.

'Don't be so stupid. What do we do with the bodies? Your answer to every problem is to shoot somebody.'

'It usually works. Take their boat out into deeper water and sink it. Easy. We will be long gone from this place before anyone even misses them. There are eight of them, we have three automatic guns. They will be dead in ten seconds.'

It seemed to Hunter that the man doing the talking had changed his mind and was giving serious thought to the idea but as killing the three men right then was not in their plan he decided to speak.

'We will stay here until we decide to leave. We are going to water ski and parasail. Maybe do some diving. You will stay clear or the next time you come here we'll put you in hospital for a week.'

The men exchanged glances and then they burst out laughing. When they got their mirth under control the man in the bows said, 'If you are still here tonight we will sink you.'

The driver said, 'Abu, let us just do it now. We have the ship coming tonight. We cannot have these animals watching what we do.' He spat into the water. 'Look at those women. They are whores, filth. Look how they dress. They need to be taught a lesson. I would like to teach them.'

'That may be an idea. We will see if they are still here tonight. If they are we can return, kill the men, have the women and then sink the boat with their bodies inside. What's eight more after all the immigrants who have died?'

Hunter called out. 'Now get lost!'

'Remember what I said! You had better not be here tonight!'

The boat made a sternboard, turned and raced back towards the shore. They watched it go.

'What did he say, boss?' Badonovitch asked.

Rima did the translating.

'So something is going down tonight,' said Hughes. 'We'd better get ready.'

'We will,' Hunter said, 'but in the meantime we'll have some fun. Do a bit of chain yanking.'

They sorted out the parasail and tossed coins to see who would be flying first. Lizzie won.

The sail they used was unlike that available to enthusiasts of the sport. Theirs was a shallow V shape of expandable aluminium, each arm 1.5 metres long and .75 metres wide. Stretched over the aluminium was a strong nylon sail into which helium could be injected giving it extra lift and was the reason the contraption, designed and built at TIFAT, was so small.

Lizzie dressed in a wetsuit jacket and pulled a mono-ski onto her right foot. She slid into the water, drifted apart from *The Mercury* until her towrope was no longer slack, yelled 'hit it' and the boat took off. She was holding the sail above her head, the wind caught it immediately and raised her serenely into the air. Seconds later she kicked off the ski and concentrated on her height and course relative to the speedboat. She watched as the *Fiore* went alongside her ski and recovered it.

'Lizzie,' transmitted Hunter, 'drop the rope and do your own thing.'

She pressed the release switch in the left-hand grip and the rope fell away. She stopped being towed and immediately her speed reduced drastically. She allowed the wing to head gently down until she was at about 15 metres above the sea and then she injected more gas using a button in the right grip. A few seconds of helium sent the wing soaring upwards and at 50 metres she used the deflate button in the left grip to control her rise and fall.

Masters had won the second toss and five minutes after Lizzie was airborne soaring free 100 metres away from her.

Hunter was driving *The Mercury* and took the boat in close to shore. With him were Badonovitch and Hughes. The former had a Glock 21 cocked and locked while Hughes had a sniper rifle with state-of-the-art telescopic day and night all-weather sights. The weapon had been designed to achieve a first round hit at 600 metres and harassing fire out to 1,100 metres. In David Hughes' hands it resulted in a first time hit every time out to at least 1,000 metres.

They went in close while Masters flew a few metres above the edge of the roof of the house. There were screams and yells. Men were pointing and shaking their fists and then al-Baghdadi appeared and calmed things down. He stood watching as Hunter took the boat around in a circle, Master's flew over the house one more time and then headed out to sea following the speedboat.

Hunter flipped a middle finger at the house. Childish and pathetic he hoped it gave the impression that they were mere holidaymakers enjoying themselves.

The afternoon continued in the same vein. They switched to water-skiing when Lizzie showed herself to be something of an expert. Mono skiing, she went in close to the shore when two of the men from the house were standing next to the water's edge. The beach was on her left and she signalled to Hughes, the lookout in the boat who was keeping an eye on her safety, to go closer to the shore. He told Hunter who was at the helm and waved his arm in acknowledgement. It was obvious what she was intending to do.

Hunter took the boat in a wide circle while Lizzie stayed upright on the ski. When they were parallel with the beach and she was a mere eight to ten metres away with the two men shaking their fists at her, she leaned over to her right, shifted her weight and went at an angle that took her much closer to the shore. Water was spraying out from under the ski and hit the two men in a deluge. They yelled in fury and jumped back. One of them tripped over and landed on his back at which point Lizzie gave a loud laugh.

Hunter decided they'd tweaked the hyena's tail enough and they returned to the *Il Bel Fiore* in time for a late tea of Italian pastries and an English brew.

Sitting around the table Hunter said, 'Okay, we need to make some plans. Something is happening tonight and we want to see what it is.'

The sun was a diameter above the horizon and there was a refreshing breeze coming from seaward. It was a balmy evening and

Hunter couldn't help thinking it was made for fun and frolics not murder and mayhem.

Hughes said, 'I think we need to move down the coast a few miles.'

'I agree,' said Masters. 'Then we walk back along the shore and see what's going on.' He shrugged. 'We take it from there.'

'Yeah. Okay let's work out the details.'

They spent the next hour doing precisely that.

Lizzie had her mobile phone in her hand and said, 'There's no signal.'

'Who were you calling?' Hunter enquired.

'Hiram. He should be kept in the loop.'

'I'll do that. I have sat-nav communications with him.'

It was fully dark when they flashed up the engines and began to shorten in the anchor.

'Nick,' said Masters, 'it sounds like we've got company coming.'

There was a half moon in a cloudless sky and they could see the dark outline of the speedboat heading their way. It was coming slowly, not making much noise.

Badonovitch was in the bows and said, 'Anchor aweigh.'

Hunter engaged gears and the boat began to slide majestically through the water. He switched on the navigation lights and turned off the deck lights, spun the helm to starboard and aimed for the open sea.

With their night vision goggles they could see the boat as clear as day. There were four men, all armed, sitting in her. They watched as one of the men stood up and pointed at them. He said something but the man at the helm shook his head. The boat turned and headed back the way it had come. David Hughes watched them go, the sights of his sniper rifle fixed firmly on the back of the head of the driver. Four targets, eight seconds. Their would-be attackers had no idea how close they had come to dying.

The *Il Bel Fiore* heaved to a mile south, very close to the beach. They anchored and when the boat was settled and all lights off Hunter contacted Walsh and brought him up to speed on events.

'We had a drone in the air about thirty minutes ago. We have a clear infrared picture that we are sending to you right now. There are still only eleven of them so they shouldn't be much trouble.'

'Thanks Hiram, got it.' Hunter sat looking at the picture that had appeared on his iPad. 'Three patrolling, the rest scattered around the house.'

'If you marry them to the architect's plans you will see that there are two in the kitchen, three in the large lounge, two upstairs in separate bedrooms and one in the smaller room.'

'Okay, thanks. Let me know if anything changes.'

Hunter told the three women and Ahmad Samara to stay with the boat until they were called for. The Libyan argued vociferously.

'You promised. You said that I could be the one to kill al-Baghdadi. That's our deal.'

'First of all, Ahmad,' said Hunter, 'I don't make deals like that. I am only concerned about two things, the safety of my men and the success of the mission. Nothing else matters. If there is anything else it comes well down my list of objectives. I'll do my best to ensure you get your wish I promise you that. When we've done what we've set out to do I'll call you. If it is humanly possible we'll keep the man alive until you get your hands on him.'

With bad grace Samara nodded. 'All right.'

'Lizzie, you take us ashore. When you get back raise the anchor and circle about here. Keep a close eye on the radar but don't show any lights unless you see a vessel that may come anywhere near you. Then put on the steaming lights. I doubt that will happen but you never know. Also take this sat-nav. It's preprogrammed so all you need do is press 'one' and you'll be connected to Hiram as well as me. Okay?'

'Okay, thanks Nick.'

Lizzie drove the speedboat as close to shore as she dared and the team climbed out. They were dressed in camouflage trousers and shirts. Over their heads they wore a thin cotton balaclava, with holes for their eyes, nose and mouth. They moved like evil spectres ready to create mayhem. The water was up to their knees but it was warm and easy to ignore. They'd been in much tougher situations than a stroll along a Mediterranean beach with wet feet. They spread out. Hunter took point and was nearest to the sea. The others stretched back at three metre intervals and at an angle of about 30 degrees. Their NVGs made the shore and sea as bright as daylight.

It was only just coming up to 22.00 and they were taking it slow and easy. Over their earpieces they heard Walsh say, 'Something's up. Three of the men are going into one room. No, they are under the house. Ah, two engines have flashed up. They're taking their speedboat and backing out.'

'Where are they going? Coming after us on the boat?' Hunter queried.

'Nope. They're heading straight out to sea. We're just moving the drone now. There's a ship about five miles offshore. It's barely making any headway.'

'How big?'

'Tramp steamer I'd say. The sort of thing you find servicing the smaller ports around the islands. Let me swap the infrared.' There was a pause. 'Yeah, I've got it loud and clear. I'm not sure what I'm seeing here so let me switch back to infrared.'

The team continued moving forward. They were now about half a mile from the house.

'Nick, you're not going to like this. The deck is jammed full of people. I think they are going to be smuggled ashore in al-Baghdadi's boat. At a guess I'd say there are a hundred people, maybe more. It's your call. What do you want to do?'

'The primary objective hasn't changed. Al-Baghdadi has to be stopped, any info lifted and the trail followed.'

'What about the ship?' Walsh asked. He didn't need to spell it out. The men on the ship would supply other end users in the never ending demand by desperate people to escape to Europe. Who was going to arrest the perpetrators, try them in a court of law, sentence them and put the guilty where? Those were the questions to which there had never been any satisfactory answers, especially from the European Union.

'Leave it to us. I'll see how it goes.'

'Nick, if we call in the cavalry you know what will happen. The crew and their passengers will swear blind that they had been rescued. That the crew are lifesavers. Good guys. We've heard it all before.'

'I know. You're right. So trust me, we'll take care of it. I just don't want any witnesses around.'

They stopped a few hundred metres from the edge of the grounds. The wall to the property came down as far as the water's edge and stopped abruptly. The top of the wall, they knew, was covered with jagged glass and above that were three strands of razor wire. But such defences were as ludicrous as the Maginot Line. Just as the Germans merely drove around the huge and impressive fortifications built to keep them out so all the team needed to do was walk into the water and around the end of the wall.

'Where are the men?' Hunter asked Walsh.

'None near you. They are all under the house, presumably waiting for their guests.'

'Thanks. Let's go.'

The team reached the wall and walked carefully and slowly into the water and around it. Hunter still led the way.

'Nothing has changed,' said Walsh who knew not to expect a transmission from Hunter. When so close to the enemy, silence was the order of the day.

They worked their way out of the water and while Hunter stood next to the waters' edge the others made their way carefully over the rocky ground. Next to Hunter was Hughes, then came Masters, then Badonovitch and then Perez. It was obvious that the finished property did not comply with the architect's drawings. There had been no indication of the three metre high wall that now stretched the length of the property on which sat the front of the house. There was a wooden door about a third of the way along as well as steps under the house. Anyone approaching the house from the front would not be able to see what was happening under the house.

They moved forward slow and painstakingly. They stopped every few paces to survey what was ahead of them. They looked for trip wires and other possible sensors but saw nothing. They were halfway across open ground when Walsh said, 'Someone's coming. From straight ahead.'

Neither the present or previous owners had made any attempt to landscape the grounds. The result was uneven land with rocks and a few boulders of all shapes and sizes. It took only seconds for all five men to find a rock to hide behind.

The approaching man was as clear as though it was high noon. He was cradling an AK74, the later model of the infamous AK47, the most manufactured gun in history with over 100 million in circulation.

The team waited patiently. The man walked past the rock behind which Badonovitch was hiding. The ex-Spetsnaz stood, took a step, put his left hand over the mouth of his quarry and jammed his Ka-Bar through the man's neck and up into his mouth. He held the body while it shuddered in its death throes and then lowered it to the ground. He extracted the knife, wiped it on the body's sleeve and slid it into its sheath on his right thigh.

Nothing was said. It wasn't necessary. One dead smuggler and now just ten to go. Plus from the way the man had walked towards them they had learnt there were no hidden tripwires or sensors.

They reached the edge of the building and stopped. The jetty, sticking 10 metres into the sea was a mere 40 metres or so away. What they hadn't seen before and also hadn't been shown in the architect's drawings were the cages that were built along the back wall.

Walsh said, 'There's nobody near you.' Then he added, 'The speedboat's alongside the cargo vessel. We've counted fifteen heads have climbed down into the boat. It's just left the side. Picking up speed now. Only minutes away.'

While Hunter watched the boat approach the others kept watch on what was happening around them.

The middle of the area was suddenly lit by overhead lights. The new NVGs the team was using instantly reacted to the change and stopped any form of blindness that the older type couldn't handle.

They pulled their goggles down around their throats out of the way. The speedboat approached the jetty and tied up alongside. Six of the smugglers stood cradling their guns and hustled the immigrants along the jetty and pushed them into the furthest cage. One man tried to protest but was clubbed to the ground before being kicked until he crawled into the cage. One of the smugglers was about to close the door when another stopped him, went into the cage, grabbed a young girl by the wrist and dragged her out. She screamed and the man slapped her across her face. She stumbled, he pulled harder and dragged her to the end cage nearest to where the team was hidden and alongside the steps leading into the house.

Patience was a virtue and one learnt a long time ago by the men watching what was happening. The speedboat made three more trips when Walsh announced, 'I counted wrong. There are now twenty heads on the deck of the ship, all immobile apart from four who seem to be patrolling the edge of the deck.'

A figure appeared at the steps and stood watching what was happening. It was al-Baghdadi who from the smile on his face appeared to be very pleased with himself. He looked more closely at the four young girls in the nearest cage and then glanced at the other cages. Two were full of people while a third was half-empty.

Hunter needed to decide whether to make a move or not. The speedboat was alongside with its crew of three and five of the smugglers were standing around in various poses of unconcern.

Hunter watched as one of the smugglers looked in the team's direction. The man shouted out in Arabic, 'Gilad! Gilad! Where is the lazy swine?'

It was obvious they had suddenly missed their dead comrade.

'Go and find him,' al-Baghdadi yelled out.

One of them walked directly towards Hunter. In three paces the man would be alongside Hunter's hiding place but in the dark, the loom of the lights not reaching that far.

The man called, 'Gilad. Where are you?'

Al-Baghdadi looked their way, spun around and started to run for the steps.

10

David Hughes had lined up his shot as soon as al-Baghdadi had appeared. He didn't need telling. His suppressed shot hit the fleeing Saudi in the left knee, shattering it and bringing him down in a scream of pain. The remainder of his men looked at their fallen boss but had barely had an opportunity to take in what was happening when the team opened fire. All were upper torso or head shots. Badonovitch took out two, Masters did likewise, while Hunter stepped out from behind his rock into the path of the man and rammed his Ka-Bar into the man's throat and through his spinal cord. The man gurgled and dropped, the knife sliding clear of the corpse. Perez had the clearest targets and while the kidnappers appeared to be wondering what was going on he took down three of them. One of the kidnappers moved fast. He threw himself into the speedboat and opened fire with his AK74 spraying the area he thought the team was hiding. Bullets hit the rocks and stones around them but caused no damage.

The noise of the AK was deafening in the confined space. The prisoners in their cages were screaming and yelling, some were crying hysterically, all were down on the ground, fighting to get to the back of the cages, to hide behind those less able to defend themselves.

Hunter could see Al-Baghdadi. The man's mouth was opening and closing, his eyes were squeezed tightly shut and he was holding his knee.

'Nick,' said Walsh, 'the ship is turning towards open water and moving away.'

'Roger that.' Hunter was nearest the water's edge, he could see the stern of the speedboat clearly along with the top of its two engines. He took a two-handed grip of his Glock, aimed and opened fire, squeezing the trigger in a controlled and rapid manner. Eight times he pulled the trigger, eight bullets hit the engines and the last one ignited the petrol. It exploded in a fireball and the smuggler leapt to his feet, his clothes alight. Hughes put him out of his agony with a bullet to the head before he could jump into the water.

The flames on the boat died as quickly as they had erupted. Hunter transmitted to the *Fiore*, 'Lizzie, send Ahmad and Rima here in the speedboat while you head out to sea. 'Hiram, give Lizzie a heading to follow the ship. Hiram, we're going to search the house. It shouldn't take too long. Then we'll go after the ship. Can you keep an eye on her?'

'No problem.'

'Lizzie, stay on her starboard quarter and don't get too close.'

'Okay, Nick.'

Walsh said, 'Lizzie, turn onto a heading of one eight zero degrees. The ship is now doing eight knots and is three point five miles south. If you increase speed to ten knots we'll see how things go.'

'Yes, sir,' said Lizzie. 'That's Ahmad and Rima away now.'

Hunter walked across to the steps. Al-Baghdadi looked at him and said, 'Please. Please, the pain. Stop the pain.' The man had spoken English.

Hunter pretended not to understand and stood looking down at him.

'You must help me. I need a doctor,' he moaned.

In Arabic Hunter asked, 'What were you going to do to those young girls?'

Al-Baghdadi said in surprise. 'You speak Arabic!'

'Why shouldn't I?'

'I thought you were English or Italian. You must help me. I am also a Saudi. We are brothers-in-arms. We are of the one true faith. We are against all infidels. You must, for the love of Allah, help me.'

'You may be right. But you must tell me what you were going to do with these people.'

By now the screaming and crying had subsided to an occasional wailing as the people in the cages watched what was going on.

'They, they are for moving into Europe. For freedom and for a better life. I swear. I am just helping these people escape the horrors of the wars and famine of Africa and the Middle East.'

'But why here? Why the cages?'

'It is safer. We take them to Palermo and set them loose a couple at a time. It is best that way.'

'I see that is a good plan.'

Al-Baghdadi nodded eagerly. 'Exactly. I am rich. I can show you. I can prove I do not do this for the money. Such a small amount is paid for transporting these people. It is not worth my time. But my goodness will be my passport to heaven as I serve the one true god.'

Hunter nodded.

It seemed that only then did it occur to al-Baghdadi to ask an obvious question. 'But who are you? Are you working with the Italian police? Their customs? What?'

'Boss,' Badonovitch said, walking across the uneven ground, 'they are all dead. Here's Ahmad.'

The Mercury hit the jetty and stopped. Hughes caught the rope thrown to him by Rima and secured the boat alongside. Ahmad leapt ashore and rushed over to there Hunter was standing He stopped when he saw the body on the ground.

'You have him,' he said hoarsely.

'He's all yours, if you want,' said Hunter. 'Or I can just put a bullet in his brain right now.' Hunter drew his Glock and pointed it at al-Baghdadi.

The Saudi had been looking from Hunter to Badonovitch in some surprise but that turned to shock when he saw Samara.

'Do you know me?' Samara asked al-Baghdadi.

'No!' A moan escaped the Saudi's lips and he said, 'Please, you have to help me. The pain! Do something for the pain.'

'You killed my family. You raped my sister.'

'I don't know what you are talking about. Ah!' Al-Baghdadi

suddenly stiffened as a bolt of pain shot through him and more tears came to his eyes.

'Are you sure you want to do this?' Hunter asked the young man.

'Yes. I am sure. These people are not here to be freed in Europe, they are here to be sold as slaves. They will be sold one, possibly two at a time. They will be taken all over Europe and made to work for a pittance if anything at all. They will be coerced into obeying what they are told and the four young girls there,' he nodded at the nearest cage, 'they will be sold as sex slaves after this man has had his way with them.'

'It's not true,' gasped al-Baghdadi. 'Never! I give you my word. You are British! I can tell from your accent. You can arrest me. Hand me over to the courts. Let me argue my case before a judge. Yes, I am smuggling people but it is for their own good. To give them a better life.'

'For some reason I don't believe you. Ahmad, he's all yours. Make his death slow and painful.'

'It will never happen,' said al-Baghdadi between clenched teeth. He began to grind his teeth together. Suddenly he began to convulse and foam at the mouth. In seconds he was dead.

The others had joined them and they looked down at the body.

'Poison,' said Samara. 'He has prevented me from taking my revenge.'

'Or getting him to answer any questions,' said Hunter. 'Somebody must have a powerful hold on people like this that they'll commit suicide.'

'They are promised a worse death if they talk and will have been told graphically what would happen to their family at the same time,' said Samara. 'I know. They did it to me.' He looked at Hunter, 'I would not be helping you if my family had not all been killed.'

Hunter nodded. 'I can understand that. This is probably for the best. Torturing a man to death, even one who deserves it, leaves an ugly scar. Right, let's take this place apart. Rima,' Hunter called out, 'come and help us.'

Twelve minutes later they met at the backdoor with a laptop and three mobile phones. It was all they could find.

'Ahmad, I want you to keep looking. There might be something else to find.'

'What about the people in the cages?' Samara asked.

Hunter took a deep breath before replying indirectly by speaking to Walsh. 'Hiram, it's too dangerous for Ahmad to release all these people. There's no knowing how some of them will react. They are safe where they are and can stay there for an hour or two. Once Ahmad leaves call the authorities and get some help to deal with them. I think that's the best we can do under the circumstances.'

'I agree.'

'Ahmad, you heard. Don't release any of those people. They are scared and scared people can do stupid things. Also there may be a jihadist or two amongst them who will think nothing of killing you if they think it will help them get away. Okay?'

Samara stared stonily at Hunter.

'Do you understand?' Hunter spoke harshly.

With obvious reluctance Samara nodded slowly.

'Good. Let's stop that ship.'

The team hurried down to the speedboat and climbed onboard. Hunter was gratified to see that Lizzie had topped off the fuel tanks from the spare cans they had brought without being told.

Walsh gave them a heading and Hunter increased speed to 40 knots.

'Nick, the ship is about six miles ahead doing about nine knots with the *Fiore* on station a mile astern. You'll be there in about seven minutes.'

'I can see both stern lights. What's the situation on the deck of the ship?'

'It's empty apart for a man pacing amidships. He's going from port to starboard and back again.'

'What's happened to the immigrants?'

'They must have been taken below. Can you see the lights of the ship?'

'The stern light is as clear as day.'

'You're one mile out and closing fast. Something's happening. Wait a sec. More people are coming onto the deck. They're coming out from the hold. What in hell is going on? Any ideas how you're going to get aboard?'

'Sure. We're getting ready. Don, take the wheel, full speed and get about half a mile ahead of the ship.'

While Masters manœuvered *The Mercury* into position they quickly assembled both parasails. Hunter and Badonovitch stripped and put on wetsuit jacket and trousers followed by the latest bulletproof vests.

'This will do,' said Hunter and Masters brought the boat to a halt. Hunter slipped into the water on the starboard side, Badonovitch on the port. Masters engaged the engines and moved the boat away while the two men each slid a foot into a mono-ski.

'Hiram, is there anybody on the bows of the ship?'

'Negative. What are you going to do?'

'Parasail. Hit it Don!'

In seconds both men were in the air and had dropped the towrope. They injected helium and soared high. They watched as *The Mercury* closed in on the *Fiore*. The speedboat gently touched the side of the larger vessel and David Hughes, complete with his sniper rifle, climbed onboard.

Walsh suddenly transmitted, 'Oh, Christ. People are being herded over the side of the ship!'

'Lizzie,' Hunter said, 'you heard Hiram. Follow and pick up the people in the water!'

They heard the sound of gunfire.

Hunter transmitted, 'Going in now.' He was about 10ft above the deck and Badonovitch about 5ft higher and 10ft further back. Suddenly an AK74 opened up, shredded Hunter's sail resulting in him coming down with a hard thud onto the deck. He landed on his feet, bent his knees and fell flat onto his front. He was twisting onto his side when a bullet hit the steel deck next to him and bounced up hitting him in the stomach. The bulletproof vest saved his life but the wind was knocked out of him as though he'd been kicked by a mule. He gasped for air, rolling towards the front of the superstructure. He expected at any second to be stitched with a magazine of bullets but nothing happened.

Hughes said, 'One less ugly, boss.' The sniper had dealt with their attacker. Hunter had his breathing under control though it still hurt if he took deep breaths. He was aware how close that had been. If the smuggler had been on the other bridge wing the outcome would have been very different.

Badonovitch was suddenly next to him. 'You okay, boss?'

'Yeah, a bit winded that's all. Luckily it was a ricochet.'

Then Lizzie transmitted, 'Nick, we have to stop. We've reached the first of the people in the water.'

'Roger that.'

As was the nature of bridge superstructures, it stretched 20ft into the air. The Captain's cabin would take up the first 10ft or so while the top half would be the bridge itself. It was also angled outwards from bottom to top by about 15 degrees. It meant they could only be seen if somebody put their head over the bridge wing and looked down.

'Dave, can you see anyone else?'

'Negative Nick. But you're moving away.'

'Can you get any closer?'

'Negative, Nick,' Masters said. 'We need to pick up the people first.'

'Hiram what's the situation on deck?'

'There are six people left and I don't think they are going anywhere. Nick, the ship is turning. I think they're going to attack the *Fiore*. Somebody coming out on the starboard bridge wing.'

Hunter looked up, his automatic held in a two-fisted grip, pointing at the bridge wing. The man appeared and leant out, looking down, his AK74 pointing down. He wasn't wearing NVGs so he began to empty his magazine into the deck, starting from the starboard side. He only managed to fire four rounds when Hunter took aim and squeezed off two shots. One hit the man in the throat, the other in his head. He flew backwards out of sight.

Walsh transmitted. 'Port wing. Stepping out now.'

Badonovitch was ready. The target leaned over the side and pulled the trigger of his AK. Nothing happened. In his fear and excitement he hadn't pushed the selector from safe to automatic. Badonovitch fired a double tap with the same result as Hunter.

'We'd better shift it,' Hunter said.

The bridge door was right next to them. It had a heavy handle that needed to be lifted to move two large lugs in the watertight door. Hunter did the lifting, pulled open the door and Badonovitch stepped into the bright lights of a corridor. They removed their NVGs and stood still, listening. All they could hear was the throb of the engines.

A door on their left, the starboard side, said Master, the door on their right First Mate.

They checked both. The cabins were empty as they had suspected but it was never a good idea to have someone sneak up from behind.

From outside the ship had looked to be in poor condition, inside it looked dilapidated. It was the sort of vessel nobody would miss if it sank. That was an option sometimes employed by the smugglers when getting rid of any evidence. It rarely happened in the Mediterranean but wasn't that rare in other parts of the world, like the Indian Ocean, where the trade in slaves for Saudi princes was quite common.

'The ship is moving in a circle,' said Walsh. 'They must have turned the wheel and with nobody to straighten her course the ship will continue circling. At least that keeps them away from the boat and the people in the water.'

'Roger that,' said Hunter.

At the end of the short corridor was a door with the sign Engine Room. Hunter pointed, 'We'll take out the lights and the engines.'

Badonovitch nodded. He grabbed the handle to the watertight door, swept it up, pulled the door open and Hunter stepped over the combing and into the raucous noise of old engines thudding out their power.

They stepped onto a latticed platform and looked down. There were two large diesels and in the furthest corner a control room. The top half of the room was reinforced, thick glass, the bottom half was metal. They could see a man sitting with his feet up, a magazine in his hands. He was cocooned in his own private world, oblivious to the drama that was going on outside.

The noise was horrendous and they moved quickly. They could see the man was alone. There was a narrow ladder and Hunter turned his back to the room and went quickly down. Badonovitch covered him. With only one man to deal with Hunter went alone.

He reached the door to the control room, flung it open and stepped inside. The man looked up startled and possibly had a chance of living if he hadn't reached for the automatic lying next to his chair. It was very stupid, as he didn't even have time to pick it up before Hunter put two rounds into the man, either side of his chest. He hadn't gone for a head shot. Too much brains and blood would have been spilt and possibly made the next part of his job that much messier.

A glance at the controls told him which levers controlled the ship's speed and he pulled them to stop. Immediately the engines began to slow and much to his relief, the noise abated.

The switchboard cupboard controlling the lights throughout the ship was on the aft bulkhead. Hunter opened the doors to take a look. The circuit breakers were the old-fashioned handles with two forks. There were two rows of six and he quickly pulled each one down. Suddenly the lights went out and he put on his NVGs. He ran across the engine room and scurried up the ladder. One or two of the smugglers were probably already on their way to find out what had happened.

Badonovitch had watched both sides of the corridor but nobody had appeared. The two of them continued along the corridor. On one door was the sign 'Crew's Room' and opposite it was the Galley. There were three further doors each side containing two bunks, two wardrobes and two sets of drawers three deep. All basic, all worn, all uncared for, all empty. Hunter pointed at the corner of one of the cabins that had obviously not been used in a long while. The rats' droppings were clearly seen.

The ship was now deathly quiet but then they heard the unmistakable clatter of an AK74 blasting off stopping only when the magazine was empty. Seconds later it started again.

'We'd better shift it,' said Hunter. 'They can only be aiming at our guys.'

11

They stopped at the door at the end of the corridor. The watertight door was pinned back and they were looking at a wooden door with a porthole in the centre at eye level.

'Hiram, what's the score outside?'

'The ship is stopping.'

'I've cut the engines.'

'Nick,' Lizzie said, 'they're shooting at us but we're still too far away.'

'Roger that. Hiram, what about the rest of the crew?'

'The six are still on the deck. They don't seem to know what to do. Hang on, two are walking forward. Where are you?'

'Behind the door at the back of the superstructure.'

'Then I think they're coming your way.'

'Thanks, Hiram. Drones make life a lot easier.'

On the port side of the corridor were the toilets; on the starboard side were the showers. The doors to both were open and Badonovitch stepped over the low combing on the port side while Hunter took the starboard. They were only just in time.

The door to the deck was flung open and two men rushed in. The first man ran past but the second man suddenly stopped and turned when Hunter said, 'Hello.'

The startled look changed to shock when Badonovitch put his hand under the man's chin, bent his head far back and rammed his knife into the smuggler's throat and into his brain stem.

Hunter stepped out and yelled, 'Oi!' at the back of the man who was at the far end of the corridor and about to reach the stairs to the bridge. Instead of diving around the corner he stopped, looked back over his shoulder and Hunter shot him twice in the side, the silenced Glock hardly making any sound. The crewman's body smashed against the forward watertight door.

'Both down, Hiram. What's going on now?'

'The four crew are standing at the guardrail. Hang on. They're firing at the *Fiore*. The boat is still too far away. These men are clowns, Nick.'

'Yeah, I see them. Dave, when I say, take them out.'

'Will do Nick.'

Hunter took a couple of rounds of ammo from a spare mag. 'Stand by Dave.'

He threw them onto the deck behind the four men who jerked around. 'Now.'

Eight seconds later Hunter announced, 'All four down, head shots.' Silenced rounds from an unknown enemy usually left the targets unable to decide what to do until it was too late as happened in this case. Even hardened men froze unless they were trained to react instinctively, before cognitive thought slowed their movements.

'Nice shooting Dave,' said Hunter.

'It's only four hundred metres, boss. With this little baby even you could have hit the targets.'

Hunter chuckled knowing it wasn't true. That distance, from an unstable platform at a target the size of a head, was extraordinary marksmanship. He rubbed his midriff. The ache had gone.

'Hiram, we're going to do a quick clean up, leave a *Marie Celeste* job. We can't do anything about the blood but if there are no bodies the authorities will have nothing to go on. That should mean they'll shrug their shoulders and get on with patrolling and saving lives.'

'Why not launch and sink a couple of lifeboats,' suggested the Colonel. 'That'll confuse matters even more.'

'Good idea.'

'What are you going to do with the people you've got onboard the *Fiore*?'

'I don't know yet. Have you spoken to Ahmad?'

'Yes. He hasn't been able to find anything else. He's on the road walking back to base. He says he doesn't want picking up. Doesn't want to talk to anybody. To think was the way he put it. He wants to be alone for a while.'

'Okay, I've got to go.'

'I'll let him play Greta Garbo for another fifteen minutes then pick him up.'

Hunter grinned. The iconic "I want to be alone" from the 1932 film *Grand Hotel* had passed into Hollywood legend.

Hunter said to Badonovitch, 'If you find some ready use lockers there could be something we can use as weights.'

'On it, boss.'

'I'm heading to the engine room to restart the engines.'

It took a couple of minutes to get the diesels going and to reconnect the electric power. He then headed for the bridge. 'Lizzie, I'm going to straighten the ship's course and reduce speed to steerageway. When I have, come alongside on the port side. You'll see a Jacob's ladder hanging down. Tell Dave and Don we can use their help.'

'Right, Nick.'

Hunter went along the corridor, stepped over the dead body at the end and took the stairs one at a time. He held his Glock in a two-handed grip ready to fire. There was always the possibility that one of the two men shot was injured and not dead. There was nobody on the bridge and a quick glance showed the two dead men without most of their heads. Blood, brains and bits of bone were scattered across both bridge wings.

A quick look showed the controls to be basic and simple. He turned a dial and centred the rudder, then engaged the autopilot on a heading of 180 degrees. According to the electronic display the ship was travelling at six knots and he adjusted the speed to two knots.

'Okay, Lizzie, come alongside. Are your passengers behaving themselves?'

'Yes, Nick. I think they are too shocked. The firing we heard earlier was the crew shooting two of the men. Only . . . Only they weren't that competent with their . . . their guns,' she stumbled over the words. 'The swine shot a woman as well. They killed three people to make the others jump into the water more quickly.'

'Tell Rod to be careful in case of any trouble.'

'Trouble?'

'We don't know who's onboard. How many people have you picked up?'

'Sixteen.'

'Men, women and children?'

'Em,' she paused, 'let me see. Seven young children, three women and six men. Youths really.'

'Okay, the women and children shouldn't be a problem but the men could be.'

'What do you mean?'

'Some of the people arriving here aren't friends of the west. They'll do anything to get into Europe to fight holy jihad. They could be on the boat posing as immigrants. Tell Rod to watch them closely. Where have you put them?'

'Below, in the stateroom and dining area. We gave them bottles of water and the kids some orange juice. Also I showed them where the rest of the food is and to help themselves. I think the women are sorting something.'

'Okay, good. Lizzie, do not let any of them come onto the bridge or try to get out from between decks.'

'How do we stop them?'

'Tell Rod to use force if he must. Get the forward hatch as well as the stern skylights locked down. If there are no external locks or bolts use rope. Look, I know this sounds melodramatic but believe me it's for the best. You cannot trust those people. Do not go below under any pretext. If you hear children crying let them. Lizzie, I am deadly serious.'

'Okay, Nick, understood.'

Then Masters said, 'We're onboard Nick.'

'Good. Give Jan a hand getting rid of the bodies. I'm going to search this place.' Hunter found a pair of binoculars lying on a chart table situated on the port side of the bridge. He wrinkled his nose at the smell of stale cigarette smoke and the dirty ashtrays on the shelves underneath windows. He could never understand why people were prepared to live in such a mess when it would be so easy to keep the place reasonably clean and tidy.

Badonovitch appeared at the port door. 'Boss, that's the lot over the side except for the two up here.'

'Okay, I'll give you a hand.' At the back of the bridge was a locked, glass-fronted cupboard. Hunter shook his head. More proof of the amateurism of the terrorists, if proof was needed. Holding his pistol by its muzzle he smashed the glass with its grip and dragged out a length of fire hose. He unscrewed the end from its connection point to the firemain and carried the heavy hose out to the port wing. He wrapped the hose around the body of the dead man who was of slim build and average height. He tied the ends of the hose together, easily picked up the body and slid it over the side. He managed to do so without getting any of the blood or gore on him.

Badonovitch joined him, 'One body heading straight down, boss. With luck it won't stop until it reaches hell where it belongs.'

Hunter smiled. A spot of macabre humour at times helped, even though it was rarely funny.

'Hiram, is the coast clear? Nothing coming this way?'

'Clear at the moment Nick. The drone has another thirty minutes on station. Is that long enough?'

'Yeah. I'm going to search for the ship's papers. There may be something of use on this rust bucket. Lizzie, just hang back and follow us closely. Actually, Don you and David get back to the boat. Then send Rima back with *The Mercury*. She can latch on to the Jacob's ladder, in case we need her in a hurry.'

As usual the chances of needing to get off the ship rapidly were remote but Hunter rarely left things to chance. Sod's law was a good axiom to apply when on an operation.

'Jan, you search up here. Lift every scrap of paper you can find, including the log if they keep one. I'll go and search the Master's cabin.'

The cabin wasn't much tidier or cleaner than the bridge. It was obvious that the occupant had been a heavy smoker.

The room was ten metres wide and five metres deep. The bulkheads were plain white metallic paint with not even a photograph to break-up the bleakness of the cabin. The carpet was threadbare and didn't quite reach the full width of the deck. A prayer mat was lying in the middle of the cabin. It looked to be new and was the best preserved item there. A desk was bolted to the deck on the port side and in an alcove on the starboard side was an unmade bed. The sheets looked as grubby as the rest of the ship.

A look through the drawers of the desk and a cupboard next to the bed revealed nothing of any interest. Hunter stood in the middle of the room and looked around. There was nothing to attract his attention. Presumably the ship's owner or owners had been paid in advance, the crew would have also been paid and the immigrants would have funded the whole rotten enterprise.

If the crew weren't the owners then there had to be a means of contact with those who were, Hunter reasoned. Perhaps al-Baghdadi owned the boat. Or was it someone further up the food chain? One thing they were certain of and that was ISIL had tentacles that reached into the very highest of societies to be found in both Saudi Arabia as well as Iran. In fact the tentacles spread out and down from those societies, born in a quagmire of twisted Islamic beliefs and corrupted power.

Hunter dropped to the deck and looked under the bed. He could see something. He put his hand in and dragged out an imitation leather briefcase of standard size. He looked closely at the top and sides of the case. He could see nothing untoward.

He sat staring at the case for a few moments. The big question was what if the case was booby-trapped? Would they bother? If any information was sensitive enough then ISIL would do everything to protect it. If that meant killing the owner of the case or anyone stupid enough to open it without taking suitable precautions then so-be-it. There was plenty more cannon fodder available. It was just a question of finding the right people all of whom needed three qualities. A skill of some description like a Master's ticket, a desire to kill the infidel and a willingness to die for Allah. More than a willingness but a yearning to die after achieving one particular ambition, which was to kill one or more non-believers.

Knowing that in some respects money was no object when it came to protecting the ISIL hierarchy, at the lower end life was cheap.

He took a closer look at the case. It was plain black, two spring locks holding down a flap, no pockets. He turned it over but it was just plain black plastic. He examined closely the two plates either side of the bottom of the case. The left side was a thin, brass coloured metal plate two inches square with two studs. On the right was the same. Hunter frowned and was about to pop the clasps when he paused and looked more closely at the plates. Then he saw what was bothering him. On the left side the studs and plate were all one, cast as a unit, the right hand side the studs were separate from the plate with a hair's breadth gap around the studs. He gently pressed one of the studs. It moved a fraction.

Now he saw that the studs were slightly lighter coloured than the rest of the plate as though they had been gripped and turned. Constant use would mean the metal coating would wear off eventually which was precisely what was happening. He took hold of the stud between his forefinger and thumb, pushed in a fraction and gently turned it anti-clockwise. The stud popped out on a spring about half an inch.

Logic told him that the studs pressed in would set the explosive, otherwise the case wouldn't stand on its side. He was hoping he was right when he tackled the second stud. That also popped out half an inch.

He flicked the locks open. He was about to lift the lid when Badonovitch appeared at the door. 'Boss, I got the log and a few other bits and pieces plus I've taken the recording of the ship's track for the last three months.'

'Excellent. Did you find a bosun's locker when you searched the stern deck?'

'Yes, I think so.'

'Nip down and see if there's a reel of sailmaker's thread, will you?'

Badonovitch didn't ask any questions but hurried down the stairs and along the corridor. He was back within minutes with a reel of sailmaker's thread, thin, tough and used to mend sails and canvas awnings.

'What do you want it for?'

'I think this case is booby-trapped. There are two studs on the bottom that I've loosened.' Hunter pointed.

'Yeah, I see.'

'So I'm going to tie this end here,' so saying he tied the end of the thread to the right hand clasp, 'pass it over the back of the chair, giving it a vertical lift and take it to the door. Coming?'

'Right with you.'

The two men stood behind the door and to one side so that the metal bulkhead stood between them and the case and Hunter pulled gently on the thread. He could feel the lid opening. They waited but nothing happened.

'I'll take a look,' said the commander, 'you stay here. If there's a time delay there's no point in both of us passing through the Pearly Gates at the same time.'

12

Hunter approached the case slowly. He looked inside by craning his neck and bending forward. There was a laptop and on the right a mobile phone nestled next to it. On the left was a small electronic device sitting next to the plate with the moveable studs. He recognised it immediately. It was a state-of-the-art explosive device that was set off when a button was released from the top of it by lifting the lid. It was perfectly safe until the side buttons were pressed in and the explosive set. The lid and base of the case also had a close fitting lining that fit snugly around all three items.

Hunter lifted out the device, walked across to a porthole, opened it and threw the explosive into the sea.

'Right, let's go. Hiram?'

'Yes, Nick'

'We're out of here.'

'Okay. We've picked up Ahmad.'

'Good. Did he find anything else?'

'He said not.'

'Then in that case can you let the appropriate authorities know what's happened? Have you worked out a cover story?'

'Yes. Intercepts led us to believe something was going down. We didn't know what but subsequent traffic has led us to believe illegal immigrants had been taken ashore. We won't say anything about a gun battle. I'll leave it for them to discover.'

You may as well call up the Italian navy and tell them about the ship while you're at it.'

'Will do. What are you going to do now?'

'Get off this ship for a start. I'll speak to you later.'

Hunter checked the time. It was already 02.26. 'Let's go, Jan.'

They left the cabin and stepped through the door to the foredeck. Hunter breathed deeply in appreciation. 'That's better. The air in that cabin was lousy to say the least.'

They collapsed and folded their parasails. Hunter's was beyond repair but they weren't going to leave it behind. They threw the sails over their shoulders and went back through the ship. They handed down their gear before clambering down the Jacob's ladder and into the speedboat.

They arrived back at the *Fiore*. Badonovitch took the bow rope down to the stern and tied it off, leaving the speedboat to trail a couple of metres behind.

Hunter went onto the bridge. 'Any problems?'

'No,' said Perez, 'although a couple of the men have been yelling.'

'Yelling what?'

'Demanding to be let loose. That they should not be kept there like animals.'

'You are kidding, right?' While he was speaking Hunter was stripping off his wetsuit and pulling on a shirt and shorts.

'Nope. They . . .'

There were sudden yells from below decks and what sounded like scuffling. Children began to scream and cry. For Hunter it was too much. He'd had enough. They'd put their lives on the line, saved their passengers from drowning and there wasn't an ounce of gratitude in some of them. A response that he knew was being replicated all over Europe.

He stepped down into the main saloon. There was a leather sofa lining the starboard bulkhead and the length of the table, two chairs on the opposite side and one each end. The seats were taken by the six men who sat around the dining table. The women and children were sitting either on the four seats in the lounge area or on the deck. Some of the children were crying.

The six men looked at Hunter, one of them said something and the other five laughed. He spoke Arabic. Hunter realised they were Somalis. Although Somali was the main language of the country Arabic was the official national language.

Hunter stepped the two paces to the man seated at the end of the table who had spoken. He grabbed him by the back of his neck, lifted him to his feet and slapped him across the face. The man's head jerked to one side and Hunter smacked him on the other cheek.

In Arabic Hunter said, 'You speak about me or my crew like that again and I will throw you overboard.' He changed his grip to take the man by the front of his jacket shook him and said, 'I understand Arabic, you little piece of pig. We saved your lives and this is how you repay us.' He let the man loose. 'You lot,' he looked at the other five, 'stand up!'

They didn't move. At that moment Badonovitch and Masters stepped past Hunter who hadn't been aware of their presence, grabbed a man each and dragged them to their feet. The others quickly stood. Fear was now etched on their faces, their arrogance having quickly evaporated.

'Ladies,' Hunter turned to the women, 'please come and sit here.'

The women looked at the men and the man Hunter had just thrown aside gave a slight shake of his head. Hunter caught the gesture. He clenched his fist and swung his arm backwards and hit the man in his teeth. The Somali flew backwards, hit the seat with a thump and the back of his head smashed against the bulkhead.

Hunter reached across and dragged the man to his feet. He shoved him onto the deck, grabbed his left arm, pulled it up behind the man's back and twisted it. The man screamed.

'Ladies, please sit around the table and have the children with you.'

Hesitatingly they stood up and moved to the table. The seven children were four girls, three boys and all seven appeared to be under ten years of age. The three women were probably mid-twenties, though Hunter found it hard to tell. All of them were black.

Hunter stood nonchalantly with his right foot pressing down on the face of the man he held and looked at the women. 'Are you from Somalia?'

The women looked fearfully at each other and then at the other men.

'Don't look at them,' Hunter focussed his attention on one of the women, 'look at me!' He spoke loudly. 'Are you from Somalia?'

The woman he was looking at said, 'Yes. We,' she indicated the other women, 'are Christians. We fled Somalia because of persecution by Muslims. ISIS is there and is killing people who refuse to convert to Islam.' She spoke English with a pleasant accent. 'Even people who convert are treated harshly. The women are raped and the men and older children are turned into slaves.'

'And these men?'

The woman hesitated before looking at the five men standing in a group. 'They are Somali. They are also Christians. That man, the one under your foot is a Muslim and a member of ISIS.'

'How do you know?'

'I heard him talking to some of the crew on the ship. They think because we are women we are of no importance. That we can be ignored as though we are nothing.'

'If these five men are Christians why were they acting the way they were?'

The woman looked frightened for a moment.

'You don't need to tell me,' said Hunter. 'They were planning to take over the boat.'

The woman nodded slowly. Then she looked defiantly at Hunter. 'We thought it was the only way we can get to Europe.'

'You agreed?'

'Yes. How can we trust you? How do we know you are not going to sell us as slaves?'

'Why would you think that?'

'We heard the crew talking. That was what was going to happen to us.'

Hunter nodded. She was right. They had no reason to trust him and the others.

'You have to take my word for it.'

The woman translated what Hunter had said. It did nothing to alleviate the fear on their faces.

The man on the deck squirmed and said in heavily accented English, 'She lies. I am not ISIS. I run away from ISIS. I want to live in peace in UK.'

The woman who had been speaking said, 'He's lying. I also saw him at the camp near Tripoli. He was talking to other men we know to be smuggling people. I tell you I am speaking the truth.'

'I believe you,' said Hunter. Which left him in a dilemma. There was no way he was going to let the man loose in Europe. Being ISIS the man would attempt to kill innocent men, women and children, of that he had no doubt. But there was no way an arrest could be made, a trial take place and a guilty verdict reached. The man would argue asylum, scream about his human rights and demand all sorts of benefits some of which he would get, some he wouldn't. But he would get what he wanted above anything and everything - a European Passport at some point in the future. If he settled in Germany or Italy he could wait. Five years or ten were immaterial to him. His fervour would never wane, his love of Allah would never diminish. His hatred of non-Muslims in general and the people of the west in particular would increase with time. And one day he would strike.

Hunter knew all that as sure as he knew the sun would rise in a few hours time.

One of the other women spoke in Arabic. 'I also saw him. I knew I recognised him but wasn't sure. Now I know. He was also in a town in Puntland.'

'Where's Puntland?' Hunter asked.

'It is a region of Somalia and where there are many ISIS as well as al-Shabab. It was in the town of Qandala where I was a schoolteacher. He was with others.' Her voice quivered and then she went on more strongly. 'They herded people into a nearby church and set it alight.

Women and children as well as men. There were not many men left in the town as they had all run away for fear of being forced to fight for ISIS and al-Shabab. They are vile, evil, disgusting men who are not human.'

The man on the floor began to struggle. 'It is not true. I would never do such a thing. Never!' He tried to twist his head and look at Hunter but he couldn't. Hunter's foot was too heavy on the man's face.

'I believe them,' Hunter said in a reasonable tone. 'What you did was evil and against the Koran. It is against the word of the prophet and you will be condemned to hell for all time for what you did.'

The man suddenly changed. 'I am destined for paradise. To sit with God. I shall be greeted by seventy-two virgins and treated like a king. I have killed non-believers in the name of the prophet, peace be upon him. I want the world to return to the time of Muhammad. To a time of peace and where the one true faith rules our lives.'

Hunter was watching the looks on the faces of the others and saw nothing but horror. Then he said, 'It says a lot for the virility of Muslims like you.'

'What does?' The man couldn't stop himself from asking.

'That seventy-two virgins last all eternity. You're a pathetic, inadequate little man.'

The man on the deck began to squirm harder so Hunter increased the pressure on the man's arm until he screamed. Hunter then bent down, picked the man up by the scruff of his collar and dragged him up the stairs to the bridge.

'Jan, get *The Mercury* please.'

The Russian went to the stern, untied the speedboat's headrope and pulled *The Mercury* alongside. Hunter literally threw his prisoner over the side and into the bottom of the boat. He landed with a yell of pain. Hunter climbed down after him but before he could say anything Badonovitch followed and pushed *The Mercury* away from the side of the *Fiore*.

'Where the hell do you think you're going?'

'Let's go, boss.'

Hunter was about to argue but thought better of it. There was no point. Badonovitch was as stubborn as a mule when he wanted to be. And when it came to working with Hunter he was always there, for which Hunter was very grateful.

Hunter started the engines, engaged the gears and headed south into deeper water. He opened her up for 10 minutes before bringing the boat down off the plane and to a gentle stop in the water.

Badonovitch had been sitting next to their prisoner with one foot on his neck and whenever he tried to move he merely pressed down hard until the squirming stopped.

'I'll do it,' said Hunter.

'Do what?' The man was terrified. He began to shake. 'No! You cannot. I demand asylum. I demand you hand me over to the authorities!'

'Are you begging for mercy?' Hunter asked coldly.

'No! Yes! Yes, I beg you. Do not kill me!'

Hunter was holding his silenced Glock in his left hand, pointed nonchalantly in the general direction of the man.

'You may be right. What do you think, Jan?'

'I think we should be fair to the people he killed, to their memory.'

Hunter's nod was to starboard and the tough ex-Spetsnaz reached down, grabbed the man by an arm and a leg and threw him over the side. He landed in the water, surfaced spluttering and Hunter put a bullet through his brain.

'He had a better death than he deserved,' said Hunter.

Badonovitch undid the shackle connecting the anchor and a few metres of chain to a nylon rope, tied the chain around the legs of the body and dropped the anchor over the side. The body vanished.

In minutes they were back alongside the *Fiore*. They tied off the speedboat and climbed onto the larger boat.

None of the others said a word. Then Lizzie asked a question that had been bothering Hunter. 'What do we do with our passengers?'

'I'm working on it.'

He took a chart covering the area he was interested in from one of the folios and studied it.

117

'I'm going to drop you guys off at the town of Acireale. You can get to the base from there easily enough.'

The team were all on the bridge, sitting at the table, coffees or teas at their elbows.

'What will you be doing, boss?' Badonovitch asked, sitting back and folding his arms.

Hunter recognised the gesture. It was the precursor to bloody-minded mulishness.

'Never mind. I'll deal with our passengers. You guys all return to base.'

The team all exchanged looks and then Masters laughed. Hughes and then Badonovitch followed him.

'What's so funny?' Perez asked, the puzzled look on his face reflected in the looks of the women.

'What they are saying in their childish and puerile manner,' said Hunter, 'is that I won't be going alone.'

'You got it in one, boss,' said Masters, shaking his head. 'That was really funny.'

Hunter knew better than to argue so he shrugged and said, 'So be it on your own heads.'

'It always is,' said Hughes. 'I take it we're going to the mainland?'

'Yeah. It'll give them the best chance.'

'That's what I figured,' said Hughes.

'Will someone please tell me what you clowns are talking about?' Lizzie asked.

Masters answered. 'You didn't think for one minute Nick was going to hand these people over to the authorities did you? To what? A rotten life in some camp somewhere? You've seen the state they're in. They're scared, traumatised and in real psychological pain. No, he's thought of something. So what is it, boss?'

Hunter shrugged. 'It's not much of a plan but I reckon if we drop them off on the mainland, give them some money, they can at least get deeper into Europe. Maybe Germany or Sweden where they'll be looked after. I don't know what else to do.'

'I'll come with you,' said Lizzie.

'Me too,' said Rima.

'I want to get off,' said Lance Corporal Wendy Black. 'I didn't sign up for what we've been doing tonight.' She shuddered. 'All those deaths. And what happened to the man you took with you?' She looked directly at Hunter.

'He's feeding the fish. What did you think?' He spoke harshly. It had been a long night for all of them. 'You heard what the women told us. What would you have us do?'

'Arrest him. Have him tried for war crimes. Or . . . Or crimes against humanity . . . Or something. Anything is better than what we've done.'

'How do you work that out?' Captain Elizabeth Montgomery stared at the other woman. 'We're at war. We're being invaded by some despicable people who will kill us if they get the opportunity. Please tell us how we can deal effectively with the situation we are facing? What would have happened to that man? Let me tell you, he would probably have been lost in the system and would have resurfaced in the future and killed somebody. Maybe a lot of people. Like stealing a lorry and driving it through crowds. Like throwing petrol bombs at buildings. Like throwing bricks over a bridge onto a motorway and causing God alone knows what carnage. So tell us what we can do to stop all that.'

Wendy's shoulders sunk. 'I can't,' she said in a small voice. 'I just know it's wrong.'

'Tell me, Wendy,' said Hunter, 'what should we have done with those armed fanatics at the house? Bearing in mind they were trafficking men, women and children as slaves, some to the sex trade, some as domestic help and some in lousy conditions on farms across Europe. What should we have done?'

'Arrested them.'

'Don't talk rubbish. You've no idea what we were facing. They were willing to die, even wanted to die, which gives them a vicious strength we don't possess in the west. We value life too highly.'

'You talk of valuing life,' she replied bitterly, 'but you've just killed many men and one in cold blood.'

'He wasn't a man,' said Masters, 'he was evil and beneath contempt.

13

Hunter took Wendy Black ashore in *The Mercury*. He put the bows onto a sandy beach.

'The road is just up there. Will you be all right?'

'Yes.'

'No hard feelings, Wendy, only we'd appreciate it if you kept quiet about this evening.'

There was no reply and the Lance Corporal walked away without a backward glance.

Just then the sun slid over the horizon with the promise of another warm and sunny day. He turned away from the beach, moved slowly into open sea and accelerated until *The Mercury* was up on the plane. It took a mere ten minutes to reach the *Fiore*. Once back onboard he poured himself a mug of coffee, and found the chart he needed to navigate their course. He had decided that their destination was Catanzaro Harbour, on the Italian mainland, nearly 150 miles to the northeast.

He checked on the passengers some of who had gone to sleep in the other cabins, stretched out on bunks. Others slept where they had been sitting. The smell of body odor was unpleasant and reminded Hunter of a cowshed though less pleasant. He would sort something out later in the morning when their passengers were awake.

The team was scattered around the bridge and the aft deck where they had made themselves comfortable and were sleeping the sleep of the just.

Lizzie was at the helm keeping a lookout, the boat on autopilot.

'Why don't you get some sleep,' Hunter suggested, 'I can take over here.'

'I'm okay. What about you? You've had a pretty hectic night.'

Hunter smiled, checked their position and adjusted their course by ten degrees to starboard. 'It goes with the territory.'

After a few minutes of companionable silence Lizzie said, 'What's the difference between ISIS and ISIL? Do you know?'

'There isn't any. ISIS is the Islamic State of Iraq and Syria while ISIL is the Islamic State of Iraq and the Levant.'

'So what's Daesh?'

'It's the Arabic acronym for the same people.'

'It's all pretty confusing.'

'Yep. And one thing I am absolutely sure about is that many of the people involved don't know why they are doing what they are doing.'

'What do you mean?'

'It's a form of religious brainwashing. Look at the demographics of the people who make up the majority of the fighters. Many can't read, certainly have never read the Koran and have been told by their Imams what to think and do. Did you know that most imams in their rotten world have also never read the Koran?'

'You're kidding me.'

'No. It's ignorance that allows them to do what they do.'

'I still don't get what they want. Do you?'

'A worldwide caliphate where Islam is the only religion and sharia law is used to control the people.'

'It'll never happen.'

'You're right of course, but here's something to think about. Ask a so-called true believer and they will tell you that if it takes a thousand years they will achieve their dream. What sacrifices they make to get there they don't care. You've heard that many want to return the world to what it was like at the time of Muhammad?'

'Yes, but that's ludicrous. Everything is moving forward. A thousand years from now who can possibly imagine what the world will be like?'

'You're right of course. Changing the subject, care for a coffee?'

'Please, white, one sugar.'

'Coming up.' While he poured he continued, 'So far what I've told you is pretty scary, right?'

'And how, but we all know this stuff only we don't admit it either to ourselves or to others.'

'That's inevitable. There's many reasons for that from being too frightened of the consequences if we did admit it to the simple need to make a living, bring up a family, in short, just to live.'

'Wow, that's pretty philosophical. Especially at this time of the day.'

'You're right. This is the kind of conversation we normally have in the evenings, after a few drinks, pontificating on the state of the world and where we're going in it.'

Lizzie nodded. 'I've heard the other guys, the SEALS and their friends talking about the same stuff. So what's the answer?'

'Here's the depressing thing, I don't think there is one.' Hunter paused, sipped his coffee and then said, 'All we can do is keep fighting and keep trying to contain the situation.'

Picking up a pair of binoculars Hunter scanned the horizon. There were numerous vessels in sight, mainly steaming astern of them, crossing the Mediterranean with whatever cargo they'd been commissioned to deliver. It was a display of a peaceful world but just a few miles from where they were, bad things were happening to a lot of people.

'Lizzie, I told you that there are many Muslims who wish to return the world to the days of Muhammad that is around the year six twenty or six thirty.'

'So?'

'How can they do that?'

She shrugged and said, 'They can't. Like I said, the world moves on.'

'Yes, for us with our rational thoughts and arguments. But what about the fanatic? Those who believe with every breath they take that they are right. That the world should return to the seventh century. What about them?'

'I'm not sure what you mean.'

'Sorry, I'm not making myself clear. How do you think that they think they can achieve it?'

Lizzie thought for a few seconds before shaking her head. 'No idea.'

'These people think they can bomb the world back to those times.'

'What do you mean? Bomb it back? That makes no sense.'

'Not to you and I, but we're being rational, the enemy we are dealing with is irrational. So they have decided there is a way to achieve their aims and that is with nuclear weapons. I don't mean dirty bombs, plutonium based or with some deadly virus, I'm talking the real thing. The US President had a meeting about this very subject not long ago. Whatever was decided was and is classified secret but believe me, our leaders are crapping themselves and rightly in my opinion.'

'I'd heard something about it.'

'Okay, but here's the thing. Knowledge is moving all the time. Things only the western world once knew are known the world over. What I mean is, the knowledge to build a nuclear bomb is spreading. North Korea is a good example. Do you know who finances worldwide Islamic terrorism?'

'Sure, we all do. Our so called friends the Saudis.'

'Sorry, of course you know. The world knows but nobody dares say anything at an official level because of oil and the sheer clout of the Saudi royal family and its investments.'

'What you really mean is the amount they spend on armaments.'

'That too. So let's take an example. North Korea is a basket case. The people live in a different century from the rest of the world, oppressed and worshipping a man as a god. No matter what he does to them they still venerate him. Suppose he decides he needs money. A substantial amount to import food to feed the people. What has he got to offer?'

Lizzie looked at Hunter in horror and said quietly, 'A nuclear weapon.'

'Yep. So who do we stop? How? When?'

'What do you mean?'

'Should we stop the money or the supplier? The same dilemma we have when it comes to drugs. If we use drugs as an example then the decades we've been fighting the suppliers hasn't worked. But we can't stop the customers wanting the stuff, whether that's heroin or cocaine or any other banned narcotic. And the reason we can't stop the customers is that they are spread across all strands of society. Wide and deep, in reality. Which is the problem we have with Islam. A great religion for the majority, rotten beyond belief for the minority but still very wide and very deep.' Hunter paused and then continued. 'So we try and cut off the supply. How? Nuke North Korea? That isn't going to happen and nobody is going to invade them, that's for sure. And let's be fair, other countries will acquire nuclear weapons, as the technology becomes more widely known. The world can scream blue murder but it's inevitable.'

'If we can't cut off the supply we need to cut off the customers.'

'That's the inevitable conclusion we keep coming to. So do we bomb Saudi? Iran? Who?'

Lizzie shook her head. 'I'm a lowly captain. This is all way above my pay grade. Good for late nights over a few drinks, like we said, but not when you're looking for answers.' She sighed. 'There aren't any.'

'At the very highest levels in the military, amongst the special operations people and the security services this stuff is discussed, argued and believe it or not plans are made.'

'What sort of plans?'

'Ah, that I don't know. You may be a lowly captain but I'm merely a lowly commander. In the meantime we keep fighting the way we are doing. There's no choice. But we're fighting skirmishes, lots of them and they're becoming more prevalent. Will it all escalate into the big one? Nuclear war on a scale orchestrated by the Islamic fundamentalists but actually fought by the west.'

'What do you mean?'

'Suppose a bomb goes off, a nuke, say in Paris or London or Washington, anywhere. And we know who's responsible. We know who supplied it and who fired it. Do we wipe those people off the face of the earth? Suppose it's Iran? We nuke the country back to the Stone Age and then what happens? We use intercontinental ballistic missiles while it was all started by a bomb with a tenth of the power, even though it's a nuclear bomb. Do you see? We'll have done the job for the so-called caliphate.'

'That won't send us back to the Middle Ages.'

'Maybe, maybe not, but it'll be as close as makes no difference. It's the nightmare scenario that's been threatened ever since the weapons were developed.'

Lizzie nodded. 'I know. We've discussed some of this in staff college.'

'Okay, but here's one thing. Every incident we can identify we have forces trying to track the perpetrators who are the leaders. The people who control what's going on. Just like we do with the drugs trade. That's why we want to follow the trail from Sicily to wherever it leads us.'

'Do you know where that will be?'

'No. But I've got a very good idea.'

'How can you have? The men are all dead. The trail is finished.'

'Ah, no. You're making the same mistake a lot of people make. Mainly from reading the wrong sort of books or watching the wrong sort of films.'

'What do you mean?'

'The secret, if one can call it that, is to interlock all the information available like a jigsaw puzzle. This is one incident amongst many. We've been working on a number of leads and contrary to popular belief we've been co-operating with the security forces of most of the western world.'

'What about with Europe? I thought now that you Brits have left the European Union the world will cave in as terrorists roam freely across the land and people die from continuous attacks.'

'That's what the politicians like us to think. That's what those who want us to rejoin the EU keep screaming about but of course they are completely wrong.'

'They are? How so?'

'Governments do not talk to governments about operational matters when it comes to the war against terrorism. Hell, nobody in any security service anywhere in the world would trust politicians to keep their big mouths shut. Their egos prevent them from keeping a secret. They need to be seen to be in the know, a part of the inner circle of government, the ones trusted to help in the fight against terrorism. No, like I said, the real war is fought at the operational level. And believe me we have a close and very active relationship not only in Europe but with our friends in America and again I don't mean just with the USA but South America also. Actually, wherever there are Islamic attacks we have co-operation. The only problem is who do we trust? No, I'll change that to who can we trust? That's the real burning issue.'

'Where do you think this trail is leading?'

'Straight to the money I hope.' He picked up the binoculars, scanned the horizon, checked their position, course and speed and altered the boat's heading a further five degrees to starboard.

'At this rate we'll be at Catanzaro Harbour at 18.00.' He called Walsh using the satellite communications system. 'Hiram?'

'Nick, you okay?'

'Fine. Got a little job to do. I'll fill you in when we get back which will be sometime tomorrow evening I suspect.'

'Okay. No names, no pack drill.'

'Good. The problem is the tough little Lance Corporal Wendy Black didn't like what we've been doing nor what we're planning to do and insisted on being put ashore.'

'I see.'

'Has she ever been on an op?'

'No, of course not. She's one of our staff that helps to keep things moving. You know how it is. All the way from paperwork to logistics and I have to say she's damned good at it. When she got back I was intending to tell her that I'd recommended her for a second stripe with the probability of a third within two or three years.'

'Well she needs a good talking to. We don't want anything we've been up to broadcast. She's a member of the SEALS and she needs to shape up.'

'Okay, leave it to me. Nick, watch your back.'

'Thanks, Hiram. Bye. Lizzie, why don't you get some sleep? I can manage here.'

Yawning, she said, 'Are you sure?'

'Positive.'

Lizzie went below while he found the chart for the harbour and took a closer look. He then checked where the railway station was located.

An hour later Masters took over the helm and Hunter went below. The passengers were awake, some sitting around the table in the saloon and others on the comfortable chairs. There was an apathy about them that Hunter found gut wrenching.

'What's your name?' he asked the woman he knew to have been a schoolteacher.

'Haboon.'

'Is that your first name?'

'Yes.'

'Okay, first things first. You all only have the clothes you stand up in but everything smells. Lizzie and Rima can give you ladies some clean clothes; we can fit you men out with jeans and tee shirts. You need to wash the kids' clothes and put them up on deck to dry. It won't take long. In the meantime you will all take showers. Do not stand under the shower with the water running. There isn't enough water for all of you. Wet yourselves, switch off the water, use the soap and shampoo and then rinse your bodies.' He was speaking Arabic and asked, 'Do you all understand?'

They nodded.

He began opening the portholes. 'Let's get some fresh air in here.

I'll open the skylights from up top.' Perez had taken Hunter's advice and had tied down the skylights using lengths of rope. 'Haboon, look through the cupboards and make some drinks. There's orange juice, tea and coffee. Do you know what a croissant is?'

She shook her head, 'No.'

Hunter opened a cupboard and took out three packets of 10 croissants. 'Place them in the oven for ten minutes to warm them. Find plates and knives and lay them on the table. Find butter and honey or jam if you prefer. Stop sitting here like . . . like bovine cattle.'

'What's bovine cattle?'

'Never mind.' Hunter was immediately ashamed of himself. These people had been through a lot. In fact a lot more than most people could ever expect in the twenty-first century. The last time there was such a problem with so many people on the move in Europe was during the Second World War.

Haboon slid off the seat and stood up. She rocked gently and Hunter put his hand out to steady her. 'Sorry,' she said.

'There's nothing to be sorry about. Have the croissants for now and later we'll have some eggs and . . .' he was about to say bacon but changed it to, 'baked beans.'

She smiled and said, 'Bacon will be lovely. I told you we are all Christians.'

Hunter nodded. 'I forgot. How did that man manage to get amongst you?'

Shaking her head Haboon said, 'You have to understand the fear we live with. We . . . We've been conditioned? Yes, I think that's the right word. Conditioned to do as we are told. We have taken many months getting this far. We have seen some terrible things. Mass murder, children and women being raped and beaten.' She shuddered. 'It is the stuff of nightmares. Many of the people are traumatised to such a degree that they will never live a normal life again. The children have seen such terrible things so often that they think such behaviour is normal. They only understand violence.' She trailed off, her eyes welling tears, her thoughts seeming to overwhelm her.

'It's okay Haboon, it's okay to cry. I've seen some of the things you have but my experiences pale into insignificance by comparison.'

Nodding, she asked, 'What are you going to do with us? Hand us over to the authorities?'

'If you want. On the other hand I was planning to put you ashore on the Italian mainland, get you to a railway station and send you north, deeper into Europe. Do you have any papers? Passports or identity cards?'

'No. They were taken from us and destroyed. It is to stop the authorities sending us back when we claim we are stateless. And the youngsters have been told to pretend to be younger than they really are. To get more sympathy. You say we can take a train but we have very little money. In fact I have none and I doubt the others have anything of any value.'

'Leave that to me. I'll take care of it.'

'How?'

'I just can. Okay? Just trust me.'

'I do.' She waved her hand at the others, 'I don't know about them.'

Hunter looked at the faces staring silently at them and saw the fear etched there. 'They don't need to trust me right now. Or ever come to that. I'll do what I can to help.'

'Nick,' Masters called down, 'we've got trouble!'

14

Hunter said, 'Got to go.'

Once on the bridge Masters pointed out the starboard window. Hunter recognised the ship as an Italian coastal patrol craft. Then he heard the radio.

'*Il Bel Fiore*,' was followed by instructions in Italian, which Hunter guessed was to heave to and allow a boarding party to come aboard.

Hunter picked up the handset and said, 'Warship, this is *Il Bel Fiore*, I do not understand. Does anyone speak English?'

'Yes. Heave-to for an inspection. Over.' The accent was thick but understandable.

'Don, go below and get everyone into the cabins forward and tell them to keep quiet. Help Haboon to put the dishes and the rest of the stuff away. Better still, get one of the women to help to lay the table up here. Get eggs cooking, get bacon frying. Get the coffee on the go. We're just an ordinary bunch of holidaymakers enjoying a boating cruise.'

'Will do. I'll wake Lizzie as well.'

'Do that. She can help.'

'*Il Bel Fiore*, do you understand? Over.' The accent was now laced with irritation.

'Yes. I am sorry, can you tell me the problem? Over.'

'We are going to search your boat. We want to know who you are, where you've come from and where you're going. I hope that is clear enough? Over.'

'Yes, but why? We've done nothing wrong. Over.'

While he was speaking Hunter speed dialled Colonel Hiram B. Walsh. 'Hiram? Hang on a second, will you?'

'Jan, make sure the kit is stowed. We don't want anyone noticing something out of order. Remember that these are our guys doing an ordinary and boring job. Be polite and smile. Okay, Hiram, sorry about that.'

'What's up, Nick?'

'We're about to be boarded by an Italian coastal patrol ship. Long story but I don't want us searched.'

'What have you been up to?'

'Like I said, I'll tell you when I see you. Our ID usually only works with senior officers and the security services. Hell, most armed forces personnel at enlisted level have barely heard of TIFAT.'

'What's the name of the ship?'

Hunter focussed his binoculars on the side of the ship, 'Pennant number P407, name, em, yeah got it, the *Vedetta*.'

'Okay. I'll get onto it straightaway.'

'Thanks, Hiram.'

'*Il Bel Fiore*, if you do not stop it will be the worse for you. Over.'

'Sorry, warship. This is *Il Bel Fiore* and we are stopping now. Over.'

Hunter nodded to Masters who took the way off the boat but kept her in gear so that the autopilot kept the bows on a steady course.

While he watched the ship's seaboat being launched, Hunter was aware of the bustle behind him as the table was laid and bread, jam, cold meats and other breakfast dishes were quickly spread out. The smell of freshly ground coffee wafted through the air. It all looked innocent and homely.

The Italian seaboat came closer and Hughes indicated to the coxswain to come to the *Fiore*'s starboard beam. The boat came gently alongside and one of the men in the bows threw up the boat's painter. Hughes grabbed it and tied it to a cleat next to the ladder.

'Welcome aboard,' said Hughes. 'Please come on to the bridge.'

The two sailors carried holstered automatics on their right sides. One was a lieutenant the other was a petty officer.

Holding out his hand Hunter said, 'Lieutenant, welcome aboard. My name is Commander Nicholas Hunter, Royal Navy.'

The lieutenant had somehow managed to strut as he stepped over the side, now he wasn't looking so sure of himself.

'You . . . You are a Commander in the Royal Navy?'

'Yes. Here is my identity card.' Hunter handed it over and watched as the man took a close look.

'It says here Commander N. Hunter, RN, TIFAT. What is TIFAT? What does that mean?'

'That is the organisation we are seconded to. The International Force Against Terrorism.'

'I have never heard of it.' He shoved the ID back at Hunter and said, 'I think this is rubbish. You are insulting my intelligence. We have instructions to search this vessel and we will. If you cause any trouble you will be arrested. I want first to see your passports and the ownership papers for this boat.'

'Nobody here owns it. We've hired it for the week to do some cruising. We have the papers here.' Hunter stepped across to the chart table, opened a drawer and extracted an envelope. He took out a few sheets of paper and handed them to the lieutenant. A glance showed them to be the boat hire agreement.

Next, each of them placed their passports on the table for inspection. The lieutenant quickly thumbed through them, pausing longest when he saw that Badonovitch was Russian.

When he had finished he announced, 'Now we will search the boat. Petty Officer, go below and search the cabins.'

'Wait a moment,' Hunter said, 'what for? What are you looking for?'

'Illegal immigrants.'

'Don't be so bloody stupid,' said Hunter, 'why in hell would we have illegal immigrants onboard? This is ludicrous!'

'Nevertheless, my orders are clear. Every vessel, no matter where from or who owns it is to be searched. This will only take a few minutes and you can be on your way.'

Which was all well and good in theory but in practice was not going to happen. 'Lieutenant, I am a Commander in the Royal Navy and I outrank you by a considerable degree. You will therefore leave this boat immediately and allow us to continue on our way.'

There was one desperate measure he could employ. Physically force the men off the boat after disarming them and send them back to their mother ship. Then sneak the immigrants over the side and into *The Mercury* and run them ashore. The coast was only five miles away. The chances of the Somalis escaping were remote but at least they might get away though that wasn't the biggest issue the team needed to deal with. All sorts of opprobrium would be heaped onto their heads. The General would rage but still move heaven and earth to cover for them, somehow.

There was one other option and that was to give up the immigrants. The reason for them being onboard could easily be dealt with. Rescued from the ship, in fear for their lives, they were taking them to the authorities on mainland Italy. Reason? TIFAT business and nobody else's.

The lieutenant's radio came to life. The lieutenant answered, listened for a few moments, said 'Si, Capitano. Si.'

The lieutenant saluted Hunter and said, 'Commander, we have been ordered to return to the *Vedetta* with sincere apologies for any disruption we have caused. My Captain has also said that the work of TIFAT is an inspiration to us all.'

Hunter nodded. 'Please convey to him our thanks.'

The two Italians climbed down into the seaboat, Hughes threw them the end of the painter and they watched as the boat puttered away back to the grey hulled patrol craft.

'What do you reckon happened, boss?' Badonovitch asked.

'Hiram, I suspect.' The words were barely out of his mouth when his phone rang. 'Hiram.'

'Nick. Have they gone?'

'Yes. What did you do?'

'I contacted their admiralty. I know the Admiral in command of their Mediterranean fleet. I managed to get hold of him. Told him it was you. That was all I needed to do. He said to leave it to him. It sounds like he came through okay.'

'What's the Admiral's name?'

'Giovanni Romano.'

Hunter chuckled. 'He's a sort of old friend.'

'How did you get a friend who's an Admiral?'

'His son was in trouble. Got mixed up with the wrong crowd. I sorted it.'

'How do you mean, sorted it?'

'You know how these things work. He dealt a bit of dope, made some pocket money on the side while he was at Milan University. By the time he graduated he was shifting coke. It was one particular gang that with a combination of persuasion and coercion dragged him deeper into the drugs world.'

'How were you involved.'

'Through his sister. She asked me to help him. So I did.'

'What did you do?'

'Made it clear to the gang that they were to leave the boy alone. It didn't take much of an effort.'

'Okay, Nick, you can tell me the rest when I see you.'

'Will do. We'll see you tomorrow.' He broke the connection.

'What was that all about?' Lizzie asked.

'Nothing, a bit of history. Let's get back on track.' He stepped to the console, turned the dial to 10 knots and watched as the revs increased and the boat's speed did likewise. He checked their position and course and said, 'I reckon our ETA is still around 18.00 plus a few minutes.'

There were no ships in the vicinity and the grey-hulled warship was already a dot on the horizon. Hunter appreciated the thankless task the Italians were embarked upon. They had thousands of miles to patrol, and even with other ships from different countries the fleet was far too small to be very effective. They rescued people from sinking boats, fished dead bodies out of the sea and dealt with people often on the verge of collapse who easily panicked in their need to be saved. Much of it was gesture politics, as usual.

Rima went below and brought the immigrants up to the bridge. They were dressed in clean clothes while the kids wore shorts and tee shirts far to big for them but good enough to protect their modesty. Cutlery and crockery was placed on the table in the stern as well as on the bridge table. Down below twenty eggs were placed into a saucepan to boil while one of the women began to fry sausages. Rod Perez sliced and buttered bread while Badonovitch poured fresh orange juice and passed the mugs and glasses around to everyone. The children's clothes had been hand washed and were now hanging out to dry. In the warm air that wouldn't take long.

Hunter stood at the helm, watching the horizon. There were ships and boats but nothing came close. They were now three miles off the coast and he could see the beautiful sandy beach that ran the length of the coastline. On the other side of the coast road was the town of Siderno, forgotten or ignored by most tourists and in need of a financial injection to revitalise the place.

After they had eaten, the Somali women, with Rima and Lizzie's help, cleared the table and washed up. A soporific peace blanketed the boat and they each made themselves comfortable below and above decks and dozed into the afternoon. Hunter stayed awake until 13.45 when Badonovitch took over the watch. Hunter went below to the empty forward cabin and thirty seconds after lying down on a bunk and closing his eyes he was fast asleep.

At 17.45 Hunter was awake and after shaving and showering he went up top. He could see the breakwater of Catanzaro Harbour, which, according to the satnav readout was just over four miles away. The harbour was circular, about 300 metres in diameter. Half of it was the natural coast while the seaward side was a wall made from blocks of stone heaped together about 18 or 20 metres wide and four metres above sea level. Along the top, on the inside, was a three metres wide cement path. The harbour hadn't been there very long. Cynically Hunter thought it had no doubt been paid for with money collected from the European taxpayers and distributed by the European Union. All at great expense and for the benefit of the EU bureaucracy alone, allowing them to justify their existence. He grinned. That was no longer a British problem.

Helping himself to a mug of coffee, Hunter asked, 'What's the Pilot say about harbour control?' He was referring to a book detailing everything a seafarer needed to know about the area, both at sea and on land.

'There isn't any,' answered Masters. 'Docking office open until 18.00, docking fees paid prior to departure.'

'Good.' He sipped his coffee, looking at the expectant black faces staring at him. Now that they were approaching land their fear was blossoming, threatening them, their sojourn in a world of near normality nearly over. Hunter was sorry beyond words for them but there was nothing more he could do. Except carry out the next stage and wish them all well.

'Listen all of you,' he said in Arabic. 'In a few minutes you'll need to go below and stay there quietly. If anyone wanders over to look at the boat and you are seen then you can be sure they'll report the fact that you are onboard to the authorities. We are going to arrange a few things so that you can at least get to Rome from here.'

'I told you,' said Haboon, 'we have no money.'

'And I said,' Hunter smiled at her, 'that I'll take care of the problem. According to the Internet there is a train for Rome leaving at 22.54. It's a slow train and doesn't arrive there until 06.31 after one change of train. We'll get you a bag each, some new clothes and toiletries. We will take you to the station a few at a time. Decide who is travelling with whom. I want one of you women with one man and share the children between you. The two men left travel together. But here's the important thing. Do not sit altogether in the same carriage. You must sit in different carriages and you must ignore each other. You will only be asked for your tickets by the ticket inspector, nobody will be asking you for any identification. You are ordinary passengers going about your ordinary business. You have been on holiday and

137

now you are going home to Rome. Don,' he turned to Master, 'get what measurements you can like shoe size, leg length and waist size. They look okay dressed in our clothes on here but it would be better if they're not seen in public.'

Badonovitch took the boat through the outer entrance, the inner entrance and then turned to port taking them around the horseshoe bend that was the clever protection from storms from just about any direction.

There were boats at anchor or attached to buoys scattered all across the harbour in what seemed to Hunter to be in a haphazard fashion. However, much to his relief, the southern wall had only two boats tied to it, which left plenty of room for the *Fiore*.

They were soon berthed starboard side to, which meant they wouldn't need to turn around when it came time to leave.

'Right, let's go,' said Hunter. 'Rod, you stay here and keep an eye on things. Don't let any of them come up here.' He pointed at the harbour wall, 'There are plenty of people strolling around and are bound to come this way to take a look.'

He was right. Already people were heading towards them. The *Fiore* was an interesting boat to look at and it was new in the harbour and so attracted sightseers.

Badonovitch and Haboon left together, then Masters and Rima, then Hughes and Lizzie. Hunter went on his own. A few minutes walk took him into the town where he found a bank with a cash dispenser outside. He inserted his credit card, pressed the requisite buttons and extracted 5,000 euros. The maximum the machine would pay out in one transaction.

Five minutes later he found a second dispenser and repeated the process. He was walking past a shop specialising in mobile phones when on impulse he went in.

The shop was packed with phones of all makes and complexity. 'Do you speak English?' He asked the young lady behind the counter.

'Yes. Some. May I help you?'

'I am looking to buy a fully charged, basic, pay-as-you-go mobile.'

'We have a number of basic phones but only a few that are fully charged. They are for demonstration purposes.'

'That's what I figured. Can you show me them?'

Reaching under the counter the young woman placed three phones side by side and pointed at each one. 'This is only for phoning and texting as is this one. This one also takes photographs.'

'What's the difference in price?'

She told him and he replied, 'I'll pay you for twenty hours use if you sell me this phone,' he pointed at the one that took photographs, 'at the same price as the others.'

She didn't hesitate. 'Okay.'

When he left the shop he grabbed a cruising taxi to take him to the railway station. The journey took less than five minutes and maybe wasn't too far to walk. In the station he used the cash to buy train tickets. All singles - eight for adults, seven for children.

He walked back towards the harbour but stopped in the town centre at another cash machine. He topped up the cash he was carrying to just over 11,000 euros before continuing to the *Fiore*. It was his own money but if anyone asked he would tell them it was courtesy of TIFAT. He never broadcast his generosity to anyone. He joined Perez on the boat.

'All quiet?'

Perez grinned. 'Yes. Good as gold. Poor buggers.'

'Yeah, they are that.'

'You know Nick, it's not until you're up close and involved that you have any idea what these people are going through. In the abstract I say send them back, in the particular I want to rescue them, save them, Christ, I don't know, protect them. Does that sound nuts to you?'

Hunter smiled. 'Nope. It's what we all feel. In some respects it's why we do what we do. Here are the others. They have enough bags between them.'

15

In many ways it was heart wrenching to watch as the kids opened their bags and exclaim over the few items inside them. The most popular were their trainers – a top brand over which they exclaimed and smiled. The boys were fitted out with trousers, tee shirts and lightweight jackets. The colours and styles of all three were different. Dressed the same, even if travelling in different parts of the train could possibly lead to questions being asked. It was highly unlikely but there was no reason to take a chance no matter how small. It was why the shopping party had been split into three - different clothes from different shops.

Haboon was dressed in a white blouse, a pleated and flared striped skirt of many colours and flat comfortable shoes. She looked at Hunter with tears in her eyes and managed to whisper thank you in a husky voice.

The men accepted their clothes with far less enthusiasm, almost resentment that Hunter guessed lay in the fact that they were having to accept charity. He thought he understood their attitude. He had learnt that they were clever, educated individuals. Two of the men were electronic engineers, two were mechanics who had done an apprenticeship together in a large and thriving garage and one had been training to be a doctor and had been in his third year when the roof had fallen in. In his case it had been quite literally when a barrel bomb exploded near his home. It also turned out that one of the women, like Rima, could speak half-a-dozen languages including excellent English even though she had kept quiet the whole time she had been on the boat.

The bags contained a second outfit, similar to the first, plus underwear and toiletries.

'I told you I'd take care of the money,' said Hunter, 'and here it is.' He handed 1,000 euros to each of the men and 2,000 euros to each of the three women. Total 11,000 euros. 'I'm giving you women more as I want you to look after the children. Will you do that?'

They nodded nervously.

'Good. You'll be going soon so just relax for the next couple of hours. In the meantime, Haboon you can help to make sandwiches for your journey. We've also got Coca Colas and some bottled water for you to take. In case you get hungry during the night, oh, and some chocolate as well.'

Lizzie and Hunter were standing at the foot of the stairs watching their passengers when she said, 'I hate them. With all my heart I hate them.'

'These poor people?' Hunter looked at her in some surprise.

'No, you idiot,' she hit the top of his arm with the back of her hand, 'the people responsible for this.'

'I know how you feel,' he replied quietly. 'I hate them as well.' Turning, he went up to the bridge and Lizzie followed.

'I want to kill every one of them,' she said fiercely, speaking slowly.

'I understand.'

She looked closely at him, 'Yes, you do. I thought of you as a cold blooded killer, one who enjoyed what he does, but you're not are you?'

Luckily the rest of the team was sitting around the table at the stern and so Hunter felt he could open up.

'No. It really is a case of someone has to do it. The question we need to ask all the time loudly and clearly across the west is how do we stop the criminal gangs and the terrorists? We need to face down the politically correct and demand that they answer the question. Not in a wholly unrealistic, holier-than-thou way of by arrest, trial, imprisonment but how do you actually do it? How do you prove a man is a people smuggler? Where should the trial be held? What do you do with him if he is found guilty? The chances of which being about as remote as finding life on Pluto. Did you know that a whole industry has grown up in the past couple of years to prosecute our soldiers for so-called war crimes in Afghanistan all those years ago? That has now been extended to action in Iraq, Libya and Syria and anywhere else the parasitic lawyers can think of.'

'No, I didn't.

'It can't happen in America, your soldiers have congressional immunity from spurious claims. Yet we've paid out tens of millions of pounds in damages to some of the worst scum on earth.'

'Terrorists?'

'No. The lawyers representing them. And all of it taxpayers' money.'

They exchanged smiles. Hunter wondered briefly about bedding a more junior officer and thought what the hell. If it happened, it happened.

'Where did the money come from?' she asked.

'What money?'

'The money you gave to the Somalis.'

Hunter replied, 'TIFAT funds. I have access to a special account that allows me to draw down cash should I ever need it. It comes in handy sometimes for paying bribes and fees.' He wasn't going to tell her or anyone else the truth.

'What does this come under?'

'Philanthropy.'

She stared at his for a few seconds and he smiled back.

'Hiram told me a few things about you and I don't believe you.'

'Moi? You don't believe me? I am wounded to the quick.' He put his hand on his heart.

'You're a real ham, but I do like you.'

'So there's hope for me yet?'

'Don't push it.'

Sunset was at 20.50, as near as dammit an hour away. Allowing an hour and a half for full dark and that would be the time to head for the railway station. Hunter had decided that it would be better to walk than take a taxi, as it would give the kids a chance to stretch their legs after being cooped up for so long.

The next hour and a half seemed interminable but finally it was time to go. It was now fully dark and as there were no lights illuminating the wall there were no sightseers. Hunter went first and a minute later Haboon, one of the men and three of the children followed. Hunter was there to lead the way and to make sure they reached the station safely.

Ten minutes later Badonovitch strolled along the wall followed by one of the women, one of the men and two of the children.

Another ten minutes and Masters quit the boat and was followed by one woman, one man and two children.

After that came Perez and the remaining two men, the mechanics, who the team had only just discovered were brothers.

At the station Hunter checked which was the northbound platform and crossed the bridge to get to it. He had taken his time, but even so had arrived with half an hour to spare. The platform was empty and he walked back along the platform to the bench seats where Haboon and her 'family' was sitting. They looked scared out of their wits for which Hunter couldn't blame them.

He smiled reassuringly. 'Don't worry. Nothing is going to happen. Nobody is going to demand that you show some form of ID. You look respectable, you have money and you are travelling home to wherever you decide you are going. The train is due at 22.54 and thanks to a man by the name of Mussolini will probably be on time.'

'Who is this Mussolini?' Haboon asked.

'A bad man who did very bad things in Italy in the 1930s but he did get the trains to run on time.' Reaching into a jacket pocket he took out the phone. 'This is a pay as you go phone. It's good for twenty hours of use and is fully charged. I want you to have it.'

'Why?'

It was a good question and Hunter had no answer so he shrugged.

'Just in case. My mobile phone number is in speed dial one. If you need any help then call me. I probably won't be able to come to help but I know a lot of people all over Europe who I can call on.'

'But why are you doing this,' she hesitated then added, 'Nick?'

The fact was he had no idea. He just knew that if he left them at the station it would seem like abandoning them. Which in many ways it was but what else could they do?

'Because you just might need me.'

Just then Badonovitch arrived followed a few seconds later with his charges. The Russian walked past Hunter while the others sat a little way away on another bench. Masters arrived with his four and then Perez with the two men. They sat scattered along the platform. And right on time they heard a train approaching from the left and at 22.50 it drew majestically into the station. The doors opened but nobody alighted. The 7 children, 3 women and 5 men climbed into different carriages with only Haboon giving a backward glance.

The men from TIFAT remained sitting and at 22.54 precisely the train started its journey. As soon as it left the station they headed down the hill.

Back onboard the boat they found Hughes and the two women drinking white wine, a bowl of salted peanuts on the table between them.

'Did they get off okay?' Lizzie asked.

'Yeah, no problems,' Hunter answered.

'I hope they'll be all right,' said Rima, taking a sip of her wine.

'There's nothing else we can do to help them,' said Masters, reaching over Hughes' shoulder and taking a handful of nuts. 'I'm for a whisky chaser. What about you guys?'

There was general accord and while Hunter found glasses, Badonovitch the bottles of beer, Masters found the Macallan, a bottle of cold sparkling water and ice.

Hefty slugs of whisky were poured; all five men added ice though Hunter was the only one to add water also.

'Cheers,' said Perez and all seven of them clinked glasses.

Lizzie said, 'Here's to our passengers. May they get where they are going and achieve what they hope for.'

Hunter said, 'It's frightening when you think that we helped as few as fifteen people when there are millions in dire straits. And we didn't do a lot for them when all's said and done.' He sipped his whisky and then took a drink of beer from the bottle.

From there the conversation turned to European politics, an agreement that leaving the European Union was the best thing that could happen to Britain and a further agreement that the country was safer. Safer from attack by terrorists by allowing the UK to have better control of its borders.

They turned in around 02.00 none of them the worse for wear. It wasn't in their nature to drink so much that they were incapacitated, added to which they all had hard heads.

Hunter slept on the bridge and woke with the dawn. He changed into running gear, stepped ashore, did a few stretching exercises to get the kinks out and started running. He ran fast, burning off the anger he still felt about the way the immigrants were being treated first by the smugglers and second by the incompetent and useless EU government.

By the time he arrived back at the *Fiore* he had run at least ten kilometres, possibly more. He stepped onboard the boat, kicked off his shoes and dived into the water. It was cool and refreshing and he did a fast crawl across the harbour and back. When he levered himself onto the deck he was in a better frame of mind. In the world that he inhabited there was a lot he could do by continuing down the track he was already on. He would take out the smugglers at every opportunity himself. Mentally, he then berated himself for he disliked the use of euphemisms. He would kill them whenever he had the opportunity. And in doing so he would do the best he could to work his way up the food chain to the paymasters and the instigators of the crimes. And, he thought, he had a pretty good idea where it would lead him.

16

They ate a leisurely breakfast after which Hunter paid the overnight berthing fees and moved the boat to the fuelling point where they topped up with diesel and fresh water. Lizzie and Rima went shopping for further supplies and returned with fresh fruit, cured meats and freshly baked bread all from a local panetteria. They also bought bottled water, cartons of fresh orange juice and bottles of beer.

'I can never get over the choice of bread and cold meats in the local bakeries. It's a pity we don't have more of the same in the States,' said Lizzie.

'The same goes for the UK,' replied Hunter. 'Our problem is we're not prepared to pay for the better quality food that could be available. As always, the masses level down.'

'Hey boss,' said Badonovitch, 'you shouldn't be so philosophical this early in the day. Keep it for the evenings.'

'Yeah. Okay, we all buttoned up? Diesel and water finished?'

'Ready to go, Nick,' said Masters.

They cast off and Hunter steered them out of the harbour, checked there were no other vessels likely to get in their way and engaged the autopilot. He steadied their heading on due south, their speed at ten knots and relaxed in the captain's chair, a mug of coffee in his hand.

He decided it was time to report to General Macnair in Rosyth.

He was through to him in minutes. 'Hello sir.'

'Commander.' The voice was frosty but it was what Hunter had been expecting.

'I suppose you've been wondering where we got to, sir.'

'Something like that.'

'Ah, well, I'm afraid you're not going to like it.'

'Why? What have you been up to?'

'Er, we brought a handful of immigrants to a town in Italy and sent them by train northwards.'

'You did what?'

'Precisely that sir.'

'Care to tell me all about it?'

Hunter explained what they had done.

'Okay, you shouldn't have but I would have done the same if I'd been in your shoes. Where's the rest of the team? Back at base?'

'Er, no sir. They're here.'

Macnair chuckled. 'I might have guessed. Tell them from me that they're all officially reprimanded and unofficially Bravo Zulu.' Bravo Zulu was shorthand radio speak for well done.

'Thanks sir. What shall I tell them to do? Return to Rosyth?'

'Yes. Did you find out anything about the smugglers' operation?'

'We purloined a laptop and the ship's papers. Don will bring them back for Leo or Gareth to have a go at.'

As far as Hunter was concerned Leo and Gareth were geniuses when it came to computers but then he was always ready to admit he was something of a Luddite.

'What will you be doing? You've another week of leave owing at least.'

'Yes sir. Fact is, I thought I might stay a bit longer. I've hired the boat for a week and there's the best part of four days of hire still to go.'

'I see. Whoever she is I hope you have a pleasant time.'

There was no fooling the old man; he knew Hunter too well. The connection was broken. The others had heard his side of the conversation so he told them what the General had said. Apart, that was, for the last sentence.

The men exchanged grins.

It was a gentle cruise along the Italian coast and down to Sicily.

The weather remained pleasant; there were a few high clouds, wispy cirrocumulus, with no hint of rain in the air. They stood naval watches - morning, afternoon, first dog, last dog, first, middle and finally morning. When they were not on watch they mainly lolled under the after deck awning but they did remove the for'ard awning for those who wanted to top-up their suntans. It was peaceful, idyllic and soporific and as was always the case with the team, the calm before a future storm, whenever it hit.

When they arrived at the marina the team collected their gear and headed for the airport and military transport back to Scotland. In the meantime Rima, Perez and Lizzie reported to Walsh.

Just after 13.00 that afternoon Walsh appeared at the marina.

'I gather the trip was a success,' he greeted Hunter as he stepped onboard.

Sitting with his feet on the table on the after deck Hunter nodded. 'I guess you could call it that.' He swung his feet to the deck and stood up. 'Can I get you something? A beer? A coffee?'

'The sun's over the yardarm so a beer will slip down a treat.'

Hunter went below, dug out two beers from the fridge, flicked off their tops with a bottle opener and returned to where Walsh was sitting. He handed him a bottle.

'Thanks Nick.'

They tapped bottles and both took appreciative drinks. They were sitting under the stern awning out of the sun where it was still 30°C even in the shade.

'Finish that story about Admiral Giovanni Romano.'

'What do you want to know?'

'The moment I told him you were involved he said to leave it with him and you know the rest. So come on, give.'

'It was a few years ago. I told you his son became mixed up with a gang of pretty nasty people. He was probably more stupid than criminal, though I'm not absolutely sure that was the case.' He shrugged. 'Anyway, I was going out with his sister at the time. Nothing serious, just a good time and a lot of fun in bed. I'd met him a few times and on the whole he seemed a nice enough lad. The third time I saw him was at a restaurant. We were sitting outside having dinner when he turned up. Usually when I've been around he's had the courtesy to speak in English, which they both spoke fluently. This time it was Italian. A lot of arguing then Flavia, the girl . . .'

Welsh interrupted, grinning, 'I figured that out for myself.'

'Yeah, well, she took out her purse and gave him a wad of euros, he took the money and stalked off without so much as a thank you.'

'Nice guy.'

'Flavia was pretty upset and told me about him being part of this gang and heading for serious trouble.'

'So Sir Galahad rode to the rescue?'

Hunter shrugged. 'You know me, Hiram. I can never resist a challenge. There was something engaging about Enrico so maybe he was more stupid than guilty. I don't know. Anyway, Flavia said something about somebody needing to help him before it was too late but then we dropped the subject.'

'So how did you get involved?'

'Two days later I saw him again. It was a coincidence. I was down near the docks on my way to visit one of our ships. An RPC.' An RPC was Request the Pleasure of your Company, which meant a low key cocktail party in the wardroom. 'He was talking to three men. They looked to be Chinese, though I wasn't sure. Then two of them grabbed Enrico by the arms and the third one was about to hit him when I yelled and they stopped in their tracks. However, they didn't let him go. The man who was going to do the hitting told me to go away. He said it in English and told Enrico to tell me the same thing in Italian. Enrico knew who I was and wasn't about to tell me to go away as I was his only chance of avoiding a beating.'

'So what did you do? As though I can't guess.'

I kept walking towards them, the one who did the talking turned towards me and took out a flick knife. He waved it in front of him at waist height. You know what I mean. The macho, look how tough I am, I'll gut you if you don't go away.'

'What age were they?'

'The ones hanging on to Enrico's arms I would say were early twenties, the man with the knife in his forties. It turned out that they were father and two sons.'

Walsh nodded. 'So you took the knife off him, beat the bejesus out of them and you walked away arm in arm.'

It was Hunter's turn to grin. 'Pretty much. I broke the arms of the man with the knife. Compound fractures of the ulna and radius. The other two hardly had time to react when I did the same to them.'

'What did Enrico do?'

'Nothing. He stood there like he was in shock. I asked him what it was all about and he told me about the drugs. I searched them and found all three had coke on them. Enrico told me that the three men were the only people he knew about. He had met the brothers at university, got slowly enmeshed with the whole rotten world of drugs and ended up being coerced to sell the coke to the end user.'

'Come on Nick. How can you coerce somebody to do something like that?'

'A number of ways. If you use the stuff then you can be blackmailed and threatened. He told me that they'd threatened him as well as promising to throw acid in Flavia's face.'

'Did you believe him?'

'About the threats? Yes. By now he was shaking like an aspen. So yes, I believed him. He told me they were father and two sons. I had a dilemma.'

'How so?'

'The father was a tough swine. He said he would find me and kill me. He would get his revenge on Enrico and Flavia and I would regret getting involved.'

'So I guess you dealt with the problem.'

'Hiram, what can anyone do? I believed the man. We were near a dry dock. A big one. There was a large tanker in the dock and no water. We were in shadow. Seeing Enrico had been more by luck than judgement. I dragged the father by his collar to the edge of the dock and then I dragged his two sons over. The father told me he would kill us all. It's incredible how stupid people are. I nodded to him and threw one of the sons over the edge. He fell about thirty maybe thirty-five metres. He didn't even have time to yell before he hit the bottom. I grabbed the second son and threw him as well. Then I stopped.'

'Why?'

'I wanted the man to feel real pain. Not physical but emotional. He was looking at me in horror. I don't think he could believe that I could be as ruthless as he was. I remember his mouth opening and closing but no words came out. I grabbed him by his collar and dragged him a few feet to the edge and shoved his head over. It was pitch black so I said down there are your sons. Mashed to nothing. You are joining them. In spite of his arms he tried to struggle. He was jabbering in Chinese and sobbing at the same time. I shoved him over.' Hunter paused.

'What happened then?'

'I missed the RPC. Instead I took Enrico home to his father's house. The Admiral was a one star back then but I know he's a two or three star now.'

'Three,' said Hiram, automatically.

'Yes, well, you know to get to that rank you need to be pretty tough and the Admiral was certainly that. When we got to his house he sent Enrico to bed, like a naughty schoolboy. He took me into his study, sat me down and gave me a large glass of Vecchia Romagna, which I remember was rather pleasant.'

'Italian brandy, at least ten years old. Excellent after dinner.'

'You learn something new everyday. I told the Admiral what had happened. Not only was he grateful he said that he owed me more than he could ever repay and if there was anything he could ever do then I was just to call. So you did and he came through.'

'Okay, the most important question. What happened to Flavia?'

'I saw her a few more times before I left Italy and haven't been back since. Last I heard she was married and Enrico is now a lawyer.'

'You should know that the Admiral said that nothing has changed. The debt is still there and will be all his days.'

'Italian melodrama,' Hunter said, 'from watching and listening to too much opera. What happened at the house?'

'It's like an ants' nest of police, military personnel and a few men in dark suits. The usual.'

'And what's happened to the immigrants?'

'They've been taken for processing. They'll try and identify them, get names and nationalities if they can, then fingerprint them and find somewhere to keep them.'

'In some sort of camp I suppose.'

'What else can we do?'

'Nothing. I just wish the camps could be better organised, better built and better stocked.'

'What we should do is build suitable accommodation on the edges of their own countries and have UN forces in serious numbers protecting the places.'

'That's a big job,' said Hunter.

'No it's not. Not compared to what we have now. Have you seen the rooms built out of shipping containers?'

'No. I can't say I have.'

'What you do is line and fit out containers as bedrooms, kitchens, lounges and toilets with showers. You have them fully plumbed and have electric sockets and lights wired in. You then make a few minor adjustments to the outside of each container, mainly welding plates and poles to the outside that slot into each other. You can literally put a one-bedroom structure together in about two hours. But here's the thing. You can slot as many of them together as you like. You can go three or four stories high. You can create one, two, three or more bedroomed structures. And you create them somewhere useful, like Italy and Greece. Or better still we go back into the war zone with an overwhelming UN force and clear suitable areas and build a city if we need to.'

'Hiram you sound positively evangelical about it.'

The Colonel looked a little sheepish but hid his discomfort by finishing his beer, hitting the table with the bottle and saying, 'I could use another.'

Hunter obligingly rose to his feet and returned a minute later with two bottles. 'Keep talking.'

'All that's needed then is water, sewage and electricity. Electricity could be a mixture of solar and wind power, quick and easy. Sewage could be proper cesspits pumped clean every now and again, whatever it takes, and water can be a desalination plant on the edge of the town, next to the sea. It might sound as though it would be expensive but it would be a damned sight cheaper and far more humane than what we have right now. And you know what it would take?'

Taking a swig of beer Hunter replied, 'Yeah, political will and honest politicians. Both are sadly lacking, the latter particularly in Eastern Europe and the Middle East, oh and Africa.'

'You got it in one, Nick.'

'Surely others have thought of this?'

'Of course they have. I just happened to read about somebody having taken three containers and welded them into a place to live. Two containers on the ground floor, one above and a small patio come garden next to it. When I read it I thought why not? So I wrote a paper on the idea and passed it up the command.'

'What happened?'

'I was told that I was a Colonel responsible for the safety and welfare of a large group of men and women and for implementing political policy by military means.'

'In other words, shut up.'

'You got it.'

'But being somewhat bloody-minded you decided to look further into it.'

'I checked out the feasibility and possible costs. Compared to what it is costing us now, as well as what the future will hold because of unrest, racist riots, terrorist attacks and every other rotten thing that's lurking in the forest it's peanuts.'

'I can see that. So you haven't given up?'

'No, I damned well haven't.'

'So what are you going to do?'

'Write the plans up as if it were a military operation. Work out the costs per unit, identify where and how the containers can be fitted out, identify where to put the first village, town, city, call it what you will and tell the world after I first send copies to the heads of every government in the world.'

'If you try really hard, really push scream and kick, you may stir the governments and civil servants into apathy, which will be a highly significant step.'

Grinning, Walsh stood up. 'Thanks for the beers and the understanding ear.'

'I think it's a brilliant idea and if there's anything I can do to help let me know.'

'Will do, and thanks.' Stepping ashore Walsh paused, looked back and said, 'Incidentally, Lizzie has seventy-two hours down time coming to her and I signed her off for it just before I came here. Enjoy yourselves.'

17

Hunter sat with his second beer warming in his hand and watched as Captain Elizabeth Montgomery walked towards the boat, carrying a green canvas bag dangling from her left hand. She was wearing a knee length, light blue skirt and a plain, white sleeveless blouse. Hunter stood up and leant on the guardrail. He smiled at her and she smiled back.

'Permission to come aboard.'

'Please do,' he grinned. Then, leaning over the guardrail he took her hand and helped her onto the boat. He placed her bag on the bridge. 'You look lovely. Am I allowed to say that to a more junior officer or does that come under the heading of sexual harassment by a senior officer?'

'You can say it as often as you like,' she smiled.

She stood close to him and looked up into his eyes. Hunter felt his mouth go dry. She was really very attractive.

'Can I get you something to drink? White wine? There's some Chardonnay in the fridge or an Italian Prosecco?'

'I know there is, if you can remember that far back, I bought it.'

'Hmm, so you did. I was forgetting. Something came up and distracted me.'

'So it seems. However, enough innuendos. Or as Miss Moneypenny said, someday you have to make good on them.'

'If I remember correctly, *Goldeneye* in 2007.'

'So you know your James Bond.'

'My favourite. An action man who is smooth, suave, sophisticated, knowledgeable, tough and let's not forget, a Royal Naval officer to boot, hence his rank of Commander.'

'So a lot like you?'

'I'm as smooth as deck tread,' he was referring to the very rough sandpaper often used to cover decks to reduce the risk of slipping.

'But you're not denying your other qualities?'

'I could, but I shouldn't.'

'Why not?'

'I wouldn't like our relationship to start out on a lie.'

She smiled again. 'So it's a relationship we're entering into?'

He pursed his lips for a few seconds, then said, 'At least for the next few days.'

'Good. That was all I was thinking as well.'

'So what is it to be?'

'The Prosecco, please.'

'Coming right up.'

Hunter went below. In the fridge he found the wine, removed the foil and wire and eased the top off. It came out with a satisfying pop. He located an ice bucket, placed the bottle inside and emptied a tray of ice on top.

He then found a bag of pistachio nuts, a bowl for the shells and a fluted glass for the wine. He returned to where Lizzie was sitting and placed the items on the table. He poured the wine, handed her a glass, they clinked bottle on glass and smiled at each other. There was tension in the air between them that Hunter found intoxicating.

They sipped their drinks and then Hunter said, 'Shall we have dinner here or find a restaurant?'

'What are you suggesting we cook?' Then she added, 'Can you cook?'

'My repertoire of cooking is a rather spectacular spaghetti bolognese, scrambled eggs with cheese or fillet of pork in a cream sauce with fried pears and vegetables. I can of course, barbecue just about any meat under the sun but preferably after it has been marinated in suitable herbs and spices. With that I can also mix a bowl of salad and make my own salad dressing.' He frowned, nodded and then said, 'Yep, that's the sum total of my culinary skills.'

'That's at least one meal better than me. My spag bol is mediocre at best. So we'll barbecue?'

'Ah, there's a problem.'

'What's that?'

'No meat.'

Lizzie laughed. 'So what you've been leading up to is that we find a restaurant.'

Looking at his watch, Hunter said, 'I am. It's 19.20. Shall we take a stroll?'

'Let me finish this drink. You're not in any hurry are you?'

'To eat, no.' He smiled, stood up and added, 'I'm going below for a shower. I'll be ten minutes.'

In the master en-suite cabin he stripped off and stepped under the shower. A few moments later the shower door opened and Lizzie stepped in. In a husky voice she said, 'I thought you might like your back washed.'

It was after 21.35 when they found a small Italian bistro with tables outside on a small patio. There was a lit candle sitting in a straw covered, bulbous Chianti bottle, small bowls of olives, a bowl of olive oil infused with garlic and some other spices and freshly baked bread.

Taking a piece of bread, Hunter dipped it into the oil and ate it. Lizzie helped herself to an olive. A waiter appeared and they ordered a bottle of Chianti and then perused the menu. When the waiter returned Hunter ordered shrimp scampi with pasta while Lizzie had prune and olive chicken.

'Where are you from?' Hunter asked. 'Your accent is obviously American but which part of America?'

She shook her head. 'My father was a one star and I was brought up on American bases from Maryland via the Philippines and Germany. So my accent is something of a mish-mash.'

'Is your father still serving?'

'No. He retired last year. Retired to a house in Florida, plays golf every day and is wondering what to do with the rest of his life.'

'What age is he?'

'Fifty-eight. He has a lot of years ahead of him but he does need to get involved with something. I suggested local politics.' She shrugged, 'He says he'll consider it.'

'It's a problem for everyone who is in a profession where he or she retires early. If you don't get involved with something you fade away.'

'What do you intend doing?' Lizzie asked.

Hunter looked surprised. 'I won't be going anywhere for a few years yet.'

'But you can't keep doing what you do. It's not possible. You'll start to slow down, lose the edge you need in special services. I suppose like Hiram you can move up a few notches and direct and control rather than be at the sharp end.'

'You're right but that really is at least a decade away, I hope. What about you? Are you going to stay until you have to go?'

Lizzie shook her head emphatically. 'No. When I joined I had visions of becoming a General. One star even two. Getting to the top in a man's world had a sort of surreal appeal but then I thought about it and realised that the sacrifices were too great. No, I'm thirty-three and looking for a good man to love, honour and obey at least some of the time. In exchange I want to be cherished and looked after and all the other happy ever after scenes from Hollywood feel-good films.'

'Weren't you married?'

'Yes. Who told you?'

'Oh, I heard it from somewhere.'

'Hiram, I bet. He's a great guy. Pity he's happily married and of course he's also too old for me by about fifteen years. I was married. It lasted two years. He was a lawyer back in Washington DC. At first he was happy with my career, then he began to make noises about me being away and then I found out he was screwing just about everything in a skirt.'

'I'm sorry to hear that.'

'That's okay. Better to find it out sooner rather than later.'

'So you filed for divorce?'

'After I met him at our marital home, kicked him as hard as I could in what you British call his goolies and left him to be ambulanced to hospital. I told him if I ever saw him again I'd cut them off instead of just kicking him and that was the last I heard apart from when I got the final divorce papers with his signature on them.'

'When was this?'

'Two years ago. He was a louse. What about you? You come close to marrying?'

'Yes. A few years ago.'

'Who was she?'

'Believe it or not, an Israeli Mossad agent. Ruth's her name. I thought I had finally met the right woman but it wasn't to be.'

'What happened?'

'She was injured while we were on an operation. Nearly lost her leg but the surgeons saved it, put her back together and although she wasn't as good as new she walked with only the slightest of limps. Anyway, she went back to Israel and refused to leave. I went out after her and tried to persuade her otherwise, but it didn't work. The last I heard she was still with Mossad, doing desk work and was married to an assistant professor of economics at Tel Aviv University.'

'Since then?'

'Since then I've known a few women, enjoyed a footloose and fancy free existence which I plan on not changing for a while yet.'

'Is that for a while or never?'

'For a while, beyond doubt. I'd like children, a proper family life and to settle in one place. I still have to meet the right woman.' Then he added, 'No offence.'

'None taken. When I meet the right man I expect a heavenly choir, a lifting of the heart and a soaring soul that says this is the man for me.'

'Is that likely?'

'No. It's more likely that I meet a man who gradually grows on me and me on him and when the conversation lags he asks me to marry him. As my body clock will be ticking loudly and I'll be thinking, may as well and I've also run out of things to say I will say yes. If he is the right man we'll spend the remainder of our lives working hard at keeping it altogether and not be one of the dreadful statistics bandied about when it comes to divorce.'

'Sounds as though you've thought things through.'

'Nick, what else is there to do during sleepless nights on an army base?'

'Point taken.' He broke off and looked up, 'Ah, this looks rather good.'

The waiter, placed the food in front of them with a flourish, offered parmesan cheese and ground black pepper both of which Hunter accepted and Lizzie declined.

They ate in companionable silence. 'This is delicious,' said Lizzie.

'So is this.' He smiled at her across the table and then swept his eyes around the patio and onto the street.

'You know, you are the most alert man I have ever met.'

He focused his eyes on her, knowing what she meant. 'It's second nature.'

'Is that why you moved your chair so that you could sit with your back to the wall and watch what's going on around you?'

'Yes. There are a lot of people out there who would like to do us harm.'

'Us?'

'Members of TIFAT in particular but western military personnel in general with Americans at the top of the list.'

'I didn't think you were that well known.'

'As far as the general public is concerned we're not, but believe me our enemies know who we are.'

'What can they do about it?'

'In essence, nothing. But you never know what can happen. A chance sighting by the wrong people and they come after you. And remember we're not talking about somebody who cares whether they live or die. So they are very hard to stop.'

'Is that why,' she lowered her voice and said in a soft tone, 'you're carrying?'

'Yes.'

Lizzie was referring to the Glock hidden under his left armpit. 'I have the right credentials to prove I am allowed to have it but I don't want to be seen with a gun as it would lead to all sorts of complications.'

'I asked Hiram about you guys. He says that you have a mandate agreed by the permanent members of the United Nations Security Council to take the fight to the terrorists and now organised crime but on condition you operate under the radar.'

'He would know. He was there from the very beginning.'

Lizzie looked at him in some surprise. 'I had no idea. He never said a word.'

'He wouldn't. I have a great deal of respect for Hiram. He helped not only to form us but to get the right agreements in writing from the very beginning. He never trusted the UN nor domestic politicians to keep their word. If it suited them they'd throw us to the wolves.'

'So you have a sort of 'double O' licence to kill but sanctioned by more than the British government.'

'Something like that.' He suddenly smiled. 'Enough doom and gloom. Would you like a sweet or cheese and biscuits?'

'Neither, thanks. I've had enough.'

'Me too. A night cap? A brandy?'

'How about back on the *Fiore*? It has a very conducive atmosphere for what I have in mind.'

'Funnily enough I was thinking the same thing.'

After breakfast the following morning Hunter and Lizzie wandered around the shops of Catania stocking up on food and drink. Back on-board Hunter pulled out a chart covering the east and south of the island. He used dividers and a roller ruler to measure distances and times.

'If we take it easy, say at eight knots, we can easily reach this bay here, just south of Siracusa,' he pointed with a pencil. 'We go around this headland and anchor for the night in relative shelter. Any bad weather would have to come from directly south to hit us and that isn't likely.'

Lizzie looked closely at the chart. 'Between Punta Milocca and Plemmirio.'

'Yes. According to the Pilot,' he read closely, 'the bottom is mainly sand with a few rocks. Good holding ground, sheltered and private. What more could we ask for? It's sixty-five miles and if we leave in an hour we should get there for about 19.00.'

'Sounds like a plan.'

They navigated the boat to the fueling jetty and topped up the diesel and water tanks and then headed out to sea. This time they didn't bother taking *The Mercury* with them. Water sports weren't on the agenda.

The weather was still as balmy as it had been for the last couple of weeks though the forecast hinted at showers sometime during the night.

It was an uneventful and very pleasant cruise south. The autopilot dealt with the drudgery of steering a straight course and the radar took care of needing a lookout. If any other vessel came within three miles of them an alarm would sound and Hunter could be at the helm in seconds.

So they lay under the sun for part of the time, but mainly relaxed under the stern awning. Nearing Syracuse Hunter needed to disengage the autopilot and steer the boat around various vessels approaching and leaving the port. The majority of other boat users ignored the rule of the road for seafarers where you gave right of way to vessels to starboard. One incident almost had Hunter boarding the other boat that cut across the *Fiore*'s bows from the port side, missing them by a few feet when Hunter thrust the boat into astern and piled on the revs.

There were half a dozen young men and women in the stern, loud music blaring out, drinks in their hands, jeering at Hunter. He took the way off the boat, engaged ahead and turned to follow the idiots. A couple of minutes later he thought what the hell and changed back to their original course.

'I wondered what you were going to do,' said Lizzie, standing next to him.

'I was prepared to . . . to . . .'

'Kick the crap out of them?'

'Something like that. But then I thought why bother? You and I at anchor with a barbecued steak and all the trimmings is a lot more attractive than satisfying my wish to teach them a lesson. If they carry on like that they'll be learning that lesson the hard way.'

'But your way could save them from a much more serious, harsher lesson.'

'I thought of that. But it's none of my business.'

'Suppose they hit another boat? Sink it and people die, what then?'

Hunter sighed. 'You're right. I'll do one thing.'

He used the radio to call Siracusa Harbour Control. They answered immediately. He reported the other boat and explained his concerns. He was thanked, informed that they knew the boat and its owner and would deal with the matter. Ten minutes later Harbour Control gave Hunter the courtesy of informing him that the boat had been stopped, its occupants arrested and the boat confiscated - at least temporarily.

They sailed around the headland and as they did Hunter took the way off the boat. Lizzie stood next to him and chuckled and then they both burst out laughing.

'It's like Piccadilly Circus,' he said.

'Washington at rush hour. So what shall we do?'

At first glance the bay appeared packed with boats crewed by people with the same idea.

'It's not as bad as it looks.'

'And how do you figure that one out, Commander?'

'According to the chart there's deep water as close as eight metres to the shore.' Pointing at the chart with a pencil he added, 'That's caused by a scouring of the seabed out to here with the current sweeping this way.'

'What current? There's hardly any.'

Hunter smiled. 'We're talking about thousands of years of water movement, let's call it, rather than a current. So this shelf has taken a very long time to form.'

He eased the helm to starboard and took them in closer to the shore. 'Keep an eye on that echo sounder and let me know if it goes below six metres.'

The digital readout was showing 15 metres, then Lizzie said, 'Down to thirteen metres, twelve, eleven.' After a few seconds she said it's steady on eleven.'

'Good.' The coast was a mere 30 metres away and they were following the curve of the coastline. 'I'm taking us further in.' He eased the helm to starboard and nudged closer to the shore, the boat's speed at a low and steady two knots.

'The depth is dropping, that's eight, seven, six metres.'

'Okay, we'll keep it there.'

The *Fiore* was halfway around the bay and the nearest boats were 30 or more metres away.

'Why do you think none of the other boats have come this close?'

'They are amateurs with virtually no knowledge of the sea and anything maritime. I doubt they have charts and I doubt they'd understand them if they did. They don't know that the rise and fall here is about one metre. Our draft is three metres, it's low water according to the Tide Tables so we can approach until we're sitting in about five metres to be on the safe side. Also how many of the boats you can see have two anchors in the water?'

Looking around for a few seconds she said, 'None.'

'That means they're going to swing right around if the wind and tide changes even a small amount.'

'What does that matter?'

'Given the nature of the seabed the anchor can be dislodged especially if you look more closely and see that many don't have enough cable or rope out.'

'I see what you mean. Why's that do you think?'

'Maybe they don't have enough anchor cable or maybe they dropped anchor, it took hold in flat calm circumstances and they thought that's enough. Like I said, amateurs who are not prepared for 'what if'.'

'And in this case 'what if' is what?'

'What if the weather changes?'

'Is it going to?'

'Yes.'

'How can you be so sure?'

Hunter smiled. 'Sailor's intuition and the fact that I heard the weather forecast on the maritime channel about twenty minutes ago.'

'I didn't hear it.'

'You were down below. It was a Sécurité broadcast. A storm heading this way due in the middle of the night. Force five to six.'

'Shouldn't we make a run for it and return to Siracusa?'

Hunter shrugged. 'We could, but we'll be perfectly safe here.' He spun the helm to port, put the port engine into astern to increase their rate of turn, centred the helm and disengaged the gears when the *Fiore*'s stern was pointed at the beach.

'Can you go forward and drop the port anchor? I'll tell you when to drop the starboard.'

'Sure.' Lizzie went to the bows and released the anchor. It paid out all the way and the *Fiore* settled in five metres of water. He adroitly maneuvered the boat to starboard and then called out, 'Let go!'

The starboard anchor dropped, gripped and held. The boat ended with the anchors at 90 degrees, the stern pointed at the shore ten metres away and the depth five metres.

'Show off.'

Hunter shrugged and smiled. 'I enjoy a challenge.'

18

Hunter barbecued the steak while Lizzie prepared a salad. They sat in the stern and watched the sunset, enjoying their meal. Whitecaps were beginning to appear. A slight breeze had started, coming directly over the bow and every few minutes it burst into a short-lived gust.

'Here it comes. Give it an hour and it will be belting rain and blowing a gale.' He shivered. 'I'm going to put on a pair of jeans and a sweater.'

They both did the same and then sat in companionable silence, listening to sixties' ballads, the sort of stuff, Hunter admitted, his parents enjoyed.

'I see a few boats have left,' Lizzie said, scanning the bay.

'The intelligent ones.'

'So what does that make us? Stupid?'

Hunter chuckled. 'No. Careful. We'll be perfectly safe. I'm going to hang every fender we have over the starboard side. Every other one at deck level, the others halfway down. That will give us maximum protection.'

'Why? Are you expecting something to ram us?'

'Yes. That boat over there. It won't ram us but it will be hitting us sometime during the night if the weather continues to deteriorate. It'll bounce around, scrape over the starboard anchor cable and onto the beach.'

'You sound pretty sure of yourself.'

Shrugging, he said, 'Knowledge mixed with experience.'

'You like it don't you?'

'Like what?' Hunter sipped his red wine. 'This is rather a fine Chianti.'

'Don't change the subject. We could easily have gone to Siracusa but you preferred to stay here. You've taken all reasonable precautions, I grant you that, but you didn't go the whole way when you could have.'

'So what does that tell you?'

'That you're an adrenaline junkie. You like pitting yourself against the odds. But, and it's a big but, you also take all necessary precautions but only up to a point.'

'What do you mean by that?'

'What I mean is you'll climb a mountain but you'd use pitons. You will take all manner of risks but will do all in your power to mitigate them. Hence two anchors and the fenders. No offence.'

Hunter was grinning broadly. 'None taken. Do you have a degree in psychobabble?'

'Yes. You could call it that. I have a degree in psychiatry. The deal was I'd serve at least five years in exchange for the education paid for by the army. During my vacation time I trained with the army and found I enjoyed it more than looking into peoples' minds. And before you say anything I couldn't have been that good at it otherwise I wouldn't have married the loser I did marry.'

'I would never have suggested such a thing!' His mock horror at the suggestion made Lizzie smile.

'Yeah, sure. You're too much of a gentleman. Anyway, I volunteered for the SEALS where I have two roles. As an assistant to the Colonel but also to keep an eye on the troops. Watch their mental state. Continuous assessment as opposed to regular interviews.'

'Makes sense.'

'What about you? You been psychoanalysed?'

'Nope and I don't intend doing so either. However, now you're here and we've been together for a few days what do you think?'

Lizzie paused for a few seconds, sipping her wine, frowning, looking steadily at him. 'I think you're about as normal as it is possible to be and still do your job. You have a deep-rooted conviction that you're doing the right thing, something I concur with by the way, and most importantly you're not afraid to do whatever it takes to keep us safe. By us I mean the general population. I also think the rest of your guys I met are very much like you. You all have a very high threshold to do your duty but, and here's the kicker, your duty is as you see it, not as you're told it should be.'

Suddenly there was a more powerful gust of wind and the boat pitched a few degrees as the sea rolled in and out again.

'I think that's pretty astute of you. I'll go along with everything you've said and I'll add one more thing. We are needed like never before only most people don't know it and many people will deny it. They will scream the rule of law and that everything we do must be within the law. It isn't always possible, as you know all too well.'

'I agree,' Lizzie nodded. 'But who guards the guards themselves?'

'*Quis custodiet ipsos custodes*? The question asked by the Roman poet Juvenal from his work *Satire VI*.'

'A classic education as well?'

'No. I'm quoting my boss, Malcolm Macnair. He had the education. We've had this discussion on numerous occasions usually over a few late night whiskies. Believe me Lizzie, we don't take it lightly.'

The wind was backing which meant that it was no longer being disrupted by the land. The electronic anemometer on the room was now registering 15 knots steady but gusting 25.

'I think we're in for a bigger blow than I anticipated. We're already at force six and the storm is nowhere near us yet.'

'It could bypass us.'

'It could but I don't think it will.'

'How do you know?'

'Call it a seaman's intuition. How are you when it comes to being seasick?'

'No problem.'

The *Fiore* lurched and Hunter just managed to catch the half empty bottle of red wine before it tumbled to the deck.'

'So what shall we do for the night?'

'Well, lying in bed isn't much of an option, I'm afraid, so I think I'll sit wedged into the captain's chair with the engines running, in neutral and ready to react just in case.'

'Won't the anchors hold?'

'They will up to a point.'

'And that point is?'

'When that boat over there breaks loose and hits us, albeit relatively gently. The extra weight might prove too much.'

There was a sudden increase in the wind and Hunter looked at the anemometer. It hovered around 30 knots for a few seconds before dropping back to a steady 22. 'A steady force six gusting force seven. A really nasty Mediterranean blow.'

The sea was undulating in long waves, 10 to 13 feet high; there were white foam crests and airborne spray. The boat gave a sudden lurch and tried to rear up like a stallion held down by its reins.

'We'd better secure down below.'

It only took a few minutes and then they returned to the bridge.

'We're in for a wild night. You okay about that?'

Lizzie laughed. 'Don't you get it? I'm enjoying this as much as you. You men aren't the only ones who are adrenaline junkies.'

The boat lurched again and she grabbed Hunter's arm to steady herself while he held on to the back of the captain's chair.

'Why don't you lie down on the sofa bed. Pull up the safety board so you don't roll off.'

'Good idea.' She lay down and fitted the board. She curled up, jamming her knees against the board and her back against the padded sofa. 'Not quite what I planned for this evening.'

'I'll make it up to you tomorrow evening when I promise you either a flat calm sea or being alongside a secure harbour.'

'Promises, promises but I'll hold you to it.'

They stopped talking and Hunter checked the radar screen. They hadn't moved an inch from when they had first anchored. He used a marker pencil and placed a spot on each of the 15 boats still at anchor in the bay and watched them for a while. Six of the radar paints moved off the marker spot. It meant they were dragging their anchors but nowhere near to the *Fiore*. His reaction was serves the idiots right to damnation he couldn't just watch what was going to happen in the course of the next hour or two.

'Lizzie! Lizzie!'

'What? Sorry Nick, I must have dozed off.'

'That's okay. I'm just going to blast the whistle a few times and see if I can get a response from these bozos.' The whistle was actually a klaxon and made one hell of a racket. Hunter pressed the button five short times, paused a few seconds and did it again. The signal was used at sea to tell someone they were sailing into danger, literally a wake up call. He aimed a high power LED flashlight at one of the boats about half a cable away and switched it on. The boat was a modern, luxury craft about 30ft long. Hunter guessed it slept four. It had an open bridge, a single anchor and it was slowly heading towards the rocks on the other side of the bay. There was nobody in sight. He guessed the crew were probably below decks cowering from the storm and being very seasick.

'Goddammit, what's wrong with those idiots?'

'So you can't sit and watch them?'

'I guess not.'

He aimed the torch at another boat that had also dragged its anchor. It was similar to the first, also with nobody on the open bridge. The third boat was larger, it was the farthest from the shore and being more open to the elements had consequently dragged its single anchor the farthest. That meant it was possible that the anchor was no longer so firmly embedded in the seabed. Hunter checked the radar. He estimated that the boat would hit the shore in about fifteen minutes.

'What shall we do?' Lizzie was standing next to him, holding on to the arm of the chair.

'First, we put on life jackets, second we put on the foul weather harnesses which are in that bench seat and third I shall head out and raise the anchors.' He started the engines and while they warmed through he slipped on the harness Lizzie handed him.

'Is the harness necessary?'

'Right now, no. But you can't tell if it will suddenly get a lot worse and if we do go onto the open deck then yes, we hook onto the wires running along the top of the guardrails.' He engaged the gears. 'Okay, take the helm. Ease her forward and take the weight off the anchors. I'll start hauling them in.'

Hunter went into the bows. The wind had dropped slightly but he knew worse was to come. Spray was hitting the front of the boat and washing over him in a deluge of salty water. He shivered. A sunny Mediterranean day was not to be confused with a wet and stormy night when the temperature had plummeted. He should have worn a foul weather jacket but hadn't brought one with him. So much for being prepared, he thought.

Two minutes later the anchors were aweigh and secured. Hunter returned to the bridge and took the helm. 'When we get next to the boat there,' he pointed, 'yell at them while I blow the klaxon.'

At least all the boats had white, all-round anchor lights showing at their mastheads. It was now fully dark and it was only thanks to the lights that Hunter could see where to go. He adroitly took the *Fiore* next to the boat that was dragging its anchor the fastest.

He went starboard side to and nudged the other boat, knowing it was safe to do so thanks to the fenders they had placed earlier.

Now they were up close he saw that the boat was a modern 40ft cruiser with an enclosed bridge and an open upper bridge. Hunter blew the klaxon five short bursts and Lizzie yelled at the top of her voice. Finally a man appeared, looked at them and waved at them to go away.

'You're dragging your anchor,' Lizzie yelled. She pointed at the coast. 'You're headed for the rocks!'

The man looked the way she was pointing and suddenly leapt to the controls. Hunter put the *Fiore* into reverse and dropped back. He didn't trust the man to do the right thing. The man started his engines and engaged the gears, he pushed the throttle too hard and the boat shot forward. The anchor caught and the boat twisted round until her bows were pointed back at the shore. The boat shot forward again and did the same thing only this time with her stern pointing at the rocks.

'Take the way off!' Hunter yelled. The frustration of dealing with such a fool was getting to him.

The boat suddenly stopped and the man looked out of the window at Lizzie as though at a loss as to what he should do next.

Hunter had already briefed Lizzie what to say and she yelled, 'Stay at anchor and keep your bows pointing into the wind. If you don't you'll end up on the rocks!'

The man stared at her and then flicked her his middle finger. Lizzie looked at the man in shock and then turned to Hunter who shrugged.

'Leave him be! It's his funeral!'

Hunter repeated the process five more times when the remainder of the crews on the other boats came to life and realised what they needed to do.

By now the first boat had moved closer in and Hunter could see that she would be aground in about five minutes. He couldn't believe he was watching something so stupid. The man had actually switched off his engines. He approached the boat and shone the torch at the bridge. There was nobody there. The man he had seen had gone below.

The anemometer was showing a steady wind speed of 35 knots gusting to over 40. The weather was now a full-blown force 8 gale.

Lizzie stood next to him, hanging on to the chair. 'What shall we do?'

'If they hit those rocks they'll drown.'

'So why did he flip me the bird?'

Hunter shrugged. 'A moron, drunk, high on drugs, all of the above.'

'So what shall we do?'

'Damn, damn, damn.' He looked at her and said, 'I can't leave them. We don't know who is onboard. Family? Kids? Girlfriends? We can't condemn people because of one individual.'

'Sir Galahad to the rescue?'

'At times like this it's more like Don Quixote who has lost his sanity and sets out to undo wrongs, bring justice to the world and revive chivalry. The key words being lost his sanity.'

'No, definitely Sir Galahad. So what are we going to do? Whatever it is it had better be soon.'

'Lizzie, you take the helm.' He looked at the depth gauge. 'Six metres. Plenty of water and according to the chart right up to the rocks.' The boat suddenly pitched higher, slamming back onto the surface.

'The seventh wave?' Lizzie said loudly.

'It's a myth! I'm going to get the berthing rope. Hold us here.'

The *Fiore* was pointing at the other boat, her stern now to the open sea, the wind and spray. Hunter went into the bows, opened the locker where the bow rope was stowed and dropped the eye over the forward cleat. He ran the rope out along the starboard side, dangling it over the outside of the hull and superstructure. He re-entered the bridge and took the helm.

'I'm going to put the bows next to their bows, turn us hard and when the hulls kiss I'm going step over to their boat and take the berthing rope with me.'

'No you're not,' Lizzie said, 'I'm going. I'm not some delicate female who needs to be babied. I'm a sodding Captain in the US Marines and I know what I'm doing. You can drive this thing better that I can so you'd better stay on the helm. I can do the other bit.'

Hunter was about to argue but knew she was right. 'Okay! Let's do it.' He was about to say be careful but thought better of it. Instead, he said, 'We'd better hurry. We've got about two minutes.'

Lizzie went onto the starboard side, picked up the end of the rope and grabbed a stanchion to steady herself. She lifted the top of the guardrail and swung open the gate.

Hunter gently increased the revs and took the *Fiore* forward until her bows nudged the other boat. He then spun the helm to port, pulled the port engine into astern, increased the revs on both engines and spun the boat as though she was on a carousel. Her starboard side touched the other's port side and Lizzie stepped onto the other boat. She climbed over the guardrail, picked her way over the paraphernalia of discarded ropes, fenders and even a folding table and made it to the front of the boat. She dropped the eye of the rope onto a cleat and waved to Hunter. In the meantime he had already reversed the previous manoeuvre and was already turning the stern of the *Fiore* to point back to sea.

He now had both engines in reverse and gradually increased the revs. The rope tightened and took the strain as the stern of the boat touched the rocks. The wind suddenly picked up and Hunter pulled the speed controls to their stops. The engines howled, the screw bit and they moved slowly away from the rocks. As soon as they were a few metres out he reduced the revs considerably. There was a gap of about three metres between the bows of the boats with Lizzie stranded on the other vessel.

It wasn't a satisfactory state of affairs but there was nothing to be done about it. He watched as she tried the only door onto the bridge, which was on the port side. It was locked. She then went round to the stern and up the ladder to the upper bridge. She waved once and then dropped out of sight.

He saw lights come on in the boat and after a few minutes Lizzie and a man appeared on the bridge. Hunter could see him start the engines and then looked at Lizzie with horror on his face.

19

Hunter worked out what was wrong. Lizzie must have done the same as she pushed the man to one side and stood at the controls. She looked at Hunter and drew a finger across her throat. She'd had to cut the engines. Hunter surmised that the props must have hit the rocks.

With the lights on in the bridge Hunter could see what was going on. The man was yelling at Lizzie and she was yelling back. He looked to be in his thirties, maybe older, round faced, medium height, podgy was the word that came to mind. Suddenly the man turned and went below. Lizzie looked across the intervening water and shrugged.

Hunter called her using his mobile phone and watched as she answered it.

'You okay?'

'Yeah, fine. The man's a fool. I told him that once we reached the middle of the bay, you'd come back alongside and we could take them off in case something goes wrong such as the rope breaking. He pointblank refused.'

'Why?'

'Said it was his father's boat and his father would kill him if he abandoned it.'

'For crying out loud, that's stupid.'

'Any ideas how you argue stupid?'

'What nationality is he?'

'From his accent I would say he was French. Sorry, but I didn't ask.'

'That's okay. Does he speak good English?'

175

'Yes.'

'I'm coming back alongside. You jump over here, take the *Fiore*, while I deal with the moron.'

'Are you sure?'

'Lizzie, you're not staying there. We can't be certain the rope will hold. It probably will but Sod's law teaches us otherwise.'

'Okay. I'm ready when you are.'

He repeated the original manœuvre, and Lizzie easily stepped back onboard. She took the helm and Hunter crossed over to the other boat. Lizzie then took the *Fiore* back into position, holding the other boat off the rocks.

Hunter entered the bridge and tried the door to the main cabin. It was locked. It was a double door, each about 18ins in width, the lock in the middle. He'd had enough by this time so he stood back raised his right leg and kicked the doors open with the sole of his foot. The doors smashed back, bouncing against the bulkhead. The boat lurched and he grabbed the top of the hatch and waited until the pitching reduced again. When it did he went below.

He wasn't surprised to see the place was a mess. There were bottles, red wine, plates and cutlery lying on the deck, the bottles rolling back and forth. Cushions were also amongst the mess and lying on one of the bench seats was an inert body. Taking a closer look, Hunter saw it was a young girl, probably late teens or early twenties. She was dressed in cutaway shorts and a tee shirt. She was on her side, her eyes were closed, her mouth was open and she was dribbling into the vomit her head was nestled in. He shook her shoulder but got no response. He felt her neck and was relieved to find she still had a pulse though her breathing was very shallow.

Leaving her where she was he took another look around. It was more luxurious than the *Fiore* and probably less than two or maybe three years old. It had cost a packet, there was no doubt about it.

The deck swayed and he grabbed the table to save himself from taking a tumble. He worked his way forward, past a well-fitted galley and dining area and through a door leading to forward cabins. There were four doors, two either side. He looked in the first cabin on the port side. It held a double bed with two people lying on it. One he recognised as the man Lizzie had the altercation with.

He was groaning, curled up on his left side, vomit on the bed sheets. Next to him was another young lady, she was on her back, asleep, snoring gently. The cabin was plush, everything of the highest quality and workmanship. A door on the left was slamming. Hunter opened it to find a shower and toilet as well as the smell of vomit. Someone had tried to reach the toilet but hadn't made it. He couldn't help wondering what sort of inadequates were prepared to put up with such a state even if it was only for a few hours.

He left the bodies where they were and checked the other cabins. The one on the starboard side was a mirror image of the first one, including two comatose people. The next door led to a shower and toilet, with bottles and tubes containing all sorts of gunges lying and rolling across the deck. In the fourth cabin was a young man propped up against the bed's headboard, a bucket next to him with his hand holding it steady.

'Qui êtes vous?' He was in his twenties and looked the worse for wear but at least he was compos mentis.

'Do you speak English?'

'Of course. Who are you?'

'My name is Hunter. I'm a Commander in the Royal Navy and right now the only person standing between you and oblivion. What's your name?'

'Max Fossett. What are you talking about? What do you mean the only person standing between oblivion and me?'

'That may sound melodramatic but it may be the case. Have you any idea what's happened?'

'What are you talking about?' He had a faint accent as though he had spent a long time in an English speaking country.

'You dragged your anchor. You were about two minutes from going onto the rocks and having a watery grave when we got a rope to you and pulled you clear. The idiot asleep in the other cabin knew it because we told him before the situation became dangerous. He gave us the finger.'

The man groaned. 'That sounds like Simon.' He crawled off the bed and stood up, swaying until he took hold of the headboard.

'We need to get you and the women off. The rope holding the boats together could break. I'm not saying it will but it could. If it does, it'll take about ten minutes before you hit the rocks. We've towed the boat a bit further to the north than where you were but we can't go too far because there are so many other boats at anchor. If you break lose, and if you are very lucky, this boat will end up on the beach. If you hit the rocks then this will flood and you could drown.'

'I understand.' He slid his legs over the side of the bed, reached for a pair of trainers and dragged them on. He was already dressed in jeans and a tee shirt and unlike the others there was no sign of any vomit. 'I asked Simon if we were safe and he said we were.'

'He was wrong. Come on, we need to get off. Just in case. What's up with the others? They seem comatose, not asleep.'

Fossett groaned. 'Alcohol and coke do not mix.'

'Coke as in cocaine?'

'I am not talking Coca Cola.'

'Then why aren't you in the same state?'

'I have never used the drug and I never will. I wouldn't have come if I had known the stuff was onboard.'

'Yeah, well that's as maybe but we need to get off.'

The boat lurched again and Fossett grabbed the bucket and dry heaved a few times into it. 'My mouth is like the bottom of a parrot's cage.'

Fossett staggered into the galley, pulled open the fridge door and extracted a bottle of cold water. He drank the contents of the bottle and said, 'Ah, that's better.'

There was another sudden lurch. Hunter said, 'Give me a hand to carry the two women out of the cabins and into here. If the rope does break we won't have so far to carry them.'

In the first cabin Hunter asked, 'What's his surname? Simon what?'

'Simon Dubois.'

Standing over the inert form Hunter slapped his cheeks twice each side, hard.

'Wake up Dubois! Wake up!'

The man groaned but didn't open his eyes. Hunter then noticed the white powder on a saucer on a non-skid mat lying on a bedside cabinet.

'Let's get the girl.'

Fossett threw the sheet off her and was about to pick her up when Hunter said, 'Lift her under her arms, I'll take her feet.'

As they picked her up she groaned and her eyelids fluttered. 'What . . . What's happening?' Then her head fell back and she was unconscious again.

'What the hell have these idiots been sniffing?'

'I told you, cocaine.'

'I don't know much about the stuff, but they shouldn't be this wasted.'

'What can I tell you? Knowing Simon he probably adulterated it with a little something else.'

They placed the girl on the floor of the main saloon and then carried out the second one. The man in the second cabin was groaning and was half-awake. Hunter smacked his face and told him savagely to wake up. The man groaned and opened his eyes.

'Qu'est-ce que c'est. Arrêtez! Arrêtez!'

'Wake up Lucas! We have to get off the boat,' said Fossett.

The man known as Lucas groaned and turned over. There was an unused bucket by the side of the bed and Hunter picked it up, went into the shower room and filled it with cold water. He stood next to the bed and threw the water into Lucas' face. He spluttered and opened his eyes. He said something in French.

Hunter smacked his cheeks again, hard and screamed at him. 'Wake up. We need to get off the boat.'

The man groaned and sat up. He swung his feet to the deck and sat there holding his head. Fossett said something in French and the man looked up at the other two.

'Do you speak English?' Hunter asked.

'Yes, of course.'

'Then move it. Look, I'm out of here. I've had enough of you idiots. If the rope doesn't break all well and good, if it does then you're in serious trouble.'

The boat lurched, harder and deeper than ever and then the movement of the boat changed subtly. Hunter knew instinctively what it was. After all the threats it had happened. The rope had snapped.

'We'd better get going. I'm damned sure the rope has parted.'

Hunter hurried into the saloon, picked up one of the girls, threw her over his shoulders in a fireman's lift and headed up the stairs. Already the boat was drifting closer to the shore. The anchor wasn't holding her and he reckoned they had about five or so minutes before they struck rocks.

'Lizzie!' He yelled and she put her head out of the bridge door and waved. 'Come round and get us!'

Lizzie waved in acknowledgement and repeated the manœuvre Hunter had carried out. The boats' hulls kissed and Hunter stepped across to the *Fiore* and placed the girl on the deck in the bridge. As he did so Fossett joined him carrying the other girl while Lucas stumbled onto the deck empty handed.

Hunter shoved him to one side and Lucas fell to his knees with a screech of pain.

'You're useless,' Hunter said, stepping back onto the other boat. He looked astern. The rocks were about two minutes away. He went below and picked up the girl on the couch. The boat lurched and he fell to one side before regaining his balance. He heard a scraping noise on the outside of the hull.

The *Fiore* was still alongside and Lizzie called out, 'Nick, I have to go or we'll hit as well!'

Hunter stepped across the widening gap, grabbed the guardrail and hauled himself onto the deck. He put the girl on the deck on the bridge and turned to look at the other boat.

The sea and its currents could play weird and wonderful tricks. It did this time. The other boat's stern touched the rocks, her bows swung round, the bows touched, the boat swung round clear of the rocks and the stern hit the beach. The backwash pulled the boat into a few feet of deeper water and then swept back in, pushing the boat hard against the sand, forcing her onto her port side.

Lizzie took the *Fiore* clear of the rocks and beach. Hunter pointed to an open stretch of water, she took the boat there, held her steady and he dropped the port anchor. She manœuvred the boat; he dropped the starboard anchor and then evened out the length of the cables. The *Fiore* was sitting comfortably to her anchors, her pitching was gentle, and the sea swell was abating.

Hunter, Lizzie and Fossett were sitting at the table on the bridge. The storm had passed and in typical Mediterranean fashion the sea was almost as calm as before the storm started. It was 04.25 and the sky was lightening in the east.

The three of them had bottles of cold beer in front of them.

'Quite a night,' said Lizzie, 'is it always this exciting with you?' She smiled at Hunter.

He shrugged and said, 'No. This was nothing.'

Lizzie laughed.

'I want to thank you,' said Fossett. 'If it hadn't been for you I understand from Lizzie that things could have turned out a lot differently.'

'Yeah, well she's right. If you'd gone in where you were before we pulled you off you'd have sunk and the state you lot were in you'd probably have drowned. At least, out of them all you may have survived but I doubt it. The sea was smashing into those rocks and your chances . . .' He didn't finish the sentence, merely shook his head.

'Why did you help us?'

Shrugging, Hunter replied, 'The code of the sea I guess. You always help those in peril on the sea. Just like the hymn says.'

The man known as Lucas suddenly groaned, rolled over and sat up. He said in French, 'Christ, where am I? Last night. I remember getting off the boat.'

Hunter stood up, grabbed Lucas by the belt and pulled him to his feet. He hustled him to the guardrail and pushed his back to it.

'Why didn't you help that girl last night?' Hunter asked.

'What girl?'

'The one on the sofa. The one who was unconscious. Do you remember seeing her?'

'Yes.'

'Why didn't you help here?'

'I . . . I needed to get off. I might have been killed.'

'What about the girl?'

He shrugged. 'What about her? I didn't know her. Not really.'

'Can you swim?'

'What?'

'I said can you swim?'

'Yes.'

'Pity.' Hunter grabbed Lucas by the throat and pushed him over the side.

He hit the surface, spluttering, yelling something Hunter didn't understand. 'The beach is that way!' Hunter pointed.

He received a mouthful of abuse in return. Smiling at the man in the water he watched as he swam towards the shore.

Returning to the bridge he sat down at the table and raising his bottle, said 'Cheers,' and took a drink of cold, refreshing beer.

'Why did you do that?' Lizzie asked.

'I don't like garbage on my boat, even if the *Fiore* is rented. He was lucky I only threw him over the side. Are those three women going to be okay?' He looked at Fossett.

'I've no idea. I don't know what he gave them. Like I told you, I don't do drugs.'

One after the other the three women came back to life, groaning and swearing never again. All three were English. Two were cousins, one a friend.

'What are your names?' Hunter asked.

'I'm Mary.'

'I'm Cathy.'

'And I am Carole with an e.'

'So what happened to you?' Hunter asked. 'You were out for the count. It can't have been the cocaine.'

'Cocaine?' Mary looked aghast. 'We don't use coke. Never. Not in a million years.'

'Somebody did. I saw some on the bedside table in one of the cabins.'

'It wasn't us,' said Cathy.

'Max, care to tell us what the hell is going on?' Mary scowled. 'We went to sleep on one boat and woke up on another.'

'I'll let these good people tell you.'

Carole looked from Lizzie to Hunter.

'You tell it, Lizzie. I'm going to make some tea. I'm sure you ladies could use some.'

The three women nodded.

Lizzie told them what had happened and how close they had been to a serious accident if not death. While she was telling the tale Hunter reappeared with mugs of tea, a carton of milk and a jar of sugar.

'Help yourselves. What was your involvement in all this?' Hunter glared at Fossett.

'What can I say? Simon and Lucas invited me to the boat for a party and a cruise to the bay. I thought why not and went along. I met these three charming young ladies,' he smiled and waved his hand at the three women, 'for the first time. It started out pleasantly enough. We anchored in the bay, had a few drinks . . .'

'Champagne,' said Cathy.

'Asti Spumante,' Fossett corrected.

'Yeah,' said Mary, 'then it all gets hazy.'

'I went to bed. I'm not a very good sailor and the boat was beginning to roll.'

'I remember,' said Mary. 'Simon made fun of you.'

'That's typical of Simon.'

Hunter and Lizzie exchanged glances. The three girls were pretty, fair hair down to their shoulders, wide mouths, big smiles, blue eyes and a look of intelligence about them. They could have been sisters instead of two cousins and a friend.

'What do you three do?' Lizzie asked.

'Do?' Mary frowned.

'Work?'

Cathy answered. 'The three of us are in our third year at Hull university training to be nurses.'

'Do you know what happened to you?' Lizzie asked.

'Yeah, I can guess,' said Mary. The other two girls looked puzzled and she added, 'Rohypnol, GBH, ketamine.'

They looked horrified and Carole said, 'The lousy swine. There was no need to do that.' Her hands were shaking and Hunter realised it was with anger. 'I'll kill him!'

'Did you give him cause to use the stuff?' Lizzie asked. 'Sorry,' she held her hands up in surrender at the furious look Carole turned on her, 'bad choice of words. There's never, ever an excuse to do something so disgusting. What I mean is had you hinted you wouldn't be going to bed with them?'

'It never came up,' said Cathy. She shrugged, 'I guess it was too early in the evening. To be honest there was no way I was going to bed with any of them,' she looked at Fossett, 'and that included you.'

'I still had to make up my mind but I can say there was no way that Simon was going to get his hands on me,' said Mary.

'Or me,' said Carole.

'Maybe he realised that and hence the use of the drug,' said Hunter. 'I suppose you can thank the weather that things didn't get out of hand.'

'Out of hand?' Mary repeated. 'Is that what you call it? How many other times has he done this?' She glared at Fossett. 'Do you know?'

'No. Look I know Simon only to bump into him in a bar or a café. He asked me if I'd like to come for a party and I said yes. Please believe me, I had no idea about the drugs. If I had I would have stopped him.'

'I still come back to the question,' said Mary, 'how often has he done it? I can't believe we're his first victims.'

'Sir Galahad rides again?' Lizzie looked at Hunter.

'Don Quixote,' he replied.

20

The three girls went below to get some sleep. Lizzie helped Hunter move the *Fiore* closer to the shore while Fossett stood and watched.

It was now light enough to see the other boats. Many of the owners and crew came on deck to wave and yell thanks to Hunter and Lizzie though a few didn't bother. Engines were being flashed-up, anchors raised and already a few vessels were leaving.

'I guess they've had enough sea time for now,' said Lizzie.

'I can't say I blame them. It doesn't take much for fun to turn to tragedy. It can happen anytime and anywhere, not just at sea. It just tends to be more deadly when the nearest land can be a mile away and that's straight down.' He focused his binoculars on the boat that was now pretty much high and dry, with the sea lapping at the side of her hull. He could see the damage that had been done to the propellers as well as to the steel bracket at the end of the prop shaft that took the weight. It had been ripped off.

Dubois and Lucas were on the beach. Dubois was sitting with his head in his hands while Lucas was lying down, his forearm over his eyes.

'What are you going to do?' Fossett asked as Hunter placed the binoculars in a holder next to the helm.

'Change into my running gear and have some exercise.'

Hunter went below and a few minutes later returned wearing a pair of shorts and carrying running shoes and a tee shirt in a plastic shopping bag. He handed the bag to Lizzie and dived smoothly into the water. When he surfaced he held up his hand and she placed the bag in it. He had a mere 30 metres to swim to the shore and aimed to be about ten metres from his target. When he reached the beach he put on his tee shirt and shoes and walked towards the two men who didn't notice him until he was standing over them.

Dubois looked up and spoke in French, a great deal of hostility in his voice. Hunter spoke reasonably good French as he did a number of other languages. However, he had found it useful to pretend not to understand especially if there were two or more people speaking together. They often said things they shouldn't.

Lucas sat up and focused his eyes on Hunter. 'He's English.'

Dubois gave the translated version of his earlier tirade while Hunter stood looking down at him.

The man wasn't in a very good state. His clothes had traces of vomit, his eyes were bloodshot and his hands were trembling slightly. Hunter figured Dubois was in his thirties, about 6ft tall, round faced, a chin that was becoming a jowl and with a beer drinker's belly. His skin was naturally tanned and he appeared to have Arabic blood, not uncommon in a country with more Middle Eastern inhabitants than any other in Europe.

'You're lucky to be alive. If I hadn't helped you would have ended up on the rocks and probably drowned. So how about a little gratitude?'

'You are responsible for what happened to my boat. If not for you this would never have happened. I demand your name. I will report you to the authorities. I will have you arrested for the damage my boat has sustained and for risking my life.' There was no mention of the lives of the others.

'I don't think so. My version of events will be believed and I shall have you for endangering the lives of the others.'

Lucas slowly stood up. He was closer to Hunter's height, his pecs bulged from too much weight lifting but his lower torso had been ignored. Upper body strength was one thing, all over strength and fitness something else entirely.

A fight should never be fair. That was a mug's game. Get your retaliation in first and it could all be over in seconds. It was a good maxim Hunter lived by.

Lucas took two unsteady steps towards Hunter, stopped and said, 'Va te faire foutre.'

Hunter shrugged, and made up his mind not to put the man in hospital or to cripple him for life. He decided he would put the man off sex for a few weeks if not a couple of months.

Lucas stood with his legs astride, leaning forward, a diatribe of French flowing from his mouth. Hunter kicked him hard in the groin, bending his toes back, using the sole of his foot. Even so, just like kicking a rugby ball, he followed through with every ounce of energy he could muster.

Lucas didn't scream. He couldn't. He toppled like a tree, to one side, his hands clutched between his legs. He was gasping for breath and his colour was turning an interesting puce. It would be a long time before he was in any condition to do anything as mundane as get to his feet. He lay curled up, groaning.

Hunter bent down, grabbed Dubois by his shirt and dragged him to his feet. 'You gave those girls Rohypnol, or something similar. Why?'

Dubois looked from his friend to Hunter who had hold of his shirt and was rocking Dubois back and forth.

'I . . . I don't know what you are talking about.'

'Yes you do. You gave those girls some sort of drug that knocked them out. You were going to abuse them.'

Dubois summoned up his courage, looked down at his friend whose colour was fading back to normal and said, 'They are nothing. Just three girls I met at a nightclub.'

Which was about the worse thing he could have said.

Hunter grabbed Dubois by the throat using his left hand and smashed him in the solar plexus with his right fist. He put his weight behind the blow and simultaneously let go of Dubois' throat. The man collapsed. He had also turned puce. Hunter stood and looked down at him, his anger under control. He used his anger to channel his strength, an ability he had found very useful in the past.

Dubois gasped but he managed to say, 'Why did you do that?'

'I detest people like you. You are a bully and like all bullies you are a coward. Now get up.'

Staying where he was, Dubois said, 'Why? What do you want?'

'We are going onboard,' he waved at the beached craft, 'and you are going to give me the drugs you have, including the cocaine.'

'No! I will not give them to you. They are mine!'

'Get up!' Hunter kicked Dubois in his side. Not hard, but enough to make the man wince.

He didn't move and Hunter kicked him again, harder. 'The next kick will take your teeth out. That's a promise.'

Dubois ponderously climbed to his feet and staggered towards the boat. Closer up Hunter could see the damage was worse than he had thought. Both shafts were twisted, one propeller was missing and the other had lost one of its blades.

'Why didn't you let us help you? We could have prevented this.'

The man didn't reply.

'I guess it's a rhetorical question. You'd used coke. It gave you a false sense of well being, of strength. The feeling that you can do anything you like and get away with it. It's one of the reasons you use the stuff.'

The deck was at an angle of 45 degrees. It was easy enough to climb on and Hunter followed Dubois. They made their way inside the bridge, walking with one foot on the deck and one foot on the bulkhead. The area was surprisingly clear of any paraphernalia such as navigation books and charts. Either they were stowed away properly or there were none onboard. Hunter guessed it was the latter.

Below decks it was a different story. The saloon, galley and seating area were festooned with debris of one sort or another. Empty bottles and broken glasses littered the deck and bulkhead. It was the oddest of sensations to be walking in the boat when it was at such an angle.

'Where are the drugs?'

'Here, in this drawer.' They were in the galley. Dubois tried pulling a cupboard drawer open but it was jammed. Hunter took hold of the handle to pull while the other man stepped to one side. Out of the corner of his eye Hunter watched as Dubois did what his body language had broadcast a few seconds earlier. Snatching up an empty bottle he began to lift it above his head. To Hunter it was as though time had slowed down.

When the bottle was halfway to his head Hunter grabbed Dubois' wrist, pushed his arm away, leaned back and helped the momentum of the blow. Dubois' elbow hit the corner of the work surface while Hunter pressed down hard. The crack of the elbow breaking was loud in the silence of the cabin. The silence lasted a nano-second as Dubois began to scream. He fell back, holding his shattered elbow with his left hand, tears streaming down his face. Hunter almost casually slapped him across the face.

'Shut up. You shouldn't have tried it. Now, are the drugs in this drawer or not? If you lie to me I'll break your other elbow.'

'No. Oh Jesus, no,' moaned Dubois.

'Then where are they?'

'In my cabin.'

'Show me.'

'I can't move. Oh God. My elbow.'

'Tough. If you can't move you're of no use to me.' Hunter pulled open a cupboard door, took hold of Dubois' left leg and put his foot inside the cupboard. He pushed the door closed and jammed the ankle in place. He then put his foot on Dubois' knee and pushed down slightly.

'Ah! What are you doing?'

'Either you show me where the drugs are or you're of no use to me and I'll break your leg by stomping down hard on your knee. You will walk with a limp for the rest of your life in discomfort if not actual pain. That will be after the doctors have rebuilt the damage.' He pushed down harder.

'All right! All right! I'll show you where they are.'

Hunter opened the door and pulled Dubois to his feet. Awkwardly they made their way forward to the cabin where Hunter had found him.

'Now where?'

'In the closet. There's a false bottom. Lift it up.'

Doing as he was directed, the bottom of the closet lifted out easily enough. Hunter had no idea what to expect. He had been thinking in terms of a few grams of coke and a similar amount of a date rape drug. Instead he took out two bags of white powder that he estimated were at least a kilogram each and a third bag of white pills.

'Is this Rohypnol?'

There was no reply.

'Is it?' Hunter yelled.

'Yes.'

Hunter knew something about the drug. If taken with alcohol or certain opiates the mixture could affect a person's breathing to such an extent that they stopped and never started again. A small amount of the drug affected people's judgement while too much made them oblivious to danger and threats.

'This isn't for personal use. This amount makes you a dealer. Where did you get it from?'

Dubois shook his head. 'I don't know,' he managed to gasp out, pain etched in his face. Although Hunter threatened him he remained adamant he did not know his supplier's name.

'Where will I find this man and what does he look like?'

Dubois then proceeded to describe Abu Mohammed al-Baghdadi and the house on stilts.

Hunter stared at Dubois and then asked, 'What nationality are you?'

'French.'

'You were born in France but your family aren't European.'

'My mother is French, my father is Saudi Arabian.'

They took the *Fiore* to Siracusa where they dropped off Fossett and the women. Ten minutes later the boat was back on the open sea and heading south. Now they were alone Hunter brought Lizzie up to date on the information he had coerced out of Dubois.

'What are the chances of stumbling across a scumbag like Simon Dubois who just happens to be in business with al-Baghdadi?' Lizzie asked.

'It sounds like a leap but think about this. Dubois is getting into the drugs business. He needs a supplier and the supplier needs a distributor. You know how it works, all the way to street level in ever decreasing doses. Now, with that amount of coke and Rohypnol, Dubois is mid-level in the distribution side of the organisation. But who's above him? Who can he really trust? For him it's not a difficult decision to make. A fellow Saudi.'

'But you said he's French.'

'He is but his father is a Saudi and that's where the bloodline takes him. Maybe his father is in the business as well though I can't see it somehow.'

'Why not?'

Hunter shrugged. 'No logical reason, just an instinct. Statistically first generation immigrants are not only grateful for the chance they have of a new life in the west but they are also determined to be successful and contribute to that life. Resentment and problems raise they ugly heads in the second generation who think they are being unfairly treated because of their skin colour, ethnicity, religion and anything else they can dream up. When I left Dubois in his cabin I took the boat's papers from a drawer in a cupboard on the bridge. They show him as the registered owner and living in a place near Marseilles. I'll get TIFAT onto it and see if he does live there and where his parents are.'

'So you reckon Dubois did business with al-Baghdadi because his father is a Saudi and al-Baghdadi is a Saudi.'

'Yes.'

She thought about it before nodding, 'I guess that makes sense. Where are we going?'

'We have two more days, unless you want to return to base?'

'No, definitely not, but let's have a nice quiet time.'

Grinning, he said, 'It's a deal. In the meantime I'd better phone Rosyth and tell the General the latest.'

He used the sat nav phone. 'Sir? I have a bit of info that may be useful.' He gave the General a shortened version of events.

'That makes sense. The laptop we lifted from the house has some interesting information on it. It's like a pyramid, somebody is at the top but it works down to a widening base of individuals who are smuggling people as well as drugs.'

'Sounds like a well-organised business. If you have a distribution network in place why use it only for one commodity?'

'That's what we think. But they're not simple people smugglers. It's a far more refined operation. They are definitely selling people into slavery.'

'Are we sure?'

'Yes. Leo and Gareth have done their usual amazing job and been sucking the laptop dry.'

'We need to get further up the pyramid if we're to do any damage to the network. Cut off the head if we can.'

'You're right but let's just hope the head isn't that of a hydra.' The Greek myth was that whenever the head of a hydra was cut off two grew in its place. 'Be that as it may, I want you to stay where you are for a little longer. I may have a job for you.'

21

'You hear that?' Hunter asked Lizzie when he broke the contact.

'Yes. I wonder if Hiram will give me a few extra days?'

'He will.' Hunter made the call. 'Hiram?'

'Hi, Nick. How are you? Busy?'

'Yes, but not in the way you're suggesting.' He told the story to Walsh who remained silent throughout.

'Nick, honest to God, only you.'

'Coincidences do happen.'

'I guess. So what can I do for you?'

'A couple of things. I think we can put the last twenty-four hours down to duty so we were wondering if Lizzie could have an extension to her leave. Say forty-eight hours?'

There was silence for a few seconds and then the Colonel said, 'Yeah, what the hell. But I need her back after that.'

'Thanks, Hiram. Also, we're a few miles south of Siracusa heading south and I've still got the coke and Rohypnol. Can you send a chopper to pick it up and have it analysed? Maybe we can identify where it comes from. Although at a guess I'd say the Rohypnol is European manufactured but it would be useful if we knew where the coke originated.'

'Yeah. Makes sense. I'll get a helo there in an hour.'

'Okay. Thanks again Hiram.'

The helo arrived on time and the drugs were transferred by hanging a bag on the bottom of a sky hook. Hunter checked the boat's position, altered course ten degrees to starboard so that they followed the coastline more closely, adjusted the speed to a gentle six knots, set the alarm on the radar should any vessel come within three miles and went to sleep on the sunbed in the stern. Lizzie slept next to him. It had been a long night.

What woke him was his phone ringing. He wasn't one to come slowly awake, to try and work out where he was and what he was doing. One second he was asleep the next he was wide-awake.

'Hi Hiram. I didn't expect to hear from you so soon.'

'I've got the analysis of those drugs.'

'That was quick.'

'This is a fair sized base. We have our drugs problems like everywhere else and it's important to get the stuff analysed asap.'

'So what can you tell me?'

'The rape drug is an adulterated form of Rohypnol, which according to our tech lab people is made in France.'

'How can they tell?'

'Don't ask me. Something to do with certain trace elements in the compound. They can even hone it down to a region.'

'The south? Marseilles area?'

'Yeah. How did you know?'

'Dubois comes from there. So I guess he's manufacturing as well as distributing.'

'Looks like it.'

'And the coke?'

'Originally grown in Columbia but here's the thing, cut in Saudi.'

'In Saudi?' Hunter made it sound as though Walsh had said Mars.

'Looks like it. As you know pure coke is pretty lethal and is cut with a variety of substances. In this case baking powder plus a laundry detergent. And according to the lab technicians it's made in Saudi Arabia.'

'A laundry detergent? Are you kidding me?'

'Nope. It's pretty common along with boric acid and some laxatives.'

'God Almighty! How stupid can people get to use this rubbish?'

'Let's not underestimate the ability of mankind and womankind come to that, to be utter, total and complete idiots. Which I reckon is an insult to idiots.'

'Okay. Thanks for that. Can you tell the General or should I?'

'I've already sent him the info.'

'I think we'd better do something about Simon Dubois and his chum Lucas.'

'What do you suggest? We can't exactly arrest them. We have no jurisdiction and the police can't do anything because there's no evidence against them as you've got it. In fact, they'll probably come after you.'

'I was thinking more along the lines of keeping a close eye on them.'

'I'm ahead of you there. They've both been taken to hospital in Siracusa. Rima and Wendy are there to keep an eye on them.'

'Are you sure you can trust Wendy after what happened?'

'Yes. I had a long talk with her. I also read her the riot act. It came in two parts. One she keeps her mouth shut or else and two she has a loyalty to the Corps and she knew what she was signing up for.'

'What's the or else?'

'I wasn't specific.'

'I guess you've done the right thing. Keep her close and keep her involved. If you turned her loose she could become bitter and twisted and blab where she shouldn't.'

'That's the way I read it. But I'm glad my actions meet with your approval, Commander.' There was no disguising the humour in the Colonel's voice.

Hunter grinned. 'Aye, aye, sir.'

'If anything else comes up I'll let you know.'

'Thanks, Hiram.'

He'd had the phone on speaker and said, 'You heard all that?'

'Yes. So all we've got to do is enjoy the cruise.'

'Don't you think you'll find just lying around boring? There isn't so much as a game of Scrabble onboard.'

Lizzie was wearing a bikini. She undid the clasp on the back of the top and shook it off her shoulders. 'I can think of something.'

It was 20.05 precisely when the *Fiore* passed the breakwater of the small port of Portopalo. On the starboard side was a marina with at least 50 boats of all shapes and sizes anchored in the bay and tied up two abreast along the outer wall, all port side to. That was unusual as normally boats berthed with an anchor down and their stern transoms parallel to the jetty in a fashion known as a Mediterranean Moor.

The end of the wall nearest the marina entrance was vacant and Hunter adroitly placed the *Fiore* port side to while Lizzie handled the head and stern ropes to secure them alongside. They finished berthing, had a shower and sat in the stern with a glass of white wine each.

Lizzie was wearing black trousers and a white blouse while Hunter was in khaki trousers with leg pockets, a black tee shirt and a white safari jacket. He wore the jacket to hide his Glock.

'According to the Pilot for the port there's a restaurant about a hundred metres away that specialises in seafood,' said Lizzie, looking up from the book she was reading. 'Though it doesn't say if it's any good.'

'It wouldn't. The Pilot gives only facts and very useful ones at that, but never comments. And let's face it one person's McDonald's is another person's three star restaurant.'

'I wouldn't go that far.'

Hunter sipped his wine and said, 'You wouldn't? No, you're probably right. Shall we try it?'

They strolled along the wall; the sea was to their right, high value boats berthed on their left. There were people sitting on open bridges enjoying the last of the sunlight, though most of the boats were unoccupied and locked up tight. Halfway along they passed a large metal box, the sort used to trans-ship goods on container ships. From the painted sign it looked as though some enterprising person had created a takeaway seafood bar.

They passed a low, flat roofed building that appeared to be a series of offices attached to which was a two-storey building that was the fish market. On their left was the reason for the market as the inner harbour contained dozens of small fishing craft. They then strolled past a badly paved road leading into the town. The next building was one storey high and had a single, sloping, red tiled roof. It proved to be the restaurant. Surprisingly there were no tables outside so they went in. The restaurant easily held 100 customers, the tables were set well apart, the chairs looked comfortable and the atmosphere had that feel about it that suggested good food. This was confirmed by the fact that it was practically full and explained the empty boats in the marina.

They were directed to a table near the door and as usual Hunter moved his chair to sit with his back to the wall with Lizzie on his left. That gave him a clear view of the room and the door.

Like many restaurants in ports all across the Mediterranean the house special was seafood.

'I have to admit I'm hungry,' Lizzie said.

A waiter appeared, greeted them in Italian and handed them a menu each. He said something else and pointed at a chalkboard with the day's specials written on it.

Hunter ordered a bottle of Frascati wine and as soon as he did the waiter repeated the earlier message only this time in English.

Ten minutes later after an indecisive perusal of the menu they settled on mussels in a tomato sauce followed by prawn and chorizo linguine with lime. They weren't surprised to find the food was delicious and as a result the evening passed very pleasantly.

After they had finished eating and were enjoying an excellent coffee Hunter spotted two men who appeared to be taking an interest in them. They were swarthy looking, Middle Eastern or Southern Italian, it wasn't that easy to distinguish. Then he deduced they were probably Middle Eastern and Muslims - they had a carafe of water on the table. He reckoned no self-respecting Italian would have dinner in a restaurant and not have a glass or two of wine. He ignored them using his peripheral vision to keep an eye on them. After ten minutes he was sure that he and Lizzie were the objects of their interest.

Smiling, Hunter said, 'Lizzie, don't look but there are two men a few tables away who are watching us though they are pretending not to.' He sensed she was about to turn her head towards them when he smiled a big beaming smile and hissed, 'Don't look!'

She looked startled for a moment and then leant forward also smiling. 'Sorry. It's just you took me by surprise.'

'That's okay. It's a natural instinct to look.'

'Are you sure?'

'Positive.'

'What are we going to do?'

Shrugging, Hunter replied, 'See how things pan out. It'll be an interesting end to an otherwise busy twenty-four hours.'

Calling for the check Hunter paid using cash and added a generous gratuity.

'Are we going?'

'In a minute, I want to give them time to pay their bill so they can follow us. Though I doubt it's necessary.'

'What do you mean?'

'They must know where we're berthed. They didn't follow us from the *Fiore* that I'm sure about. They also didn't come in here until half an hour after us. Add that lot up and I think they found the boat, figured we'd come here and came in. I saw them standing at the door looking around before being shown to a table. At first I thought they were looking to see if there was an empty table but now I figure they were looking to see if we were here.'

'So again, what are we going to do?'

Smiling, Hunter stood up. 'Like I said, see what happens.'

He made a show of pulling her chair away, thanking the waiter who had returned to clear their table and then leading the way to the door. Outside they walked slowly along the side of the inner harbour before reaching the outer wall. Hunter had taken a silencer from his pocket and attached it to his Glock, holding the weapon with his right hand under his left armpit.

Stopping, he put his left arm around Lizzie's waist and half turned her so that he was facing back the way they had come and kissed her. It was more a planting of his lips on hers rather than a kiss because he said, 'They're trying to blend in with the wall at the corner of the restaurant and not doing a very good job of it.'

'Amateurs?'

'Seems like it. I hate amateurs.'

'Why?'

'They're unpredictable. At least with professionals you have a better idea what they might do.'

'You're a professional so what are we going to do? Shoot them?'

'Maybe. Let's play this out.'

He turned and they continued their perambulation, slow and easy. Twenty paces later he did the same again. The two men were the same distance away, following more openly.

Turning, his left arm around Lizzie's waist, he said softly. 'They're more open. They're not making any effort to hide from us.'

'Maybe they believe we'll think they are just two men returning to their boat.'

'Yeah. Like I said, amateurs.'

'So what shall we do?'

'When we get to the seafood bar I'm going to hold you against the side of the container for a second and I want you to laugh out loud and say in a loud voice, 'Not here!'

'What then?'

'I'll say why not let's go behind here, also in a loud voice. We'll slide out of sight and if I am not mistaken they'll come fast thinking they'll find us in a compromising position behind the container. Okay?'

'Okay.'

They reached the end of the metal box and Hunter pushed Lizzie up against it. They followed the script and went round the corner. Instead of going behind the container Hunter dropped to his knees and carefully peered around the edge. The two men were now hurrying forward, at an angle towards the water and were quickly out of his line of sight.

'Stay here.' Hunter stood up and half a dozen strides took him to the other end of the metal wall. He looked around the corner and found both men with their backs to him.

'Don't move and I won't shoot you.'

The men spun around, the nearest one was holding a revolver that he started to lift. Hunter didn't hesitate. He wanted to question one of them so he only needed one to be alive. He knelt down and shot the first man through the forehead. The bullet continued its upward trajectory missing the second man by inches. The sound of the shot was like that of a sheep on a distant hill burping. The new silencer was highly effective.

Blood and brains splattered into the face of the other man who staggered backwards and fell with the shot man on top of him.

'I've got a few questions I want to ask you.'

22

Hunter kicked the prone man in the side of the head. Not too hard, he didn't want to break his neck but hard enough to leave him unconscious. Both men were slight, maybe in their twenties, well dressed, soft hands, clean shaven.

Hunter went through the pockets of the dead man and extracted a wallet, a mobile phone and a French passport. He grabbed the dead man by his jacket, dragged him to the water's edge and dropped him in. The body would be found soon enough but hopefully not before the morning. He then recovered the dropped revolver and put it in his jacket pocket. He picked up the other man, propped him against the container and put the man's right arm around his neck.

Lizzie appeared. 'What are you going to do?'

'Take this guy like he's a drunken friend. In case anyone sees us.'

'And the other man?'

'Right now he's either pleasuring the first of seventy-two virgins or is being tormented by the demons of hell. Alternatively, he may just be dead.'

'They'll find the body as soon as it's light. The police will come calling.'

'Let them. We won't be here.'

Hunter took long strides, the other man's toes barely scraping the ground. The boats still had a few revellers sitting on them but most of them were buttoned down for the night. They arrived at The Fiore; Hunter changed his grip on the body and drew the man across his shoulders in a fireman's lift.

'Take the fore spring and back spring off, please while I start the engines.' Two minutes later only a stern rope and bow rope secured the boat.

'Lizzie,' Hunter spoke barely above a whisper, 'let go the bow rope and then the stern rope.'

She did as he instructed and stepped onboard via the stern. Hunter engaged the gears and the *Fiore* eased away slowly from the dock wall.

The man lying on the stern deck groaned.

'Tie him up and put a gag in his mouth.'

In ten minutes the stern of the boat was passing the harbour entrance and heading out to sea.

'I think there's a certain irony,' said Lizzie, standing next to Hunter, 'in that it's a beautiful cloudless sky with a full moon, a flat calm sea and a balmy night.'

'What irony?'

'That this is all so delightful, perfect in some way and yet look what we're doing.' She shivered.

'You okay?'

'Sure. A goose just walked over my grave. See?' She held up her arm. 'Goose bumps.' After a few moments she added, 'Where are we going?'

'Southeast.'

'What's to the southeast?'

'Deep water.'

'Oh.' There was no need for Hunter to elaborate. She understood all too well what he meant by it.

'Does it give you a problem?'

'What? No. Are you asking because I'm a woman?'

'No. Because you're a rather lovely lady and maybe you have a soft heart.'

'Are you patronising me?' There was anger in her tone.

'God no! I'm really sorry if that's how it sounded.'

Sighing, she said. 'That's okay. Like you said, it's been a long twenty-four hours.'

They stood in companionable silence for a few minutes and then he put the boat in autopilot, checked the radar, set the alarm system and sat at the table. Lizzie sat opposite him

'What are we going to do with him? Apart that is, from kill him?'

'Lizzie, if that's a problem I'll understand. I can drop you off back at Portopalo and return for you in a few hours.'

Shaking her head Lizzie said, 'There's no need, honestly. Nick I've already said, I'm a Captain in the US Marines and I'm attached to the SEALS. I know and understand the war we're fighting. Those men were going to kill us. What do we do with him? Let him go? Arrest him? On what charge? It's the usual argument Nick, how do we deal with people like these? Believe me I have no scruples when it comes to this fight. You said it a few days ago. We're at war only the enemy doesn't wear a uniform. They attack, kill and maim people, hide their weapons and claim to be civilians more being harmed than harming. So believe me, whatever you decide is all right with me. Only . . .'

'Only what?'

'Only don't torture him. Don't cut off his fingers and his toes or whatever it is you do.'

Hunter actually laughed. 'I won't. A couple of years ago we discovered a far more subtle way to get these people to talk. Though it depends on their religion and how devout they are.'

'What do you mean?'

'Wait and see.'

Lizzie went below to one of the cabins while he composed a message to TIFAT, which included the passport details of the two men. He also scanned in their photographs in case there was a match.

He checked the prisoner's ropes to make sure he couldn't get loose, or move anywhere, and settled down to sleep on the bridge. He slept like a log until the sun was just hitting the horizon. There had been no disturbances during the night, no other vessel coming within three miles of them and a quiet prisoner who's mouth was tightly gagged.

Checking his e-mails he saw he'd received a reply to the e-mail he had sent earlier. He quickly read it and murmured, 'Well, well, well. How very interesting.'

Hunter went below to the galley and returned with a packet of bacon. In spite of his discomfort the man had fallen asleep. Taking a bucket from the aft locker, Hunter filled it with seawater and threw it over the man's face. The man shot awake drawing in air through his nose, not getting enough and slowly turning red. Hunter untied the gag and threw it to one side. The man gasped, his chest heaving, tears in his eyes. Hunter stood watching him, his face impassive.

'Do you speak English?'

The reply was a torrent of abuse, all in French, and spoken in the kind of venom that only the French language seemed capable of creating. After a minute or so Hunter refilled the bucket and threw more water over the man. He spluttered and started the tirade again so Hunter kicked him in his side and he stopped.

'Here's the thing, either you speak English or I will cut each of your fingers off until you start speaking in English.'

'Je ne parle pas l'anglais.'

'Then you're no use to me.'

Grabbing the man by his coat he moved him to the rails and was pushing his head over the side when the man said, 'Wait. I speak English.'

'Why am I not surprised? Let's start with your name.'

'You know my name. You have my passport.' His accent was strong but it wasn't French. Hunter had heard it often enough to be pretty sure it was Arabic, besides which, the e-mail had confirmed the man's nationality.

'The passports are false.'

'Rubbish! They are real. I am a French citizen. Why did you shoot my friend?'

'Because he was going to shoot us'

'That's a lie!'

Hunter's phone rang and he looked to see there was another message from TIFAT.

Hunter went back inside and telephoned Rosyth. He was put through to the Operations Centre.

'Leo?'

'Hi, Nick. You got my message?'

'Yeah. How positive are you?'

'Ninety plus percent.'

'That's good enough for me. Thanks Leo. Give my love to Isobel.'

The IT department had come through again. They had been into the French passport office computers, checked names and dates of birth and established that both passports were false. Leo had taken it another step further. Using a new programme he had developed he invaded the computers in every major airport in Europe. The vast majority of people weren't aware of the reason there were lanes to follow to passport control, whether leaving or arriving in a country even if there were no people in the queue. It was to give time for the cameras in the ceiling to photograph their faces. The photographs were then fed into a face recognition data base and seconds later, if there was a match, a well oiled machine went into overdrive and the person taken away for questioning. These were the databases Leo had invaded. Three months earlier both men had flown Egyptair from Cairo to Charles de Gaulle Airport, Paris.

Only they had arrived on Saudi Arabian passports. Then their names had been Mustapha al-Baghdadi and Abu al-Baghdadi. The names were too much of a coincidence and they agreed they must be members of the family of Abu Mohammed al-Baghdadi, the now dead people smuggler.

'Are you a good Muslim, Abu?'

The shock on the man's face would have been comical under less demanding circumstances. It was the sort of comic reaction found on stage in a vaudeville comedy only then it's intentional; this was a shocked reflex action.

'What, you didn't think we'd find out who you are? You are Abu al-Baghdadi and the man I threw into the water is Mustapha al-Baghdadi and you are both related to the dead Abu Mohammed al-Baghdadi who, I am pleased to tell you, died a horrible and painful death. How am I doing? Got your undivided attention yet?'

The man on the deck was staring at Hunter as though hypnotized by a cobra. 'Explain your relationship. Are you brothers, cousins, uncles, nephews, what?'

The man just lay there staring at Hunter, his mouth open, not saying a word. The RN Commander nudged al-Baghdadi in the ribs with his foot.

'Answer me!' Hunter leaned low and spoke in a harsh voice.

'We are cousins.' The voice was a croak.

'You are all cousins?'

'No. I . . . I mean Abu Mohammed and Mustapha were brothers. I am their cousin. Our fathers are brothers.'

'Why did you want to kill us?'

'We didn't! By Allah, I swear we didn't. On the life of my mother.'

'So what were you going to do? Why did you follow us from the restaurant? Why did Mustapha have a gun ready to use if not to shoot us?'

Silence greeted the question until Hunter nudged him again.

'It . . . It was for protection.'

'What's that supposed to mean? Protection? From whom?'

'From you.'

'Why did you need protection from me?'

'We were told to watch you. That was all. But to be careful. That you are a dangerous man.'

'You're a liar Abu. Mustapha had his gun out and was going to kill us. What is it with you people that you are unable to speak the truth even when confronted by the truth? You're an Arab. Lying to you comes as naturally as breathing. Is it a cultural thing?'

There was no answer. The man looked down at the deck, licking his lips.

'Why were you following us and why were you going to kill us?'

'We were not going to kill you. I swear it on the Holy Koran!'

'So let's get back to the question. What were you going to do?'

'Nothing. Just follow you and report where you were.'

'You're a liar. You were there to get revenge, pure and simple. How did you know where to look?'

'I . . . I do not know.'

It was obvious to Hunter that the man was lying. This time he kicked al-Baghdadi much harder in the ribs. 'Here's the deal, Abu. If you tell me what I want to know I will let you go free. If you do not you will never get to paradise.'

'I will. It is written that if you kill a non-believer you are guaranteed a place in paradise. I have killed many non-believers.'

The boast was made simply and proudly, with no thought for the consequences of his statement.'

'Does that include women and children?'

'What?' The realisation of what he had said suddenly hit him. 'No! No women and no children.'

'I don't believe you. You are a coward and like all cowards you prey on the weak and vulnerable. You are not a man. You are not a holy warrior, as you like to think of yourself. You are nothing but a cockroach who does not care for the well being of those less fortunate and more vulnerable than yourself. You are like all your family. You are the foul al-Baghdadi family that needs to be wiped off the face of the earth. I will ask you again. How did you know to look for us in Portopalo?'

Swallowing hard, al-Baghdadi shook his head. 'I will never tell you.'

'I was afraid of that. Tell me Abu, are you a good Muslim? Do you pray five times a day? Do you observe the strictures found in the Koran?'

'Of course! It is the word of God as told to the prophet Muhammad, peace be upon him.'

'So you do not drink alcohol?'

'Never! It is the drink of the devil.'

'You never eat bacon or pork? Pig's meat.'

'The word of Muhammad says, "And the swine, because it divideth the hoof, yet cheweth the cud, it is unclean unto you. Ye shall not eat of their flesh, nor touch their dead carcass".'

'So you know your Koran. Have you read it or is this what the imams teach you?'

'I have read it. I have attended lessons on the Koran in my hometown.'

'Where's that?'

'I will not tell you!'

'What will happen to you if you touch the meat of a pig?'

'What do you mean what will happen to me?'

'Just that. What will happen?'

'I will become unclean. I will need to cleanse myself.'

'How?'

'It states that if you become unclean from contact with a pig you should cleanse yourself seven times, once using water and earth.'

'What if you eat pork?'

'Then you wash your mouth out with water six times and on the seventh you mix it with earth.'

The backward looking stupidity of a religion anchored in the sixth century never ceased to amaze Hunter. Especially when there were far more enlightened versions of the Koran that had more relevance in the twenty-first century.

'I will ask you again. How did you know where to look for us?'

'I will not tell you.'

Hunter went into the wheelhouse and returned with a sealed packet of bacon in his hand. As he did, Lizzie appeared dressed in shorts and a tee shirt.

Their prisoner appeared to have regained some of his courage because he said, 'Look at this woman. She is a whore. She dresses like a whore and she acts like a whore. Not like Muslim women who dress modestly and behave modestly.'

'That's not very nice Abu,' said Hunter.

'Abu?' Lizzie looked at Hunter with raised eyebrows.

'Yes, it seems Abu here is a member of the al-Baghdadi family.'

'What are you talking about?'

'Let's have a coffee and I'll bring you up to speed.'

Lizzie made the coffees while Hunter sat watching al-Baghdadi who lay still on the deck, his eyes closed, mumbling under his breath. He seemed to be praying. With their coffees in hand Hunter recounted the information supplied by TIFAT.

'So how did they find us?'

'I'm about to ask again.'

'Nick, I meant it when I said no cutting off fingers and toes!'

'Don't worry, I may threaten to do it but it's not my style.' He finished his coffee, pouring the dregs from his mug over the side.

'Do you see this, Abu?'

The man kept his eyes closed, his mumbling becoming more coherent. It was a prayer he was saying in Arabic.

For the third time Hunter threw a bucket of water over their prisoner. He stopped his prayer and glared at Hunter.

'Do you see this?' Hunter held a packet of bacon close to the man's eyes. 'You see that word maiale? It's Italian for pig. And in case you are in any doubt as to what this meat is there's a picture of a fat contented pig prior to being slaughtered.'

Al-Baghdadi shrunk from the package. Real fear was etched deeply in his face.

Hunter pulled open the sealed bag and shoved the package under the other man's nose. The man tried to push himself further away.

'Take it away. Take it away. By Allah, take it away.' He was actually moaning.

Although he had been expecting a reaction, Hunter was amazed at the man's response. He took the meat out of the packet and held it next to the cheek of the man who appeared to be on the verge of becoming hysterical. Suddenly there was the smell of urine in the air and Hunter looked down to see that their prisoner had wet himself.

'Lizzie, please fill the bucket with seawater and throw it over this swine. Aim mainly for his crotch.'

Hunter stood looking at al-Baghdadi while Lizzie did as she had been asked. After the third time he said, 'Thanks. That'll do.' He knelt down and held the bacon next to the man's cheek. Al-Baghdadi was shaking with tears forming in his eyes.

'Here's the deal, Abu, either you tell me what I want to know or I will tie this meat around your neck. I will then wrap you in a canvas sheet and throw you overboard. You will never get to paradise, will you?'

'Please, please. No do not do it. You will condemn my soul forever.'

Hunter's smile was not pleasant. 'I know I will. Think on that Abu. What a long time forever is.' He glanced at Lizzie who was sitting on the steps to the wheelhouse, watching in fascination.

'How did you know where to find us?'

'We didn't. It was luck. We have people looking for you.'

'How many people?'

'I swear I do not know.'

'Then guess.'

'Perhaps as many as twenty.'

'And they all work for al-Baghdadi?'

'No. They have been hired to look for you. That is all. It was luck we found you. No, not really luck. It was a logical place to look.'

'How did you know to look for us?'

'How did we know? We were told to.'

'Yes, but why? Nobody knows who we are.'

'I don't know!'

Hunter took the packet of bacon to within an inch of the man's face. 'I'll ask you again.'

'All right, all right! I will tell you. Somebody told us.'

'Who told you and who is us?'

There was no reply.

Enough was enough and Hunter pushed the bacon into the man's face, across his nose and mouth. Al-Baghdadi fainted. Lizzie didn't need to be told. She threw cold water over the inert form and on the second time he came to. He began to sob.

'It was a woman. She phoned and told us.'

211

'Phoned where?'

'To the house in Cassis.'

'Where's that?' Lizzie asked, looking at Hunter.

Shrugging, he replied, 'No idea.'

23

It took a few seconds on Google maps to find the town. It was ten miles southeast of Marseilles in southern France.

'Who lives in the house?'

The man was moaning and Hunter slapped his cheek. 'Shut up. Who lives there?'

'My father.'

'What's the full address?'

He gave it to them. In spite of further questioning they learnt nothing more of any interest apart from one vital fact. According to Abu al-Baghdadi it was solely a family business. They had started out transporting people, some as slaves others simply migrants looking for a safer and better life but now they had expanded the business to drug dealing.

They sat at the table in the wheelhouse. Al-Baghdadi they left lying on the deck trussed up, in pain from the ropes and in anguish from the pig meat.

'He's real scum,' said Lizzie. 'You heard what his family has done. Correction, are doing. They think Islam justifies any and everything because it is all aimed at non-believers. They have no compassion. No . . . no love in their hearts for others not of their faith. Or at least, their sect of Islam.'

'Wahhabism.'

'Islam Saudi style. No tolerance. No understanding for any faith other than their interpretation of Islam and a religion reinforced by whippings, stoning, beheadings, and imprisonment. Some of it for the most spurious of reasons, like a woman not wearing the burka and the full face veil.'

'The religious police in Saudi are vicious thugs of the worst kind.'

'So what are we going to do with him?'

'I told you. Kill him.'

'I mean how.'

'How much misery do you reckon he and his family have inflicted?'

'God alone knows. But it must be a hell of a lot. The slavery, the drugs, the deaths of people trying to cross the Mediterranean. We know how horrendous it is.'

'I'm not going to shoot him, knife him or strangle him.'

'Getting squeamish?'

'No I don't want any blood on the deck and I don't like the idea of putting my hands around his scrawny neck and squeezing it until he dies.'

'So what are you going to do?'

'Precisely what I promised him.'

Standing next to al-Baghdadi, Hunter said, 'You've smuggled people across rough seas, you've let men, women and children drown and so it's only fitting the same happens to you.'

'I am not afraid of death. I welcome it. I will go to paradise for what I have done in the name of Allah. So you can do your worst.'

It was as though the incident with the bacon had never taken place.

Hunter took out a roll of canvas, one of the spare awnings and cut a thin length off. He went across to al-Baghdadi and sat on his chest.

'So you think you are going to paradise to be met by seventy-two virgins and to live in a perfect environment?'

'That is my fate,' was the strained reply.

'Well, I hope you meet the pig this bacon was taken from when you get where you are going. Which, by the way, isn't likely to be paradise.' He took the bacon and wrapped it around al-Baghdadi's neck and used the canvas to tie it in place. The man went into a spasm resulting in a state of neurogenic motor immobility also known as catatonic shock.

In one of the lockers was a spare stanchion for repairing the guard-rail if it was damaged in some way. He tied it to the now inert form and rolled the body over the side. It floated for a few seconds and then sank beneath the surface. The man didn't struggle, made no attempt to yell or scream. Hunter watched the body disappear, Lizzie standing next to him.

'Good riddance,' was her pronouncement.

'Yes. But you realise the consequences of what he told us?'

'Do you mean with reference to a woman phoning the house in Cassis?'

'Yes. Who could have made the call?'

'Who do you think?'

Lizzie sighed. 'One of three people.'

'Three? I thought only two. Rima Kameo and Wendy Black.'

'You're forgetting a third person.'

'Who?' Hunter frowned.

'Me.'

'Christ, Lizzie, that's ludicrous.'

'Thanks Nick, but I thought I had better bring it up before you thought of it. So what are we going to do? We can't be sure it's either of them.'

Standing at the helm, Hunter turned the dial on the autopilot and reversed course. The boat settled down on a northerly heading at ten knots.

'Any ideas?'

Lizzie shrugged. 'Check their phones and see if one of them phoned Cassis.'

'Isn't that a bit obvious?'

'I guess you're right. She, whoever she is, could have sent an e-mail, or texted from a pay-as-you-go and thrown it away.'

'There are plenty of options but al-Baghdadi said a telephone call.'

'He could have been mistaken,' said Lizzie.

'Possible but not likely. If it had been an e-mail he would more likely have said the information came via e-mail. Don't you think?'

'Possibly. No, probably. Oh, I don't know. Let's not forget Wendy Black's tirade and her attitude to what was happening.'

'Which I think goes to prove her innocence.'

'How do you figure that out?'

'She drew attention to herself. A lot of attention. Hiram had plenty of reason to send her Stateside.'

'A double bluff?' Lizzie suggested.

'But if he had she wouldn't be of any use to the al-Baghdadis.'

'I don't see it, do you?'

'No. So that leaves Rima.'

Lizzie shrugged. 'It seems like it. Though I can't believe it.'

'You mean you don't want to believe it, which is entirely different.'

'I guess. But she's just out of training. She speaks seven languages. She's highly educated. She was a schoolteacher.' She tailed off and looked at Hunter. 'So why is she doing the job she is? It's ludicrous. She can get a high paying job just about anywhere. American companies are desperate for people with language skills.'

'To say nothing of European firms. Yet she joins the army as a grunt? It doesn't make sense. Could she have applied to officers' school?'

'I doubt it. I suspect she's too old. But the army will take enlisted men and women to age thirty-five and the marines up until thirty-four. But why would she join?'

'A sleeper? Long term infiltration with specialist knowledge?' Hunter suggested.

'Like five years from now killing and harming a lot of soldiers.'

'These people think long term, we know that.'

'These people?'

'Islamic fundamentalists who hate our guts.'

'What shall we do?'

'I'll call Hiram and tell him what we know. And in the meantime, what are we going to do?'

'Do you have your passport?'

'No. Only my army ID.'

'In that case we'd better return to base.'

'Then what?'

'Return the boat to Catania, speak to Hiram and head to Cassis. We can't use the boat anymore as we're now top of al-Baghdadi's hit list. If he wanted revenge before he wants it even more now.'

'Only he doesn't know what's happened.'

'Not yet. But if we return to base.' Hunter stopped speaking. 'That gives me an idea.'

Hunter phoned Walsh. 'Hiram? You'd better sit down.'

'Why? What's up, Nick?'

When he had finished Hunter was treated to a full 30 seconds of silence.

'Are you still there?'

'Yes. Yes. I'm just thinking through what you've told me. It makes sense. Goddammit.'

'Don't do anything until we get there, will you? We'll let you know when we're on base. You find a reason to bring Rima into the office, we'll arrive and I'll tell you again what's happened. I won't mention Cassis but I will tell you Abu and Mustapha are dead. I'll drop it in suddenly. Hiram, please look at me when I do, do not look at Rima unless she gasps or makes a noise or something. Something that draws attention to her.'

'Don't worry, Nick. Go and teach your grandmother to suck eggs.'

'Yeah, sorry Hiram.'

'Apology accepted. Hey Lizzie, you listening to this?'

'Yes sir.'

'Then I'm sorry about your little vacation. But it's typical of Commander Hunter.'

'I'm sure that cannot possibly be the case, sir. Anyway, I wouldn't have missed it for the world.'

Walsh chuckled. 'Nick has this magic hold over women who are happy just to be with him.'

'It's called being a gentleman, sir. Something I miss when with the SEALS.'

Walsh laughed. 'Yeah, that's the Royal Navy for you. When will you get here?'

'We'll be at Catania port around 18.00. I can give you a closer ETA this afternoon.'

'Okay. I'll have a car for you. So enjoy the rest of your cruise.' He broke the connection.

'Like some breakfast?' Lizzie asked.

'I'll make it. Scrambled eggs, flavoured with cheese, fresh tomatoes and toast be okay? Sorry, no bacon.'

It was an idyllic journey. Flat calm sea, a breeze from the west, sunshine with a few clouds and very few ships or boats to get in the way.

They dozed under the stern awning, made love and dozed again. It was 16.00 when Hunter phoned Walsh and confirmed they would be at Catania at 18.00.

'Okay,' said the Colonel. 'By the way, Nick, I've been looking more closely at Rima Kameo's history.'

'Find anything interesting?'

'An anomaly. I think the idea of such an educated woman speaking so many languages joining the army allowed her to slip under the radar.'

'What anomaly?'

'It's not a lot to go on but she mentions a sister and then a few months later at her second interview she says she has no family. That they've all been killed by jihadists.'

'It's not a lot.'

'Maybe, maybe not. But it's not the sort of mistake you make, is it?'

'No, but it could have been the notes taken by the interviewer that were in error,' said Hunter thoughtfully.

'I considered that but again, not very likely. The forms and questioning are designed to be foolproof so that mistakes like that can't happen.'

'I guess you're right.'

'We've locked in to her mobile phone, in case she uses it. I've told her that I'm reviewing the excellent work she's been doing as part of my recommendation for officers' school. I told her I also want to question her to ensure she is fit to be an officer.'

'What if she's using a pay as you go?'

'There are few places to keep it. She has a room, a locker for her sports kit and nothing else. So there's not a lot to search. I want you and Lizzie to search both. If you find a phone tell Leo the number and he'll do the rest.'

'Okay. See you later.'

Next, Hunter contacted the brokerage where he'd hired the *Fiore* and told the man to expect him at 17.30 or thereabouts. The boat was in immaculate condition and the diesel tanks were two-thirds full. The diesel was a bonus as the tanks had been virtually empty when he'd hired it.

After berthing, the broker spent a few minutes checking the boat over and quickly announced he was satisfied. He was also delighted to take possession of bottles of wine and beer, as well as various packets of food in the fridge and freezer. Lizzie took the coffee with her. She had a coffee-making machine in her room.

A waiting car took them to the naval station and deposited them outside Walsh's office.

They discussed what they were going to do before Hunter and Lizzie made their way to the accommodation block where enlisted personnel lived.

24

Lizzie had already acquired the pass key for the rooms from the corporal on the front desk. She hadn't told him why she wanted it, she didn't need to. She outranked him by a mile.

Rima Kameo's room was as immaculate as if she were still in training. Everything was folded neatly away and her bed was made to army regulations. It didn't take five minutes. Lizzie found a phone in the chest of drawers underneath a pile of freshly laundered shirts. Hunter switched it on, got the number and phoned TIFAT.

'Okay, Nick, got it,' said Leo. 'Whenever she uses it we'll be listening.'

'Let's go,' said Lizzie.

'No, hang on. Let's keep looking.'

'What for?'

'A laptop or even another phone.'

'Why another phone?'

'Because that was too easy.'

'We found it hidden in a drawer.'

'Hardly that. Supposing we're right. Supposing she is a mole worming her way into the US army with the intention of committing serious harm sometime in the future?'

'So?'

'She's an important asset. We know we are dealing with an enemy who thinks long term as I keep saying. Ten years means very little to these people. A worldwide caliphate in a hundred years, a thousand years, is their dream. And let's not forget they believe they'll be in paradise watching it happen, rejoicing in the part they've played.'

'Such rubbish.'

'We know it's rubbish but they believe it's true. It's that belief that not only sustains them but motivates them to keep going.'

'Okay, supposing what you say is true, which I believe incidentally, how does it apply here?'

'We refer to our enemies as ragheads plus a few other less polite terms.'

'I've heard them all Nick, and used a few in my time.'

'There are many intelligent, educated, motivated people amongst them. That Rima speaks seven languages shows how intelligent she is. If we're right about her then she will have applied that intelligence to her situation now. Supposing suspicion did fall on her, it could only be for doing one thing.'

'What's that? I don't understand.'

'Reporting something to someone. Contacting the enemy about something important.'

'Would getting revenge by killing us be that important?'

'Maybe. I don't know. But forget that for now. Let's work on the assumption she is that switched on, what does she do?'

'Have a phone in a drawer that's easily found. It's pay as you go but it's a back-up in case she loses or damages her normal phone.'

'A very good reason to have a second phone, on the face of it.'

'But in fact it's a decoy.'

'Possibly.'

'Makes sense, you're right. We'd better keep looking.'

This time they were more careful. They felt under drawers making sure nothing was taped there, they raised the mattress, looked behind the headboard, checked the desk and found nothing.

They had replaced everything pretty much as they had found it but if Rima was as clever and careful as they thought she might be then she would know that her private space had been invaded.

The floor was solid concrete with a cheap carpet covering it and didn't look as though it had been moved in years. Even so they checked underneath but saw nothing.

Lizzie sat sideways on the chair in front of the desk, her arms folded. 'I guess that leaves her sports locker though I can't see it somehow.'

'Is she a keen sportswoman?'

Lizzie thought about her answer for a few seconds before saying, 'Not really. I think she uses the gym from time to time. You know, the running machine, though I haven't seen her play any team sports.'

'So she's a bit of a loner?'

'I guess. I hadn't really thought about it. But now that I am thinking about it the more obvious it becomes. Yeah, she keeps herself pretty much to herself.'

'Let's not twist the suspect into fitting the crime. All we have so far is pure conjecture. Pure circumstantial.'

'Yeah, but my money is on her. Look, Nick, we found the phone let's leave things like that. We're over thinking her ability.

Hunter was standing next to the door and he nodded. 'You're probably right.' He turned his head just as Lizzie stood up and pushed the chair underneath the desk.

'Hang on,' said Hunter. He stepped across to the chair and knelt down. The back of the chair was horizontally slatted wood held in place by four brass coloured screws in each corner. The seat and back were padded with green, fake leather.

Squinting closely at the screws he said, 'These screws are brass coloured but stainless steel underneath.'

'So?'

'So these are scratched.' Reaching into a jacket pocket he extracted a Swiss army knife and opened a screwdriver blade. He removed three screws and then carefully worked on the fourth while holding the back of the chair in place. When he'd removed the fourth screw he said over his shoulder, 'Lizzie, wait outside, will you?'

'Outside? What for.'

'In case this is booby-trapped.'

'For the love of God, Nick, that's not very likely. I wouldn't want to sit on a chair knowing it was rigged with explosives.'

'I know and neither would I. So just humour me, okay?'

'All right. But I think you're being over cautious.'

When Lizzie was outside the door he turned his attention back to the chair. He eased the back off and smiled. There were no wires, no detonators, no explosives; just another pay as you go phone fitted snugly in the foam.

'Found anything?'

'Hang on a second.' Carefully he eased the phone out and held it up for Lizzie to see.

She stepped quickly back into the room. 'So we were right,' she said softly.

'It looks like it.'

'But no explosives? No booby trap?'

'No. But you can't be too careful.'

Switching on the phone, he made a call. 'Leo? It's Nick. We found a second phone. It was hidden very carefully. This is the number.'

'Okay, Nick. I've got it.'

'Happy listening.' Hunter switched off the phone, replaced it in the foam and screwed the wooden back into place. 'Let's go.'

Outside the accommodation block Lizzie said, 'I'm sad we found it. I didn't want to believe it. I liked, I mean, I like Rima.'

'I know what you mean. I liked the little I saw of her as well.'

'What will happen to her?'

'That's down to Hiram. He could let her run for a few more weeks. See if she leads us anywhere.'

'Such as where?'

'She may be the one who gave us away but this is a sideshow. Compare it to the bigger picture of having an officer in the US army working for you. Getting her even to where she is has taken patience as well as planning.'

'I see what you mean. Like why has she become involved in a people and drug smuggling operation risking exposure when there could be far bigger fish to fry in the future?'

'Precisely. If you had her language skills and became an officer what would you choose to do?'

223

Lizzie pursed her lips while she thought about her answer and then said, 'The Marine Intelligence Corps.'

'That's what I figured as well. Think of the potential for damage in both directions.'

'Both directions? What do you mean?'

'Giving away intelligence secrets as well as doctoring information coming in. Creating misinformation, if you like.'

'She could do a lot of damage.'

'Yep. We're experts on the subject.'

'TIFAT?'

'No. We British. We had high level spies reporting to the Russians throughout the forties, fifties and well into the sixties. Highly placed, well connected and traitors. Just Google names like Kim Philby, Guy Burgess and Anthony Blunt. Despicable traitors who should have been shot.'

'We've had a few as well. Do the same for names of people who have spied for Cuba, China, East Germany. There are a hell of a lot of them. What always gets me is why they do it.'

'Belief? Money? Blackmail? Threats? Hatred?'

'Or a combination. Which do you figure is the most powerful motivator?'

Shrugging, he said, 'I think hatred. If you hate enough you're capable of anything. I think we had better check her sports locker for the sake of thoroughness though I doubt we'll find anything there.'

The gymnasium held a bank of sturdy lockers, each bearing the name of its user. They found Private First Class Kameo's, from the office Lizzie collected a duplicate key and they opened the door to the locker. It was 3ft high, 1ft deep and 1ft wide, standard issue in the American Army. There was a tracksuit hung neatly over a hanger, a box of 4 racquet balls plus a racquet, and a towel lying in the back of the locker.

'Nothing,' said Lizzie, 'which is pretty much as we expected.'

Hunter was standing looking over her shoulder and said, 'What's that under the towel?'

Lizzie lifted a corner of the cloth and said, 'A box for trainers.'

'Have a look inside.'

She slid the box out and opened the lid. 'See, trainers.' She then weighed the box in her hand. 'Hang on, there's something else in here.' Lifting out the shoes she placed them on the bottom of the locker. The cardboard box looked empty but it was still far too heavy. She shook it but there was no noise and nothing appeared to move.

'Let me feel,' said Hunter. He took the box and said, 'There's definitely something here.' He used his knife to pick a corner of the box free and pull the bottom of the box away. Nestled in a cardboard frame that fitted the weapon was a small automatic plus a box of ten shells.

Hunter shook it out of the box and held it in his hand. The gun was smaller than his palm. He took a closer look. 'It's a Beretta Pico.'

'I've heard of it. It's supposed to be one of the best close-quarter protection automatics in the business.'

From the bottom of the grip to the top of the hammer was a mere four inches while the barrel was five inches long. He pressed a button and the magazine dropped out of the grip. 'Six rounds. Pretty light as well. The frame is some sort of polymer, while the firing mechanism and barrel is made from steel. A nasty piece of kit.'

'You have to be pretty close for it to be effective,' said Lizzie. 'More than a dozen paces away and you'd be lucky to hit your target.'

'That's why it's called close-quarter protection.'

'Yeah, okay, wise guy. So why has Rima got it and why is it hidden? You know some of the guys have a favourite weapon they use but they are kept in the armoury and withdrawn only when on an operation or on the range.'

'She could have the gun for any number of reasons.'

'Like shooting people.'

'Or committing suicide,' Hunter said thoughtfully. 'It depends how much of a fanatic she is and how far she would go not to tell us anything.'

'Is she likely to use it?'

Shrugging, he replied, 'We'll have to find out.' He took a closer look and saw how to access the firing pin. He used the bottle opener blade on his knife to bend the pin out of shape.

'Why not just remove the bullets?'

'What if she's used the gun often enough to be able to feel the difference in weight and replace them?'

'There is that but the gun doesn't look as though it's been fired that often.'

'You may be right.'

He replaced the gun and the box then used his mobile to speed dial. 'Hiram?'

'Nick? Where are you? We thought you'd be here by now.'

'Got held up.'

'Traffic in this place? Typical. But you're on your way?'

'She's dirty.'

'Great Nick. So you'll be here in a few minutes. See you then.'

'How are we going to play this?' Lizzie asked.

'She's our friend. She's on our side in the fight against the terrorists, people smugglers and slave traders. Let's not forget that. So we treat her nice as one of the team.'

Five minutes later they were in Walsh's office. Rodriguez Perez was sitting at his desk, Walsh was at his and opposite him sat Private First Class Rima Kameo.

'Nick, Lizzie, welcome. Take a pew as you Limeys like to say and bring us up to date.'

Hunter scowled and nodded in Rima's direction.

'Rima is in on your exploits. I've told her some of it but I thought she should hear what you have to say. Let's face it, she's part of the team and I've just been telling her I'm putting her name forward for Army Officer Candidate School at Fort Benning. I'll have her fast-tracked for selection. She's too valuable to stay as an enlisted person. Her skills will be better utilised further up the tree. She'll have better and easier access to information she'll need in our fight against the terrs and the smugglers.'

'Okay, Hiram, you're the boss.'

Hunter placed a chair to the side of the desk so he could see the other three without turning his head. Lizzie moved her chair so that she had a more full-on view of Rima's face.

They began telling their story. Interrupting one another, correcting some of the detail.

'So let's get this straight. Abu al-Baghdadi wouldn't tell you what you wanted to know?'

'No. There's somebody further up the pecking order, we know that, but he wouldn't tell us who or where they were based. He said it was somewhere in France but he had never been there.'

'Did you believe him?'

During their reporting of what had happened, Hunter had kept a surreptitious eye on Rima. He was interested to watch as she reacted to what he was saying. There was nothing too obvious, she had her emotions pretty much under control. However, she had lost some of her colour, her hands were on her lap, clenching and unclenching in her agitation and the look she shot Hunter from time to time was one of pure malice. Or maybe, Hunter thought, he was imagining it.

'So once you decided there was nothing further to be learnt from this Abu al-Baghdadi what did you do?' The Colonel enquired even though he knew the answer.

'I wrapped rashers of bacon around his neck and shoved him over the side.'

Rima gasped out loud. Her hands were shaking and she looked positively ill.

'Are you all right?' Walsh asked, sounding full of concern.

'Sorry, sir. Yes, sir. It's just . . . It's just I was feeling a bit under the weather earlier on and now with this story . . .' she tailed off and then summoned up a smile and added, 'But I'm okay now.'

'Good.' Walsh turned his attention back to Hunter. 'Good job Nick. I think this calls for a celebration. How about 20.00 in the O Club?'

'Will Rima be allowed in?' Lizzie asked, frowning.

'In civvies as my guest, yes. There's only one person on this base who outranks me and I have it on good authority he's away for a few days. So I guess that makes me the ranking officer and I'll invite who I damned well please. You okay with that Rima?'

'I . . . I'm not sure, sir. It may not be a good idea.'

She had some of her colour back but she was still looking like she wanted to be sick.

'Maybe we'd better celebrate another day,' said Hunter.

'Nonsense,' replied Walsh, 'we have something to celebrate and we should do so. Rima, why don't you go back to your room, have a rest, a shower, a cup of tea or something and meet us at the club? Afterwards drinks and dinner will be my treat at a very nice restaurant in the middle of town.'

'I don't drink, sir.' Rima spoke in a small voice.

'That's okay. Fizzy water or whatever you care for will be on me. I promise you some of the best seafood to be found around the Mediterranean. Right ladies, we'll see you at 20.00. Nick and I have a few more things to go over.' As if by way of reinforcing the message, he added, 'Pity we never found out where the house is in France. Still you did a good job as far as it went.'

The two women left and Hunter told Walsh about the Beretta. The Colonel sat in silence for a couple of minutes, the fingers of his left hand drumming his desk. Hunter remained silent. He had a pretty good idea what his friend was going through.

'We're back to the same dilemma we always face,' said Walsh.

'Yep. What do we do with her?'

'We've enough evidence to put her away for a few years but after that, what then? If she's a committed jihadist she gets out and starts killing people, or planning attacks, or working to smuggle more Muslim fundamentalists into Europe and the States.'

Hunter nodded. 'A lot will depend on what she says on the phone, assuming she calls someone.'

The words were barely out of his mouth when his phone rang. He looked at the display and pressed receive and loudspeaker.

'Hello Leo. What have you got for us? Hiram is listening in.'

'Hi guys. She used the second mobile. The one you found hidden in the seat.'

25

'Who did she call?'

'To someone in Cassis.'

'Do we know who?' Walsh asked.

'Yes, her uncle.'

'Her uncle?' There was no disguising the shock in Walsh's tone.

'Hiram? It's Malcolm Macnair here.'

'Hello Malcolm. What do you make of this?'

'First of all, your vetting procedures need tightening up.'

'No argument from me.'

'I take it she's a declared Muslim?'

'You got it in one. So minority quotas kicked in, she's a westernised Muslim and looks good on the stats. You know the routine. Helping to fight for all that is good and decent in the world like democracy and fair play and tolerance of other people and other religions. And we're so tolerant we have certain people join the military without proper vetting. Instead of taking a much closer look at them we skip aspects of their lives and family that could be important.'

'But how did she get into your mob? Your operations are like ours and way above top-secret.'

'I don't know. I'm getting hold of her docs and seeing who did the vetting. We don't do any ourselves. We don't have the manpower or the skills so we rely upon others. Besides, vetting takes place before joining. Rima was seconded here because of her amazing language skills.'

'I can appreciate that,' said General Macnair. 'What are you going to do with her?'

'No idea is the short answer.'

'Sir, what did she say?' Hunter asked.

'Nick, I'll answer that,' said Leo. 'She was crying bitterly when she told her uncle about you wrapping bacon around Abu al-Baghdadi's neck. She really broke down.'

'What did her uncle say?' Hunter asked.

'He went ballistic. He ranted and raved. Told the girl that her job was no longer to stay quietly in the marines, not to infiltrate higher up the ladder but to kill you and Lizzie and anyone else.'

'Leo, what language were they speaking?'

'Arabic. I would say that they are both Saudi Arabians from their accents.'

'Okay, thanks. What did Rima say to that?'

'She tried to argue the point. That the long term was far more important than short-term revenge.'

'So she's got a good head on her shoulders, if one can call it that,' said Walsh.

'She's no fool,' said Macnair.

Leo continued. 'Her uncle overruled her. Apparently, the person who went to his grave with the piece of pig was his son.'

'Excellent,' said Hunter. 'I hope the man is in mental agony and torment.'

'He is that.'

'Has she agreed to it?' asked Walsh, 'And if so, when?'

'Yes. Tonight at the O Club. She told her uncle that she has sixteen bullets and she would make every one count starting with you guys. She would then shoot as many people as possible before she's stopped.'

'What did her uncle say to that?'

'He said sixteen bullets should mean sixteen dead Americans.'

'Do we know where the house is?' Hunter asked.

'Yes. We have it pinpointed.'

'Good. Sir, any chance of some of the lads joining me?'

'Jan, David and Don are on their way, fully kitted and spurred.

230

They're landing in Central France and driving down. They'll be at Cassis tomorrow morning.'

'I'll see about flights,' said Hunter.

'We already have, Commander. You fly from Palermo at 06.25, land at Rome 07.30 and then catch the 10.55 to Marseilles arriving at 12.20. Both flights are Alitalia.'

Hunter smiled and thought typical Macnair. Never one to let the grass grow under his feet.

'Hiram, you'll need to decide what to do about the woman and decide fast.'

'I know.'

'What's the gun they're talking about?'

'A Beretta Pico,' replied Hunter.

'Small, compact, six shot,' said Macnair. 'Good for close quarter work, lousy from the other side of an average sized room. I suppose you can wait until she takes the pistol out, aims and shoots one of you. You can have her arrested for murder.'

'The gun won't fire, sir,' said Hunter, 'I've bent the firing pin.'

Macnair chuckled. 'I might have guessed as much.'

'Hiram, she takes out her gun, aims and pulls the trigger then one of you has the right to shoot her,' said Macnair.

'Curious isn't it,' said the Colonel, 'but if she were a man I wouldn't hesitate to put a bullet in her brain but as it's a woman I'm squeamish.'

'We all have the same notions of chivalry, I guess you can call it,' said Macnair.

Hunter quipped, 'But let us not forget Kipling's *The Female of the Species.*'

'True enough. More deadly than the male,' said Macnair.

'You Limeys and your poetry,' said Walsh.

'A good poem encapsulates an incredible number of truisms like nothing else can,' said the General.

'Okay, I give you that. Malcolm, as to what we do we'll have to see. A military court has a lot more freedom to hand out justice without so much of the crap we get in a civilian court. In a military court life can mean life, we know that often isn't the case with a civilian court.'

'There's a massive problem we all seem to be forgetting,' said Hunter, 'and that is she knows too much. That is to say too much about recent operations. We don't want the general public knowing about them. There'll be hell to pay. Think about the fuss the left wing media will kick up aided and abetted by the politically correct anal retentives.'

'That's a good point,' said Walsh. 'I guess we cross that particular bridge when we come to it.'

Leo said, 'We're now listening in to the phone in Cassis so we might pick up something useful. Although it's more than likely he uses a different phone for a different contact or for a small number of contacts. If he has any sense that's what he'll be doing.'

'His reaction to what happened to his son and his orders to Rima suggest he isn't that sensible. He's sacrificing her for revenge,' said Hunter. 'It'll be interesting to see how she behaves at dinner. It takes a lot of skill and nerve to act in a way that is opposite to what you're feeling. I suspect she'll want to get it all over with as quickly as possible. So we can expect a move from her early on.'

'How would you go about it Nick?' Leo asked.

'I'd go to the heads, come back with my gun in my hand, get up close and bear in mind you're standing and everyone else is sitting, and start firing. We're not paying her any attention, there's just the four of us, so four rapid shots up close and it's job done. If we're sitting in a quiet place in the room, or if the club is pretty empty I wouldn't shoot anyone else I'd walk out and head for the hills. With the right planning and luck the chances of getting away are pretty good. On the other hand, would she have an opportunity to kill so many people again? And that may be her only consideration.'

There were a few seconds of silence before Macnair asked, 'Is there anything else? No? In that case I wish you a most interesting evening.'

'Where's Ahmad?' Hunter asked.

'He's being vetted. He's done a good job so far but we need to make sure he is who he claims to be. Is he coming into Europe as a sleeper? Nowadays that's a big question and damned difficult to answer with any degree of certainty.'

Nodding, Hunter said, 'Yeah. That's the problem. Distrust and discord as far as the eye can see.'

Hunter had been allocated a room in the senior officers' accommodation block. It was basic by hotel standards but not bad by the military's ideas of comfort. The room had a single bed, a wardrobe and a chest of drawers. There was also a desk and a kettle with instant tea, coffee and pasteurised milk in little tubs. It was also en-suite with a shower and toilet.

He caught up on some sleep for an hour and then at 19.30 showered and changed. He wore a short-sleeved, white shirt, a pair of grey trousers and his lightweight, cream coloured safari jacket. As usual, hiding his Glock from inquisitive eyes made his choice of clothes somewhat more limited than that of people who didn't wander around with a gun under their arm. His shoes were specially made. Light coloured suede; the toecaps were lined with steel.

A quick inspection in a mirror and he was out of his room and strolling towards the O Club. Perversely he was looking forward to seeing how the evening panned out.

Walsh had described the club as military soulless and Hunter saw exactly what he meant when he entered the large room. It held about 60 tables each with four chairs and had a bar running the width of the room along the farthest wall. The outside wall was half brick, half glass, the walls were painted a drab uniform light green, there were doors to the toilets and swing doors to the kitchen, one in and one out.

There were half-a-dozen men sitting on barstools, and four women at a table. All wore civilian clothes. Walsh was sitting at a table in the corner of the room away from the other patrons. He waved when Hunter entered.

Walking over, Hunter asked, 'Can I get you something?'

'It's waitress service. Grab a seat and someone will be along shortly.' Walsh was dressed in a white shirt and blue trousers with no jacket - he wasn't carrying a weapon and had no need of one.

Rod Perez arrived. He was wearing a jacket in order to hide an automatic under his left armpit.

A waitress appeared. 'Sir, what can I get you? Another ginger ale?'

'Yes please, with ice.'

'Yes, sir. You gentlemen?'

'Same for me,' said Hunter.

'And me,' said Perez.

At that moment the two women arrived. Lizzie looked stunning in a white blouse and green, pleated skirt, a false smile on her face. Rima had tried to look attractive in a brown shirt and dark brown trousers but her face was pasty white and she looked as though she was not at all well.

Hunter stood and arranged two more chairs so that they could all sit at the table.

'You both look lovely,' said Hunter with a beaming smile. 'Or am I not allowed to say such a thing in this man's army? Sexism and all that?'

Lizzie managed to grow her smile a few millimetres though it still looked false. 'I'm sure we can allow the occasional compliment, don't you agree Rima?'

Rima nodded. Her hands were clasped around a small leather bag she had on her lap and she didn't look directly at any of them.

'Are you all right, Rima?' Hunter asked. 'You look a bit off colour.'

'I'm fine,' her voice croaked, she cleared her throat and in a stronger voice said, 'I'm fine, honestly.'

'What will you have to drink?' Walsh asked. 'Lizzie?'

'White wine please.'

'Rima?'

'Just a soda water with ice.'

'Coming right up,' the waitress said cheerfully and walked away.

While they waited for their drinks Hunter smiled at Rima and asked, 'I gather you're from Syria, Rima, is that right?'

'Yes. Yes. I came to the west nearly nine years ago.'

'When did you decide to join the army?'

She frowned and appeared to be considering her answer before saying, 'It must be a year ago.'

'Did you have any problems?'

'What sort?'

'You know. We call it positive vetting. Checking you're not a terrorist or a criminal.'

'Oh!' She chuckled without mirth. 'Nothing like that. I had to apply for American citizenship and as soon as I got it I applied to join the army. I think it is my ability to speak so many languages that enabled me to enlist.' She looked at Walsh and said, 'And the Colonel is telling me to apply to Fort Benning for officers' school.'

'She'll be a shoe-in,' said Walsh.

The waitress appeared and distributed the drinks.

They all raised their glasses and clinked them apart from Rima. Hunter said, 'Cheers, Rima a long and happy life.'

Nodding, she raised her glass, tapped it against his and took a sip of her soda water.

'Excuse me, sorry, I need the bathroom.' Rima hastily stood up, 'I won't be a minute.'

They watched her go.

'Pretty much as we expected,' said Hunter. He looked at Lizzie, 'Can she have discovered about the firing pin?'

'No. She went to the locker room just before we came here. I watched her. She didn't know I was following her. There were a few others in the room and so she took the box back to her room. I knocked on the door a minute later and she came out with her bag over her shoulder.'

'Good.' Hunter looked over Lizzie's shoulder. 'Here she comes. She has her hand in her bag. This is going to be interesting.'

Rima stopped at the table, withdrew her hand from her bag, pointed the Beretta at Hunter's head and pulled the trigger. She pulled it again and again and again.

Walsh grabbed her hand with the automatic in it and pulled her onto her seat. He casually backhanded her across the mouth, not hard, not soft, but enough to cause her lip to bleed and for tears to well up.

Rima was sitting next to Walsh, opposite Hunter, alongside of whom sat Lizzie. The table was next to the window and Perez sat facing the glass. He reached into Rima's lap, squeezed her hand until she opened it and removed the Beretta.

'Nice little toy,' Perez commented, 'but nonetheless deadly close up. You're a traitor to your country.'

Rima's head had been bowed but now she looked up and stared at each of the four faces around the table.

'I am no traitor,' she spat. 'I honour Allah, I praise the prophet Muhammad, *peace be upon him*, and I will work tirelessly to destroy the Great Satan America. You with your bombs, your total disregard for Muslim lives, the genocide you are committing in my country in the name of your so-called democracy.' Her face had become twisted with hatred. Hunter recognised it as a deep, passionate hatred of the west of a type he had seen many times. It was unthinking, unexamined with no real substance to it except it burnt white hot with a passion people in the west couldn't fathom.

Walsh said, 'Do you remember saying that you solemnly swear to support and defend the Constitution of the United States against all enemies, foreign and domestic: that I will bear true faith and allegiance to the same. Do you remember?' He spoke very harshly.

She turned her head to look at him and stared him in the eyes. 'I made an oath a long time ago. One that is superior to all other oaths. And that is to Allah and my country. To destroy the United States. You can arrest me, kill me, but for every one of me a thousand will rise up, ten thousand, until the decadent west no longer exists.'

Hunter was watching her with interest. It was like a switch had been turned on. Hatred and bile spewed from her mouth as though a dam had burst having kept back the waters of her vitriol for a long time. He watched as her right hand slowly crept towards the long stemmed wineglass next to her. If she was lucky and took hold of the glass by its base, smash it on the table, breaking the thin glass of the bowl she could possible harm one of them. A lunge for the face, the neck or eyes being the target and some serious damage could be done. She was staring at him so he figured he was the target. He decided to wind her up.

'Abu al-Baghdadi was your cousin, wasn't he?' Hunter said, both his hands resting on the table in front of him, his fingers loosely intertwined.

'Yes,' Rima said in a husky voice.

Hunter realised that Walsh and Perez were aware of what was going to happen. Rima was transmitting her intentions as though using a megaphone.

'He died,' said Hunter, 'begging for his life. He died a coward. What I didn't tell you was when I wrapped the bacon around his neck he went into a catatonic fit and literally froze. He knew he would never go to paradise. He would never be met by seventy-two virgins and have a contented existence for eternity. Incidentally, how does that work for women?'

'What? What do you mean?'

'You know, all those virgins for men, what do women get?' Hunter snapped his fingers as though inspiration had suddenly struck. 'Of course, you get nothing. You're not even second class citizens in your pathetic countries.'

That was the moment she decided to make her move. She had been goaded to act and act she did. She picked up the glass by its stem, smashed it on the table and tried to ram the jagged end into Hunter's right eye. Hunter grabbed her wrist as it came at him and twisted it hard. She let out a gasp of pain and dropped the glass.

'I hate you! I hate you all!'

'Why did you do it?' Lizzie asked. 'You are living in what is an open, inclusive and pretty tolerant society. Why throw it all away?'

'Your tolerant society,' Rima sneered, 'is a myth. You mean it is a society for debauchery where the women behave like whores, where godlessness is all about you, where you do not pray to the one true god and his prophet, you all disgust me.'

237

'What were you going to do if you had killed us?' Lizzie asked.

Rima turned her venomous gaze on the other woman. 'That is for me to know.'

'Were you going to kill as many people in this room as possible, just like your uncle ordered you to?' Lizzie asked

Rima's mouth dropped open, shock clearly etched into her face. 'How . . . How do you know?'

Perez took out his iPad, pressed a couple of buttons and placed it in the middle of the table. There was the sound of a phone ringing. Then Rima's voice came over the loudspeaker. She shrank back from it as though it was a venomous snake. Her gaze flicked from the iPad to the two people opposite. Hunter and Lizzie were looking at her with implacable faces.

The conversation that followed was in Arabic. After a minute Hunter reached out and stopped it.

'We have the whole conversation and we know what your instructions were. We know where your uncle lives, in fact we now know a great deal about him. I will be leaving tomorrow morning to meet your uncle, I will ask him a number of questions and then I shall kill him. I will also kill everybody else in his household.'

Rima came out with a mouthful of vitriol all in Arabic. Hunter let her rant for about a minute before he spoke to her in the same language and told her to shut up.

'What are we going to do with her?' Lizzie asked.

'Gitmo,' was the Colonel's reply.

Guantanamo Bay Naval Base was a US military establishment consisting of 45 square miles of land and water on the southeastern tip of Cuba. In 2002 the base was changed and a prison was added to the site. The prisoners held there were captured terrorists from Afghanistan, Iraq and any country where the inhabitants were hell bent on destroying the USA and western culture. The prisoners were not subject to court proceedings, a trial fair or otherwise and had no rights of any value. The problem the Americans and other western countries faced was the one that raised its ugly head time and time again. What did you do with these people? If they were let loose the chances of them continuing their war on the west was practically guaranteed. Which meant innocent men, women and children would die in order to satisfy the notions of justice when applied to people who didn't deserve any.

Hunter nodded at Walsh and looked at Rima. 'You will go to Guantanamo Bay and stay there for a very long time.'

Rima clenched her teeth hard, her jaw moving back and forth like a mad person. Suddenly she began to shake then froth at the mouth and then she fell forward, her forehead hitting the table.

26

Rima died in a little over two minutes. She shook and frothed, her eyes turned up in her head and she went a chalky white. Then she stopped breathing.

The others watched her dispassionately. None of them intended doing anything to help. What could they do? Mouth-to-mouth was untenable. How poisonous was the substance she had taken? They weren't about to find out.

'It was her choice,' said Walsh.

Lizzie had also lost her colour and said, 'A bullet would have been kinder. Poor girl. Why did she do it? Why did she sell us out like she did? I liked her. I'd hoped she'd become an officer and she could have come back to the unit. I even envisaged being friends with her.' She shuddered. 'The fanatics have a tight control over some aspects of their religion and use that control ruthlessly.' She turned bleak eyes on the others, 'We can't fight fanaticism like this. It's impossible.'

Hunter nodded. 'I agree with a lot of what you say, but we have no choice. What's the alternative?'

'It means decades of war,' said Lizzie.

'Look at the Farc in Columbia,' said Walsh, 'fifty years of warfare.'

'But that's regionalised. This is worldwide,' Lizzie protested.

'You're right, Lizzie,' said Hunter, 'but right now I don't see what choice we have.'

She sighed. 'Neither do I.'

Walsh phoned the infirmary and two attendants in an ambulance appeared in minutes. He instructed them to take the body to the morgue and that he would deal with the situation in the morning. Rima was placed on a stretcher, covered with a blanket and quickly removed. The autopsy could also wait.

'Are we going to dinner?' Hunter asked.

'I don't see why not,' said Walsh.

Lizzie looked at the three men and then shook her head. 'Count me out. I couldn't face anything to eat. I think I'll go back to my room.' She left the table, got as far as the door and then turned around and marched back. 'I haven't eaten all day. I am feeling peckish.'

'What changed your mind?' Hunter asked.

'The realisation that she got what she deserved even if it was self-inflicted. She was a traitor to America even if she saw us as the enemy and her loyalty was to her faith.'

'It's more complex than that,' said Hunter, 'if you think about it. She knew her family was and is involved with people smuggling, slavery and drug smuggling. All done in the name of Islam. It's perverse.'

'Shall we head for the restaurant?' Walsh asked. 'It's only a twenty minute walk and the evening is fine and warm.'

They set out, the conversation continuing along the same lines.

Perez made the observation, 'Nick's right, it is perverse but it's also a part of their armoury. Drugs and slaves for the financing of their war on the west and jihadists amongst the asylum seekers. If the estimated figures are correct then there are a lot of jihadists invading Europe.'

'According to EUROPOL,' said Walsh, 'over five thousand are already in Europe. Do the maths. Say they average ten deaths and injuries each, that's a lot of innocent people with devastated lives and bereft families.'

'I've always maintained,' said Hunter, 'that we cannot solve the problem. Only other Muslims can and they seem reluctant to really face down the people intent on destroying us.'

'I heard the American Secretary of State a few months ago,' said Walsh, 'during a televised debate about the problem. A Muslim woman was arguing that it was wrong for all Muslims to be classed as terrorists. The Sec pointed out that nobody was doing anything of the kind. He also pointed out that not all Germans had been Nazis, or that all Russians had been Communists who supported Stalin. But look at the results when ordinary, decent people did nothing. The fight against terrorism was being left to the west, even though there were more Muslims killing Muslims than anyone else.'

The others nodded glumly.

The restaurant was as good as Walsh had suggested and they banished all discussion of death and terrorism while they ate and drank. The conversation was general, along the lines of places they'd been and people they had met.

Hunter and Lizzie caught the 06.25 flight, which departed 15 minutes late. They changed at Rome and finally arrived at Marseilles only twenty-five minutes late.

They collected their luggage and made their way to the concourse. The team was a mere half an hour away and so they settled for a cup of coffee from one of the kiosks on the ground floor of the airport building.

When his mobile rang twice then cut off they walked outside to the pick-up area. The team arrived in a Ford SUV a minute or two later, Don Masters at the wheel. Hunter sat beside him and Lizzie squeezed into the back. If the team was surprised to see her they didn't show it by as much as a glance.

After greetings they headed for Cassis, using the A50 motorway. The road wasn't busy but even if it had been with three lanes each side the traffic would still flow freely.

'We're booked into a Hôtel de la Plage Mahogany,' said Master, 'on the Avenue de l'Amiral Ganteaume.'

'I looked it up on the Internet, boss,' said Badonovitch, 'and as you say, it doesn't look too shabby.'

'How far to Cassis?'

'Door to door, thirty-five klicks,' said Hughes.

'Let me check on something.' Hunter used his iPad and a few minutes later said, 'Change of plan.'

'What?' Masters glanced at Hunter.

'Hotels are too restrictive. I've just found an Airbnb house with four bedrooms, two public rooms and three bathrooms. It also has a garage and a forecourt.' He pressed a few buttons, extracted his credit card and paid for seven days' rental, the minimum available.

'Makes sense,' said Masters. 'More freedom of movement and far fewer people to note when we come and go.'

'I'll key in the address and let the satnav do the guiding,' said Hunter.

'Have you seen the Google photographs of al-Baghdadi's house?' Badonovitch asked.

'Yeah. It looks quite a place. High in the mountains, no houses nearby, swimming pool, tennis court and what looks like a large outhouse.'

'That's the servants' quarters,' said the Spetsnaz. 'Or that was how it was listed when the property was sold a couple of years ago. Leo downloaded the details of the place. That includes photographs as well as architect drawings.'

The satnav steered them to the waterfront and along to a small cul-de-sac with four detached houses either side. In accordance with the booking instructions Hunter was dropped off at a small café-bar situated on the corner of the street and went inside. A middle-aged woman took him along to the third house on the right.

She explained that the house belonged to a friend and that she was looking after it for the summer months. If there was anything they needed then they were just to ask at the bar where she was to be found most days.

A three metres high wall surrounded the house, there was a double wooden door into a garden and incorporated in one of the doors was a postern door. The woman unlocked the postern and led the way into a well-kept driveway stretching a dozen metres to a garage. The garage was detached, the house to the left of it with a footpath connecting them. The woman explained that he was lucky to get the house, as there had been a last minute cancellation.

She led the way inside to a spacious, cool hallway. She then proceeded to give him a tour of the place. The rooms were light and airy; two bedrooms faced the front, two the back of the house. The bathrooms contained showers and toilets but no baths. The kitchen was well equipped though the larder was bare. On the back patio was a gas barbecue.

Hunter checked an inventory with the woman who left thirty minutes after they had arrived. Five minutes later the car pulled onto the drive and then into the garage.

The team unloaded their gear into the house. Weapons were handed out and certain pieces of equipment checked over.

Lizzie observed, 'All the gear needed to start a small war.'

Badonovitch corrected her with a smile, 'To end one, you mean.'

She smiled in return and said, 'I guess I do. If it's okay with you guys I'm going for a shower.'

'No, carry on,' said Hunter. 'Our bedroom is top of the stairs on the right.'

Nobody made any ribald comments. They knew Lizzie and Hunter had been away together and so sharing a bedroom was no surprise. However, as soon as she left the room Masters spoke.

'Nick, why is Lizzie here? The General didn't say anything about her coming as well.'

'He didn't know though I expect he does by now. It was Hiram's idea. A couple strolling about the place will cause a lot less interest and speculation than a man on his own. Especially when we saw the photographs of the house. It's isolated and we need to do a bit of rubbernecking as well as take a close look at the plans and photographs.'

'Isobel is working on it now but we should have right up to date photographs transmitted here this afternoon. There's a satellite that covers the area for about an hour this afternoon, another one this evening and a third during the middle of the night.'

The satellites weren't geosynchronous hence the reason they were only on station for an hour at a time.

'Let me ask the General for a couple of French drones,' said Hunter.

He speed dialled his boss who picked up on the second ring.

'Commander, I trust all is well,' Macnair greeted Hunter.

'Yes sir. Fine as far as it goes. I was wondering if there's any chance we can get our hands on a drone or two? Hiram's too far away but the French might be able to help.'

'I'm sorry Nick, it's too dangerous?'

'Too dangerous? What do you mean?'

'You remember General Pierre Charney?'

'Of course. Put in to head the DGSE. Of itself an unusual appointment which we talked about at the time.'

The Direction Générale de la Sécurité Extérieure was France's equivalent of MI6 and the CIA in that it operated outside France in the wider world. It came under the jurisdiction of the French Ministry of Defence and reported directly to its minister. Internationally it was highly respected and recognised as one of the forefront organisations helping in the war against terrorism. The reason it was an unusual appointment was that the head of the organisation normally came up through the ranks to become the Director.

'I met with Charney a few days ago in Boulevard Mortier in Paris.'

'At DGSE HQ?'

'No. Around the corner in a restaurant. He'd arranged a private room.'

'It sounds very mysterious,' said Hunter, frowning. 'What's that to do with requesting a drone?'

'I'm coming to that. About five years ago the French government in its wisdom decreed that positions within departments and organisations that are exclusively run by the government for the government were to be staffed in proportion to the ethnicity of the country.'

'So not the best people but according to what? Religion? Where their families come from?'

'All of that.'

'So how does that effect the DGSE?'

'The percentage of the population in France who are Muslims is seven point five percent. The total number of people employed by the

DGSE is five thousand two hundred. So they are having to hire and train as near as dammit four hundred people. Also according to General Charney they estimate that more than five hundred jihadists have left France to fight for ISIS and ISIL in Syria and Iraq. Some are trying to return to Europe, radicalised and trained. Ten percent is fifty, one percent is five people who will kill innocent Europeans if they get the chance. And we know it only takes a lorry or a bus to wreak real havoc. These are some of the facts given to me by the General. But here's the kicker. The DGSE over the last five years have just about achieved their target numbers. And what's been happening is raids and arrests have dropped in the most dramatic manner. Literally, a raid is planned, the DGSE arrive to make the arrests only to find their targets have fled, often just minutes before the police arrive.'

'I get the picture.'

'Hence General Charney's appointment. The previous Director was too frightened to step out of line and so he investigated everyone equally. This has taken time and manpower and of course is ludicrous. Charney made it clear that if he was given the job he would focus on the men and women of the Muslim faith who have joined in the past five years.'

'That makes sense.'

'Of course it does.

'Has he had much success?'

'It depends what you mean by success. He has identified a number of operatives who are basically jihadists and need to be weeded out but that is proving very difficult.'

'Why?'

'Think of the uproar if it got out that Muslims were being targeted by the security services of France? There'd be riots and God alone knows what else.'

'Then what's General Charney doing about it?'

'He's a canny operator. He's laid a false trail of investigations of all personnel irrespective of colour, ethnicity and religion.'

'Do his political masters know?'

'No. When he was offered the job he told the minister that he would deal with the problem on condition he was left to get on with it.'

'And the minister agreed?'

'He didn't have much choice. So Charney was appointed, which resulted in ructions in the DGSE but they seem to have gotten over it.'

'And what has he found out?'

'That there are rather too many radicalised individuals in the organisation.'

'But he can't get rid of them?'

'It's proving pretty difficult.'

'I can see that. How does all this affect the request for drones?'

'He can't be sure he can supply any without it becoming known to the enemy.'

27

'Okay, I see that. Thanks, sir.'

'Did you know that Marseilles has gone from being given the accolade as the cultural capital of Europe to being considered the most dangerous city on the continent?'

'No, I didn't.'

'There's a vast amount on the Internet about it. It has a Muslim population estimated to be between thirty and forty percent, is the European drug smuggling hub and has massive no-go areas that are no longer controlled by the authorities. In the ghettos the order of the day is to use AK47s on rival gangs and innocent people to ensure control stays in the hands of the few. And by the way it is also now a centre for people smuggling and slave trading.'

'How in hell has this happened?' There was no hiding the exasperation in the RN Commander's voice.

'It sneaked up on us, Nick, like it has in the past. Think of Nazi Germany, Spain's Franco, Italy's Mussolini. We can go on but now the issue is fundamentalism, people smuggling, slavery and drugs.'

'And we're the frontline.'

'Yep, my boy, you've got it in one.'

'So how is General Charney going to handle his problem?'

'He's doing his best to isolate people in jobs where they can do no harm. Even so, he's already facing a backlash of complaints and demands for fairer promotion prospects and better appointments.'

'He's between a rock and a hard place.'

'Of that there's no doubt. I don't envy him the task but he's making a start.'

'Okay sir, so no drones. We'll manage.'

The connection was broken and as soon as it was Hunter's phone rang. It was Walsh. 'Hello Hiram.'

'Nick, I thought you might like to know that Rima's poison was implanted in one of her back teeth, like al-Baghdadi.'

'It takes a weird sort of courage to be carrying that in her mouth. She could have broken her tooth at any time.'

'Possible, though according to the medical examiner it would have taken a lot of effort to break the tooth. She'd had root canal treatment, creating a space under the tooth and then had it crowned with a substance known as bis-acryl resin. It had been weakened though not by much. When she ground her teeth together it broke and leaked so it took her longer to die than it was meant to, I guess.'

'Do we know what they used?'

'A compound of various alkaloids but we don't know which ones. We don't have the facilities here for such an analysis but I don't suppose it matters.'

'You're right. Thanks for that. We're going out on a recce shortly so I'll be in touch.'

'Happy hunting, Nick.'

There was a television in the corner of one of the rooms and Masters connected it to his iPad. He brought up a picture of a drawing of the grounds and outline of the house. 'This area is about five acres, or in French money, two hectares. It sits at the top of this hill with amazing views over the town, out to sea and west almost to Marseilles.'

'It must be worth a fortune,' said Hunter.

'It is.'

'Who owns it?'

'Isobel and her team are working on that right now. As far as the local officials are concerned it belongs to a corporation based in Paris.'

'Presumably that's owned by another corporation based in some tax haven or other,' said Lizzie.

'Close,' said Masters, 'but in fact it's an investment trust. So far Isobel has traced ownership through three trusts.'

'Has she a gut feeling where it'll end?'

'Leo has. He reckons Saudi,' said Hughes.

'Why am I not surprised?' Hunter frowned. 'Do we know the name of the man living there apart from the fact he is al-Baghdadi?'

'We think his full name is Hamid al-Baghdadi and is distantly related to the Saudi royal family.'

'That doesn't mean much,' said Hunter, 'in a family of over fifteen thousand people claiming some sort of connection.'

Masters said, 'This wall is three metres high and the top is covered with sharp blades of stainless steel. They are embedded into the stone and as deadly as razor blades. There has been some discussion at international level about their use but they haven't been banned yet.'

'Why?' Lizzie asked. 'Surely people have the right to protect their property?'

'It's a question of reasonable protection and deadly protection. If someone breaks into your house and you kill them you will be done for manslaughter for using unreasonable force. If someone tries to climb over the wall, cuts themselves badly and bleeds to death the argument is that's unreasonable force.'

'You are kidding me,' said Lizzie.

Hunter shook his head. 'We're almost at the stage that if you're attacked and your assailant hurts his knuckles on the top of your skull you get done for causing grievous bodily harm.'

'Now I know you're kidding.'

'More like using hyperbole to make a point. So we have these razor sharp blades, what else?'

Masters pointed. 'There is only one gate and it's here. You can see that this road is a cul-de-sac and single track with passing places outside the walls of each of the houses. The other houses have gates at the front while this is the only one with the gate at the back where the road has been extended. From the photographs it's obvious the change has been made in the last few years, the original gates being along the front. This is a guard post big enough to hold at least three people. According to the satellite images we've seen there are five people in the grounds at any one time. If that changes Isobel will let us know. You can see here the tennis court and the swimming pool. Both are at the back of the house. This is all lawn except the patio. That's the drawing, now let's take a look at the satellite images.'

Masters went through the various images taken from different angles and with various magnifications. There were palm trees, bushes and paths, one of which circumnavigated the ground alongside the wall.

'Now let's take a look at the diagrams of the house and the servants' quarters.' He changed the picture on the TV and went through each room in turn. There were six bedrooms, four of which were en-suite. Two shared a bathroom at the end of a corridor. Downstairs were four rooms, two lounges, a smaller room possibly a study or office and the kitchen/diner.'

'Is there a basement?' Hunter asked.

'No. At least, not on the plans,' Masters answered. 'But you never know what might have been added since it was built.'

'How old is the place?'

'Thirty-four years ago planning permission was granted and it took two years to build. It was owned by a businessman, has changed hands three times and is now owned by this corporation.'

'Do we have any idea how many people are there?'

'We have an idea but can't be sure. We think there are a total of ten maybe twelve guards plus servants.'

'I take it they're armed?' Badonovitch said.

Masters replied, 'Bound to be. No point in them being there otherwise.'

'Okay, if they are as brazen as to have arms on the property how is it the National Gendarmerie haven't raided the place, confiscated the weapons and locked a few of them up?' Hunter asked.

Masters shrugged. 'The French NG? You know it stands for Not Good and that's putting it mildly. Bribery and corruption is rife all along the coast otherwise how can so many illegals get away with living here?'

'Fair point. Do we have the plans of the electricity supply?'

'Here it is, Nick,' said Masters. 'You can see that all the houses have cable that meets at this junction box near the bottom of the hill. Access to the box is directly overhead through a manhole cover.'

'Good. In that case Lizzie I want you to deal with the problem.'

'How?'

'I'll tell you after we've taken a look.'

They broke for a bite of lunch after which Hughes and Badonovitch went shopping in Marseilles. They needed gear from one of the large superstores selling building materials and associated equipment.

'Don, can you get in some fresh supplies? Enough food and drink to last a few days. Lizzie and I are going for a walk.'

'We are?'

'Yes. Let's go and be eyes-on at the house. I want see how alert the guards are. Also it'll be interesting to check on their nationality.'

They strolled up the hill arm-in-arm.

'There's the manhole,' said Hunter.

They stopped next to it and looked down.

'So what will I be doing?'

'See the slot in the edge for a crow bar? You lift the cover and drop a thermal explosive down. You don't even need to look where it lands. Anywhere near the box and it will melt like an ice cube in boiling water.'

'A thermal explosive?'

'It's one of Don's creations. He's a genius when it comes to all things that blow up in various ways and with various methods of detonation. He'll show you.'

The houses they passed were walled with double gates set back about four metres from the road. However none of them had blades or even broken glass along the top of the walls. At the crest of the hill the road turned sharp right and in the crook of the bend sat the target house.

'Impressive wall,' said Lizzie.

'Those blades on the top look pretty nasty.'

'I hadn't noticed the six inch blades under the overhang at the top of the wall pointing out at about forty-five degrees.'

They rounded the bend and stopped. The road came to an end, the gate to the grounds was on their right and they both turned to look down the hill and across the rooftops of Cassis. It was a warm, clear afternoon and the view was spectacular.

They stood there for a few minutes, Hunter facing the house with his arms around Lizzie's waist. He could see through the metal railings of the gate and could make out the guardroom on the left. The house itself was in the far corner of the garden, leaving a significant expanse of ground between the gate and over to the right of the house. The garden looked to be well tended with two lawns separated by a footpath, round plots of flowers and a couple of tall trees. There were cameras on poles above the gates angled to cover the gates and the road where they were standing. It took two minutes for someone to appear and yell at them. Hunter ignored him. He was about five metres away and gesticulating with both his hands, making a shooing motion, as though trying to herd a gaggle of geese. At least that was the ludicrous picture painting in Hunter's head as he looked at the man.

He was speaking bad French and Hunter just looked at him, ignoring him. The man looked over his shoulder and said something. A second man appeared and stood alongside the first. Hunter deliberately turned his back on them and stood side-by-side with Lizzie admiring the scene.

'They should be here any second,' he said.

The words were barely out of his mouth when they could hear the two men walking across the road in their direction. They were speaking Arabic together. Hunter heard one of them say that if they didn't leave he would break their heads. The first man yelled again at them to go away.

When Hunter sensed that they were directly behind he turned suddenly and faced them. Both men appeared to be in their mid-twenties, average height, average weight, swarthy looking and of Middle Eastern extraction.

The first man placed his right hand on Hunter's left shoulder and tried to push him away. Hunter grabbed the man's wrist with his left hand to make sure it stayed in place, put his right hand over the man's elbow and jerked down hard. The snap of the man's elbow breaking was drowned out by the man's screams.

The other man was further to the left and Hunter swivelled on his left foot and brought the heel of his right foot smashing into the side of the man's left knee. He put all his weight behind the blow and the knee collapsed with the bottom of the man's leg sticking out at right angles. The man stood still for about a second and then collapsed, screaming in agony.

Hunter kicked the first man in the side of the head and the second man, because of the angle, under the jaw.

'We'd better go,' he said nonchalantly, 'before they come out waving guns.'

'How do you know they'll be armed?'

'Because these two are. Look at the bulges under their coats. Let's go.'

He placed his right hand under his coat and gripped his Glock. Lizzie walked on his right, leaving his field of vision to his left and towards the grounds clear. They walked quickly without appearing to do so. After a few minutes, halfway down the hill Lizzie spoke.

'Why did you do that?'

'Do what?'

'Attack those men like that. I'd have thought it would have been better to keep a low profile.'

'A couple of things. The first is there are two less uglies we'll have to deal with. I don't think either of them will be in a fit state to do anything when we appear on the scene. But there's the thing and you just said it. Nobody would expect me to have done what I did and still attack the house.'

'A sort of double bluff, so to speak.'

'Something like that. After all, showing our hand like I did is the work of an idiot and I suspect that's the interpretation al-Baghdadi will put on it.'

'He could call the police.'

'He won't.'

'You sound very sure.'

'I am. It's one thing to have bribed the National Gendarmerie, if indeed he did, it's another to have them crawling all over the place investigating an attack by a stranger. Especially as they would have to explain why they had left the grounds and told us to leave. We were on a public road. They had no right to tell us to move away. No, reporting us to the police would probably cause more problems than it solved.'

'So you reckon they won't be on a higher alert?'

'I don't think they will be and like I said that's two fewer guards we have to deal with.'

They arrived at the edge of the town and then made their way to the house. The others were already back and Lizzie told them what Hunter had done. The three nodded in approval.

'Good move, boss,' said Badonovitch. 'Pity we didn't see it when the satellite went over.'

'Do we have a precise time for the next one?'

'Isobel texted 03.20 for one hour,' Masters replied.

'Good,' said Hunter. 'In that case we'll get into position at 03.00 and wait for her to contact us. There are cameras covering the gates but we couldn't see any others. I wondered if the corners of the house had any but I couldn't see them if they are there. Did you get the aluminium ladders?'

'Yes,' said Badonovitch. 'They come in three sections and are quick and easy to fit together.'

'And the cloth?'

'All done.'

'Good.'

They spent the evening checking their equipment and memorising the plans of the house. They went to their beds at 22.30 and Hunter slept like a log while Lizzie lay awake wondering what the night would hold.

Finally, it was 03.00 and the team was awake, dressed and ready to move out.

'The timer set?' Hunter asked Lizzie.

'Yes. For three minutes.'

'Good. Then let's roll.'

They took the one car. It was a bit cramped with all the extra gear onboard but they were only in it for a few minutes. It was another warm, quiet night, with no wind and a clear sky. Moonrise was scheduled for 04.13 and so the night sky was dark while the surrounding streets were lit with orange lights. Here and there was an occasional house light, either forgotten to be turned off or belonging to an insomniac. Light pollution was alive and kicking along the Mediterranean coast and so Lizzie was able to drive without lights.

She stopped the car next to the first house on the hill, backed in so the tail was near the gate and waited for the others to climb out. The internal lights of the car had been switched off. The men looked what they were – a paramilitary team loaded with gear. They each wore black, long-sleeved shirts, black trousers with side, back and leg pockets. They also had on their balaclavas. Their desert boots were black and had rubber soles that ensured the minimum sound of footsteps on concrete. Their kevlar vests were hard-plated and reinforced - the very latest in technology. The vests were also wrap-around which meant they protected the shoulders and sides of the body.

They each carried a Glock fitted with highly effective silencers. A comms check between them plus with Rosyth established a loud and clear response. They wore the latest in night vision goggles that in one mode worked as an image intensifier and in a second mode as an infrared detector. The former gave the image a green tinge while the latter could locate warm bodies through walls if required.

In a leg pocket they carried an unusual item – a six inches long wooden handle of the type found attached to a club hammer.

They moved like ghosts. If anyone had seen them they would have thought that inhabitants from Hell had visited earth.

At the grounds they went to the farthest corner from the house and began to assemble the aluminium ladder. Each leg was three metres long, and into the top of one of them they slotted a one metre length of solid aluminium half a metre wide. The uprights, the rungs and the short platform had been wrapped in brown cloth, which matched the colour of the paint on the walls. The cloth helped to hide the bright aluminium and reduce any possible noise if the pieces were accidentally dropped or smacked against the stone wall.

'Ready to go,' Masters whispered.

'Wait,' said a voice from Rosyth.

They stood silently for a few seconds and then they heard someone hawking and spitting. One thing the team had in abundance was patience. Any job took as long as it took and nobody would be hurrying – unless things changed and speed became of the essence.

'Okay, go.'

They placed the leg with the solid platform against the wall and Masters quickly climbed it. Hughes handed up the other leg and Masters swung it over the wall. He slotted it onto the other side of the platform. The result was a stable bridge - a quick and easy way into the grounds.

Hunter transmitted, 'Okay Lizzie, go for it.'

Hunter and Badonovitch went over while Hughes stood at the top, resting his torso over the ladder, his sniper rifle at the ready.

Over their earpieces they heard Lizzie say, 'Fire in the hold. Three minutes.'

They knew she would now be back in the SUV ready for a rapid extraction should one be needed.

The three men were against the wall, hidden behind a large bush of some sort of flowering shrub with large pink petals.

'Listen up,' said the voice in Rosyth, 'there are two people approaching. There are three at the gate, one next to it and two inside the gatehouse. As near as we can tell there are a further twelve people in the house. Eight are prone so are probably sleeping and four are seated in the large lounge behind the staircase. From their posture I would say they are seated at a table.'

Just then the lights in the street went out plunging the area into darkness. They switched on their NVGs. Now they saw every detail of the grounds and house in a pale green hue.

The two men approaching came around the corner of the house. They were about 50 metres away. The path they were walking was packed earth, they were talking and one was smoking. They each had an AK74 slung over their shoulders, barrel down with their hands nowhere near the stock. It would take vital seconds to grab, point the weapon and fire. By which time they would be dead. When the lights went out they began to talk loudly in Arabic.

Then one of them yelled out, 'Husaam, what is happening?'

A voice at the gates came back, 'I don't know. I will take a look.' A few seconds went by before he called out, 'All the street lights as well as the house lights are out.'

'How can it be?' The first man asked loudly.

The voice in Rosyth said, 'The people at the table in the house are moving. They appear to be heading for the door. Yes. Two have gone to the back and two to the front.'

'Sayid,' a voice at the front door called out, 'is everything all right? What has happened to the lights?'

'They have all been extinguished in the street. It is a local power cut. It happens sometimes even here in France.'

'Make a careful search of the grounds. Make sure there are no intruders. If you see any kill them.' The voices were Arabic and Hunter whispered a translation.

The voice came over their earpieces. 'The four men have regrouped in the lounge. They have sat down at the table. One of the prone figures upstairs is on the move. He's entering the lounge. He is gesticulating. I guess he's shouting. Can you hear anything?'

'No,' replied Hunter.

'Oh, oh, the men have stood up and are heading for the front door. The fifth man is following.'

The team watched as four men appeared at the front door and then they heard the man behind them say loudly, 'You will search the grounds. And be quick about it. Do not forget what happened this afternoon!'

Hunter said. 'Okay, they've been told to search the grounds. That means there are nine of them, plus seven upstairs and the man behind the door. He could be al-Baghdadi.'

They watched as the men spread out in a haphazard line and started across the grounds. None carried a torch neither did they wear NVGs and all looked to be relatively young and nervous. It was an eerie sight to see six figures walking directly towards them, guns in their hands, looking around but not towards where the team was crouched.

The voice in Rosyth said, 'The man at the door has closed it and returned inside. He is in the lounge the others vacated. Distance to targets ten metres.'

The enemy was so close that they must be able to see the team any second.

Hunter whispered, 'Me one, Jan three, Don four, Dave six.'

The order of firing made sense as the targets were furthest away, behind numbers two and five and therefore not in their line of sight.

'Three, two, one.'

Hunter's first shot was into his target's head, which was blown apart. The sound of the shot was like a sheep burping from the other side of a wide valley. The target went flying backwards. So did number three, number four and number six.

Numbers two and five hadn't realised what had happened but number five began to look behind him. Hughes blew his brains out while the other three all put a bullet into the head of number two.

Hunter walked across the ground to take a closer look and administer the coup de grâce if it was needed. It wasn't. There was blood, brains and pieces of skull all over the place.

'Still three at the gate,' said the voice. 'That leaves seven upstairs and one in the lounge.'

Hunter and Badonovitch went clockwise, Masters went anti-clockwise.

A few minutes later Masters transmitted, 'I'm at the back of the house. The curtains are open and there is still only one man sitting at a table.' Seconds passed and then Masters said, 'I've taken a close look at the glass. It's definitely bullet proof and I would say three and a half inches. The serious stuff.'

He took out his Ka-Bar and scraped at the cement between two of the bricks underneath the window. The knife was razor sharp and the cement fell away easily. He felt the knife slip and said, 'Okay, usual sloppy job. The glass is fitted but the surround is unprotected. On my way.' He continued around the perimeter. 'Ten metres to target.'

'Ditto,' said Hunter.

Now two men were standing at the gate, looking at the road, the third was standing in the gatehouse. The two looking out through the gate couldn't see a thing locally, it was too dark, but they could see the lights on in the rest of the town.

'Nick,' breathed Badonovitch, 'look at the glass.'

'Yeah, I see it.Don, it's reinforced.'

'I figured that was the case.'

'Don, you take the booth, we'll take the other two.'

'Roger that.'

Masters crouched low and moved slowly towards the booth. The bottom half was stone, the top half was glass. It needed precise timing. Masters would get to the door of the booth and pull it open and at the same moment Hunter and Badonovitch would kill their prey.

All went according to plan up to the last few seconds. Then it all turned to rats.

28

Hunter's target moved at the last second. Hunter's shot scraped the side of the man's face and he gave out a yell. The second man wasn't so lucky; Badonovitch's bullet blew the target's head apart. Masters grabbed the door handle and dragged the door open and shot the man standing there twice in the chest. The man fell back and hit the panic button with his back. While Hunter fired a second shot into the head of his target a siren sounded in the house. It wasn't loud enough to disturb the neighbours but was loud enough to wake the household.

'What's happening?' enquired the voice over their earpieces. 'The bodies upstairs are on the move.'

'Problem,' replied Hunter. 'An alarm has sounded and we need to move fast.'

There were four windows upstairs, each one a bedroom. Downstairs were another four windows, two to each lounge. In one of the rooms upstairs a figure appeared at the window. He obviously thought he was safe thanks to the bulletproof glass. However, David Hughes had an answer to the problem

His sniper rifle was fitted with a sabot, a device used in a firearm to keep a round in the centre of the barrel when it was fired. The gap between a barrel and a bullet, called the windage, is necessary to allow the bullet to move along the barrel. Firing the bullet in a sabot raises the muzzle velocity of the projectile considerably. When the bullet reaches the end of the barrel and hits the air the sabot is pulled away. The bullet itself is known as a flechette and is a pointed steel projectile with a vaned tail for stable flight. It was armour piercing and at the range Hughes was shooting, deadly accurate. He had changed the ammunition when Masters had reported the existence of the bulletproof glass. The ammo was a new modification for the sniper rifle although it had been used in the American M40 recoilless rifle.

His first shot went straight through the window and blew the target across the room.

'One down,' said the sniper.

A second man appeared in another window and looked out, but before Hughes could fire he ducked down. David Hughes began a systematic aim and fire at the windows, each shot shattering the glass though hitting no human targets. AK47s suddenly erupted into the air, bullets sprayed everywhere, none aimed at any of the team. Even so, it was highly dangerous; a lucky shot was just as deadly as an aimed one.

Over their earpieces came the information. 'The man downstairs is running for the backdoor. Three of those upstairs are on the move. It looks like six alive and the one running out the backdoor.'

'I see him,' said Masters. There was a pause of a few seconds before the sergeant said, 'He's down. A bullet in the leg. He could be al-Baghdadi. Approaching him now.' There was no need for anyone to tell Masters to be careful.

That left six.

The windows had been blown apart so that now left the walls. They were less bullet proof than the glass. Hughes was given an instruction.

The voice in Rosyth said, 'Dave, the upstairs end window to the right of the house, behind the wall to the left of the window someone is spraying bullets.

'I see him.' Seconds later, 'I think I got him.'

'Yep. He's down,' said the voice.

Hunter and Badonovitch were against the wall on either side of the front door.

'There are three people on the ground floor. One is going into the lounge on the right, the other into the room on the left. The third man is staying in the hall. He looks as though he could be hiding under the stairs.'

Bullets erupted through the window on the right. Each side of the door was a colonnade supporting a sloping roof about two metres long by three wide. A bullet hit the stone at the wrong angle, bounced off and hit Hunter in the back. He stumbled forward letting out a muted 'Oof!'

'Are you okay, boss?'

'Yeah. A ricochet got me. No damage done.' He was aware that twice in one op was pushing his luck.

Hunter turned and looked at the window and could see a man partially hidden by the wall. Three shots from his Glock sent the target flying. Badonovitch took a fragmentation grenade out of his leg pocket, pulled the pin, stepped around the colonnade and tossed it underhand through the window. He stepped back as more bullets sprayed the grounds. The explosion was deafening; bits of the house came flying through the window surrounded by fragments of iron.

'Nick,' came the voice, 'you need to hurry. We don't want the local cops showing up. It would be highly embarrassing.'

'It'll be the National Gendarmerie as they're the only ones to be armed. They need to get here from Marseilles so we've a few minutes still. Don, is it al-Baghdadi you've got?'

'Affirmative Nick. I've bandaged his leg and reduced the bleeding so he should live long enough for us to talk to him. I've also used the handle.'

'Good work. Can you get him to the car?'

'Yes. Don't you need help?'

'We're good.'

'Dave,' said the voice, 'on the first floor, the first window on the left kneeling at the window, behind the wall. He's spraying the grounds.'

'Yeah, I can see the flashes.' Hughes fired through the wall, effectively blowing the man apart.

The shooting stopped. A voice began to call out in Arabic. The man was calling people's names. The voice was high and reedy; it sounded as though fear had the man by the throat.

'There are two left, one downstairs and the second heading for the back stairs.'

'I'm on it,' said the Spetsnaz, running along the front of the house. Hunter transmitted, 'Rosyth, how far from the front door to the target?'

'Five or six metres.'

Hunter pulled the pin from his fragmentation grenade and threw it into the hallway. The explosion ripped the place apart.

'He's down,' Rosyth reported.

'I'm at the corner,' said Badonovitch.

'The man will be out the door any second.'

'Here he comes, straight towards me.' Badonovitch waited for the man to run past. Real warfare wasn't a game where there was much honour. It was kill or be killed. As the man reached the corner he slowed down to check if the way was clear. Badonovitch had his weapon at head height and pulled the trigger twice. 'He's dead.'

'Nick, there's nobody left alive. Take two minutes and check for computers, memory sticks, mobiles whatever.' This time it was General Macnair transmitting.

'Yes sir.'

'Dave, pack up and hit the trail. Jan and I will check the house.'

The two men hurried through the front door. They ignored the bodies and body parts, having seen death in such forms many times. Each room contained the usual furniture to be found in any house until they entered the fifth room at the back, opposite the kitchen.

It was a study with a large desk, leather chairs, book-lined walls, a sideboard laden with liquor and a laptop in the centre of the desk. They ransacked the drawers and Badonovitch found two mobile phones. Hunter found three memory sticks.

They stepped out of the study and Badonovitch said, 'There's a door under the stairs.'

'We'd better take a look.'

Cautiously, Hunter opened the door. It led to a set of steps going down into the basement. Slowly he led the way, Badonovitch right behind him. The stairs were narrow concrete, and they could see that the ceiling was thick concrete. The air was warm and fresh which suggested an air-purifier was in use. They stopped at the bottom of the stairs and found themselves in an area about three metres wide and stretching away for a good 20 metres. They could hear noises, like animals moving about. The area where they were standing was devoid of anything, no machinery, no discarded items, nothing. On either side they could see metal doors, about three metres apart. Hunter pointed to the right and he went to the left.

They looked through the bars of a metal door. Thanks to their NVGs they could easily make out the inside of the cells. The one Hunter was looking at was just under three metres wide by three metres deep. In it was a cot, a toilet and a shower. There was also a metal chair at the back of the tiny room. Sitting on the edge of the cot was a young girl staring fearfully at the bars on the door.

'Christ, Nick, there's a young boy in here.'

'A girl here.'

'What shall we do?'

'There's nothing we can do. Let's get the hell out of here and leave it to the authorities. It's their problem. Either they're slaves for sale or slaves made to work in this place. Either way we can't do anything. Did you get that Rosyth?'

There was no answer. The walls were too thick, which explained why they hadn't been warned there was somebody else on the property. Infrared images were highly effective in the right place at the right time.

Both men took the stairs two at a time. They reached the front door when Lizzie spoke to them.

'I can see flashing lights and hear the faint sounds of sirens getting closer.'

'How far?' asked Hunter as he and Badonovitch rushed along the corridor and into the open air.

'Two minutes.'

'Is Don with you?'

'Just arrived. He's shoved the prisoner into the trunk.'

'Okay, you get back to the house. We'll run it.'

'Are you sure?'

Before Hunter could reply, a strong retort on his lips, Masters said, 'Got it, Nick. On our way.'

Hunter and Badonovitch sprinted out of the gates and headed down the hill. Halfway down and the first police car arrived. They stepped into the shelter of a gate and waited as the car flew past. It was obvious that whoever had reported the attack had told the police which house it was.

Much to Hunter's surprise there was only one car. The two men ran further down the hill until the loom of more lights and the increasing wail of sirens forced them into hiding again. This time there were two cars followed by a blue van the type used by the National Gendarmerie to transport their armed squads. Now there was serious firepower up on the hill.

They didn't see anybody as they ran. The locals were too intelligent to risk being out when guns were firing and explosions were erupting. Terrorism had taught people to keep their heads down.

Ten minutes later they arrived at the house.

'You okay?' Lizzie greeted them.

'Fine,' replied Hunter. 'Got a sore back, that's all.'

'Why? What happened?' she asked.

'A ricochet bounced off my vest. It's nothing.'

'It could have been your head,' said Lizzie in alarm.

'Then there would have been no damage done,' said Badonovitch, straight faced.

The others laughed and Hunter chuckled. Ribald comments were a good antidote to what they had been through. They were all on an adrenaline high and good-natured banter along with a couple of drinks was just what the doctor ordered. But first there was business to deal with.

'We found people locked up in cells in a basement,' said Hunter.

'What did Rosyth say?' Lizzie enquired.

Hunter had made a brief report when they were running down the hill.

'That we made the right decision to just leave them for the French authorities to deal with. Where's al-Baghdadi?' Hunter asked.

'He's tied up and gagged in the garage.'

'What about his wound?'

'It's not too bad. The bullet went right through. I've plugged it so he won't bleed to death,' said Lizzie.

'Don, any problems using the handle?'

'No. His mouth was wide open as he tried to scream so I stuffed the handle across his mouth and used a piece of bandage to keep it in place. I think I broke a few of his front teeth but he won't be able to grind his jaw and get at the poison. Assuming he has any.'

'Good work. I'll go and see him and give him a shot. Keep him under for a few hours while we get some rest. In the meantime, how about a couple of beers and a malt? Mine's the usual.'

For Hunter that meant whisky, ice and a splash of soda. He checked the time. As always it came as a surprise to find that the whole operation had only taken fifty-three minutes from the time they had left the house until their return.

The wailing of sirens hadn't abated, there were flashing police car lights up the hill and still more coming.

They heard a loudspeaker and after a few seconds they could make out what was being said. The people were being advised to stay indoors for their own safety and that the police had everything under control.

Hunter went through the connecting door into the garage. The garage could comfortably hold two cars, even with all the paraphernalia associated with a large house used to teenage kids running about the place. As it was there was only the one car and sitting behind it, away from the door, was their prisoner.

He was on an upright metal chair bought specially for the purpose. His legs were securely fastened to the legs of the chair with half-a-dozen tie wraps, and his arms were similarly secured along the arms of the chair. His body slumped and his head lolled forward. Hunter stepped across to the man and lifted his chin. The club hammer handle was jammed in his mouth and held there with bandages. The man was still alive even if his breathing was laboured. There was blood around his mouth and his leg. Hunter checked the leg and could see that Lizzie had done a competent job. The man wouldn't die any time soon of a bullet wound. He could die of asphyxiation, which was not what they wanted to happen.

Hunter slapped the man's face a few times but got no response. So he filled a bucket with cold water and poured it over the prisoner's head. The head jerked up and the man looked wildly about him and then stared at Hunter. The look was one of pure hatred.

'Nod your head if you can speak English.'

The man just stared, making no indication one way or another.

Holding up a syringe, the Commander said, 'This is a slow acting poison. You can either indicate to me if you understand what I am about to say or you can pretend you don't and as I will have no further use for you I will inject you with it. Death will not be pleasant but I won't hear a thing as I will be upstairs relaxing. So I'll ask you again, do you speak English?'

There was the faintest of nods.

'Do you speak Arabic?'

Again there was the faintest of movement indicating yes.

'Good.' He spoke in Arabic. 'Your men are all dead. We killed them. Also we killed others in your family, Mustapha and Abu Muhammad and Abu. Was Abu your son?'

The man looked up with dead eyes but he made no indication that he had even heard the question so Hunter asked it again. Still no response.

'Okay, I've had enough. You've decided you want to die and I'll help you or you can answer me. Was Abu your son?'

The man slowly nodded.

'Rima killed herself using the poison hidden in one of her teeth. You have the piece of wood in your mouth to stop you getting at it. I don't know if you have seen the poison at work but her death was terrible. It was sheer agony and the kind of end nobody deserves. But you don't care about that do you? You don't care about the living deaths you subject people to as slaves, treated like rubbish, hurt, humiliated and abused! And for what? To fund your so-called holy jihad against the west and the infidel while in reality you are living the good life with everything you want and slaves to do your bidding. You are filthy hypocrites.'

The man just stared at Hunter who was tempted to put a bullet in the man's head and leave it at that. Only he didn't want to leave any blood in the place.

'Did you hear what I did to Abu?'

The man continued staring and then slowly shook his head.

'I put his body into the sea wrapped in a piece of canvas and do you know what else was with him?'

After a few seconds there was another slight movement of the head.

'An open packet of bacon. Yes, bacon from a pig. I put it there after forcing some into his mouth. So no paradise, no seventy-two virgins, no spending eternity with Allah.'

The man's reaction was similar to his son's. He strained against the tie wraps, his body going rigid with shock, he was moaning a low, anguished sound, tears rolled down his cheeks. Hunter stood and watched, completely unmoved. Then he added a few more tie wraps to the man's legs and arms and finally held up the syringe in front of his prisoner's eyes. Then he rammed it into the man's thigh and pressed the plunger. He walked out without a backward glance.

A beer and a couple of whiskies beckoned.

29

There was no need to keep a watch on the prisoner but they weren't ones to take chances. They placed an easy chair in the garage and played rock, paper, scissors to see who slept there. Hunter lost and so he spent the rest of the night sleeping in the chair in the garage with Hamid al-Baghdadi who was out for the count thanks to the drug he had been injected with. It was good for at least five maybe six hours.

It was just after 09.00 when the police knocked on the door. Lizzie answered wearing running shorts and a low cut tee shirt. She wasn't wearing a bra.

'Yes, gentlemen?' She greeted them with a smile. 'Can I help you?'

They wore uniform showing that they belonged to the Police Municipale, the local police found in the towns and cities of the country and under the direct authority of the mayor. Lizzie realised they weren't serious cops. They were going through the motions. If it had been serious then they would have been the para-military police, the National Gendarmerie.

The man in front saluted, swallowed and tried hard not to look at Lizzie's cleavage.

'Madam, do you speak French?' His accent was thick, his words were hesitant.

'Pardon me, but no. I am an American.' She said it as though that explained everything. After all, few Europeans expected an American to speak anything other than their version of English.

The second officer spoke. 'I speak English.' He stepped forward and saluted. 'Madam you may have heard the . . . the noise last night.'

'Goodness me, yes.' Lizzie put her hand to her throat in a display of shock.

'Did you see anything?'

'Only the cars rushing past. You know with their lights flashing and their sirens making enough noise to wake the dead.'

'Wake the dead?' The policeman frowned and then said, 'Ah, yes, I understand.'

'My partner is here, we can ask him if he saw anything.' She looked over her shoulder and called out, 'Nick! Nick darling, there are some nice policemen here to ask us questions.'

Hunter wandered into view with a mug of coffee in his hand and a bewildered look on his face. 'Yes, honey, what is it?'

'Nick, these two guys are asking about last night. If we saw anything.'

'Yes, I did, damn it. I saw cars and vans screeching up the hill, lights flashing and sirens sounding. It woke me up and stopped me from getting back to sleep for hours.' He yawned. 'I'm knackered. We came here for peace and quiet,' he suddenly frowned at the two men. 'Care to tell us what's happened?'

'No, monsieur, madame, it is just a local problem. Thank you for your time.' He gave half a salute and they left.

Lizzie closed the door. 'Think they bought it?'

'Sure, why wouldn't they? I'll speak to my boss later and find out what he knows. He'll be in touch with the French as soon as is reasonable to ask for a report on what's happened.'

'What are we going to do about our guest?'

'Extract a few teeth.'

Just then Don Masters wandered into the kitchen. 'Ah, I smell coffee.'

'There's a very good machine in the corner,' said Lizzie, 'and freshly brewed coffee in the jug. I've put some bacon under the grill and there are eggs to fry. However,' she added, 'I'm a Captain and not a cook for a bunch of enlisted.'

Hunter couldn't decide whether she was being serious or not and so he said, 'I'll do the eggs, scrambled with cheese through them. But first, Don, you and I have a little task to perform. It's not very pleasant put we may as well get it over with before al-Baghdadi recovers conscious.'

In the garage the prisoner was still out. His head was to one side and drool was dripping from his mouth. At least he was still breathing a fact Hunter had monitored during the early hours of the morning.

Taking a pair of long nosed pliers, Hunter lifted al-Baghdadi's head back and used a torch to look inside his mouth.

'His teeth are disgusting. Nicotine stained and there are three missing. And there's also a fair amount of blood on his teeth. The handle must have prevented the saliva from cleaning them.'

'There's a tap in the corner, Nick. I'll get some water.'

There were a dozen empty wine bottles in a box ready for ditching and Masters used one. Hunter pushed the man's head back and poured water into his mouth, before pulling his head forward to let the water dribble out.

'God, it's disgusting,' said the Commander. 'Let me see. Ah, got it. Don, put your hands either side of his head and hold it steady.'

Masters went behind the chair and gripped al-Baghdadi's head. 'What have you got?'

'There's a back bottom molar that looks comparatively clean and almost healthy.' He held the jaw and put the tip of the pliers on the tooth in question. He squeezed gently, got a firm grip and moved the tooth ever so slightly back and forth. He took his time, increasing the movement a fraction at a time. He didn't want to break the tooth and fill the man's mouth with the poison. Steadily the tooth moved more and more and when Hunter eased upwards the tooth came cleanly out. He placed the tooth to one side and re-examined the mouth. Too many back teeth were missing for it to have been any other tooth.

Satisfied, Hunter said, 'He's lucky to have a top tooth to grind the poisoned one on. Okay. He'll bleed a bit but leave him. He should come to in about an hour.'

'Should we gag him?'

'No. We don't want him to choke. Can you stay here for ten minutes? I'll send Jan or Dave in after they've had breakfast.'

Masters made himself comfortable in the armchair, leant back and closed his eyes. 'I'll just doze here, Nick, Jan can take his time.'

Hunter returned to the kitchen. Badonovitch and Hughes were seated at the table drinking orange juice while Lizzie had bacon under the grill.

'So how about these famous scrambled eggs of yours,' teased Lizzie.

'Coming right up.'

Hunter busied himself breaking a dozen eggs into a bowl, adding butter, milk and grated cheese. He sprinkled in some black pepper and whipped the concoction together. These mundane chores were in stark contrast to what he'd done a few minutes earlier and what he'd be doing later, and the irony was not lost on him.

David Hughes made fresh coffee in the large cafetiere and put a jug of milk in the microwave for a couple of minutes.

'Toast, eggs, grilled tomatoes and bacon coming right up,' said Hunter.

They ate in companionable silence then when he'd finished Badonovitch said, 'The eggs aren't vomit making, boss, thanks.'

Lizzie stared at Badonovitch.

'It's okay,' said Hunter, 'that's a compliment.'

Hughes was grinning and said, 'Also endorsed by me. I'll go and relieve Don.'

Hunter reported their situation to Macnair.

'Okay, question al-Baghdadi then get rid of the body,' was the callous reply. There was no question whether the man was to live or die. The former wasn't an option.

'From his reaction when I told him about his son and the bacon I know just what I need to do. Except,' Hunter said thoughtfully, 'I'll take it one step further, just to ensure we get the right answers.' He changed the subject. 'How's Chris getting on?'

He was talking about Captain Chris Bletchley late of the Royal

Marines Special Boats Service and now seconded to TIFAT. He was also engaged to Hunter's sister, Louise.

'Fine. I was going to tell you about his op. I told you General Charney was suspicious of two officers within the DGSE, well Chris has confirmed they are jihadists.'

'What does the General say to that?'

'He's asked us to deal with part of the situation. There's a jihadist cell in Paris and according to Chris they are planning an attack.'

'When?'

'He's pretty sure it will be in two days time.'

'Has he identified the complete cell?'

'We believe so. Four immigrants plus the two DGSE officers.'

'When you say deal with, what do you mean exactly?'

'General Charney has been ordered by his minister to arrest the immigrants and put them on trial.'

'And what about the two DGSE officers?'

'According to Charney the minister wants the two officers to disappear.'

'I'm surprised a politician suggests such a move.'

'He didn't, Charney did.'

'And the minister is going along with it?'

'Under certain conditions.'

'Let me guess. The main one being the minister's name is not involved in any way.'

'Correct. We can always rely on politicians to look after themselves at all costs.'

'So how did the General get the minister to agree? To persuade him not to have the officers arrested?'

'Charney pointed out that if they did arrest the officers and put them on trial it could easily undermine the public's faith in the DGSE. They are the frontline troops against terrorism and France is sitting on a powder keg as it is. The people need to feel safe. By arresting the four immigrants and having a trial it shows how on top of things the security services are.'

'I guess that makes sense.'

'Charney told me that he intends arresting the four men in the middle of the night although he hasn't decided on the precise time yet. He needs the two officers removed first. He can't risk them tipping off the terrorists. Chris has reported that the four jihadists are armed to the teeth with automatic rifles and grenades as well as suicide vests.'

'Bloody hell! Why doesn't General Charney keep the two officers out of the loop? Send them home and just not use them?'

'That was an option but he'll have a heavily armed squad of men at the DGSE on Boulevard Mortier in the twentieth arrondissment from early evening onwards. However remote, it's possible that piece of information could get out and the cell told to run and hide, just in case. They could easily escape, even abandon their primary target and head elsewhere.'

'What's their target?'

'The Palais Garnier.'

'The opera house?'

'Yes. In two days time there is a special showing of *The Phantom of the Opera*. It's expected to play to a packed house, which means nearly two thousand people will be there. That's one of the reasons why Chris is certain of the timing.'

'That's one hell of a tempting target for the terrorists but I would have thought security would be so tight it's not a feasible target.'

'It is if you have DGSE uniforms and two officers flashing their credentials.'

'There is that. The carnage would be horrendous.'

'And let's not forget the damage done during a panic. People will be badly hurt if not killed. Chris has reported that a bullet as well as a detonator can trigger the vests so even if the attackers are shot they'll do a lot of damage. If the attack goes ahead with so many people there we can expect casualties in the many hundreds. I passed the information to General Charney and up until now I believe only he knows all this. He intends keeping it that way until the last minute. Just in case there are other officers involved.'

'And if there are?'

'Then it could all go pear shaped and the attackers could escape.'

'Sir, you said they could escape, I don't buy it. You won't allow it to happen and neither will General Charney.'

Macnair chuckled. 'Correct. So here's what you're going to do.' Macnair gave his orders.

'Okay, sir. Where are these terrorists holed up?'

'In an apartment in the Seine-Saint–Denis region of Paris.'

The area was a well-known no-go zone in the "City of Light" where Sharia law ruled and non-Muslims risked being attacked or even killed should they venture there. The local police never went into the area and the National Gendarmerie only when heavily armed and in significant numbers.

'Nick, I'll send you photographs as well as plans. We've identified four ways in and out of the building. Also vantage points for each of you. Send Don and Jan back here with the laptop and the other stuff. A helo will pick you up at Marseilles airport anytime after nine ack emma.'

Hunter grinned at the old-fashioned term for a.m.

'Does Chris know we're coming?'

'Yes.'

'Does he have a problem with me being there?'

'No, of course not. He understands the chain of command, as do you. It's his show unless you say otherwise. Okay, everything clear?'

'As usual, sir, clear as mud, but we'll do what we can. What about extraction?'

'Down to you. We can't risk telling anyone you are there. The men Charney is using are all non-Muslims. He tells me he needs more time to find out who he can and who he can't trust.'

'Won't that cause problems if the politicians discover he went into a predominantly Islamist area with no Muslims in the force?'

'If it's noticed, yes he will.'

'What will he do if it is?'

'Shrug his shoulders and claim it was not intentional just that he used the best people for the job without fear or favour.'

'Will he get away with it?'

'Quite frankly, he doesn't care. Like I told you, it's his way or no way as he made perfectly clear to the Minister of Defence in no uncertain terms when he was appointed.'

'I'll send Don and Jan this morning.'

'Good. The sooner we get to work on the laptop and memory sticks the better. Incidentally, I have more information about the people in the cells in the house. Did you check them at all?'

'No, sir. We saw a couple. We couldn't hang around.'

'Some of the cells had two even three people in them. There were a total of twenty-six people, some were used as slaves around the house and grounds and others were due to be sold.'

'These are truly evil men we are dealing with.'

'I'm afraid it gets worse. There were three cells with young girls in them. And I mean young like in prepubescent. I've been told they found a set of twin girls they think are about ten years of age. One is traumatised beyond words the other is more like a trapped animal cowering in the corner. They are both in a very bad way and will probably never be normal again.'

'What happened to them?'

'Al-Baghdadi is what happened to them. One of the other prisoners has described in graphic detail what those animals were up to. Believe me Nick, you don't want to know. They have ruined many lives and stopping them will help a lot of people in the future.'

'Thanks for that sir. It makes what I'm going to do all that much easier.'

The connection was broken. The others had heard the general apart from Hughes and so Hunter went into the garage and brought the sniper up to speed.

'You sure you won't need us, Nick?'

'Chris has Peter, Sam and Matt with him.'

Sergeant Peter Weir was an ex-United States marine and was as good a sniper as David Hughes, having qualified for the Olympics. Unfortunately, he had been unable to take part in the actual games as he was on assignment at the time.

Sergeant Sam McReady was ex-Special Boat Service and had seen action all across the globe before joining TIFAT.

Matt Dunston was an anomaly. He was tall and tough, ex-Sandhurst who became a member of the Royal Marines 3 Commando Brigade. In his early forties he had taken a turn of unimaginable proportions by becoming ordained. He was a Chaplain when he joined TIFAT but, as he liked to put it, he now fought the good fight without turning the other cheek. He was also 51 years old, which made him a bit long in the tooth for frontline duties. He liked to say that he brought intelligence and wisdom to the teams, something sadly missing in their gung-ho attitude. He was still fit and had few equals when it came to hand-to-hand combat, perhaps Hunter being one person who could give him a run for his money. He also spoke seven languages fluently – German, French, Spanish, Mandarin, Urdu, Arabic and Hebrew. Although Glaswegian by birth he had virtually no accent having been sent to Gordonstoun School on the Moray coast at the age of 11 where he spent six happy years before going to Sandhurst. His black hair and grey sideburns gave him a grandfatherly air that had proven useful on some ops. Who looks too closely at an elderly gentleman, especially if he gets into character, like walking with a stoop and carrying a cane? He had quit the marines and was now a private contractor working for Macnair. He struggled with his religious beliefs and what he was doing, having to examine his actions along with his motives on a regular basis. In many ways, although outwardly calm, he was a seething mass of contradictions. The person who helped him to rationalise his thoughts was a man he considered one of his closest friends and that was Nick Hunter.

Although the teams were interchangeable, they had gradually settled into individual teams. It meant that each team member had complimentary skills, knew each other well and had absolute faith in each other's abilities.

The new guy on the block was Chris Bletchley who was still winning his spurs.

Hunter put his arms around Lizzie's waist. 'It's time to go,' he said softly.

'My last dime in the juke box, another place, another time.'

'Jerry Lee Lewis.'

'You really are an old sentimentalist.'

Hunter smiled and riposted, 'Less of the old. I'd better go.' He kissed her cheek. 'Here's looking at you kid.' Then he turned to walk away.

Lizzie placed a hand on his arm and he looked over his shoulder at her. 'Like you said, Nick, another place, another time.' Then she smiled brightly. 'I'm already packed. I'm catching the 11.00 flight back to Sicily. Hiram needs me.'

Hunter nodded and smiled.

'I hope I haven't broken your heart,' she added.

'Of course you have. I'm totally gutted.'

Badonovitch and Masters hadn't been in the kitchen but were returning when they heard what was said. They exchanged long-suffering looks while Lizzie laughed.

'Liar! You're happy to see me go and I'm happy to be gone. No offence, Nick.'

'None taken.' He wasn't going to admit she was right. He was too much of a gentleman for that. Leave them smiling was his motto. 'I'll take the three of you to the airport in Marseilles as I've some shopping to do.'

30

Hunter returned at midday. He was carrying a parcel the size of a football carefully wrapped in half a dozen layers of plastic bags. He hadn't wanted the blood to run. The abattoir he had visited had been most obliging especially when he didn't haggle over the price. He thought 30 euros was a bit steep but then beggars couldn't be choosers.

He drove into the garage. Their prisoner sat with his head bent forward, his shoulders slumped, his eyes closed. He was mumbling to himself and after a few seconds Hunter realised it was the noonday prayer known as the Dhuhr.

'How long has he been praying?'

'Is that what he's doing?' Hughes shrugged. 'About forty, maybe fifty minutes.'

Hunter found a fresh bandage and wrapped it tightly around al-Baghdadi's mouth. The man kept his eyes closed the whole time.

'Open your eyes,' said Hunter, tapping the man on his cheek.

There was no response so Hunter slapped harder and hissed, 'Open them or you'll regret it.'

Still nothing.

'Okay, I gave you the option.'

Hunter took the package and unwrapped its contents. He placed it on al-Baghdadi's lap and then went behind the man. He placed his mouth close to the man's ear, hit him hard across the head and yelled, 'Open your eyes!'

Hunter wasn't sure what the man's response would be but at least it could be similar to his son's. Hunter had moved around to be able to see the Saudi's face and the reaction was most satisfying. The prisoner looked at the head of the pig sitting on his lap and freaked out. He began to moan and thrash back and forth. His neck muscles strained and his eyes bulged. The horror on the man's face was a look that Hunter had not seen before.

Hunter lifted the pig's head by its ears and placed it on a bench nearby and turned al-Baghdadi's chair so that when he lifted his head he would see it just a couple of feet away.

'Open your eyes,' said Hunter, hitting the man across the back of the head.

Al-Baghdadi had stopped moaning, but he sat in the same position as before only this time he was also shivering uncontrollably.

At that moment Hunter's phone rang and a glance at the screen showed it was Rosyth.

'Hunter.'

'Nick,' said the General, 'I thought I'd tell you what's happening up the hill. The Gendarmerie are packing up and leaving. I had a word with Pierre Charney and told him there was nothing to investigate. He took my meaning and called off his dogs. The local Préfecture of Police wasn't happy until the General leant on him.'

'How'd he do that?'

'Told him he'd be out of a job ten minutes from when he hung up the phone. Apparently the Préfecture didn't take a lot of persuading. As always the French are very pragmatic people.'

'You sound as though you admire them, sir.'

'I wouldn't go quite that far but I do hold some of them in the highest regard.' Then Macnair added, 'Though not many of them, it's true.'

'Thanks for the info, sir. I can stop worrying about the house being raided.'

'You were worried?'

'Hardly, sir. I'd better get back to the prisoner.'

'Got anything yet?'

'No, sir. I haven't started questioning him yet.'

'His passwords for his computer and mobile if he has one would be useful. It'll save us some time.'

'Roger that.'

It didn't take long. Al-Baghdadi couldn't answer the questions quickly enough, all the time staring at the pig's head. He immediately divulged the password to his laptop and encrypted files. Knowing them saved the boffins in the IT section at Rosyth a few hours work.

They discovered that his brother, Tadeas al-Baghdadi, was a senior member of the Mutawa in Saudi Arabia and therefore a leader in the organisation. He confirmed that their main activities were smuggling slaves and other immigrants into the west, as well as drugs and jihadists. Coupled with all that was the creation of legal small to medium sized businesses across Europe which were used to make a profit as well as launder money. The operation was on a grand scale. According to Hamid al-Baghdadi they had transported over three hundred thousand slaves and paying immigrants alone. The value of the drugs sold at street level ran into billions, though al-Baghdadi admitted he was only guessing.

'How many people are involved with your organisation?'

'I do not know.' The man's voice croaked as he continued staring at the pig's head, talking to it, not Hunter.

'Do you want some water?'

The man nodded.

Hunter took a glass of water, put it to the Saudi's mouth and poured. Most of it trickled down his chin and into his lap but he greedily swallowed what he could. The man's eyes returned to staring at the pig.

'I want to talk about the people we found in your house. Locked in the cells like animals.'

The man seemed to regain some courage as he moved his eyes to look at Hunter. 'They are nothing. They are not of the one true faith and therefore they are lower than dogs.'

Hunter had heard it all before but even so the depth of the man's venom took him aback.

Hughes and he looked at each other and the sergeant shrugged. Hunter had had enough. He took the bandage and wrapped it tightly around the man's mouth, making sure he could breathe through his nose and then both men left the garage.

The coffee was stewed and Hunter busied himself making a fresh pot. Neither man spoke for a few moments. It was Hughes who finally broke the silence.

'Nick I don't get it.'

'Get what?'

'Where the hatred comes from. The attitude to fellow human beings all over a piece of dogma that doesn't add up when closely examined.'

Hunter shrugged, 'I agree Dave. But you see the passion in the man. And we know that not only is he not alone but there are hundreds of thousands equally passionate and even millions on the same wavelength but who would never stoop so low as to behave like al-Baghdadi and his tribe. For that's what they are, of course. A tribe living off the misery of others.' He paused before he added, 'It scares the hell out of me.'

'You?' There was no disguising the surprise in Hughes' tone.

'Oh, I don't mean the battles. I mean winning the war. How do we fight such bigotry and ingrained hatred?'

'Remember what Teddy Roosevelt said?'

'Do you mean if you've got them by the balls, their hearts and minds will follow?'

'That's it.'

'Great sentiment but in this case it doesn't seem to be working.' Hunter poured the coffees in gloomy silence. Both took theirs strong, white, no sugar.

After a few minutes the Commander said, 'He's going to believe he's going to hell. He's taking that pig's head to the grave with him.'

'Grave?'

'Figure of speech. Dave can you nip down to the harbour and hire a speedboat for twenty-four hours? I've been looking at a chart online and there's a cove about ten klicks up the coast that looks pretty deserted. When the time comes we'll take him there, head out a couple of miles and ditch him.'

'Dead or alive?'

'Alive. The piece of filth will know exactly what's happening to him.' He sighed and then added, 'The connection to the Mutawa is, what's that word Jan has taken to using recently?'

'Discombobulating? That's his latest.'

The Spetsnaz took pleasure in finding obscure English words and dropping them into the conversation much to everyone's amusement.

'Yeah, that's the one. Confusing and upsetting at the same time.'

'We're not particularly surprised the Mutawa are involved, are we?'

'I guess not,' said Hunter.

The Mutawa was an Islamic organisation based in Saudi Arabia and some other Islamic states. In this case, it was part of the Islamic sect known as Wahhabism. In fact, they were the Islamic police force for the country. Their powers were legendary. Their existence was justified having been described in the Koran as necessary to ensure that correct moral behaviour was observed and that Sharia law was supreme in all cases of potential wrongdoing and blasphemous behaviour. The problem had become one of perception and enforcement. At ground level they were the arbiters of what was right and wrong and they enforced their powers with ruthless abandon.

'Have you read the analysis of the Mutawa's activities in the past and what their role is today?'

Hughes shook his head. 'What I do know about them is that many of them are ex-convicts who have memorised the Koran in order to get their sentences reduced.'

'That's part of it, though the ex-cons aren't the majority. The Saudi Committee for the Promotion of Virtue and Prevention of Vice are the body that authorises the activities of the Mutawa. There are now over three and a half thousand officers and thousands of volunteers who sometimes have police accompanying them.'

'So what do the volunteers do?'

'They claim a neighbour or someone they have a grudge against has broken the strict laws as laid down in the Koran and the next thing the person is arrested. Often on trumped up charges.'

'Surely a quick enquiry resolves the matter and that's the end of it?'

'You'd think so, wouldn't you?' said Hunter, sipping his coffee. 'But here's the kicker. In order for the Mutawa to justify their existence they need to find blasphemous and as they call it, depraved activities to justify not only their existence but also their powers. So people are arrested for being homosexual or prostitutes. They enforce dietary laws so no alcohol and no pork. They actually beat women who are not dressed according to their perception of Islamic law, which means the burqa or niqab covering the women's bodies, heads and faces. They have even been known to stop cars and drag women out and whip them for the sin of driving. It goes on and on. No western television or music, no proselytizing of other religions, which are banned in Saudi.'

'Yeah, I know and the Saudis are supposed to be our allies!' said Hughes with disgust.

'A case of the enemy of my enemy is my friend. The list goes on. If a senior member of the Mutawa is the head of the Al-Baghdadi organisation then its tentacles probably go much higher and possibly reach into the heart of the royal family.'

'As far as the king?'

'There's no way of telling but I seriously doubt it. He is a conservative and a traditionalist with regards to political reform and social change but he is a friend of the west. You should Google Mutawa hierarchy and read what's there. It'll make your blood boil while you laugh at some of the absurdities. You hot to trot?'

'Yeah. I'll see you later.'

Hunter returned to the garage while Hughes set out on his errand to hire a speedboat.

Hunter removed the prisoner's bandages from around his mouth. 'I asked you before about the position your brother has in the Mutawa. Are you going to tell me?'

'Yes,' was the croaked reply. 'He is the deputy director. He has a great deal of power.'

Hunter didn't doubt it. 'Why is he doing this? Why are you?'

The man looked surprised at the question for a moment and then his shoulders moved fractionally as though he was shrugging. 'The usual.'

'What's the usual?'

The response was a stare filled with hatred.

Hunter shrugged and turned to the head of the pig. He took a knife and cut one of its ears off. Al-Baghdadi watched in horror as Hunter turned towards him with the ear in his hand.

'Do you know what I am going to do with this?' He held it up, advancing towards the bound man.

Al-Baghdadi pushed himself back in the chair, his head bent as far back as possible, horror etched into his face. Hunter stopped with the ear an inch from the man's mouth.

'I will stuff this into your mouth or you tell me what I want to know. Do you understand?' There was no reply. 'Do you understand?' The words were spoken with a greater degree of menace.

'Yes,' the voice was barely a whisper.

'Louder, I can't hear you.'

'Yes.'

'I'll ask again. Why are you doing this? For the money?'

'Water.'

Hunter repeated the previous performance with the water. 'So answer me.'

'You do not understand. In the Kingdom wealth and power is in the hands of just a few. All are princes of the House of Saud. My brother is deputy director but he will never be director. He does not have the right influence, which in turn means the money to bribe the right people for the job. And that job will become vacant soon. My brother wants to be the director of Mutawa more than anything in the world. To do so he needs a great deal of money which he has been amassing for a decade.'

'So he's a billionaire,' retorted Hunter.

'No. There are many expenses. The organisation has increased significantly but even so Tadeas has told me he is worth only three hundred million dollars.'

'Only? How much does he need.'

'That is no longer the issue.'

Hunter was about to ask what was when he realised the answer for himself. 'Power beyond the job. Money to spend to establish what would in effect be a worldwide Islamic caliphate based on Wahhabism. I read about it on the Internet,' Hunter spoke slowly as the memories returned. 'It's what the House of Saud is doing and will continue to do no matter how long it takes. Didn't one of the imams at the Grand Mosque in Mecca say that it was the duty of all Muslims to work in whatever way necessary to make the world Islamic?' The question was rhetorical and Hunter didn't expect to receive an answer, just a hate filled look, which he got.

There was nothing more to be asked of the prisoner. Hunter placed the pig's ear next to its head, rebandaged the man's mouth and went back into the house. He needed a shower to wash away the filth. And it hadn't been from handling the pig.

When Hughes returned they took it in turns during the afternoon and evening to keep an eye on their guest. At 22.00 it was dark, there was no moon and the streets were silent. After the events of the previous night the good burghers of Cassis were taking no chances. They were all staying indoors with their doors locked.

Hunter gave al-Baghdadi an injection. It would keep his under for about an hour. He didn't want it to be any longer. The man wasn't going to die peacefully after what he had done to all those innocent men, women and children.

An item the team had bought in Marseilles was a piece of carpet about three metres by three metres. They rolled al-Baghdadi in it, used masking tape to hold it together and dumped him in the trunk of the SUV. Hunter drove them to the marina where Hughes climbed out and boarded the speedboat he had hired. Hunter drove along the coast while Hughes followed at sea.

They met at the lonely cove. Hunter carefully reconnoitred the area before he was sure there was nobody to see what he was doing. He threw al-Baghdadi over his shoulder and carried him the short distance down to the water's edge.

Hunter threw al-Baghdadi into the boat and returned to the car to collect the multi-layered plastic bag with its gruesome contents. He took the wheel while Hughes headed up to the car. Hunter engaged the gears and backed the boat away from the sand. About a mile offshore he put the engine in neutral before cutting the masking tape off the carpet. When he unrolled it he was gratified to see that al-Baghdadi was awake and his eyes were wide open.

'Hamid, I am sending you to hell where you belong.' He took the pig's head, showed it to the prisoner and then placed it on the man's chest. Al-Baghdadi bucked and squirmed, panic stricken, tears running out of the corners of his eyes. Hunter used a whole roll of masking tape to hold the pig's head in place. It was awkward and time consuming but the anger Hunter felt for the man who had inflicted such damage on so many people was off the Richter scale. Finally, he was satisfied and tied the boat's anchor around al-Baghdadi's ankles. He dropped the anchor over the side and manoeuvred the man next to the edge.

'You will be with this pig for eternity. You will see your son and nephews and whoever else in your damned family involved with what you've been doing. I am going to track down every one and they will each meet the same fate so you can all be together in hell.' There was more he wanted to say but knew there was no point. He lifted the body over the rails and watched it vanish beneath the waves.

The return journey was peaceful and at the same time therapeutic. The sea was calm, the night was balmy and the coast was dark. He eased back on the speed to enjoy the peace and serenity his surroundings offered for just a few more minutes. Then he woke up to the fact that he had things to do, rammed the throttle hard home and felt the exhilaration of the boat lifting up onto the plane and building up to a speed of 60kph.

31

There was a helicopter waiting for them at Marseilles airport when they arrived at 09.05.

The flight north was uneventful and by the early afternoon they were ensconced in rooms in a hotel in Saint-Ouen, Paris. The hotel was large and impersonal. After booking in and dumping their bags in spacious rooms they went outside to find a restaurant. They ignored the big yellow 'M' sign as well as Starbucks, and settled on a small bistro around the corner from the hotel.

'What now?' Hughes asked.

'The General said to wait until Chris contacts us, which will be sometime this afternoon. I don't know about you but after this salad and the coffee I'm heading for my pit for a couple of hours.'

'Sounds like a good idea,' said Hughes.

The salad was not as fresh as they would have wished and the coffee definitely not as good as it should have been. Hunter put it down to the antipathy harboured in the hearts of Parisians to all visitors in general and the British in particular. This was especially true now that Brexit had been triggered. Hunter figured many French people were jealous of the British as a result.

They returned to the hotel where Hunter hit the sack and promptly fell asleep. He was woken up at 17.34 when his mobile rang. A glance showed it to be Chris Bletchley.

'Hi, Nick, you got here all right?'

'No problem. Where are you?'

'Two doors along from you. I thought we'd have a briefing here at 18.30.'

'I'll be there.'

'I'll have room service bring up a few pots of coffee and plates of sarnies.'

Hunter rolled out of bed, did fifty sit-ups, fifty push-ups and fifty squats. He repeated the workout three times. It wasn't as satisfying as a run but there was nothing more he could do. At least some endorphins had been released in his brain. He knew that exercise helped to reduce stress, ward off anxiety and feelings of depression, improve sleep and boost self-esteem. However here was the quandary. He didn't have any of those negative thoughts and feelings. Was that due to the exercise or his natural demeanour? One for the psychiatrists, he always told himself.

He shaved and showered then dressed in black jeans, a dark brown shirt over which he wore his lightweight safari jacket. The Glock and holster was under his left armpit as usual. At 18.30 at Bletchley's door he tapped twice, paused, tapped twice again, paused and tapped once. It was the Royal Naval diving signal for "Have found, started, or completed work" and known as '5 bells'. For the team it also meant that it was clear to open the door. It opened but there was nobody standing there. Precisely what Hunter had expected.

'Come in, Nick,' said Bletchley.

Hunter stepped into the room. Bletchley was standing a few paces to one side, his right hand hanging down by his thigh, a silenced automatic hidden behind his leg. He had a welcoming smile reciprocated by Hunter whose smile widened when he saw Matt Dunston standing in an alcove on the other side of the room.

Bletchley was the same height as Hunter at 6ft 2ins, and had the same build with the same tough no-nonsense look about him. His hair was fair, wavy and unruly reaching over his ears. He had brown eyes, an aquiline nose, a square dimpled chin and was as fit and tough as he looked. Becoming a Special Boat Service Captain in the Royal Marines meant you had that certain something that separated you from the herd. It enabled you to live by the SBS motto, "By strength and guile". It was a characteristic the men at TIFAT all shared.

The two men shook hands while Dunston crossed the room to do the same only he also patted Hunter's shoulder. He had been the one to persuade Hunter to learn Arabic on the basis of not only knowing your enemy but also being able to converse with them and in the early days had helped him with his lessons.

'Good to see you, Nick.'

'You too, Matt. Where are the others?'

'We're waiting on Dave but Peter and Sam have been recalled. They were wanted urgently back in England. There's been a couple of incidents.'

'When and what sort?'

'A bomb went off in Leeds and another in Newcastle. Nothing big and no reports of casualties but enough to put the country on high alert. Bikini Black Special has been posted.'

Bikini Black Special was the third highest state of emergency in the UK and meant that there was a potential terrorist threat. Only now there was no "potential" in it. It had happened. It meant officers of all the emergency services being recalled and placed on high alert, ready to deal with another incident. As was usually the case, the security forces were on the back foot, playing catch-up instead of leading the fight.

There was a knock on the door of '5 bells'. The three men parted and took up a stance that told anyone who saw them that they were ready to react if necessary. They were aware that such actions appeared melodramatic to the layperson but better to look foolish than be dead.

'Who is it?' Bletchley called out.

'Hughes.'

'Come in, Dave.'

Although there was a peephole at eye level in the door none of them were stupid enough to use it. An eye over the glass and a change in the light could result in a few bullets through the door. It was a ludicrous way to die.

A waitress entered along with Hughes, pushing a trolley laden with plates of sandwiches, cold drinks and coffee.

'Just leave it, thanks,' said Bletchley, handing the girl a five euros note.

The woman half curtsied, smiled and left.

'Help yourselves,' the SBS captain said.

The accommodation was a suite with a large lounge and a bedroom on the other side of an alcove. It was an unusual arrangement but ideal for their purposes. Bletchley had already wired his laptop to a large screen television sitting in the corner of the room and was ready to brief the other two.

'Before we start,' said Hunter, 'what happened to the two DGSE officers?'

Bletchley replied succinctly, 'A bullet and no body, which was General Charney's preference. He plans an internal "Eyes Only" report for senior personnel showing the two men had been jihadists and have probably gone to Syria or Iraq to fight for Daesh. He's using the info we supplied. Recordings, photographs, phone taps the lot. He has been effusive in his thanks to General Macnair. If his own people had carried out the operation there was no chance of it being kept quiet. This way allows Charney to carry on investigating without showing his hand. He did say to the General that our services would probably be needed again.'

Hunter shrugged. 'That's inevitable. Is that Arabic TV I can hear?'

'Yes,' said Dunston. 'It's on that loudspeaker. We're listening in to the apartment. It appears that all they have to say has been said. They also spent most of today praying.'

'So what have we got?' Hunter asked.

Bletchley tapped a few keys on the laptop and a picture appeared on the TV screen. 'As you can see this is a detached building in the middle of Seine-Saint-Denis. This is an acknowledged no-go area because of the, shall we call it, sensitivities of the Muslims who live there? In reality, it's a case of the three monkeys.' There was no reason to elucidate. See no evil, hear no evil, speak no evil was the mantra of western politicians and was one that drove the security services of the west into paroxysms of rage tinged with despair.

While he spoke the other three were helping themselves to sandwiches and coffee.

'After we gave Charney the info and carried out the operation he met with us. He told us all about the area. It really is a hotbed of radicalised Muslims, some of whom have left France to fight for Daesh in the Middle East while others are planning attacks in this country and other parts of Europe.'

'Why haven't the French done anything about it?' asked Hughes.

'They don't want to upset the people living there. Poking a stick into a nest of hornets was the way he put it. It appears that many of these people are armed maybe even have explosives. And you know how it is, Nick, many are ready to die as long as they take non-believers with them.'

'It'll be all out war.'

'It will take a very large force to contain the violence if they can. Though Charney doubts they'll be able to do so. It will take an army. The army, more precisely.'

'Do you agree with him?'

Bletchley nodded. 'Yes. I would say so from all that we've heard. This is a very big operation for these people. Four highly sophisticated explosive vests in a place packed with people many of whom are amongst the high and mighty?'

'Why the high and mighty?'

The French President's wife and other members of her family will be there.'

'But they'll be closely protected.'

'Of course they will. But this is an all out attack. What I haven't told you is that once they are at the target a number of other jihadists will be joining them. They will attack with two gunmen accompanying one bomber. They are killed and the first bomb explodes. That's followed by the second, the third and the fourth. Each one trying to move deeper into the theatre. They might not get all the way in but on the other hand it is possible.'

'I take it the attack will be after the performance has started?'

'They have timed it to be just before the intermission.'

'Okay, General Charney knows all about it so what will he do?'

'First of all there'll be a ring of steel around the area including armed officers in plainclothes. They are putting in a dozen metal and explosive detectors. No bags of any description will be allowed into the theatre. That applies to all and sundry no matter how important that person thinks he is. I will say one thing for the General, he's a tough son-of-a-bitch. He doesn't care who he upsets.'

'Like our boss,' said Hughes.

The others nodded. There was no question that Macnair was tough.

Hunter said, 'That's the final line of defence. He wants these people taken out before then.'

'Correct and for a number of good reasons.'

'If he waits for the attack to take place in effect he loses control of the incident and the timing. Also, too many people will know what's happening and the attackers could easily be warned. So they'll then put off the attack for another day. And what? Leave the area for another safe house?'

'Yes. We heard them say so. No matter how you look at it these people have to be taken out where they are.'

'I understand that. If an attack takes place in, let's call it, a civilised part of the city, then non-Muslim people could and probably would rise up. They'd attack innocent Muslims just because of their religion.'

'They'll be scared. More scared than they are now. It's a powder keg, Nick, we know that. It won't take much to ignite it.'

'The ordinary people get organised and attack those living in Seine-Saint-Denis with sticks and stones and go up against guns and bombs.'

'It will be chaos, a lot of dead people, a lot of injured and enough bad feeling to last a lifetime.'

'So these four terrs need to be taken out where they are.'

'Correct.'

Hunter picked up a sandwich, took a bite, nodded his appreciation and followed it with a sip of coffee. 'So we come back to the usual problem. The General goes in mob handed and kills people. Maybe terrorists with guns, maybe not.'

'Maybe terrs with guns which are removed by others who then scream murder and genocide by the fascist police who are accused of killing innocent people.'

'However you look at it,' said Dunston, 'the General is between a rock and a hard place.'

'So he's looking for a surgical strike,' said Bletchley.

'I figured that.'

'He told me that they fear if things get out of hand here in Paris then they could escalate to other cities with large Muslim populations such as Dijon and Marseilles.'

'With either side ready and willing to start the rioting,' said Hunter. 'It's a scenario we've played out many times.'

Hunter was referring to the "war games" they played back at base. They examined different scenarios in different places and tried to find impossible solutions to difficult questions.

'The apartment the cell is using is this one,' Bletchley used a laser pointer pen on the screen, 'on the third floor in the corner. We managed to get plans of the place though they are at least fifty years old so internally there may have been alterations. There are four exits from the building,' he rotated the view and pointed each one out, 'as well as these four fire escapes. Although there's a basement, there are no doors beneath ground level. Here are the four vantage points we can use.' He changed the screen. 'The roofs of these four buildings are ideal for our purposes. As you see, around the edge of each roof is a metre wide pathway. This is to give access for roof and chimney repairs. There's one door.' He pointed to it. 'Matt checked it out. It isn't locked.'

'Checked it out?' Hunter queried.

'When we were sure the apartment was empty Matt dressed as a

Muslim and walked into the building. Open and bold, no suspicion, picked the door lock, placed the bugs and got out. The whole thing took less than six minutes.'

Dunston said, 'The door's hinges have been oiled and the lock tampered with so that it can't be locked.'

'I see the fire escapes reach the roof,' said Hughes, 'so anyone trying to get away can go up, across the roof and down the other side.'

'Correct. There's more. General Charney has told us that they think as many as three hundred Muslims in the area are jihadists and twice that number are fundamentalists who either won't be of any help or will actually try and hinder the operation,' said Dunston.

'By doing what?' Hunter asked.

Bletchley replied, 'Just by being in the street. The DGSE are not going to shoot unarmed Muslims even if they are trying to help known terrorists escape. The backlash would be off the scale from legal rights to riots.'

'What will happen if the DGSE arrive but aren't noticed until the last few minutes?' Hunter asked.

Bletchley said, 'It's obvious from what we've heard that these people aren't stupid. They have a plan for that eventuality. Suppose the DGSE split up and head for all four doors. One of the men will head for the roof. He'll be wearing his suicide vest. He will wait until members of the DGSE are near this door here,' he pointed, 'and then jump at the same time detonating his vest. It has a two second delay and will explode just after he hits the ground. Between the explosion and the ball bearings a lot of people will die. The other three will get out through the same door.'

'How many officers does Charney plan using?'

'Twenty-eight in four people carriers. Not exactly an overwhelming force.'

'You're right. Seven per target isn't overwhelming.'

'I haven't told you the really bad news,' said Bletchley.

'Oh, good! All this good news is making me wonder why we're here. So share the bad news.' Hunter looked grim.

'The area is on high alert.'

'By the DGSE?' Hunter frowned. 'I don't get it. I thought Charney wanted the operation kept secret until the last minute.'

'He does. The DGSE isn't responsible but the jihadists are. They have put themselves on high alert. We've real time imagery which I'll show you.' He pressed buttons and the picture changed. He pointed, 'See here and here and here. These men are armed. They are lookouts for the terrorist cell. As near as we can figure there are ten of them, maybe a few more.'

'This is ludicrous,' said Hunter, 'the General must just use over-whelming force.'

'He can't or won't. It's like I've told you, killing four jihadists is containable, many more and the screams of prejudice, Islamaphobia and all the rest will drown out any reasonable voices trying to explain the reality of what happened.'

'On the other hand if it all goes pear shaped,' said Hunter, 'the fallout could be enormous. Many innocent people could be killed. If this cell isn't stopped that is precisely what will happen.'

'That's an understatement,' said Dunston. 'Nick, if just one of these terrorists escapes from what we've heard about the vests there will be enormous loss of life. And I'm not talking about the Opera House but if one went off in a railway station or on a crowded train the death toll would be huge.'

Hunter stood up and paced around the room for a few seconds. 'Any ideas?'

Bletchley replied, 'The DGSE will hold the perimeter and we go in and do the job.'

'Dressed as followers of the faith and with the gas?' Hunter queried.

The gas was halothane, a synthetic and highly potent medicine that worked fast for a short period of time. It was also deadly if the wrong dose was administered. In this case the amount of gas was irrelevant. As far as Hunter was concerned the more gas the better.

Bletchley nodded. 'Easy deaths with no mess.'

'How close will the DGSE be?'

'Not close. They daren't. They don't want to spook anybody.'

'So why will they be there at all?' Hunter asked.

'If we are discovered and a gun battle does break out he assures us he'll come to our aid.'

'And you believe him?'

Dunston replied, 'Malcolm assures me Charney can be trusted to keep his word.'

'Charney was up front with the General,' said Bletchley, 'in that his men with the Police Nationale can deal with riots and operate en-masse, but they're not trained to deal with this kind of operation.' He added, 'We are.'

'I thought he was using DGSE officers only and not the police.'

'He is. Like we said, he's worried about jihadists in his own organisation but that worry is multiplied many times when it comes to the police where vetting isn't as stringent.'

'So if the PN is involved the likelihood is that knowledge of the operation escalates.'

'Not just escalates,' said Dunston, 'but he says he's sure the jihadists will find out about it.'

'So what's the plan?' Hunter asked.

32

Bletchley said, 'Matt and I will go in wearing thawbs and keffiyehs. Dave will take one of the rooftop points that we think gives the best overall coverage. Nick I want you to listen in on the transmissions from their apartment and tell us if anything happens.'

Hunter shook his head. 'It's better if I go in with . . .'

Bletchley interrupted him. 'I'm going in Nick. I made it clear to the General that this is my operation and I'll make the decisions. You can suggest and advise but at the end of the day I decide what's happening.'

Hunter didn't like it but he bit his tongue and shook his head. 'I agree you should go in,' he said mildly.

'So what are you talking about?'

'Matt is going because of his language skills in particular. His other talents go without saying. If anyone talks to you he'll be able to answer them. Correct?'

'Yes, correct.'

'My Arabic is good enough to deal with that but it may not be good enough to listen to and interpret what is said over the microphones. So it makes more sense for Matt to listen and direct us while we go in.'

'Oh! I thought . . .'

'I know what you thought. Something along the lines of protecting you because of Louise. Chris, there isn't a dog's chance in hell of that ever happening. You're a valued member of TIFAT and you'll be treated as such without fear or favour. Nothing in your personal life will interfere with operational decisions, even after you marry Louise. I hope that's clear.'

'Yes, Nick, sorry. Loud and clear.'

'Good.' Hunter grinned. 'Now I had better talk to the General.'

Hunter phoned Macnair and went over the operation in detail. 'Does General Charney know all this?'

'Only some. I'll give him a full briefing,' said Macnair. He broke the connection.

While they waited to hear from the General they studied photographs of the area, particularly those where the jihadists were staked out. Hunter's phone rang.

'Commander Hunter? This is Pierre Charney.'

'Hello, sir.'

'General Macnair has outlined the situation to me. Do you have a map of the area?'

'Yes, sir.'

The large-scale map was on the table.

'You see the building?'

'Yes, sir.'

'The roads run front and back and along the sides in a straight line for a hundred metres or so.'

'We know.'

'To the west and the south is clear land, while to the east and north are buildings, streets, branch roads and alleyways.'

'Yes, sir.'

'I'll have my men cover the open area to the west and south at least five hundred metres from the building. I cannot put a force of any kind in the other two sectors because they will be seen immediately.'

'That's what we figure.'

'I must emphasise if one of the terrorists gets out of the building he must be stopped before he reaches the labyrinth to the east and north.'

'We concur.'

'I am relying on you. Commander, I don't wish to sound melodramatic but I will go much farther. France is depending on you.

These vile monsters must be stopped but it must be with the minimum of bloodshed. In other words, four targets, four deaths.'

'We'll do our best, sir.' He didn't add it was highly unlikely. There were jihadists watching the place. They needed removing. Sometimes it was better for the higher command not to be given too much detail. They knew it all anyway, but they wanted to be in a position to deny all knowledge of events. Much like a politician.

'I am sure you will. Good luck, Commander.' The connection was broken.

There was nothing more to say. As usual the team settled down to a quiet couple of hours.

It was midnight when Dunston said, 'That's the terrorists settled down for the night. We should move in an hour. We have one more thing to do.' He took out a series of photographs that showed four different people from different angles so that not only their faces could be memorised but the shape of their heads and their jaw lines. 'These are the targets. Take a close look. I kept them until last so that they are fresh in your minds. We don't want to shoot the wrong people or miss the right ones.'

They looked closely at the photographs.

'We don't know who is who but I can tell you,' said Dunston, 'that their names are Alem, Jafar, Tariq and Ziad.'

Hunter pointed at two of the photographs, 'Both are thin, same aquiline nose and square jaws. They look Arabic and they look related.'

'We're pretty sure they're brothers, as are the other two.'

The other two were round faced, wore glasses and had thick lips. They were about as different from the first pair as it was possible to imagine.

'However, the four of them are of Iraqi heritage but first generation French. Which is what makes life for General Charney all that much harder. Killing a foreign terrorist is one thing, killing a homegrown one something else entirely.'

Hunter telephoned Charney. 'Sir, we're going in at around 01.00.'

'My men will be in position by 00.45.'

'Sir, one of my men speaks fluent Arabic and will be listening to what's going on in the apartment. He'll keep us informed as well as you using an open line.'

'Good. If we are needed rest assured I will come in with my men as quickly as possible.'

'Sir, thanks for that. I understood from General Macnair your minister . . .'

Charney interrupted him. 'Is an idiot. General Macnair knows that I will use my men if I need to. I think the idiom is I will not hang you out to dry.'

'We appreciate that, sir.'

Well, good luck Commander. I look forward to speaking to you later.' He didn't add, if you're still alive. That went without saying.

David Hughes was the first to leave. He was wearing dark clothing and had a cotton ski mask in his pocket to wear when he was in position. Underneath his jacket he wore a kevlar vest while he carried his rifle with silencer in a duffel bag slung over his shoulder. The weapon was broken down for ease of transport but he could assemble it in less than two minutes. He reported at 00.43 that he was ready and had a clear sight of three of the four doorways. The range was 400 metres. An easy shot for him to make. He also had a clear view of the roof.

At 00.45 Hunter and Bletchley left the hotel via a backdoor carrying holdalls. The night was warm and muggy, the sky cloudy, a thunderstorm in the air. In an alleyway around the corner from the hotel they dressed in ankle length thawbs with a white keffiyeh on their heads held in place by a black band around their brows.

Over the thawb they put on safari jackets underneath which were hidden a number of useful items. They were also wearing kevlar vests.

It took them 10 minutes to be in sight of the building. They stopped and stood at the corner of the building on the roof of which Hughes was staked out.

'Okay Matt, what's the score?' Bletchley asked.

'All quiet. They must be asleep. Or trying to get to sleep considering they think they haven't much longer in the land of the living. The General has reported that he and his men are in position.'

Hunter and Bletchley examined the area using heat-seeking binoculars. They'd discussed with Charney the advantage of shutting off the streetlights and even all the electricity in the area but decided that could warn the terrorists and perhaps give them the chance to escape. Under the circumstances they figured it was better to maintain the status quo. Give the terrorists a false sense of security.

Each of the two TIFAT officers carried silenced Glocks under their left armpits, they had Ka-Bars strapped to their left forearms, a second backup automatic strapped to their right calf and two flashbangs hanging on their belts behind their backs.

'See anything?' Bletchley whispered.

'No. But I've got an itchy feeling between my shoulder blades.'

'Me too, it's too quiet. Last night and the night before we reconnoitred this area and the place was pretty busy. Not heaving but people out and about and a few bars still open.'

'Bars? In a predominantly Muslim neighbourhood?'

'Yes. You know how deeply their hypocrisy runs.'

'True. But even at this time of the morning?' Hunter asked.

'Yes, even at this time. I spoke with the General about the social scene. Apparently this is the time the men like to congregate, chew khat and drink alcohol while discussing the end of the west coupled to holy jihad.'

Khat as both men knew was a drug that induced excitement, loss of appetite and euphoria. It was found and used mainly by people from the Horn of Africa and the Arabian Peninsula. The sale and use of the leaf was now illegal in most western countries.

'So where are they all?'

'Expecting trouble or just being careful?' Bletchley replied to the question with a question.

'If they had been expecting trouble we'd have heard something. Some chatter over the mics. Something. Anything.'

'Yeah, I think you're right. I think they are taking no chances. The way I read it is there are people guarding the approach to let the holy warriors get some rest.' There was no disguising the contempt in Bletchley's tone.

'Shall we go for a stroll?'

'Yep. It's a nice night for one.' Bletchley chuckled.

'Hang on do you see what I see?'

'The two men walking along the pavement? Think they're some sort of patrol?'

'We'll see if they walk around the building and back. At the speed they're going it'll take them six or seven minutes to get around.' They were in no hurry. They were used to long stakeouts and observing from afar.

'Oh, oh,' said Hunter. 'Look to the right. In that alleyway.'

'I've got them. Another two. I think its called loitering with intent.'

'How many more I wonder?'

'Nick the two men who have just appeared can't be the same ones. It's too soon.'

'Agreed.'

They stayed where they were for 12 minutes. Dunston was aware of the situation and kept General Charney in the picture.'

'It's your shout Chris, what shall we do first?'

'Take the two in the alleyway, stroll across the road and deal with each of the patrols in turn. We dump the bodies in the alleyway and head for the building to finish the job.'

'I wish I was as sanguine.'

'I'm not but we have to start somewhere.'

'You're right in all respects. Shall we go?'

The two men headed directly towards the alleyway. As they approached two people appeared.

Hunter greeted them in Arabic. 'As-salāmu alaykum.' Peace be upon you.

They were surprised when the person who replied was female. 'Wa'alaykumu s-salām.' And upon you, peace.

The anomaly to the greeting was the fact that the two people held automatics in their hands, which didn't suggest peace of any kind. Luckily the guns were pointing at the ground. Neither Hunter nor Bletchley hesitated. The two people were protecting four men who intended killing and maiming very many innocent people and they would inevitably know it.

Hunter said in Arabic, 'What are you doing out so late, my brother and sister?'

'We will ask the questions,' said the man. 'What are you . . .'

He got no further. The two officers drew their silenced Glocks and put a bullet through each of their heads. The two bodies flew backwards, landing in the dark alleyway.

'Saves having to move them,' said Bletchley. 'Let's go.'

They walked towards the building just as one of the patrols appeared. The patrol stopped and watched as Hunter and Bletchley approached. The same greeting was exchanged. This time, still ten metres away, the men from TIFAT raised and fired their Glocks twice. Their targets died instantly.

Hughes came over the airwaves. 'Better hurry. The other patrol is about to come around the corner.'

The two dead men were wearing thawbs but no head dress. Hunter and Bletchley snatched theirs off their heads and walked towards the other patrol, which had just rounded the corner.

'Matha hadath?' asked one of the men. What's wrong?

At about eight metres and before they could be recognised as not being the other patrol Hunter and Bletchley fired. Again two head shots killed the men instantly.

It took a few minutes but they carried the bodies into the alleyway and dumped them on the other two.

'Dave, how's it looking?' Bletchley asked the sniper.

'All clear.'

Dunston said, 'I can hear a phone ringing in the apartment. It's being answered. Oh hell! Something has happened. One of them is yelling to wake up. That they must get out. That the authorities are coming.'

33

'More bad news,' said Hughes, 'a mob is forming over to my right. I can count ten people. Might be more. They all seem to be carrying AKs.'

'Okay, we're going in,' said Bletchley.

'The bombers are already on the move,' said Dunston, 'coming your way.'

'No they're not,' said Hughes, 'one has just reached the roof.'

'Take him,' ordered Bletchley.

'Got him,' said the sniper, 'through the head. One down, three to go.'

Hunter and Bletchley went through the front door. They could hear footsteps coming down the concrete steps rapidly growing louder.

Before Hunter could say anything, Bletchley said, 'I don't like this. We're not on a suicide mission. Dave, we're coming back out. Nick, we go either side of the doorway and let them run out. We take them from behind. If we try here one of them might be able to explode a vest.'

They had seconds. They stepped outside and stood either side of the doorway. It was the one door that Hughes wasn't overlooking. They could hear people yelling a couple of blocks away.

'In position,' announced Bletchley.

Hunter stood one side and Bletchley the other, their backs against the wall. They held their Glocks at eye level. The door opened and two men ran out. They were half a dozen paces away when the two officers opened fire. Two double taps into the head. They didn't dare risk body shots for three reasons. The target could have been wearing a bulletproof vest, the round could have set off the explosives and finally death wouldn't have come quickly enough to ensure the explosives weren't detonated.

Where was the fourth target?

Hughes said, 'Nick, Chris, the fourth man just ran out the backdoor and is in the middle of the crowd. He's bent over. I can't see him to get a clear shot. General, you getting all this?'

'Yes.'

'What the hell happened, General?' Hunter asked.

There was a heavy sigh. 'I shall tell you later but I will tell you there was a third traitor at headquarters.'

Bletchley said, 'Okay, we're going after the fourth bomber.'

They ran after the crowd and caught up with them as they rounded a corner into a deserted street. There were eight men and three women. All of them, including the women, were carrying AKs. The bomber was in the middle of the crowd; bent over, partly hidden, just like Hughes had broadcast.

Bletchley said, 'Matt, General, we are ten metres behind a group of eleven. The target is in the middle, bent over and is not a clear shot. All of them are armed with AKs. General we need you here like now. If you can get ahead of them we might be able to stop them but it'll be open warfare.'

'Yes, yes,' the General spoke testily, 'I understand that. We are loading up now. Where are you?'

Bletchley looked at a street sign and told the General. 'I know it. We will be ahead of you in about two minutes. At the next junction there are only two ways to go, straight ahead or to the right. I will have both streets blocked off.'

'We're falling back,' said Hunter, grabbing Bletchley's arm and slowing him down.

'What's up?'

'We don't want to be too close. Trigger happy and frightened DGSE officers might just shoot one of us by mistake.'

The group was now 20 metres away and opening. Suddenly blue lights could be seen flashing ahead of them and the group stopped. Shots rang out as a number opened fire with their AK74 assault rifles. They were on fully automatic and the noise in the stultifying air was enough to waken the dead. There was a flash of lightening followed by what sounded like a series of explosions but was in fact a peal of thunder and the threatened storm hit hard. Visibility dropped significantly and within seconds everyone on the street was soaked to the skin.

The firing ceased, people were yelling in French and Arabic and then the group split.

Seven ran forward yelling, 'Allahu Akbar,' God is the Greatest, at the same time firing from the hip on fully automatic. The other five plus the bomber turned and began to run back the way they had come.

Hunter and Bletchley had no choice. They were standing next to a parked car and they knelt down beside it, took aim and began shooting. Luckily they had three things going for them. The storm, nobody expected them to be there and the fact they were using silenced weapons.

Hunter shot the first target he could see clearly in the chest, while Bletchley shot his target in the head. Both people went flying backwards. They recognised the bomber at the same time and fired directly at him, ignoring the other three for the seconds it took to pull their triggers.

The explosion killed the bomber and the three people with him. It broke a few windows and set car alarms wailing. But it wasn't a major explosion.

'What happened?' Bletchley asked Hunter.

'I've no idea. But I'm not going near there until the bomb squad has examined the body. The bomb hasn't detonated properly. It could be a misfire ready to go or a planned booby trap. Whichever it is I have no intention of finding out.'

'Me neither.'

The rain had muffled the shots being fired up the street but now they had ceased.

'General, you okay?' Hunter transmitted.

'Yes. I heard an explosion. What has happened?'

'I think it's a partial explosion so we need the bomb squad here asap. You also need to get men to the other three bombers but tell them to be careful. They should stay well back until the bomb squad has taken a close look. We can't be too careful. They may be booby trapped in some way even though I doubt it.'

'Nick, Chris, I'm going back to the hotel,' announced Hughes.

'Okay. We'll wait for General Charney,' said Hunter.

Now that the operation was effectively over Hunter was in command. That was a given. Neither man had to say anything. It was just the way things worked in the military.

They didn't have long to wait. One of the SUVs pulled up and the General alighted. He walked across to the two TIFAT officers.

'Not what I had hoped for,' he greeted them.

'No sir,' said Hunter, 'but not a bad operation given the circumstances.'

'My difficulty is I have a Muslim DGSE officer under arrest who will be tried for treason, participating in a crime to kill many people,' he waved his hand, 'and everything else the prosecutors can think of. He'll be going to jail for a very long time while the civil liberties crowd will yell stitch up, islamophobia, entrapment and anything else they can get away with.'

'I don't think it will come to that,' said Hunter, 'look at what's been happening. A lot of armed terrorists dead and four bombings stopped. The people will be celebrating.'

'No, they won't, Commander. They will want to know how it is we came so close to catastrophe. Why hadn't these terrorists been stopped sooner? How is it an officer in the DGSE was involved? And so on and so on.' The man sounded weary. 'I sometimes wonder why we bother.'

'Because there's nobody else,' suggested Hunter.

The General managed a slight smile. 'I guess you're right. Thank you gentlemen. I will arrange a clean up squad plus bomb squad. This won't be treated like a crime scene and I'll make sure there's no investigation.'

'On what grounds,' Bletchley asked, 'could there be an investigation?'

'Using unreasonable force. Why weren't people arrested to be put on trial? And so on.'

'Ah, yes, sir, I see.'

The two TIFAT men beat a retreat and twelve minutes later they were in the hotel with large scotches in their hands. While they sipped their drinks Hunter reported to General Macnair.

'Well done. A helo will pick you up at the Paris Air Base tomorrow at thirteen hundred. Don't be late.'

They arrived at the Capitaine Georges Guynemer Air Base in plenty of time. Their creds ensured they were taken through to a lounge where there were drinks and food. They settled on coffees and sandwiches. They'd been there about ten minutes when they were approached by a couple of men. One was distinguished looking, about 6ft tall with a pointed chin, slightly large nose and short grey hair. The other was 5ft 8ins with a round face and wore gold wire framed glasses.

He reminded Hunter of someone and then he realised who that was. It wasn't that he looked like the other person, it was that he had the same air of command about him as General Macnair. Hunter didn't hesitate. He stood and held out his hand to the man wearing the glasses.

'General Charney?'

The General looked taken aback for a moment. Hunter suspected that it was unusual for him to be identified as such a senior officer.

'Yes, how do you do,' Charney shook his hand and then did the same with the others.

'Let me introduce you to Romain Goulart, my number two.'

More handshakes followed.

'General Macnair told me I would find you here. I wanted to thank you personally.'

'It's our job, sir, no thanks are necessary.'

'I never believe that, Commander. We are in your debt.'

'What happened, sir? Any of your men hurt?'

The General sighed. 'Yes. One seriously but we think he will pull through.'

'And the terrorists?'

Here the General smiled. 'All dead. Incidentally, my men have checked over the devices those swine were wearing and believe me the death toll would have been horrendous.'

'Why did the fourth vest not explode properly?' Dunston asked.

Charney shook his head in wonderment. 'It was the merest of flukes. A bullet hit a wire and broke it. Part of the explosive worked while the rest was cut off. If the lot had gone up believe me we would not be talking now.'

It was a sobering announcement but then after ops wash-ups usually were. Frequently they went along the lines "But for the grace of God".

'Have you identified the bombers?'

'Yes. We have arrested members of their families, taken possession of their computers and mobiles and are currently doing in-depth investigations of everyone who is remotely connected to them. As you can appreciate, it's a massive task.'

'Has there been any fallout yet?' Hunter enquired then added hastily, 'I mean, political or media.'

'Some but so far nothing we can't handle. I suspect that will change. We'll have the right wing press screaming for blood, the left wing press demanding more aid and greater understanding of Muslim immigrants and politicians sitting in the middle watching which way the wind blows before they make any pronouncements.'

'Sounds about right sir. It's the same with us,' said Bletchley.

'Your great leader Winston Churchill had it right when he said democracy is the worst form of government, except for all the others that have been tried from time to time. So we have politicians to run things and the press to keep them honest.' He chuckled with genuine mirth while the others smiled.

'A contradiction in terms, sir,' said Hughes.

'Yes, that's for sure. I wanted you to meet Nicolas, as he will be your contact in future, day or night. We need closer liaison, something that hasn't been forthcoming for some time. It has happened of course, but people change, politicians change and before you know it barriers have been erected where there should be complete honesty and cooperation. Don't you agree Commander?'

'If you say so, sir,' was the polite reply.

The General chuckled again. 'I do say so but my words count for little. We are facing a really tough time in Europe and it is going to get a lot worse before it gets better. There is no political will to act against the extremists in the way we need to yet at the same time our politicians wring their hands and preach about the need for action. It is the same all over Europe. Britain has taken the right road quitting the European Union. With better control of your borders and the use of ECHELON you are much safer than if you had stayed. Our hope is that we all continue to cooperate at operational level.'

'There's no doubt about that, sir,' said Dunston. 'Cooperation is the only thing that'll keep us safe.'

The General nodded. 'Collectively safe, you're right. But as individual countries, if we are targeted, it will be a different picture altogether. Look what has already happened in Belgium, France and Germany without the terrorists using guns and explosives. With them we will really be in trouble unless we attack the source of the problem.'

Hunter nodded and then understood. 'You have the source?'

'General Macnair said you were very sharp. We have passed certain information to TIFAT that corroborates what you know. It's not new, merely confirmation.' He handed over a memory stick. 'I thought it would be a good idea if you delivered this personally to Malcolm. If I can help in any way then please let me know through Nicolas.'

Goulart handed Hunter a card. 'Here are my contact details. My mobile is with me twenty-four seven. My office always knows where to find me and if it is important and I am caught up in say a meeting and cancel your call you phone me straight back. I will know it is urgent and will answer.'

'Okay, thanks.'

'I think that is all, Commander. Ah, I think this is your pilot.'

A woman in green flying overalls was approaching. 'Commander Hunter?'

'That's me.'

'I'm to take you to Brize Norton, sir.'

'Right, thanks, lead the way.'

Handshakes were brief and then the team moved out. No customs and no baggage searches meant they could take what they wished with them. Which was just as well in view of what they were carrying.

The journey to Brize Norton was fast and smooth. They transferred to a RAF Atlas, the replacement for the venerable C130, for the flight to Edinburgh. Once there a helicopter took them to Rosyth. They were in HMS *Cochrane* by 18.00 in time for the bar to open.

34

Hunter was pounding the pavement. It helped him to think. He was rehashing the events of the past few days and thinking about what was still to come. The job wasn't even half done. Isobel and her team were working on the information they had supplied so far. Bank accounts, investments, personnel, there was a mountain of useful intelligence that had to be worked through, disseminated and passed to relevant bodies across Europe.

Choosing which information to pass to whom was the hard part. He and General Macnair had spent the past 48 hours trying to decide who to tell what. The problem was the course of action the various countries would be taking. The information they gave wasn't the sort that could be used in a court of law. Quite the opposite. It was the sort of information that any defence lawyer would have a field day starting with where did it come from, how authentic was the information and why should the court believe for a second that it applied to their client? Then would come the big question. Was it because the accused was a Muslim? And that was where the legal process would come unhinged.

His intention was to run 10k at a speed that would never have qualified him for the Olympics but one that would have enabled him to keep going for at least another 10k, if not more. He was running around the track circumnavigating the perimeter of the base, HMS *Cochrane* in Rosyth. It had once been a thriving Royal Naval establishment in the good old days when Britain had one of the most formidable navys in the world. But the place had been closed, as had many others around the country and had been earmarked for demolition. Then TIFAT had been created.

However, too many spotlights were being shone on TIFAT and too many questions were being asked about what they did and how they did it.

That thought caused him to glance at his watch. He put a spurt on. If he wanted to finish with a swim he needed to pull his finger out. The meeting was due in less than an hour.

He and the General had debated how to play it, even down to whether or not they should wear uniforms or civvies. They had decided on the latter. Hence, after his swim Hunter dressed in a light grey, single breasted, two-piece suit, white shirt and his naval club tie, dark blue with gold crowns. He walked into the conference room at 10.55, five minutes before the meeting was due to start.

It was a large room with a table at right angles to the door capable of seating 20 people comfortably. The walls were insipid green with the occasional waterscape that broke the monotony. At the end of the room a large window showed a view of the River Forth. The glass was an inch thick and could easily stop a rocket-propelled grenade. More importantly, it was lined with fine strands of wire that carried a continuous sound impulse that blocked out all known eavesdropping systems.

To his right sat five people, General Macnair and Isobel Sweeney, TIFAT's Head of Computer Operations, who were facing three strangers. Though strangers in name only. Hunter had read their files with some interest, particularly as he knew why they were there. He wasn't sure what the outcome would be but he and the General had tried to cover all the bases.

'Ah, Nick, welcome. Help yourself to coffee,' greeted Macnair.

'Thank you, sir.' Hunter crossed to the corner of the room and busied himself pouring a coffee, milk, no sugar. He carried the cup and saucer to the table and sat alongside Macnair.

'Let me introduce you,' said the General. 'On the left is Fred Cohen, in the middle is Ms Angela Wills and on the right is Eric

Saunders. 'This is Cmdr Hunter. He is the Operations Director for TIFAT.

For a moment Hunter wondered who would be the lead speaker and it came as no surprise when Angela Wills spoke.

'I know who he is.'

Somehow, it seemed to Hunter her tone implied a mixture of revulsion and dislike, or was it just his imagination knowing as he did what was about to happen? He sipped his coffee and looked closely at the woman. He knew she was 45 years old, married twice, divorced twice, no kids. She had short, fair hair with streaks of grey that she didn't bother to disguise. She was attractive but with a hardness around the mouth that Hunter figured put men off. Her white blouse underneath a blue jacket was buttoned up to her chin.

His antipathy towards her was instant and complete. He could feel the same emotion emanating from her and directed at him. He knew she had been a civil servant all her working life having left Oxford University with a first in politics and economics. Then nine years ago she had joined the Labour Party, been elected a Member of Parliament and was now a Shadow Minister in the Justice Department. Somehow her brief had been expanded and she was looking in more detail at the security services and how they operated. Nobody seemed to have realised what she was up to until it was too late. She had formed a sub-committee with powers to question members of the security services all the way to the top. And while other parliamentarians were looking around wondering what had happened she was doing an excellent job of undermining the fight against terrorism. Naturally it was all done in the name of human rights, support for which was rife amongst many Labour politicians in general and the Scottish National Party in particular. As far as the SNP was concerned the more disruption brought to bear on the Westminster parliament in particular and English lives in general the better.

Hunter glanced at the man seated on her left. Fred Cohen was 56 years old, obese and had been a Member of Parliament for the

Conservatives for over 18 years. To the layman's eye he looked like a mentally challenged sloth but Hunter knew the man to have been a highly regarded Queen's Counsel until he decided to enter politics. Being independently wealthy helped the transition from highly paid lawyer to inadequately paid politician.

The other man was a ferret-faced individual, with a beaked nose and dark eyes. Eric Saunders was an advisor to the Government who had been called in to help with the Brexit negotiations. The UK getting out of the European Union was the one single event that was controlling or influencing every aspect of British life and to a lesser extent that of the remainder of Europe as well.

The General wasn't going to make it easy for their visitors. He sat waiting patiently for Angela Wills to begin. Hunter watched in amusement as the silence dragged on for a few seconds. He took another sip of coffee and looked over the rim of his cup into the eyes of Fred Cohen who was staring back. Hunter smiled though there was little humour in it.

Cohen gave a slight nod as though he was acknowledging some sort of signal passing between them.

Angela Wills reached down, picked up a document case and placed it before her. She unzipped it and took out a stack of papers. She zipped the case closed and replaced it on the floor. There were ten identical reports in the pile and she handed out five of them.

Hunter glanced at the title - *Events following Brexit. Appendix 12, TIFAT.*

Wills cleared her throat importantly. 'This report is a summary of what we need to do with regards to TIFAT now Brexit is a reality. In spite of the fact that I think this is disastrous . . .'

'Wait a moment, Angela,' said Cohen, 'your opinion is not appropriate. We are here to discuss what has to be done, nothing more.' He looked across the table. 'As you know, we are from the new Brexit department set up by the Prime Minister to oversee and control our escape from the European Union.'

The man looked Hunter in the eye who got the message. The use of the word 'escape' meant Cohen was a 'Brexiter', Wills was a 'remainer'. What about Saunders?

'Thank you for that, Fred. Let me continue.'

Her voice gave Hunter the impression of fingernails being scraped down a chalkboard. If he was more sensitive he might have gritted his teeth. As it was he merely folded his arms and stared at her.

'As you know, we have been given the task of coming to many agreements with our European neighbours in what we should be doing after we finally leave the European Union. The new department is broken down into different sections, many overlapping, to negotiate and agree certain things. There are, in fact, many hundreds if not thousands of these agreements required. One of them is what we do about this place.' She disdainfully waved her hand around the room and then added, 'TIFAT.'

The three faces opposite looked at her with stony expressions. She moved restlessly. Hunter was gratified to see that she appeared to be showing signs of being intimidated.

'Yes, well, like I say, we have been commissioned to deal with the problem that TIFAT presents when it comes to our Brexit negotiations.'

'I don't understand,' said Macnair, 'when you say the problem that TIFAT presents. What problem? Would you care to explain?'

'Yes, well, I'm coming to that.' She hesitated.

If this is the best we can do when it comes to having someone negotiate on our behalf, thought Hunter, then God help us.

Cohen spoke. 'Gentlemen and lady,' he smiled at Isobel, 'I have a great deal of admiration for what this organisation has achieved in the past and could possibly achieve in the future. That is, if you were left to carry on with your job, but unfortunately we have a problem when it comes to our European neighbours.'

'Particularly the French, you mean,' said Hunter. He knew they were talking politically, not operationally. He had seen proof of that first hand with the DGSE.

Cohen nodded. 'As you say, Commander, particularly the French. Their Gallic pride clouds their judgement on many occasions and when it comes to TIFAT they are extraordinarily blinkered.'

'Except when they've needed us,' said Macnair.

'That may be the case,' broke in Angela Wills sharply, 'but the price of Brexit is the cessation of TIFAT.'

'The price of Brexit?' Hunter leaned forward and stabbed the table with his right index finger. 'What do you mean the price of Brexit? Brexit is our decision and ours alone. We will decide what we do, what we give and take. Not the French or any of the other European countries.'

'Commander, Commander, Commander,' said Wills in her most patronising voice, 'we operate in the real world. Not the make-believe fantasy world of guns and killings. But the world of law and order. Of right and wrong. And though not all my colleagues agree with me, the closure of TIFAT is a price well worth paying for certain other concessions we are able to negotiate.'

'Where do you stand in all this Mr Saunders?' Isobel looked at the little man in front of her. 'Are you wanting TIFAT shut down?'

'No! Most emphatically no! I've read some of the reports that have highlighted your exploits and even those that have been heavily redacted show how effective you have been at preventing terrorist attacks and in bringing culprits to justice.'

'That's just it,' said Wills excitedly, 'bringing them to justice. You do no such thing. You kill them. There's no inquiry, no court case, no justifying your actions. You decide who lives and dies and you just do it. Well the French in particular, supported, I may say, by the Swedes, Dutch and Danish are all in agreement.'

Hunter smiled, folded his arms and leant back in his chair. 'And what do they all have in common?'

'What?' Wills turned her gaze on him.

'You heard. What do they all have in common?'

'I fail to understand you.'

'Their governments are all left wing and are forever preaching a holier than thou attitude to human rights and the rights of the scumbags,' said Hunter.

'Be that as it may, the scumbags as you call them do have rights. Otherwise we are no better than they are.'

'For Christ's sake,' said Hunter in disgust, 'listen to you. We've heard that argument time and again until the next atrocity and then you scream for help and demand we do something about it and when we do you complain about human rights. You and your sort make me sick!'

'I won't be spoken to like this,' said Wills, glaring at the General. 'Are you going to allow this man to speak to me like that?'

Macnair shrugged. 'He's his own man. He is also a highly respected and a very,' he emphasised the word, 'highly decorated officer who has put his life on the line for his country many times.'

The two men with Wills nodded. Saunders spoke. 'I have read something of Commander Hunter's exploits and I can honestly say this country owes him a great deal of gratitude.'

Wills looked to her left and right before looking straight across the table at Macnair. 'So that's how it is.'

'How what is?' Macnair enquired.

'This whole thing has been a farce. This meeting. You have already colluded against me to do what? Make me look a fool?'

It was Isobel's turn to cross her arms and lean back. 'You didn't need our help to do that. And for the record I have never spoken to either of these men before in my life. General?' She turned her head and looked at him.

Macnair shook his head.

'Nick?'

Hunter did likewise.

'Gentlemen, have you spoken to us before now?' Isobel asked.

'No,' the two men replied simultaneously.

'We've been here before,' said Macnair. 'Other righteous politicians have done their best to have us shut down but without success. But then, you probably know all that.'

'This time it's different,' said Wills. 'I keep telling you, this is part of the Brexit agreement. In exchange, we will have certain agreements that are advantageous to this country.'

'Such as?' Hunter asked.

320

'None of your business but suffice to say it is to do with movement of people and trade as far as the City is concerned. I am not at liberty to tell you anymore at this stage.'

'What's the first duty of any government?' Hunter asked softly.

'What?' The woman frowned, staring at Hunter.

'I don't need to repeat myself. Just answer the question.'

'I'm not sure I understand what you're getting at.'

'Then I'll tell you,' he said. 'It is to keep its citizens safe. That is the first and foremost duty of any government. Everything else is peripheral. The economy, industry, taxation, you name it.'

'So? What's your point?' There was no disguising her irritation.

'My point is,' Hunter spoke with heavy emphasis, 'we are not fighting a conventional war. The enemy does not wear a uniform. Quite the reverse. Many of them are here and living amongst us. Let me ask you, Ms Wills, how many suspected jihadists do we acknowledge are living in this country and have some sort of control order on them?'

'I'm sure I don't know.'

Hunter looked at Cohen. 'You know?'

'Somewhere in the region of a couple of thousand.'

'Correct. And do you know how many people it takes to watch just one of them twenty-four seven?'

Saunders answered. 'About twenty.' Then he added, 'I found out during an MI5 and PM meeting. The Prime Minister was shocked to be told but it helped to put the issue of security into perspective.'

'What point are you trying to make?' Wills asked.

'The point Commander Hunter is making,' said Macnair, 'is that we cannot deal with the situation as it is now. And it is going to get a lot worse.'

'Rubbish!' The word was spoken with real venom. 'I am fed up listening to you people justifying your very existence. Killing indiscriminately, demanding more support that in effect means more money, personnel and all sorts of equipment.'

Saunders interrupted. 'The cost pales into insignificance when compared to the alternative.'

She turned her venomous gaze on him. 'You're supposed to be on my side. We are here to inform these people that this organisation is to close and close soon. Have you forgotten that?'

'No, we haven't. But it doesn't mean we like what we are doing. Fred and I volunteered to be here because we didn't want the General and his staff to think that we do not appreciate what they have done for us. The sacrifices they have made and the operations they have carried out is the stuff of legends and those of us who know more about it than you do are aware of the fact.' He looked across the table. 'I want to correct something. Angela has it in her head that we are here to close you down. Or at least give you notice. It isn't true. There have been moves behind the scenes to stop it happening but that's a political battle above our pay grade.'

'What are you talking about?' The woman shot back at him and then looked at Cohen. 'Is this true?'

'Yes. We all know where you stand and that's alongside the French and their allies. Hence the reason you were sent here.'

'Why is that?' Her tone was glacial.

'As a sop to the French politicians. The European chattering classes, so to speak. The PM has been delaying matters as much as she could but finally decided this meeting needed to take place. Well it has. And you chaired it. It will keep the Europeans quiet when we report that matters are in hand and that the situation as far as TIFAT is concerned has been satisfactorily dealt with. We will obfuscate, delay and pretend we are doing what they want. We will get the agreements we wish for and then tell our European neighbours, those who need telling, to go to hell.'

Wills looked wildly around the table. Her face had gone chalk white then she stood up. 'I will not have it. I will announce to the world what is happening. I will force the Prime Minister to follow the proper procedures to their proper end. And that is the closure of this place.'

'If you go public,' said Cohen, 'then we will release to the world the sterling work that has been done by TIFAT. In detail. The operations they have run, the lives they have saved and even name some of the men they have killed. The public will rightly call them heroes and saviours and every other clichéd word you can think of. I shall make it my business to ensure you're pilloried in the press and, for want of a better term, hung out to dry.'

Silence cloaked the room. Angela Wills dropped back on to her chair and sat as though turned to stone. Hunter looked at her dispassionately. She was everything he despised. Sanctimonious, convinced she was right about everything and she would be damned if she let facts get in the way of her prejudices. One thing though, he was surprised at the turn of events. He glanced at his boss. The General's face gave nothing away. He was not a good man to play poker with, but Hunter guessed he had known how things were going to go.

There was a knock on the door and before anyone could say anything it was flung open. Major James Carter stood in the doorway. He was TIFAT's Quartermaster, seconded from the Catering Corps.

Macnair looked at the man. 'Yes, Jim?'

'Sir, you'd better see this. A bomb has gone off in Trafalgar Square.'

35

At that moment a man with sergeant's chevrons on his arms appeared. 'Sir, I have a call holding for you. A lady by the name of Sarah Fleeting. She says it's urgent although I told her you were in a meeting.'

Macnair nodded. 'I'll be right there. Jim, see what? What bomb?'

'The news, it's live from London on the BBC.' The Major strode across the room, picked up a remote control, aimed it at a blank wall and pressed various buttons. A section of panelling dropped open to show a TV screen. It came to life on the BBC news 24 channel.

They watched in silence at the scene unfolding before them. Macnair watched for a few seconds before leaving the room and hurrying along the corridor to his office.

He grabbed the receiver. 'Elspeth? It's Malcolm.'

The head of GCHQ didn't bother with any greetings but got straight to the point. 'Have you heard the news?'

'The bomb in Trafalgar Square?'

'Yes.' Her voice was bleak, quivering with pent-up rage.

'I've just been told. Nick, Isobel and three people from London are watching the news even as we speak. How bad is it?'

'Before we get to that, is one of them Angela Wells?'

'Yes. How did you know?'

'Come on, Malcolm, this is GCHQ. I'll talk to you later about her after she's gone. Are the other two Fred Cohen and Eric Saunders?'

'Correct.'

'They're amongst the good guys.'

'So I've discovered. Okay London, how bad?'

'Not as bad as it could have been. We'd picked up some traffic but, as you know, the terrs have become very cute at hiding what they really mean under a layer of innocuous statements. One of the ways we can identify something is going down is the utter randomness in what they're saying. That's a giveaway. Gobbledygook in, meaningful message out. We knew something was going to happen but didn't know what, where or when. Then one of Five's operatives got lucky.' Sarah was referring to one of the officers working for MI5, the UK's security service inside the country's borders. 'He was praying at Finsbury Park Mosque.'

'That bed of radicalised extremists!' Macnair interrupted.

'Yes, well, not so much nowadays. But he heard a couple of worshippers speaking together. He was directly behind them and picked up some of what they were saying.'

'What was that?'

'He heard Trafalgar Square, today and during the Dhuhr.'

The Dhuhr was the noonday prayer, said around noon but after the sun had passed its zenith. Hence the actual timing of the prayer varied across the world, even in the countries with the same time zones.

'When did he hear it?'

'It must have been after 11.30. He left immediately and phoned it in to Thames House.'

'Surely there was time to evacuate the square?'

Sarah sighed. 'You would bloody well think so, wouldn't you?'

'What went wrong?'

'The person who took the call passed it up the line.'

'So?'

'There was nobody to actually pass it to. She ended up leaving messages on half a dozen answering machines.'

'Please tell me you are making this up.'

'No, I'm afraid it's true. Line managers were all in a meeting discussing what to do in the event of a terrorist attack. This is particularly relevant when you consider what's happening across Europe.'

'And ironically an attack takes place on the same day at the same time?' Macnair trailed off while Sarah remained silent. After a few seconds he said, 'Oh, Christ. The attackers must have known about the meeting.'

'We think so.'

'An accidental info leak or a traitor working for the Islamists?'

'At the moment we can't tell. We have our suspicions and as soon as we know anything we'd better have a little private chat.'

'Sure, anytime, you know that. You still haven't said how bad it is.'

'Ah! There I have some relatively good news. The woman who took the original call used her commonsense and phoned SO15.' The Counter Terrorism Command of the Metropolitan Police were renowned for operating effectively under the most trying of circumstances, mainly caused by their political masters kow-towing to political correctness and hysterical mass-media. That was the way the Deputy Assistant Commissioner described the constraints affecting how SO15 worked. It was a sentiment echoed by every law-enforcement, counter-terrorism organisation in the democratic world.

'So what happened?'

'It took a little while for the message to get through to the right officer. Someone with the authority to hit the 'go' button. Officers were deployed, the roads, underground and pedestrian ways were closed and people were quickly evacuated.'

'So no casualties?'

Sarah sighed. 'There wasn't enough time to do a really effective job.'

'How many?'

'They're still counting. At least a dozen dead and the same again injured. Some of the injured won't make it.'

Macnair let loose with a string of expletives.

'If we hadn't been warned the number of dead would have been much greater. As it was it was one hell of a blast.'

'A suicide bomber?'

'Yes. PE plus ball bearings.' The boss of GCHQ was referring to the terrorists' use of ball bearings packed into plastic explosive. This simple device trebled the effectiveness of the explosion.

'Anyone claiming responsibility?'

'Yes, but it's too early to be sure who was really responsible.'

Macnair knew that only too well. When an atrocity was committed there was no end to those people who wanted to claim responsibility. Separating the perpetrators from the lunatics who saw some sort of glory in such an atrocity took a little time, albeit with luck, hours not days.

'Surely SO15 can deal with whatever needs doing?' Macnair kept his tone even, not showing any of the frustration he was feeling.

'We may have a cell for you.'

'Why would you want us involved? Surely SO15 can handle it.'

'This cell is a little unusual.' She hesitated.

'Go on.'

'Have you heard of Lawyers for Justice?'

'No. Who are they?'

'A firm of lawyers based in Leicester. They're the ones who have been making life miserable for ex-military personnel, accusing them of all sorts of illegal activities in Iraq, Afghanistan and Syria.'

'Sorry, I do know who you mean. I just hadn't made the connection. It all comes under the heading of human rights.'

'You've got it. Well, we've had our eye on them for sometime. All terribly hush-hush of course. If they knew that we were paying particular attention to them they'd have a court order against us before you could blink.'

'Haven't they had some success along those lines stopping the media reporting about them?'

'Yes. They are a very astute bunch of people.'

'How are they funded? Legal aid?'

'Mainly. So far spurious claims of mistreatment by our soldiers have cost the taxpayer millions and ruined the lives of a number of our lads who were already suffering from PTSD.'

'Ruined how?'

'Broken marriages, alcoholism and two suicides.'

'God Almighty. Why haven't they been stopped?'

'They haven't stepped outside the law.'

'Then why are you telling me about them?'

'Because now they have. They not only claim for legal aid but are also funded by the Saudis. Something we have only just discovered. They have cleverly hidden payments to their firm behind dummy companies and clients making it all appear above board.'

'So arrest them.'

'We can't.'

'Illegal collection of evidence.'

'Precisely. You know no court in the land would give us a warrant to eavesdrop on one of their own, no matter how obnoxious. However, we now know they have regular contact with a man by the name of Hussain al-Baghdadi and we are sure they have been passing information from him to people in this country.'

'Not just information but money as well.'

'What do you mean? What do you know about it?'

'It's to do with an operation we had in Sicily and France recently.'

'Was the French op near Marseilles by any chance?'

'Yes. Isobel has been working on information we got hold of, which I'll share with you later.'

'Fair enough.'

'When you say passing information are you talking personal contact?'

'Yes. The jihadists are becoming more wary. They don't trust e-mail, phones or dare I say it, old-fashioned faxes. However, it seems al-Baghdadi is convinced we wouldn't dare spy on people working in a law firm, especially people with such high profiles. Under normal circumstances he's probably right, only these aren't normal circumstances. Therefore they are using couriers to pass information back and forth.'

'So what can we do for you?'

'We're using our standard systems, but now we want internal eavesdropping as well.'

'I think you should just hand over the case to us.'

'Because of Marseilles and Sicily?'

'Yes.

'I'm not sure.'

'Don't you have enough to do?'

'Sure. My desk is groaning under the weight of open files.'

'I thought everything was digitalised nowadays.'

'It is. Just a figure of speech.'

'Sarah, we're following a smuggling snake, trying to get to the head. We're close. From what you've told me I think this law firm is part of that snake. Also, in the meantime this firm will still be accusing our forces of atrocities that did not take place and continuing to make their lives a misery.'

'I know.'

'What has all this to do with the explosion in Trafalgar Square?'

'We're pretty certain LFJ as they like to be referred to, knew about the attack and we're pretty sure they know about more in the pipeline. At this stage we don't have enough evidence to get a warrant. Besides which, if we apply for one, we will have the perennial problem of showing why we need it. That comes down to the use of ECHELON and all that entails.'

'There's nothing they can do about that any longer.'

'They can still go to the European Court of Justice and create holy hell.'

'But it has no jurisdiction.'

'That won't stop them from causing righteous trouble.'

'You're right. Can you send me a breakdown of the staff at LFJ? Names, addresses, phone numbers, e-mail addresses, the lot. Saves duplication of effort.'

'Will do. It'll be with you in the next hour or so.'

'Okay, thanks. If there's nothing else, I'd better get back to this meeting.'

'Malcolm before you do, let me tell you something. The Europeans are creating holy hell to have TIFAT disbanded. The usual human rights claptrap. Here in the UK Angela Wills is leading the attack against you.'

'So I gathered. But you know we've been here before.'

'Yes, but that was internal politics. Lib Dems and other leftwing nonentities flexing their muscles on a holier than thou crusade.'

'So what's different? It's just the same idiots but from across Europe.'

'In many respects you're right. All I'm saying is tread carefully with her.'

'Okay. To be honest I'm not sure what I can do. If the powers that be decide we need to go then I guess we're gone.'

'Yeah, sure. Which means you have an alternative plan. Let me guess, re-locate to the good old US of A?'

'It's an option. I'll speak to you later.'

'Okay and thanks . . . Oh hell. Wait a second.'

Macnair heard her say, 'Thanks. Malcolm? There's been a second explosion in Sloane Square. Outside the Royal Court Theatre. Many casualties. I'll have to get back to you.' She hung up and Macnair replaced his receiver.

He walked slowly back to the conference room and opened the door. Jim Carter had quit the room. Angela Wills was pontificating on the rights of the perpetrators to be identified, arrested and tried.

It was too much. 'Shut up,' said the General, 'I'm sick to death of hearing your rubbish. There's been a second attack.'

36

Four of the remaining people looked at him in surprise. Only Hunter kept a straight face.

The General leaned on the table, on his fists, his eyes staring into those of Angela Wills. She looked back at him like a rabbit caught in the gaze of a venomous snake.

'More people have been killed. You've heard it all before. The security services have to be lucky all the time, the terrorists only once.'

Wills hadn't earned her reputation as a hardass politician for nothing. She was as tough as old boots when she needed to be, which was all the time as far as she was concerned. She leaned forward. 'I will not be spoken to like that,' she hissed. 'I will do all in my power to expedite the closure of this place and also do my best to have you and everyone who works here arrested for crimes against humanity. Or,' she floundered and then said, 'Or not carrying out due process. Something. Anything.'

'How do we stop what's happened?' Hunter asked reasonably.

She turned her gaze on him as though looking at a poisonous reptile. 'I told you. You follow due process. You arrest people, you obey the law, you take people to court, present the evidence, get convictions, place the perpetrators in jail.'

Fred Cohen broke in. 'Listen to you. Those are the arguments made last week in the European Union Parliament.'

'MEPs actually clapped,' she said.

'They're idiots,' replied Cohen. 'They don't live in the real world.

They live in a bubble of privilege that has never existed before. What does a few deaths matter as long as we can take the so-called moral high ground? Well, ask the families of the people killed and injured. See what they think.'

Macnair said, 'I am now going to show you something. Isobel.'

Isobel picked up a remote control aimed it at the wall and another section of panelling dropped open.

'I am going to share this with you. It is highly sensitive information and classified above secret.' He didn't trust Wills not to reveal what he was about to tell them but he felt he had no choice. Under the guise of parliamentary privilege she could get away with revealing Britain's most important and intimate secrets. Such was the nature of democracy in the UK.

Hunter turned his chair to watch while the other three sat glued to what was being shown.

'This is a list of some of the operations we have been involved in over the past two years. Many are missing and I can assure you these are not the most serious or damaging.'

The General ran through operation after operation. He explained the essence of what had happened but missed out one vital ingredient – the death toll. It took ten minutes. 'Any questions?'

As he expected, Wills asked the question. 'How many people did you kill? Or more precisely, have killed?'

'Wrong question,' said Hunter.

She looked at him. 'I don't think so.'

'It is. You should be asking what is your estimation of the number of lives saved?'

'And that's what?' There was no disguising the scorn in her voice.

'You can work it out for yourself. It's in the hundreds of thousands when you consider the devastation the dirty bombs could have wreaked.' The Commander sat leaning back in his chair the nonchalant look in sharp contrast to the anger he was feeling.

'That's what you say!' Wills had regained her composure and was ready to go on the attack.

'No it isn't,' Hunter shook his head. 'It's what other agencies say. We have numerous reports from all across the world on the subject of what we prevented and what could have happened. I take it you know about the summit meeting in Washington? Hosted by the President?'

'No. Why should I? Is it important?' There was no hiding the sarcasm in the woman's tone.

Macnair spoke. 'You have made it your business to interfere with the running of the security services in this country to an extent that is damaging, so you should know before you say any more.'

Isobel answered. 'It dealt with the certainty of the Islamic fundamentalists getting their hands on a dirty bomb.' She spoke softly, staring at the woman opposite. 'Not possibly or probably but certainly. Have you thought through those consequences?'

'I don't believe it. It's rubbish and you know it. Just like the fiction we have just been shown. Exaggerated and dramatised you are playing to people's fears. You are talking about something that will never happen merely to justify your existence and, more importantly, the methods you use.'

'You really are a stupid woman, aren't you?' said Hunter with obvious scorn.

'What? What did you say?' She didn't wait for Hunter to repeat himself. 'How dare you speak to me like that!' Her head turned left and right. 'Fred, Eric, I refuse to stay here and be insulted.'

Fred Cohen placed his hand tightly on her arm and said, 'I'm afraid you must. The Prime Minister knows all about this meeting. She has said Brexit means Brexit but it also means there will be no concessions on certain items. One of them is TIFAT. It's here to stay or until a British Government, along with a dozen others in the free world, decide otherwise.'

'You mean like the Americans.' Angela Wills' antipathy for all things American was well known in Whitehall.

'Of course he means the Americans,' said Saunders.

'I've told you, the rest of Europe wants to see you gone.' She addressed herself at Macnair and then sat back with her arms folded. 'And I'm here to tell you it's going to happen.'

There was a knock on the door and the same sergeant opened it. 'GCHQ again, sir.'

'I'll be right there. Talk some sense into this woman.' Macnair rose to his feet, turned and left the room.

The others looked at Wills in silence. After a few seconds she shifted uncomfortably. Hunter turned to Isobel, 'Please put the TV back on.'

Isobel used the remote and BBC 24 lit up the screen. '. . . second bomb has exploded in Sloane Square, outside the Royal Court Theatre. People were queuing to buy tickets and the pavement around was packed with people. So far all we know is that someone wearing the burka had been standing in the queue before the explosion and appears to have been at the centre of the blast. So far the reports are unconfirmed.' There was more of the same. The reporter didn't stop talking although there was nothing new to add.

Hunter reckoned verbal diarrhoea was taken to a whole new level when a microphone was placed in the hands of a reporter. Macnair returned.

He sat down heavily in his chair and said, 'Over fifty casualties, dead and wounded.'

'My God,' said Angela Wills, speaking for them all.

Silence reigned for a few seconds and then Isobel asked, 'Do we know who did it? Which group is claiming responsibility?'

Macnair shook his head. 'It's too early. We're trying to separate the facts from fiction and it's taking time. Ms Wills, I am going to spell something out for you. TIFAT will operate as usual and work within its mandate. In case you need reminding, it is to take the war to the terrorists. I will do so with every resource at my command. We do not arrest people. We do not put them on trial. Matters are too urgent for such niceties. Your task is to pretend, and I emphasise the word, pretend to work with the EU mandarins as though you are preparing the way to remove TIFAT as part of the Brexit deal. It won't happen. You will obfuscate, you will prevaricate and you will pretend that with Brexit, TIFAT will no longer exist.'

'What good will that do?' Wills' tone was surprisingly more reasonable.

Macnair didn't believe it for one moment. 'We will continue to work to protect this country and other nations from Islamist attacks. We will operate the same as before.'

She nodded, as though satisfied. Her half smile said one thing, her eyes another.

'Look, Ms Wills,' said the General, 'myself and the people working here understand where you're coming from. We are dealing with amoral people the likes of which have rarely been seen before. If they wore uniforms we wouldn't hesitate to put a bullet in their brains. As it is,' he shrugged, 'we are fighting with both arms tied behind our backs.'

It was the turn of Angela Wills to shrug. 'It cannot be helped. The rule of law must prevail.'

'Whose law?' asked Hunter. 'Our laws work because we are all of a similar mind when it comes to those laws. If you don't believe in them, if you're not prepared to accept them, then they are of no use. That's why we are not being protected from the jihadists. There's enough information out on the Internet from Muslim fundamentalists who make it clear they wish to take the world back to the time of Muhammad. Total rubbish of course, but nonetheless it is what they are trying to do. WMDs, chemical, bacteriological and nuclear based are what they want. We cannot stop them by arresting them. What witnesses are there to their crimes? Where do they stand trial? Would it be a jury trial? How long would each one take? Where would we put them if they were found guilty? In the meantime they become martyrs and a rallying point for the morons who want the same thing. You people haven't thought it through. You can talk about the rule of law, the ethics of what we can and cannot do, human rights and all the rest of it but,' he raised his right index finger in the air, 'you have no actual answers. And when we give you them they offend your sensibilities. We're past the point of pandering to those sensibilities if we are going to keep the world safe. And let me tell you something else,' Hunter leaned forward, his fists on the table, clenched, wanting to give the woman in front of him a good shake, 'we're not just talking about Europe or the USA. Supposing a dirty bomb explodes in Jakarta, or Abuja, or the Philippines? What then? Worldwide recession would be the least of it. Real warfare would erupt across the planet. There would be wars the consequences of which would be unimaginable.'

'You can't possibly know that.' Wills was back to her usual attitude, unable to keep up the pretence of listening to anything the others had to say.

'Yes we can,' said Macnair in a quiet voice. 'The intercepts we've received have made it clear what the jihadists wish to do. And that's on top of the announcements found all over social media. You people need to get real. You need to come into the real world and smell not the roses but the dung.'

'I want to ask you something,' said Hunter, 'and I'd like an answer, please. How do we stop the people smugglers? How do we stop what is happening in Calais and other European ports? How do we ensure the safety of ordinary people travelling back and forth by car and lorry? I'm not asking you for some sort of morality answer, I'm asking you for a pragmatic answer that will ensure the safety of innocent people.'

Silence blanketed the room. Five pairs of eyes stared at Angela Wills and she squirmed. She said nothing.

'Please, Angela,' said Saunders, 'it's a reasonable question. What do we do? Tell us what you and those who you represent wish the security services to do.'

'Arrest the traffickers. Put them on trial. Obey the laws we've developed over the centuries.'

'You're not listening, Angela, 'said Cohen. 'These people not only don't respect our laws they reject them. Tell us what we can do. It's a simple question.'

'That's the job of the security services,' she said, her cheeks tinged with anger.

'You say it's up to us and yet when we give you our solution you tell us we can't do it yet, at the same time you don't tell us how to stop the attacks. How do we save the lives of innocent people? And let's not forget the attacks are indiscriminate.'

There was a knock on the door and Jim Carter walked in. 'We've just got the info from the Met,' he greeted them. 'It looks like the death toll is sixty-three and rising. Dozens more have been badly injured.' His face was as bleak as his words. 'Many have lost limbs, had their faces pulped, the usual.'

'Thank you, Jim,' said Macnair. He turned his gaze back to the Labour MP. 'Well Ms Wills, how do you think we should react?'

There was another knock on the door and this time Leo Kinski came in. He was one of two people who ran Isobel's IT department. Short, overweight but working to lose the fat, he was a genius when it came to computers. 'Sir,' he handed Macnair a piece of paper, 'Sarah said it was urgent.'

'Damnation!' The General screwed up the paper and looked at Angela Wills with real venom.

37

'What is it, sir?' Hunter asked.

'I'll tell you later. Right Ms Wills, as I expected, you don't have any answers. Even so you're still not listening to what we are saying. That goes for the other politically correct, left wing individuals in the European Union Parliament as well as our own. You seem incapable of acknowledging what we are facing and if you do, you have no solutions to offer.'

'Whatever we do has to be under the conditions imposed by the European Court of Human Rights,' she argued.

Macnair shook his head slowly. 'You just don't get it. All courts have been created to protect the citizens of the country in which they operate. The laws they impose are man made. That means we can and should create laws to suit us, the ordinary people. If any law isn't working then it should be changed. Given the problems we face today what we have, self-evidently, isn't fit for purpose. So we need to make changes to reflect those problems and how they should be addressed. That means there will be no habeas corpus and we deal with the terrorists using maximum force.'

'Huh! That's just another euphemism for murder.'

'Call it what you like. We are rapidly running out of options,' said Cohen, 'and the General is right. We need to take tough action. Brexit has given us that opportunity. We can control our own borders, allow into the country the people we want and get rid of those we no longer see as desirable.'

'What about a person's right to a home life?' she countered.

'What about it?' Hunter asked. 'You know it's being abused to a degree that was never meant to happen. It's actually making a laughing stock of British law not only in the UK but also across the world. We all have some idea of the number of criminals we have living here all screaming blue murder about their human rights and the right to a family life. We have the reputation of a country that protects criminals no matter how vicious the crimes they've committed.' He shook his head. 'We're not getting through to you, are we?'

Standing up Hunter turned to the General, 'I'd better get back to work, sir. Are we wanted?'

Macnair shook his head. 'No, not yet. I'll let you know if we are.'

Hunter left the room and returned to his office. He busied himself with his coffee machine for a few minutes, replacing the coffee beans and filling the water reservoir. He was as mad as hell. Dealing with people like Angela Wills brought out the worst in him. The refusal of her and her kind to admit they were wrong was playing into the hands of the terrorists. He thought of it as a war where the security services were using a toothpick while the enemy was using a cricket bat. He admitted to himself it was an idiotic way of thinking about the war on terrorism but Matt Dunston had once said the same thing to him and he hadn't been able to get it out of his mind. In essence, it summed up what they were facing. Only in reality it was more a pea-shooter versus a semi-automatic. Yet in theory the security services ought to have been winning. It was what General Macnair's original paper had spelled out. That was the reason TIFAT had been established in the first place and yet there were forces doing their damnedest to undermine the organisation at all levels. Having TIFAT shut down was the pinnacle of those ambitions.

On the wall between the two windows that looked out over the River Forth was a painting by Geoff Riley titled *Old Man of Hoy*. As always, the painting gave him a feeling of calm. It showed the sun setting behind the rock, the sea calm, and all the splendour of the place captured on canvas. His cousin, Richard Griffiths, had introduced him to Geoff Riley's work, and in Richard's words Riley was a real artist. Not a pretend and pretentious one who called an unmade bed or a chunk of meat in a glass jar filled with formaldehyde art. As soon as he had the time he'd visit the gallery where Riley exhibited his paintings and buy a couple more. From the artist's website he had identified a painting titled *Trawler Harvester* that he fancied. It would look good hanging on the bulkhead of the saloon onboard the 50ft luxury motor sailer he now lived on. It was berthed at the jetty attached to the base and gave him a feeling of being divorced from the place while being quickly available in the event of a crisis. He took an appreciative sip of his coffee.

The time was 15.45 and he debated with himself whether to visit his parents in Balfron. As a compromise he telephoned the house. It was answered after only a few rings.

'Four four double one double six.'

Hunter grinned. The voice made up his mind for him. 'Hi Louise, I didn't expect you to be home.'

'Oh, it's you.'

'Who were you expecting?'

'You know who.'

'Wouldn't he ring you on your mobile?'

'I guess so. Sorry, dear brother, it's nice to hear your voice.'

'Yours too. I was wondering whether to come home or not. Seeing as you're there I will.'

'Lovely. What about Chris?'

'He's got the weight.'

'What does that mean?'

'He's duty officer. Somebody has to run this place when the working day is over.'

'I guess.'

'How long are you in Scotland for?'

'Two days. We flew in from New York this morning.' Louise was an airline pilot and had recently been promoted to Captain. The fact that the airline was Griffiths International Airlines, GIA, and hence her family owned a chunk of shares didn't bother her one iota. What was the point of nepotism if you didn't take advantage of it?

'Does Chris know you're here?'

'Yes. I texted him.'

'He may be trying to swap with someone.'

'I hope so. Should I tell Mum and Dad you're coming home? It'll give Mum time to prepare the fatted calf.'

'Tell her not to go to any trouble.'

'As if! You know Mum. Beef Wellington or b-b-q?'

'Are you asking me?'

'Yes. I'll let her know.'

'Dad likes a b-b-q and so do I.'

'Okay. I'll nip up to the butcher's and get some decent steak. See you soon.'

Hunter changed into black jeans, a white, open-necked, short sleeved shirt and his cream safari jacket. He left his office and was walking along the corridor when the door to the conference room opened. The general was leading their visitors towards the main door. Angela Wills was trailing the others by a few metres. Seeing her brought his anger back to the surface.

He took a side door and headed to the car park. He didn't need any gear; his parents still kept his room for him. He zapped open the doors to his Range Rover Sport climbed in and placed his Glock in the special container in the left-hand armrest. Being armed was a relatively recent innovation after members of TIFAT had been targeted by terrorists. Although they tried to keep a low profile – a very low profile in fact – their name and activities were becoming known. This was mainly due to the big mouths and loud voices of politicians such as Angela Wills.

He started the engine and was about to back out when he heard his name being called.

'Nick! Room for me?'

Bletchley was hurrying towards him, his overnight grip in his hand.

'Sure. I take it you changed duties?'

'Yeah. Matt's taken the weight.'

'Have you told Louise?'

Bletchley grinned. 'I prefer to surprise her.'

They drove through the main gates and headed for the A985. They travelled in companionable silence until they reached Kincardine and were crossing the bridge over the River Forth.

'What was the meeting about?'

'I wondered when you'd ask.' Hunter filled him in.

'What a bitch,' Bletchley summed up what Hunter was thinking.

'Yep. You got it in one.'

They passed smoothly along the M876 and then on to the M9.

'You'd better tell Louise you're coming. She's buying steak for a b-b-q.' He paused. 'On second thoughts, don't bother. Knowing her and Mum they'll have enough to feed a rugby team.'

They reached Junction 10 and headed up to the roundabout where they took the second left on the A84. They slowed down behind a stream of cars, Hunter holding back his impatience.

Hunter glanced at Bletchley and said, 'Okay, tell me what's up.'

'What do you mean? Nothing's up.'

'Yes there is. You're beginning to look more nervous by the minute. Like a virgin on her wedding night who's been told horror stories of what to expect.'

There was silence for a few seconds then Bletchley reached into his jacket pocket. He took out a small box and flipped it open. He held it up and Hunter glanced at it.

'So you're popping the question?'

'Er, yes but after I speak to your father.'

Hunter chuckled. 'He'll tell you to ask Louise.' He paused and then thought about it. 'No, you're doing the right thing. He's a bit old fashioned that way. He'll give you his permission and then you can ask her. I suggest you go down on one knee. But to save embarrassment do it in private.'

'Embarrassment? Do you think she'll say no? You know her better than anyone in the world. What do you think?'

'I shouldn't tell you this but if you don't ask her soon she'll probably brain you.'

Bletchley's smile threatened to split his face in two.

They passed the Blair Drummond Safari Park and next turned left down Kirk Lane. There was no traffic and Hunter put his foot down, winding the car up to 70mph for a few minutes. They turned right onto the A811, a single lane straight road with plenty of opportunities to pass any vehicle dawdling along. There were quite a few.

They passed through the tiny village of Arnprior and then Buchlyvie. Minutes later they turned left on the A875 and up the hill. Hunter slowed down significantly as they turned the tight left-hand bend and hit the 30mph sign, then down to 20mph. Hunter liked driving fast but was punctilious about not speeding in built up areas.

They went through the zigzag of bends as they reached the outskirts of Balfron and drove down the hill known as Buchanan St. Just before they reached Shearer's, the Esso garage, Hunter turned right into the driveway of his parents' house.

They rounded the back of the house and stopped. The house was a significant white structure with an extension at right angles the width of the kitchen. The extension consisted of an en-suite bedroom while downstairs was a sitting room with glass walls.

His parents and sister were seated at a wooden table, glasses of white wine in front of them. When they saw the car they each broke into a smile.

When Louise saw Chris she leapt to her feet with delight and hurried around the bonnet of the car just as he stepped out. She gave him a peck on the lips and a hug.

'I wasn't expecting you.'

He hugged her back and replied, 'I managed to swap my duty. Hello, sir, Sian,' he nodded at them.

Tim and Sian Hunter had stood up to welcome the two men. Before they could a golden labrador came out of the kitchen, looked around as though to ask what's going on and why are you disturbing my sleep, saw Hunter, woofed and rushed forward. The dog put his paws on Hunter's chest and tried to lick his face.

'Winston,' Hunter rubbed the dog's neck, 'how are you boy? Good dog. Down you go.'

The dog reluctantly dropped to the ground but nudged Hunter who knew the dog wanted his ears tickled. Hunter obliged.

'Mum, Dad,' he smiled at his parents.

His mother was in her early sixties, was 5ft 8ins tall, had an oval face with blue eyes. She was still slim with black, wavy hair streaked with grey that just covered her ears. She was a striking woman with a personality to match. His father was a couple of inches shorter than his son, also slim and fit looking though he never did any exercise worth the description. He claimed that being a member of the bowls club across the road was exercise enough. He had brown hair, grey at the temples, brown eyes and a dimple in his chin. Both his children took after their mother when it came to the colour of their hair and eyes. Tim Hunter joked that was because his genes didn't dare go up against the genes of the Griffiths' family.

His mother kissed Hunter's cheek and hugged him while he and his father shook hands behind her back.

Winston continued to nudge his leg wanting attention.

They sat down around the table while Louise went to the kitchen for a couple of beers from the fridge. The setting was similar to a month earlier when Hunter had first met Bletchley and agreed to help him transfer from the SBS to TIFAT. He had acknowledged to General Macnair that it had been a good move.

The coals were lit, the beers refreshed a few times and then the steaks were cooked. Tim Hunter did the cooking. He had marinated the meat in a sauce of his own making and was adroitly flipping the steaks while everybody talked. As always it was on world politics with an emphasis on Europe and Islamic terrorism. When altogether, Hunter played down any role he had in affairs of a military nature but that was for the benefit of his mother. Once he and his father were alone he opened up and told him more about what was happening in the world as well as whatever he'd been up to.

The steaks were excellent, the baked potatoes just right and the salad with a Mediterranean dressing healthy. While his mother, father and sister swapped to red wine he and Bletchley stuck to a couple of bottles of cold beer, which they made last.

After they had finished eating they sat around talking for an hour or two. The two TIFAT officers drank coffee while the other three stuck with wine. Finally it was time to say goodnight and while Louise and Bletchley headed for the bedroom in the extension Hunter collected a dog's lead. Winston was immediately up and by his side. He'd been expecting his walk, a part of the ritual whenever his master was at home. Another part of the ritual was to stroll with his father down the hill and along the bank of the River Endrick.

They walked in silence until they reached the bridge then his father said, 'Tell me what really happened on Sicily.'

So he did. That in turn led him to tell his father about France.

His father was a renowned journalist who had also written the history of the Griffiths family starting with his best seller *A Million Tears*. That was when he had met Sian, the granddaughter of David Griffiths, the patriarch of the family. It was an extraordinary tale of poverty and hardship, adventure and wealth. Tim Hunter used to joke that the family had seen it all and often done it all. In the early half of the twentieth century the family seemed to have been in the middle of just about every event of significance in the country. Hunter's great, great grandfather, Evan Griffiths had even run for President of the USA and won! However, events had conspired against him and he never had the opportunity to take up the exalted position.

'You know son, I've said it many times and I know you agree but where the hell is all this leading? How do we stop these people?'

'I don't know Dad. By doing what we are doing I guess.'

They turned around and started back the way they had come. Winston turned, gave a bark of annoyance at returning so soon and bolted ahead of the two men.

Back at the house they found Bletchley waiting at the garden table, a glass of whisky close at hand although he hadn't drunk any of it. Seeing the two men he took a gulp and stood up. Knowing what was coming Hunter excused himself and went to the toilet. He gave his father and prospective brother-in-law a few minutes and then returned to the garden.

Both men now had whiskies in front of them with a decanter and third glass waiting.

Hunter poured himself a couple of fingers worth, added soda and an ice cube from the ice bucket.

Bletchley was smiling, as was his father. 'So you gave your blessing?'

Tim Hunter shrugged. 'I had no choice. Your mother and sister would have strung me up if I hadn't. However, I heartily approve, so good luck to you both and welcome to the family.'

The three men clinked glasses.

'You're going to need it,' said Hunter.

'I heard that,' said his sister, stepping out of the doorway where she had been standing.

'I knew you were there,' replied her brother.

38

The following morning they were seated around the dining table in the kitchen listening to the Today Programme on Radio 4. They wore glum faces. While they had been enjoying themselves the evening before there had been another two terrorist attacks in England. One had been in Leeds and the other in Manchester.

In Leeds there had been a dozen deaths and at least 20 people hurt, while in Manchester there had been at least 30 people killed and many more people hurt.

The usual platitudes were being aired by the politicians none of whom knew what they were talking about. That of course wasn't unusual for a politician, but it didn't stop them pontificating on the subject in question.

There was one voice Hunter immediately recognised. Angela Wills was saying, 'We must be tolerant and understanding. We must come to realise that the people attacking us have their reasons and we must deal with those reasons. We must not blame any one culture or religion for what is happening. Much of it is as the result of the west's foreign policy in the Middle East.'

'Christ Almighty,' said Tim Hunter, 'listen to that stupid cow. She's trying to justify the attacks on innocent . . .' he stopped speaking when he heard the interviewer.

'Are you saying that these attacks are justified?' There was incredulity in the voice.

The woman seemed to realise that she had gone too far because she said, 'No! No! Of course not! You are deliberately putting words into my mouth. Nothing can justify such attacks.'

'You just blamed foreign policy. I would take that to mean justification for what has happened.'

'That is not what I mean at all. I mean the way we deal with terrorism.'

'Then what is that supposed to mean?' There was no disguising the irritation in the interviewer's tone.

'For instance, instead of arresting the perpetrators of these attacks we allow armed forces to shoot them.'

Sensing more, like a good newshound, the man asked, 'Do you have any particular force in mind?'

'Yes, of course. The so-called International Force Against Terrorism.'

'But surely it is not so-called. It has done some amazing work in the past and been responsible for saving many lives. And that's a fact if only a tenth of the stories about their exploits are true.'

'I shouldn't believe all you read in the papers,' was the scathing reply. 'It's time TIFAT was closed down and, let me tell you, that is part of the Brexit deal.'

'What? What was that you just said?'

This time she knew she had gone too far and needed to extricate herself before she said anymore. 'I'm sorry but I need to go. Thank you.'

'Well listeners, you heard it here first. According to Angela Wills the closure of TIFAT is part of the Brexit deal. How will the Prime Minister deal with that and more to the point what will it do for British and European security? Now over to Brad Bowles for the latest weather.'

'Did you know about this?' asked Tim Hunter. 'You don't seem surprised.'

'I'm not. We had a meeting at Rosyth yesterday and she was there. The General laid it on thick about our work and what we've done in the past.' He shrugged. 'What can I say? She wasn't listening. She's on a crusade to close us down. She had no answers for dealing with the problems of terrorism just the usual claptrap about arresting people, putting them on trial and imprisoning them. That is, of course, if they're found guilty.'

'Huh,' said his father, 'that won't work as we know all too well. Any prisoners will become idolised, even venerated as examples of the sacrifices needed for the greater good. That these people are helping to establish a worldwide caliphate even if it takes a thousand years.'

'Didn't a visiting imam to the East London Mosque in Tower Hamlets talk about such sacrifice and the long term objectives of Islam?' Sian asked.

'Yes, it was reported to the authorities and he was deported but only after three court appearances,' said Tim Hunter.

'He was defended by that shower in Leicester,' said Hunter, helping himself to a croissant.

'Lawyers for Justice?' suggested his father.

'The very same.'

'They're a vile bunch of people,' continued Tim Hunter. 'They've defended some of the most despicable people on the planet. Or I should say despicable Muslims on the planet. They are extremely good at their job and have been tying our courts up with legal arguments for years.'

'Amongst everything else they've been up to,' said Hunter, 'they are now creating spurious claims against our soldiers for war crimes.'

'Huh,' said Bletchley, 'I'd like to see how these people would behave if they were being shot at or if they saw a friend blown to pieces. I defy any one of them not to want revenge.'

'You're right,' said Hunter. 'Which is why we need to operate in the dark as much as possible. We need to tone down the publicity we're getting.'

'But you're not seeking it,' said Tim Hunter.

'I know, Dad, but you know what it's like. The biggest problem is loud mouthed politicians wanting to make a name for themselves either denigrating us or praising us. Either way gives them the opportunity to have their names in the public eye. The general has always emphasised that we are an information coordinating organisation but few people believe that anymore.'

'You're victims of your own success,' said Hunter's mother. There was no disguising the worry in her eyes. She knew precisely what her son was involved in, no matter how much her husband and Nick tried to keep it from her. She and Louise spoke about it when they were together. Now there was an added worry, Chris!

'Mum, Dad, we have to go.' Hunter stood up. 'Congratulations Lems, I hope you're both very happy.' Lems was the name of endearment he had used for his sister since they had been toddlers. Louise had been too difficult for him to get his mouth around. He smiled, 'I like your ring but you can stop admiring it now.'

His sister held out her left hand and used her thumb to wriggle the ring, allowing the light to catch the diamond. Her smile was laced with satisfaction and happiness.

Minutes later, after fond farewells, the two TIFAT officers were on the road heading back to Rosyth. They arrived at the base at 09.15 and reported to the Operations Room that also contained the IT Centre.

'Glad you could make it,' General Macnair greeted them, looking meaningfully at his watch.

'Yes, sir. Sorry. But Chris became engaged to my sister last night so we celebrated a little bit longer than usual.'

'Oh! Congratulations,' said the general.

'Thank you, sir.'

'Yes, congratulations, Chris,' said Isobel, smiling broadly. Then she added, 'It's nice to have some good news for a change.'

'What's up?' Hunter asked, helping himself to coffee from the ever ready fresh pot on a side table.

They were in an annex to the main room. The annex was a large conference area with seating for 50 people. It was laid out in theatre style; the leather seats were comfortable, each with the necessary cup holder. Already seated in the auditorium were Jim Carter, Matt Dunston, Sam McReady, Peter Weir, Jan Badonovitch, David Hughes and Don Masters. They all echoed their congratulations mixed with a few ribald comments.

At the front, to one side, stood a table. Isobel and two men she referred to as her left and right hand, Leo Kinski and Gareth Scarlatti were sitting there. They each had a laptop in front of them.

In the main room were 35 highly trained staff working their computers. They were sorting out the wheat from the chaff when it came to gathering information floating around in the ether worldwide. The whole team was concentrating their efforts on one target, the al-Baghdadi organisation. They had been working on the information supplied by Hunter and the team since it was brought back. They were still finding information and passing it through to Isobel who in turn was assessing how to use it. Or even if it was of any use in the first place.

'If we're ready,' said Macnair, 'we can begin. Isobel, over to you.'

'Thanks, Malcolm. The information we've gleaned from the computers, memory sticks and mobiles you brought back has enabled us to categorise the information into different sections.' She pressed a button on her keypad and a list appeared on the large screen in front of them.

Locations
Personnel
Banking
Investments
External contacts

'Al-Baghdadi isn't as bright as he thinks he is. Or maybe his success has gone to his head and has made him careless. Or maybe he thinks his security precautions sufficient to deal with any possible problems.'

'Which al-Baghdadi?' Hunter asked. 'There's so many of them.'

'Sorry, I should have said Tadeas. The passwords are layered. By that I mean one password can be used by one part of their organisation but not another. Then another password can open a website higher up the food chain while giving access to everything below it. Does that make sense?'

Her audience nodded.

'Won't they change the passwords if anything goes wrong?' Macnair asked and then added, 'Which in this case it has.'

'Yes, they have already done so. However, thanks to you guys we stole a march on them and have been able to get into their systems and effectively lift every crumb of information to be found. It's taken us quite some time to assimilate because the al-Baghdadi organisation is so big. In fact we are still working on it.'

'And how big is it?' Hunter asked.

'I'll come to that. We'll go through each of the sections in turn. Any questions as usual write them on the pad in front of you and keep them until the end.'

The men nodded. They knew the routine. They'd been through it often enough.

They broke at 10.30 for coffee, at 13.00 for lunch and at 15.30 when it was all over.

When Isobel and her team finished Macnair took the stand. 'I think we're in shock. I don't know about you guys but I know I am.'

The others exchanged cynical looks.

Macnair said, 'Isobel, let's get this straight. There are at least three maybe four hundred men and women in the organisation, from teenagers up to . . . to octogenarians.'

Isobel nodded. 'As near as we can tell.'

Macnair continued, 'They are operating in thirty different locations and maybe more across Europe as well as a dozen sites in Iraq, Libya, Syria, Egypt and so on.'

'Correct.'

'According to the bank records you've managed to hack into they have net cash assets in excess of fifty million dollars.'

'Yes.'

'They have further investments in blue chip companies worth at least a hundred million.'

'As far as we can estimate. We're still trolling the investment world looking for any other assets. As you can appreciate tracking down dummy companies, trusts and names is a time consuming job.'

'I appreciate that. Finally, the organisation has external contacts that appear to help to coordinate their activities.'

'That about sums it up,' Isobel nodded again. 'One of these contacts is the law firm Lawyers for Justice. There's quite a lot of traffic between them and Saudi though it's all in code.'

'Can you crack it?' Hunter asked.

'Difficult. It's a once only code for each message so there's no pattern.' Then Isobel added, 'Which makes it pretty much foolproof.'

'We need to bug the place,' said Hunter. 'Agreed, sir?'

'Yes. We also need to deal with Tadeas al-Baghdadi.'

'Sir, are you suggesting a hit in Saudi?' Masters enquired.

'I need to think about it,' said the General. 'It's probably too risky. It doesn't bear thinking about if anyone is caught.'

'That's our job,' said Hunter.

'I'm not talking about the personal risk but the political fallout,' said the General. 'As we all know, ostensibly the Saudis are our allies. The reality is entirely different. However, we have to play the game. Last year the country that bought the most arms of any government in the world was the Saudi Arabians. That's an estimated spend of around seventy billion dollars. Also getting into Saudi and dealing with a senior member of the Mutawa is easier said than done.' Then he added, 'No, strike that. We'd get the job done but getting out could be, shall we say, problematic.'

'In that case,' said Hunter, 'we need to coerce al-Baghdadi to come here. Give him a reason to visit the UK or even somewhere in Europe.'

'How?' Hughes asked, reasonably.

'First we need to establish the actual relationship between Lawyers for Justice and al-Baghdadi,' replied Hunter.

'Assuming there is one,' said Badonovitch who had been quiet up until then.

'We're pretty sure there is,' said Isobel. 'Why use a once only code to connect with clients unless there is something to hide?'

'There could be a number of reasons,' said Hunter, 'such as confidentiality.'

'Yes, but why a once only code?' Masters asked.

'That's simple,' said Bletchley, 'they don't trust the government not to be reading their e-mails.'

'Any reason for their paranoia?' asked Hughes.

'Yes,' said Leo. 'I looked them up on the Internet. They are well known for representing Muslims who are recognised as being fundamentalists. You know the sort of thing. Hate preachers who incite Muslims to commit jihadist type crimes, including going to the various regions of the world to fight for a caliphate mainly achieved by killing non-believers. At the last count we reckon jihadist fighters from over one hundred countries have travelled to the Middle East to fight for Daesh. Incidentally, as a matter of interest, if ISIS catches anyone using that name they have threatened to cut out that person's tongue.'

'Why?' asked Badonovitch.

'The word means either to trample down and crush or a bigot who imposes his view on others. It sounds ludicrous that the same word can mean such different things but there it is. Anyway, they hate the word and hence one of the reasons the west now uses it so much.'

'To get up their noses?' Masters suggested.

'Precisely,' answered Leo.

'What we need to do,' said Hunter, 'is establish the relationship between LFJ and al-Baghdadi and use them as some sort of lever to get al-Baghdadi to Europe.'

'I guess we can take a look,' said Macnair. 'It will be worth a try. In the meantime Isobel, I want you to raid the bank accounts of the organisation. Do the usual. Also see what you can do about acquiring any of their investments. Let's make them squeal where it hurts and that's in their pockets. Starved of funds it will be interesting to see how many of their supporters slide back into the slime where they belong and become lost to sight.'

39

On the large screen on the wall was a photograph of the building in Leicester where the offices of Lawyers for Justice were to be found. The building was modern, detached and in the corner of an industrial estate on the edge of the city.

'Do all these offices belong to LFJ?' Dunston asked.

'Yes,' replied Isobel. 'As you can see it's a two storey building with ten windows either side of the main entrance. According to the plans registered with the local authority there are twenty offices, though we think only half are in use.' She used a laser pointer aimed at the drawing. 'This is a conference room that can easily seat twenty or more people.'

'It's quite an operation for a firm of lawyers,' said Hunter.

'Not nowadays,' replied Isobel. 'There are firms with dozens if not hundreds of lawyers many of whom specialise in different areas of the law.'

'Have you been into their data base?' Macnair asked.

'Yes, a few hours ago. We found some interesting things.'

'Such as?' Bletchley enquired.

'First of all we took a look at their employees. There are thirty-two. Fifteen qualified lawyers, fifteen assistants and paralegals and two receptionists. We checked the nationalities of all thirty-two people and we found an astonishing fact. Only eight are British born.'

'And the rest?' asked the General.

'Mainly Saudis but two are Libyan, two are Iraqi, three Egyptians, one French and two Spanish. Also they are all devout Muslims.'

'All?' Hunter queried. 'The odds of all of them being devout,' he emphasised the word, 'is pretty remote.'

'More than remote,' said Isobel, 'and there's another interesting fact. We have trawled through their client lists and we are positive that the only cases they take are on behalf of Muslims. Don't get me wrong. I mean they cover all aspects of the law from house purchase to serious crimes but looking at the names and addresses of the individuals then we are confident when we say this firm only operates for people of the Islamic faith.'

'Isn't that against race relations or something?' asked Hughes. 'Or maybe it's Christianophobia, agnosticophobia or even atheistophobia?'

The others chuckled and Dunston said, 'Good one Dave. If we have Islamophobia why not the rest of the phobias as well?'

'We need to get in there and bug the place,' said Hunter, 'including phones and computers.'

'We have the new listening devices,' said Isobel, 'the ones about the size of a full stop.'

'I thought their transmission distance was limited,' said Masters.

'It is,' replied the IT boss, 'but we have some good news.' She changed the display to one that showed the building they were interested in plus a couple of the surrounding buildings.' She laser pointed. 'This building is currently empty. There's a for sale or to let sign out the front of it. As you see it's fifty metres or so from the solicitors' place so transmission distances won't be a problem.'

'What about using parabolic mics?' asked Dunston.

'We'll use them as well,' said the general. 'I want the place raped of every bit of information we can collect. These are the people who are making the lives of our serving men and women and those who have retired or left the services with full honours a misery. We are going to turn the tide on these people one way or another. I hope I make myself clear?'

The others nodded. They understood all too well.

They broke for the day. Hunter went running and swimming, working out the kinks from sitting all day. He contemplated phoning a lady friend of his but decided not to bother. He wasn't in the mood to be attentive, polite and a gentleman to boot.

Now that he lived on a modern motor sailer berthed at a jetty attached to HMS *Cochrane* he didn't have far to travel home. The boat was 35 tons of luxury, steel hulled with a heavily reinforced fibreglass superstructure. The hull was maroon; the topside of the boat was white. Internally she was solid teak with reverse-cycle air-conditioners and diesel central heating driven by the engines. There were three watertight compartments secured by watertight doors. There was a single berth forward cabin with hanger space and dresser. The saloon had a starboard side lounge with a pilot berth behind. Next to it was the computer station with the latest scanner/printer as well as a state-of-the-art communications centre. Opposite was the forward head and shower. Next was the galley with a dinette capable of seating six people. The galley had more mod-cons than a newly built house including a fridge/freezer, microwave, garbage compactor, gas cooker, a filter hood and both fresh water and sea water connections.

Further aft were two cabins each with double bunks and aft of that came the en-suite master bedroom. The boat was fitted out to a high degree of luxury but somehow still had a rugged feel about it. In the saloon was a mini-bar, well stocked but rarely used.

The bridge and fly-bridge were fitted with the very latest in navigation equipment, engine controls, autopilot, compass and everything else required to ensure a safe passage with the minimum of effort.

When onboard Hunter slept the sleep of the just.

The following morning Hunter, Dunston and Badonovitch set out for Leicester in Hunter's Range Rover. They had 340 miles to go, mostly on motorways and expected to arrive at their destination around 13.00. They stopped en-route for a natural break and to refresh their coffees.

Due to roadworks and traffic jams they didn't arrive on the outskirts of Leicester until nearly 15.00. They openly pulled up outside the empty offices near to their target and climbed out of the car.

Retribution

The day was overcast though there had been no rain. There was a fresh breeze blowing from the west and rain was threatening.

They stood alongside the car and looked around. The building they were next to was two storey, with three windows either side of the main entrance. About forty metres to the right was another building also with a for sale/to let sign. The estate looked as though it was on its way down.

They had seen the floor plan and knew there was one large room for manufacturing use plus two offices and a toilet on the ground floor. What had been made there was lost in the mists of time as the place had been empty for the best part of three years. Upstairs was a corridor running along the length of the building with four offices either side.

Hunter used his lock pick. It was a small gun into the nozzle of which could be attached different sizes and shapes of picks. The secret was to find the right one before inserting it into any lock. He was expert in its use, quickly identified the pick he needed, attached it to the gun, placed it into the lock and pulled the trigger. There was a faint humming noise and a gentle vibration and the lock turned. He extracted the pick and opened the door. The whole operation had taken less than 20 seconds.

Inside the place had a musty smell but was clean. There were no signs of mice or rat droppings. The entrance hall was just large enough to hold a waist high counter two feet wide and six feet long with two chairs behind it.

There was a door with a visitors sign on that proved to be a toilet. Dunston turned on the cold water tap. There was a gurgle, a hiss and water spurted out in short bursts before settling down to a continuous stream. A small cupboard held a switch with the legend water heater on it, which he flicked on. Nothing happened then he realised there was no electricity in the building. Back in reception he found a walk-in cupboard inside which was the electricity junction box. He grabbed the handle and lifted it with a satisfying clunk. Lights flickered as electricity surged through the building.

The other two had been opening windows to circulate the air, showing the place to be openly occupied.

Hunter returned to the car and grabbed a couple of bags, carrying them into the entrance hall. From one he took a paper banner with the legend "SOLD" written on it. He peeled off the backing, returned outside and placed it across the for sale sign.

Badonovitch brought in more bags and dumped them in the reception area. The three men explored the remainder of the building, opening windows and doors as they did. The air was already beginning to freshen and the stale fetid feel of the place was dissipating. All the windows were covered with venetian blinds, which suited the team, enabling them to look out without being seen very easily.

The building they were interested in was directly across the road with a small car park in front of it. The car park was full with an impressive array of vehicles. They were mainly SUVs, top of the range Range Rovers and Audis but here and there were a Nissan or Datsun. Even so, none of the cars appeared to be more than two or three years old. Hunter counted them. Thirty-two cars for thirty-two employees.

They had three camp beds, sleeping bags and pillows with them. They took a room each. The rooms were unfurnished apart from the biggest room with the sign BOARDROOM on its door. In it was a large table with eight chairs. They deduced that removing the table had been more trouble than it was worth though why the chairs weren't taken was and would remain a mystery.

There was a kitchen though it had been emptied of all useful utensils. Luckily, they had brought a kettle so they could at least make instant coffee, tea or instant soup. They also had packets of supermarket sandwiches, crisps and fresh fruit.

They set up three parabolic microphones aimed at the building opposite. The mics collected sound waves and focused them into a receiver. They each put on headphones to listen but the reception wasn't that good due to the distance involved and the background noises.

Taking off his headphones Hunter said, 'Tea or coffee you guys?'

They opted for tea along with shortbread biscuits. Dunston switched on his iPad to BBC News Live in case anything interesting was broadcast.

Hunter's mobile phone rang. A glance at the screen showed it was the general.

'Sir?'

'Commander, you set up yet?'

'Yes, sir. The parabolics don't work but once its dark we'll go across, plant the bugs and put the programmes into their computers.'

'Good. I thought I would let you know that Isobel has begun cleaning out the organisation's accounts she's so far identified. She's planning on leaving ten dollars in each one just to drive them nuts.'

'Why?'

'She said to put two fingers up to them.' Macnair chuckled. 'I can see her point. With luck we'll wind Tadeas al-Baghdadi up enough to hot foot it to Europe in an attempt to sort out the mess. Once you've uploaded the instructions on the memory sticks into the lawyers' computers we should be able to scare al-Baghdadi enough so that he does come to the west. I'll call you later.'

Dunston peeled open cheese sandwiches with pickle while the other two kept watch. The first person to leave was a woman at precisely 17.30. Ten minutes later a second person came out and from then on they exited the building in a steady stream. They counted the people and by 18.30 there were still 10 left in the offices. The women all wore headscarves; the men were dressed in smart suits and ties with one thing in common. They were all swarthy and of Middle Eastern appearance.

It began to rain. The weather suited them. Though they doubted anyone would be around to see them it was still better than a crisp clear night with a full moon.

Around 20.00 the lights came on one by one in the building and a short while later began to be extinguished as more people left in dribs and drabs. Each time someone exited the building a light came on flooding the entrance and the first few metres of the approach to the door. Soon all the lights were out and all the cars had left.

Badonovitch took their car behind the building out of sight. They settled down for a long evening. There was no point in keeping watch, there was nothing to see. Dunston listened to language CDs learning Chinese, Badonovitch read a thriller about the CIA snorting with derision at some of the antics of its agents while Hunter read an Agatha Christie Miss Marple story. He was a fan of the peaceful, gentle old lady with a mind like a steel trap.

They broke the evening with another round of sandwiches, this time tuna and sliced cucumber with the crisps.

The General phoned at 21.10 and Hunter put his phone on loud-speaker.

'What time is kick-off?'

'Midnight, sir.'

'Okay. I thought you might like to know that Isobel and her geniuses are breaking into the companies and trusts that own the assets of al-Baghdadi and are redistributing them to various charities around the world via an untraceable route. She did explain it to me but I only understood about one word in three.'

The team exchanged grins. They all knew that Macnair had an excellent grasp of computers and systems and what could be done with them. He just enjoyed playing the ignoramus.

'So how much has she transferred?' Dunston asked.

'About twenty million so far. That's in investments. She's already lifted all the cash. That's a few million over fifty.'

Dunston spoke. 'I think we should use as much of the money as we can to help the refugees. After all, that's where it came from.'

'I couldn't agree with you more,' said Macnair. 'We just need to find the best way to do so rather than give it to the charities that are currently claiming to be helping.'

'Médecins Sans Frontières is a good place to start,' said Hunter. 'That's one charity that's doing a lot of good worldwide and especially in the Middle East.'

'Isobel has already given them five million dollars. We're sending money to Help For Heroes and SSAFA as well as a few other charities that help our lads and lasses. Okay, back to business. There's no doubt that Lawyers For Justice is in regular contact with al-Baghdadi in Saudi. We've looked further into their activities and I can tell you they are extremely profitable. They have significant fees coming in from all over Europe.'

'Isn't that a bit unusual?' Hunter suggested.

'Not unusual,' the General corrected him, 'impossible.'

'So what's going on?'

'We think they could have their many fingers in the pie. That is, they are actually part of the criminal organisation. Okay, pretty lowly, probably the coordinating centre for some or all the organisation but an important cog nonetheless.'

'I guess that makes sense. Once we've broken into their databases perhaps we can persuade al-Baghdadi to come to Europe.'

'Any ideas?' Macnair asked.

'Send al-Baghdadi a message along the lines of being needed here to sort out the mess. Can't trust using any form of communications as they might have been hacked. If they are the communications centre for the whole organisation then having the big boss come here makes sense.'

'It could work.'

'Also, sir, do they know the money has gone and their investments are evaporating?'

'Not as far as we can tell. If they don't know yet they soon will.'

'Who runs Lawyers For Justice?'

'A woman by the name of Sabela Hamza.'

'A woman? That surprises me. Especially with the attitude Muslims have to women. It just shows how hypocritical they are. If there's nothing else sir, I'll phone you as soon as we're finished.'

'Okay. Good luck.'

'Thanks, sir.'

As he broke the connection Dunston said, 'Something's up Nick. There's a car coming.'

40

They stood at the window with the lights out, watching as two men climbed out of the car. They approached the building opposite and the external lights came on. From their swarthy complexion they looked to be Middle Eastern or possibly Pakistani. They were wearing some sort of blue uniform with SECURITY in large yellow letters on their backs.

The two men entered the building and went in different directions. Ten minutes later they met again in the foyer, pulled out chairs from behind the counter and sat down in clear view of anyone outside the door.

'Security,' said Badonovitch. 'Pretty late coming on duty.'

'Good,' said Hunter. 'The way they went in means there is no electronic security.'

'So what do you suggest we do?' Dunston asked.

'We'll use the halothane vapour. See the letterbox on one side? If we reach it we can slip the end of the tube through, switch it on and leave it to do its work. Once they're out we go in. It shouldn't take many minutes. You can see the doors around the reception area are closed.' Halothane was a synthetic and highly potent medicine that worked fast for a short period of time.

'We need to be careful with the dosage,' said Dunston, 'we don't want to kill them.'

They knew enough to keep an eye on the men, watch them fall unconscious and take them outside into the fresh air where their lungs would expunge the gas. They would inject the two men with a compound that would put them under for an hour or more.

'What if the lights trip on?' Badonovitch asked.

'We'll cross that bridge when we come to it.'

Their time scale had altered as a result of the guards showing up. Midnight came and went. The lowest energy level in a person was usually between 02.30 and 04.30. At that time a guard was at his least awareness level, often dozing, his brain partly closed down. Frequently, if they had been doing the job long enough and there were no incidents of any kind they would settle down and intentionally go to sleep. With two people it was easier. One slept, one kept watch. But that also made it harder for the guard who was awake to stay alert.

At that moment the team had a bit of luck.

'Look!' pointed Dunston who was standing at the window.

The other two joined him in time to see a fox and two cubs walk alongside the front of the building. At the doorway the lights flashed on and the foxes stopped to look in. The two guards jerked alert and looked at the foxes who stared back for a few seconds. Then nonchalantly the vixen turned her head and carried on walking.

'Both sides are used to each other,' Hunter said.

'Urban foxes are becoming a blight,' said Dunston. 'They're vermin made to look cuddly.' Then he grinned. 'But useful under the circumstances.'

'Look,' said Badonovitch, his binoculars focused on the reception area opposite, one of them has just taken something out of a cupboard.' He chuckled. 'A camp bed no less.'

'Got it,' said Hunter. 'Better and better. Okay, it's 01.22. We'll give it another hour and then go in. I'll keep watch if you two would like to get some beauty sleep, after all you need it a lot more than I do.'

The two men went to their rooms. Hunter made himself a mug of strong coffee. A low ebb applied to everyone not just bored guards.

An hour later Hunter woke up the others with the gift of a fresh mug of coffee.

'Nothing's changed,' said Hunter. 'The guy on the camp bed looks fast asleep and the guy in the chair keeps nodding off.'

They tooled up with their silenced pistols, checked they had

everything they needed and moved out. The three of them were wearing dark clothes and had balaclavas on their heads ready to pull down
over their faces. At the door they stopped as a sheet of lightening lit up
the sky, thunder rumbled and the heavens opened. The rain pounded
down and the lights in the entrance to the building opposite came on.

'Good,' was Hunter's opinion.

The team cut right and came at the building from a diagonal angle.
They pulled their balaclavas down and the hoods of their waterproof
jackets over their heads. At the corner of the building they paused but
still nothing had changed. They edged forward and at the entrance
hall Badonovitch carefully looked around the corner and into the
foyer. The man sleeping on the camp bed hadn't moved while the
man in the chair appeared to be dozing. He had his arms folded and
his chin resting on his chest. Badonovitch slid the end of a thin tube
through the letterbox and halfway to the feet of the guard in the chair.
He turned on the small gas cylinder he was holding and watched as
the pressure gauge on the bottle slowly dropped.

After a few minutes the man in the chair gave a slight jerk and slid
onto the floor. He didn't move.

Hunter used the pick lock gun and quickly opened the door. All
three men pulled on facemasks attached to small oxygen canisters
before entering the building. They checked to ensure both security
men were breathing and dragged them to the entrance. They couldn't
take the men outside as they'd get wet and once they woke up they'd
know something had happened to them.

Hunter took a deep breath and placed his facemask over the mouth
and nose of one of the guards while Dunston did it for the second. The
unconscious men were able to take two breaths before the two officers
reclaimed the masks. Badonovitch had taken a syringe from his bag
and stuck it into the thigh of one of the men. He pressed the plunger.
He repeated the process with the second man. They would be
unconscious for at least an hour, possibly two.

They kept their masks on as they made their way into different
rooms. They turned on computers and inserted a memory stick into

each one. The stick downloaded a programme that ensured anything written on the computer was forwarded to Rosyth. It also meant any one-time code being used would automatically be broken. A second memory stick copied all the information contained in the hard drives. They planted bugs into telephone receivers, on walls and behind framed pictures all of which displayed a subject connected to Islam, though nothing depicting a likeness of the prophet Muhammad. They also bugged the ladies and gents cloakrooms. The bugs were the size of a pin head. They were virtually impossible to see and if anyone saw one it looked like a smidgen of dust. The most sensitive of detectors couldn't pick them up but they did have one draw back. Their range of transmission was limited.

Hunter placed a receiver/transmitter in the cupboard downstairs, hiding it in a far corner behind cleaning utensils and dirty rags. The broadcast from each bug was forwarded to a master receiver across the road and then copied to TIFAT.

It had taken an hour. They checked on the two unconscious men, made them more comfortable on their bed and chair respectively and quit the building. Hunter relocked the door and followed the other two into the rain. Two minutes later they were back at their observation post transmitting the information on the memory sticks north.

The time was 03.45 and while Badonovitch kept watch Hunter and Dunston got some sleep. They slept through until 06.50.

'Anything happen?' Hunter asked. 'Thanks, Jan.' He took the proffered mug of tea and sipped appreciatively.

'The two guards woke up.'

'Any reaction from them?' Dunston enquired, smiling and nodding thanks for his tea.

'Yeah, it's been recorded. One of them asked the other if he was okay and was told that he was.'

'Is that all?'

Badonovitch shrugged. 'That's all boss. Except they talked about using the toilet and getting some tea. Neither said anything about being asleep.'

'Good. The General is e-mailing Sabela Hamza the senior partner to tell her about the money and investments going missing. That should set things off with a bang.'

'Boss,' said Badonovitch, 'I'll go and buy breakfast. Bacon and egg rolls all round?'

The other two nodded.

The Spetsnaz left on his errand using the back door; Dunston picked up his binoculars and focused on the building opposite. He saw a woman wearing a hijab arrive by car and enter the building. She greeted the two guards who had put away their camp bed and placed the chair back behind the reception counter. There were smiles and nods and the two men left. The woman took up station behind the counter and appeared to be the receptionist.

An e-mail arrived from TIFAT. Hunter opened it and read its contents.

'This is a list of the people who work there. All accounted for as legitimate employees on salaries who pay their taxes.'

'They need to be seen to be whiter than white,' said Dunston. 'Where did we get the info from?'

'The tax office. I can tell you they are earning good money. Even the receptionist earns more than £30,000 a year. Oh, plus a bonus that last year amounted to another £10,000,' said Hunter.

'What about the woman who runs the place?'

'The fifteen lawyers are all partners and so have a self-employed income that they declare at the end of the year. The paralegals and the two receptionists are salaried. Hell's teeth.'

'What's up?'

'According to these accounts the partners each earned more than a quarter of a million last year.'

'That's serious change for a law firm specialising in doing work only for Muslims.'

'Here's another e-mail from HQ. They've hacked into the computer of the accountants. Surprise, surprise their name is Tawfeek and Co. A good Arabic name.'

'We know the Muslim community work together and occasionally play together. So it's not surprising that their accountants are Muslims. There's another car arriving.'

Over the course of the next 15 minutes another thirty cars arrived, each carrying just the driver. All the women wore the hijab covering their heads though none wore the niqab that also covered the lower half of their faces nor the burka, a single garment, that covered the whole of the head plus body leaving a mesh for the wearer to look through. The more modern and progressive men and women who were also Islamic saw such clothes as shackles and belittling of women. Modern day slavery was another description of women being forced to wear such garments.

Badonovitch returned with a couple of bacon and egg rolls each. He had discovered a snack van at the entrance to the industrial estate that was doing a roaring trade supplying breakfast to the workers pouring into the area.

The bugs were beginning to pick up transmissions from the lawyers. The transmitter/receiver they were using operated on a different wavelength for different bugs. This meant that anything said in office A was recorded at one frequency and office B on another and so on.

Macnair phoned. 'Listen in to the bugs planted in their boardroom. You'll find it very interesting.'

Hunter adjusted the channel and put the broadcast on loudspeaker. The three of them sat around, fresh coffees in hand, listening to what was being said.

'So we're agreed,' said a female voice, 'we'll take all four cases and start proceedings against the British government naming the seven soldiers as having committed war crimes.'

'I think that's going too far,' said a male voice.

'What do you mean?'

'What I say. It's too far. It isn't a war crime. It is possibly an abuse of power. However, it is unlawful wounding at the most. We can apply for compensation but I don't think we should do more than that.'

'Haatim I want their heads on a platter.' There was real vitriol in her tone. 'I want the British people to pay for the crimes they have committed against our people in Syria, Iraq, Afghanistan and everywhere else.'

'If we do that,' said the reasonable voice of Haatim, 'we will alienate vast numbers of people in this country and what is worse stir them into some sort of reaction.'

'Huh! Such as what? Arresting us? For what? We've not committed any crime. In fact it's the reverse. They have committed the crimes. We are trying to get redress for our brethren. For our warriors fighting the fight of Allah.'

There were murmurs of agreement from others in the room.

Hunter's phone rang.

'Sir?'

'We're logged into their computers. We have their once only code. It's simple when you use a computer. The code has been uploaded and any message that's composed on the computer to be sent to certain addresses automatically causes the code to trip in. It's effective up to a point and we're way past that point. Isobel has checked out all the computers and there is only one that's connected to Tadeas al-Baghdadi and that's the one in Hamza's room.'

'That's not surprising. I have to say sir, I'm not impressed with their overall level of security.'

'We think we know why that is. From some of the e-mails that have gone back and forth it seems that Ms Hamza is convinced that the UK authorities wouldn't dare touch her with a barge pole because of the outcry that would create from human rights groups, the Muslim Council of Britain and of course the Mosques and Imams National Advisory Board. In a nutshell, she thinks she's untouchable thanks to the support she enjoys in general from the Muslim communities in the UK.'

'And does she have that support?'

'No. Most of it is in her imagination. Believe me, the majority of Muslim organisations in this country at all levels are as British in their thinking as we are. However her attitude is good news for us.'

'In that she's careless when it comes to security.'

'Precisely. Her arrogance means we have relatively easy access to the information held by them. Nick, some interesting stuff has already surfaced.'

'Oh? Such as?'

'I'll let you judge. Log on to the computer in Ms Hamza's office and put her phone on speaker. Tell me what you think this evening.'

Intrigued, Hunter said, 'Will do, sir.'

Minutes later the meeting in the boardroom ended and a few minutes after that they heard Sabela Hamza enter her office. It was obvious she was followed by a second person.

'Take a seat, Abida.'

'Thank you, Sabela.' The voice was female.

'What did you think of what Haatim had to say.'

'I . . . I'm not sure.'

'Come on, Abida, I want to know what you think. Will we antagonise the British public if we chase after these men?'

'Yes. Most definitely yes.'

'Good. That is precisely what I want to do. I want to push and push until they react. I want them using soldiers to attack us and imprison us without trial so that our brothers and sisters rise up and civil disobedience will be rife across the country. As it will in the rest of Europe.'

'But why?' The question was asked in a plaintive voice.

'Because I hate them. I never told you but an American drone bombed the town where my family comes from. My uncles and aunts and cousins were killed. That was when I decided it was time for holy jihad.'

There was the sound of a gasp, then, 'You mean a legal fight. Using the power of the courts to get justice.'

'At first but I quickly realised that wasn't enough. That what we do is less than a pinprick on the hide of an elephant.'

There was silence for a few seconds that seemed to stretch on and on. 'Sabela, what are you telling me?'

'I want you to join my war. Like the others.'

'What do you mean, like the others?'

'Everyone here has been carefully vetted. I have ensured they think like I do. You are a paralegal but you are a trained lawyer. You will become a partner and help us in our struggle. For that not only will you have great satisfaction but you will earn more money than you can dream of.'

There was more silence.

'What do you say?'

'I . . . I need to think about it. It has come as such a shock.'

There was steel in Sabela Hamza's voice when she said, 'Don't take too long. I need an answer by the end of the day.'

There was a faint gasp and then, 'All right. I'll tell you this evening.'

'Good. That's all.'

'Sabela, I have to ask, do you know what jihad means?'

'What? Of course I do. It means holy war.'

'No it doesn't. It means struggle. It means to struggle to be a good Muslim and to tell others about our faith. Jihad also means that to protect our faith from others we can use political, economic and legal means to do so. If we cannot achieve our objective peacefully we are allowed to use force but only under certain and strict circumstances. Innocent people such as women and children, even invalids must never be harmed. Note that word, never. The use of jihad today is an abomination when it comes to our faith. One other thing, jihad is not a violent concept. It is not a declaration of war against other religions.'

'Why are you telling me this?'

'Because I want to know that we will be fighting injustice using economic, political and legal means. Not killing people.'

'You may go.'

They heard the door close.

'Haatim come here. I think we have a problem.'

41

'A woman has just exited the building and is pacing up and down. It looks like she's using a mobile.'

'Aim the mic at her,' said Hunter. It was a superfluous order as Badonovitch already had the parabolic microphone aimed at the woman.

Her voice came across loud and clear as she moved away from the other building and towards theirs.

'Nigel? It's me. No listen. I just had a conversation with Sabela.' There was a pause. 'I can't explain but my instincts tell me they don't trust me.' Pause. 'Look, Nigel, the reason you sent me in here was because of what happened to that other woman in a hit and run.' Pause. 'I haven't found any proof that she or anyone else in the firm actually carried out the attack but I've already told you I think they were involved.' Pause. 'No, Nigel, I'm not suggesting I quit now I'm just giving you a heads up.' Pause. 'I understand that.' Pause. 'Nigel, I am not a field operative but a backroom analyst. You sent me here because of my legal knowledge but I'm ready to become worried.' Pause. 'I'd better go. I'll phone you tonight.'

'Nick,' said Dunston, 'I don't know who she is but she has cause to be worried. Listen to this.' He switched on a recorder.

'Haatim, I'm not sure about Abida.'

'Why not?'

'She just gave me a lecture on holy jihad and I didn't like or agree with what she had to say.' She explained what she had been told.

373

There was silence for a few seconds before the man replied. 'That means we cannot trust her.'

'I fear so.'

'What do you propose we should do about it?'

'We cannot afford another hit and run accident. We were lucky with the first one.'

The three TIFAT men exchanged looks. That answered one question.

'What about a mugging?' suggested the man they knew as Haatim.

'Possible. Where and when needs thinking about.'

'Why not just sack her?' said Haatim.

'For what reason? She has a permanent job. You can't just dismiss people nowadays. Besides, if she turned on us she does have information that at best is sensitive and at worst downright dangerous to us. What we don't want are journalists sniffing around.'

'Nor the authorities.'

'Forget about them. They're toothless. They . . . What's Abida doing outside using her mobile? Who is she phoning? Come and look,' ordered Sabela.

There was a few seconds of silence. 'Phoning her boyfriend?'

'Possibly,' said Sabela Hamza, 'but somehow I doubt it.'

'Then who?'

'How do I know?' she answered irritably. 'I don't like it.'

'You don't think she's a spy do you?'

'I've no idea. Would the authorities risk putting someone in here to spy on us? If we found out think of the stink we could cause in the media. The British Government is too frightened to risk doing anything like that. On the other hand she could be a journalist.'

'That's not possible. I checked her references very carefully. No journalist could invent such a cast iron background.'

'Then are you suggesting the British authorities could?' The woman's tone was scornful.

'That's possible but I don't believe it for a moment. They wouldn't dare. No, I think she is what she appears to be but that still leaves us with a problem.'

'She maybe knows too much. If she has been snooping she could have found out things we'd rather not have made public.' She paused. 'All right, leave it with me. I'll speak to someone who can sort the mess out.'

'By sort the mess out you mean get rid of her.'

'What choice do we have?'

The man sighed. 'I guess none. Just make sure whatever you do doesn't come back to haunt us.'

'It won't. I can assure you. What do you make of the people who have taken the offices opposite?'

'What's there to make? I haven't seen them.'

'Could they be spying on us?'

'Sabela, you see spies everywhere. No I don't. They have arrived in a car, parked it openly and entered the building.'

'Yes, you're right. Thank you.'

There was the sound of a door closing and a few moments later Sabela Hamza spoke again this time using her phone.

'Sameer? Yes it's me. I have a job for you and your sister.'

'Is it like the last one?'

'Yes, as usual twenty thousand. I want you to make it look like an accident.'

'Any ideas how? It's not that simple you know.'

'I know but that is what you specialise in doing and what you are paid well to do.'

'You are not suggesting another hit and run are you? One such accident you can get away with, two is impossible. Even the British police aren't that stupid.'

'I know. So what do you suggest?'

'What nationality is she?'

'British.'

'I mean her ethnicity.'

'Pakistani.'

'Excellent.'

'Why excellent?'

'Does she have any family?'

'No. According to her file both her parents are dead and there's no mention of brothers or sisters, or uncles or aunts come to that.'

'Even better. Buy a return ticket to Islamabad in her name. She will vanish and you can say you know no reason why she went nor why she hasn't returned. You can put it on file that she was taking a fortnight's holiday so you don't have to report her as missing for at least two weeks, probably a few days longer.'

'That will work.'

'How soon do you want the job done?'

'You have forty-eight hours.'

'Okay. Consider it done.'

Hunter phoned Macnair. 'Sir, I don't think this paralegal Abida is all she appears to be.'

'Oh? Why?'

He explained his reasoning.

'You could be right. Leave it with me. She's either Five or SO15. I'll find out.'

'Are you going to warn them?'

'Yes. They can pull her asap.'

'What will you tell them about how we got the information?'

'At the moment I won't be telling either of them about our operation, but that can always change. We have the girl's full name from their employee records so it won't be difficult to find out who she's working for. By the way Haatim's full name is Haatim Radwan.'

'Radwan? I know the name.'

'His uncle is on the American top twenty list as a radical imam in Syria. Not high enough to warrant a drone strike but moving up the pecking order, so to speak.'

'I know who you mean. Thanks, sir.' The connection was broken.

'You heard, guys, what do you think?'

'I think,' said Dunston, 'that trusting the attack won't take place for two days isn't on. Furthermore, these people can't be very bright. It will be the easiest thing in the world to show she never caught the flight.'

'As they're not that stupid,' said Hunter, 'they'll solve the problem by sending someone who looks enough like Abida to Pakistan.'

'They'll have to,' said Badonovitch, 'otherwise this won't work.'

Later that afternoon they heard Sabela Hamza say to Radwan that she had booked a return flight in Abida's name. Her next sentence proved she wasn't stupid.

'We'll send Nura. She has a superficial resemblance to Abida. Wearing a headscarf and the fact that she is leaving the country means nobody will be looking too closely especially bored passport control officers. We have Abida's passport?'

'Yes, of course. We have everyone's in case they need to take a trip at short notice, which happens from time to time.'

'Yes, yes,' she said distractedly, 'I wasn't thinking clearly. I was thinking about something else.'

'Oh? Something worrying you?'

'Not worrying, no. I . . .'

A buzzer sounded. 'I thought I told you no interruptions.' There was a pause. 'You'd better put him through. What is it Tadeas?' She asked the question in Arabic.

An agitated voice came over the line. 'Have you been into our bank accounts this morning?'

'No, of course not. Why would we?'

There followed a mouthful of expletives until Hamza managed to interrupt the flow and say, 'What are you talking about? Why are you cursing?'

'I am telling you there is no money. It is all gone.'

There was bewilderment in her reply. 'What do you mean? What has all gone?'

'The money, you fool! All the money has gone.'

'Watch who you are talking to Tadeas I don't like being called a fool. Take a deep breath and tell me what is happening.'

They could hear the man sucking in air before speaking. 'Sorry. So sorry. I am anxious. I received an e-mail ten minutes ago informing me that there is no money left in our accounts. The e-mail specified the accounts and where they are held. I checked them. Every account has only a single dollar left in it?'

'I guess,' said Hunter, 'Isobel decided not to leave them with as much as ten dollars.'

They grinned.

'What?' The shock in her voice was startling. 'What,' she cleared her throat, 'what do you mean?'

'I am telling you Sabela, there is no money. Over fifty million dollars has been taken from our accounts. Check it if you don't believe me.'

'I will! I will. I will phone you back.'

There followed the frantic clacking of a keyboard.

'What is it, Sabela? What has happened?'

'Shsh. I need to concentrate. Oh my God. Oh my God.'

'What is it?'

'The money! It has all gone.'

'What do you mean it has all gone? How? Who can have done this?'

There was silence for a few seconds before the woman let loose with a string of expletives of her own. She calmed down and said, 'You imbecile! How do I know? I do know that if I find out who is responsible I will ensure they have a slow and painful death.'

After a few seconds Radwan broke the silence. 'What about the investment portfolio?'

There was more frantic clacking of the keyboard. It was followed by a low moan. Her voice was faint and hoarse when she said, 'It has all gone. Every investment has been left with a single share. Like whoever did this is taunting us.'

'Who can have done it? The authorities?'

'No, never. They would never be allowed to commit what is after all theft. No, there are dark forces working against us.'

'No, I don't think that is the case,' said Radwan.

'What do you mean?'

'The British government would never allow this to happen. We know that. It would take court orders, trials, convictions and a host of other things before this can be done.'

'So what are you saying?'

'Someone who had access to our accounts has done this. Who knew the details? Who is the only person who can have done this and pretended he isn't responsible.'

'Tadeas.' Her voice gasped.

'Yes. Who else?'

'But why? What does he have to gain? He is not materialistic. He fights holy jihad with every breath in his body.'

'That's what he claims. He doesn't actually do anything. He sits in Riyadh abusing people he considers unworthy of calling themselves Muslim and makes a song and dance about how people should conduct themselves.'

'Yes,' she spoke slowly, 'that's true. But we're fighting for Islam. What does he want the money for?'

Her computer pinged. 'I have an e-mail.' After a few seconds she said, 'Look at this.'

'What is it?' Radwan read the message. 'What is going on?'

'It says that the people who have taken the money are listed below. Look at the names.'

'I can see!' Her voice was on the verge of hysteria. Gone was the cool collected tone of a woman in charge of events and in control of herself.

'What shall we do?' Radwan whispered.

'We will kill them,' she said fiercely. 'We need to see who is loyal and who isn't.'

'That will mean a war between our own people.'

'It cannot be helped. We must get that money back. We need it urgently. We have many people to pay and we need the money now.'

'What do you suggest?'

'Tadeas must come to Europe. We must meet with him. Look at this! Another e-mail.'

Radwan read it over her shoulder. 'It has gone into more detail. It has the names of the accounts and where the money has been sent.

Finally, Radwan asked, 'Who sent these?'

'I . . . I don't know.' There was the sound of the keyboard and then, 'I've no idea. Whoever sent this has covered their trail. I can't tell who they are.'

'Sabela, with all due respect,' he used the word 'respect' but was showing none, 'but you know nothing about computers and security systems and tracking down who has sent you what.'

She sighed. 'You are right. But what can we do Haatim? Oh my God. The company business account!' She opened the account and read what was on the screen. 'Thank Allah. The money is all there. We will at least be able to pay . . . No! No!'

'What is it?'

'It's going! The money is going even as I look at the screen.'

Radwan bent over to look more closely. 'I feel sick,' he whispered.

'Send an e-mail to Tadeas now. Encrypt it. Tell him he is to be in Paris in twenty-four hours.'

'What if he won't come?'

'Tell him he had better. Do you notice anything about the names?'

'Yes, of course. They are all loyal to Tadeas. They are his people.'

'So I want to look him in the eyes and ask questions and get his answers.'

'I still say what if he pointblank refuses?'

'Then tell him if we cannot sort this problem in the next twenty-four hours I shall have to inform the prince.'

'He won't like that. You know what his attitude is to you. In fact, his attitude to women in general.'

'The man's a fool when all's said and done.' There was no attempt to hide the scorn she felt towards the Saudi.

'The threat to tell the prince should be enough to get him to France. He can use one of his many aliases not that anyone knows who he is. Where shall we meet him? Somewhere public or private?' Radwan asked.

'I don't know!' She spoke sharply, the tension unravelling her. 'Look at my hands! They're shaking. Oh God, Haatim, if we can't sort this out the prince will be sending people after us. You know what he's like. He'll consider us all guilty.'

'Of what? We haven't done anything.'

'That won't matter. He blames everybody but himself if anything goes wrong and nothing can be more wrong than this. Everything has gone!' The last sentence was spoken barely above a whisper with horror in her tone. 'He won't believe we had nothing to do with it. He'll want to know who had access to the accounts and the answer is only you and I. Haatim, I am really scared. I need a cigarette.'

There was silence for a few seconds except for the sound of drawers being pulled open and slammed shut. 'Got them!' After a few seconds came the faint sound of someone exhaling and then, 'God, why did I ever give up?'

'Because it's good for you. However, I shall have one as well if you don't mind. Let me repeat my question. Somewhere public or private?'

'Public. No, private.'

'Make your mind up Sabela. We need to tell Tadeas as quickly as possible.'

'Wait a moment.'

The team heard the sound of a keyboard being used.

'Here's just the place. The Luxembourg Gardens at the seats by the small lake. I was there a number of years ago. It's all open space.'

The three men listening to their conversation grinned. The pressure was only just starting. There was still more to come.

42

General Macnair phoned. 'That was all very illuminating though not surprising.'

'We know the House of Saud at some level is involved with holy jihad. We've known it for a long time,' said Hunter.

'But it sounded as though this woman Hamza is more important than al-Baghdadi.'

'I think that's because al-Baghdadi is replaceable but Sabela Hamza isn't.'

'How do you work that out?'

'Sir, I suspect the prince, whichever one it is, can get others to do al-Baghdadi's job.'

'And that is?' Macnair asked.

'To find people to do the smuggling. So what if a few are killed or imprisoned? If they're killed it's no loss as far as the prince is concerned. They died doing Allah's work. They will be in paradise amongst the virgins, eating honey and drinking tea or whatever it is awaits them when they get there. But they're replaceable. If they are arrested they're not going to talk. They would be too frightened for their families. This prince would ensure a nasty death as an encouragement to the others to keep quiet.'

'True. That's been shown by the lack of cooperation we get when these people are arrested. What you're saying is that Hamza and her company are far more difficult to replace. I take your point.'

'We said earlier that just about every phobia imaginable would be thrown at the authorities if they did try anything. Even when the claims are shown to be spurious nothing is done about it.'

'They did close a firm of solicitors not that long ago for making spurious claims,' pointed out the General. 'As well as that solicitor being struck off.'

'Big deal,' said Hunter, 'he deserved a bullet in the head. And let's not forget they started up again six weeks later.'

'I wasn't aware of that.'

'Isobel mentioned it in passing. More as an indictment of our weak and feeble legal system than anything.'

'Yeah, well they're in for a shock.'

'Hamza is talking again,' said Dunston.

'Haatim, I feel sick. I've never known anything like it.' She paused. 'I . . . I want to throw up.'

'Take deep breaths. Control your breathing, let your heart rate settle.'

A few seconds passed. Then a minute. Then two. 'I feel better. Thanks.'

'Good. We need clear heads if we're to solve what's going on. Okay, we tell Tadeas we need him in Paris, then what?'

'Then we ask him to his face what's going on. We know we're not responsible, so someone in his organisation must be.'

'Apart from us the only person with access to the accounts is him. It looks as though he raided the accounts and investments and distributed the money to members of his network.'

'I feel sick again. Haatim, I'm terrified about what could happen. I . . . I'm a coward. Oh, I can fight using legal arguments. I can face anyone down and challenge anyone when it comes to a battle of words, but I hate physical confrontation. I always have. As a child I was even afraid to play hockey in the girls' school I attended.'

'Moral courage, Sabela, is far more important than physical courage.'

'Thank you for that. We still come back to what can we do about it.'

'First we need to send a message to Tadeas. He needs . . .'

The phone rang. It was Hamza's direct line. 'Who can that be?'

'We won't know until you answer it.'

'Only three people have that number. You, the prince and Tadeas.'

'So answer it.'

The ringing stopped. 'Hello?' It came out as a croak. She cleared her throat and said again, 'Hello. Who is this please?'

'Who do you think?' The words were spoken harshly.

'Ah, Tadeas, I was about to e-mail you.'

'I have no time for e-mails. I demand to be told what is happening. Where is all the money? Where are the investments? Tell me Sabela or it will be the worst for you.'

'Tadeas, by the prophet Muhammad, peace be upon him, I have no idea. We need to meet. To discuss what has happened. I will e-mail you a time and place. It will be Paris.'

'How dare you! You do not tell me what I should or shouldn't do. You will come here to Saudi Arabia. Here we can have a proper conversation when I will be able to get to the truth of the matter.'

'That isn't going to happen, Tadeas. Look, either we meet or I tell the prince what has happened.'

'And who do you think he will believe?'

'I have a surprise for you, Tadeas.'

'What surprise, woman?' Then he added, 'I knew we should not trust a woman.'

'You don't know this Tadeas but the prince is my husband's first cousin.'

There was silence that lasted a few seconds. 'You lie.' The two words were uttered but totally without conviction.

'No, I don't lie. So I want you to come here to Europe. I will send you details of where we should meet.'

'I am not coming to London. I will never set foot in the accursed country.'

'I am not asking you to. We will meet in Paris. I will e-mail you the details of the time and place.'

'I am not sure. I may be walking into a trap. You may be behind all that's been happening. How do I know?'

'Listen to yourself,' said Sabela, contemptuously. 'Why would we bother? Tadeas we have had all of our money taken as well as our investment portfolio. We need to get it back. We need to meet and discuss what has happened. There is no other way.'

There was silence.

'Tadeas, did you hear me?'

'Yes. I will make the necessary arrangements.'

'Good. Then we will see you tomorrow.'

The connection was broken.

'Are you really related to the prince?'

'Yes. Only my husband and he are not first but third cousins. Still, a little exaggeration goes a long way in the Arab world.' She paused. 'What are we going to do? Oh God, what are we going to do? We have no money. We cannot pay the staff. Where has it gone? Who has done this to us?'

'It must be Tadeas. I have already said, apart from us he is the only person to have access to the accounts. We are agreed on that, but I just don't see it. You heard him. He's as worried as we are.'

'I'm not worried,' replied Radwan. 'No. I am terrified out of my mind. If the prince doesn't believe we had nothing to do with it then he will kill our families and us. You know what he's like.'

'Psychotic doesn't come close to summing him up.'

'Then who can it have been? Assuming not Tadeas. The prince doesn't have any access. He left everything to us. Who? The authorities? Are we back to them?'

'I cannot see it. There is no chance that they would raid our bank accounts and steal our money and investments. There is such a thing as the rule of law. It has to be internal.'

'Someone here?' Radwan suggested.

'If you had suggested that a day ago I would have said impossible but now there is one candidate.'

'Who?'

'Abida,' replied Sabela Hamza.

'Yes.' There was silence for a few seconds. 'That means we cannot have her killed. We need to find out what she has done and how she has done it and more importantly, we need to get our money back.'

'I'll speak to Sameer. Explain what we want. It must be done today. The sooner the better.'

Hunter's phone rang. 'Commander? The girl is SO15. I just had word from Isobel.'

'We need to get her out of there. Wait a sec sir, something else is happening.'

'Sameer? It's a change of plan. I don't want the girl killed. I want her taken someplace quiet where I can question her.'

'You, Sabela? Do you know what you are saying?'

'Yes, of course I do. But it's important and I will ask her what I need to know and she will answer me.'

'No! I don't mean that. I mean kidnapping someone is a lot harder than killing them.'

'What you mean is that you want more money.'

'Of course. The task is far more difficult. We need to plan, find out the woman's movements, and decide when and where it will be best to take her. That is a minimum of three, perhaps four days.'

Hamza snorted. 'There is no chance of that. It needs doing today.'

'Today? Are you mad? That's impossible.'

'Sameer, I will pay you an extra ten thousand pounds.'

'I . . . I . . . No! Money is no good if you are in prison. I tell you it's impossible.'

'Twenty thousand and that's my final offer.'

'What about sending someone in her place to Pakistan?'

'That will be done today. This evening.'

'The total you will pay me is forty thousand?'

'Yes.' She still had her personal account with more than enough to pay Sameer.

'I want half up front.'

'Of course. I will send the money in the next few minutes. Sameer, I must emphasise this must be done today.'

'I understand. Where is she now?'

386

'Here.'

'Do you have a photograph of the woman?'

'Yes. In her personnel file.'

'Send me a copy along with a description of what she is wearing.'

'Haatim, do that now please. Sameer, where will you take her?'

'There's an old abandoned industrial complex about twenty miles from you. The sort of place you find burnt out stolen cars and abandoned household goods.'

'What about tramps or homeless?'

'No idea. But there isn't anywhere else.'

'Okay. What's the address?'

'No idea. You take the Oadby road and just before you get there you'll see the place on the left side. It's pretty dilapidated and waiting for the bulldozers.'

'How do you know about this place?'

'A friend of mine has put an offer in to buy it and let's just say he has made an offer that the owner can't refuse.'

'I see. Like that is it.'

'Less of the holier than thou attitude Sabela. You have more blood on your hands than a waterfall can wash off.'

There was an uncomfortable silence and then Radwan reentered the room. 'I've sent the photograph as well as a description of what Abida is wearing.'

'Did you hear that, Sameer?'

'Yes. Now send the money. I'll phone you when we have the woman.'

The connection was broken. 'Do you have that sort of money available?'

'Only half of it.'

'What about the other half.'

'I want it from you.'

'I . . .' he paused. 'Yes, all right. I'll use my mobile and transfer the money to Sameer's account.'

'I will do likewise.'

'Give me the account details.'

She read out the sort code and account number. There was silence and then the team heard Hamza say she had transferred the money and then Radwan said the same thing.

Macnair said, 'With this man Sameer's account details we can backtrack to Hamza's and Radwan's. Leo's working on it right now.'

'Hi, Nick.'

'Hello, Leo.'

'I'm looking at the account now. It's pretty healthy with forty-nine grand plus change in it.'

'What about the other two?'

'Patience, Nick. I'm almost there. Okay, I'm in the woman's account. It's a joint account with her husband, I assume.'

'How much is there?'

'Eighty-six grand.'

'So she lied to Radwan.'

'Yep. No doubt about it. Nice woman.'

'And Radwan's?'

'Twenty-eight thousand plus a few hundred.'

'Any unusual activity in either account?'

'Not that I can see. Just the usual household bills. Credit card payments. Utility bills. No mortgage payments. I'll check the land registry and see if they have mortgages though I doubt it.'

Hunter said, 'Sir, our priority here and now is to protect the SO15 officer Abida.'

'It's a priority but we have a few others as well. This man Sameer and his sister are obviously dangerous people. They need to be stopped. Besides which, they've admitted to killing someone when ordered to by Hamza.'

'What do you suggest?'

'You know what she looks like so keep an eye out for her. If you can follow her all well and good.'

'Will do, sir.'

'Nick,' said Badonovitch, 'that's the Hamza woman on the phone.'

'Sameer? I have an idea. I will simply tell Abida that she needs to take a package to the place. That you are a prospective purchaser and that we are handling the sale for a businessman living in Iraq. That you are here in the country for one day only and so you wish to see the place and the sales offer before going any further. That you will meet her there at five o'clock. I'll tell her she can finish for the day and go home as soon as she's dropped off the envelope.'

'Think it will work?'

'I don't see why not. Anyway, she does as she's told, end of story. I'll leave the rest to you but I'll be there about nine o'clock.'

43

Dunston stayed at the stakeout while Hunter and Badonovitch drove to the industrial park. They arrived there just before 13.30.

'It's not as bad as I thought it would be,' said the Russian.

They drove off the main road for about 100 metres and then turned into a cul-de-sac that opened out into a large parking area. On each of three sides stood a building with four roller doors, an ordinary door to the right of each roller and a window to the left. Many of the windows were boarded up as well as some of the doors but on the whole the buildings looked intact. There was no indication of life but they still climbed cautiously out of the Range Rover.

They checked each of the doors. They were all secured. Hunter used the pick lock gun and opened one of them. Inside it was dank and smelt of stale air. They heard a squeal and saw rats' droppings on the floor. They were in a short corridor with an office on the right and a door to the large workspace on the left. Inside the workspace was a workbench running the width of the back wall, which stretched about eight metres. The building was at least twenty metres deep with a window in the middle, a toilet on the right and a kitchen/staff room to the left. It was basic, utilitarian and depressing.

Hunter said, 'This place has never been used. There are no signs outside announcing the names of any company and this floor is clean apart from the rats. This kind of unit would normally have stains on the floor, bits and pieces of rubbish left when it was abandoned. Instead it's pretty much pristine.'

'Yeah. An investment property that went wrong?'

'Could be. Let's check the other units.'

They did so quickly with the same result.

'We'll unlock the corner door,' said Hunter, 'and see if Sameer and his sister are tempted in.'

It was the only building kitted out like a garage with a car pit on the left of the main room.

'A tempting place to dump a body,' said Badonovitch.

'In this case, two. We can then tell the General to deal with it. I'll get rid of the car in the side street we passed about half a mile back. You cover here.'

'Okay.'

Hunter left the building, climbed into the car and drove sedately away. Five minutes later he was walking back when his mobile rang and he looked at the screen.

'Yes Jan.'

'They're here. Just parked up. They've climbed out of their car and are looking around. The woman has gone to one side, the man the other. They're trying the doors. The woman is coming here. I'd better go.'

Jan Badonovitch stepped through the door into the main room that held the car pit. He stood behind the door and listened. He heard the unlocked outer door being opened and a woman call out.

'Sameer, this door is open.'

'Check it out Salma, though be careful.'

Badonovitch heard the woman's footsteps as she took a few paces along the corridor. She opened and closed the door to the office and then put her head around the door to where Badonovitch was standing. She paused and then stepped into the room. She was carrying a silenced pistol in her right hand, held waist high with her elbow tucked against her side.

She jerked her head to the right to look at the Russian but she was far too late. Badonovitch clamped his right hand over her wrist and bent it down, preventing her from squeezing the trigger or taking aim. He hit her with his left fist putting every ounce of weight he could behind the blow. When someone has a gun in their hand and is ready to use it there was no time for subtlety. The woman's head jerked backwards and her left temple hit the door jamb a mighty blow. She gurgled, collapsed and died.

Badonovitch, knowing something of the woman's history felt not an iota of remorse.

'Boss,' he phoned Hunter, 'I just killed the woman.'

'Good. Shoot the man if you have to.'

'Will do. Oh, oh. He's yelling her name.'

'Salma! Salma where are you?'

Badonovitch stepped across to the window and looked out through the grime. He could see the man standing near his car an angry frown on his face.

'Salma! What are you doing? Where are you?' He paused and then called out in Arabic. Badonovitch recognised the language but didn't understand the words.

The man reached into his pocket took something out and a few seconds later a phone in the dead woman's pockets began to ring. It rang three times, stopped and the man ran the dozen strides towards his car. He got in, started the engine and rammed the accelerator to the floor.

Badonovitch was at the front door in seconds with his silenced Glock in his hand. He took a two handed grip on the weapon, placed his feet apart, bent forward, took aim and fired four shots. The first two hit the rear tyre on the driver's side, the second two hit the opposite tyre. The tyres shredded and the car skewed left and right. Badonovitch took off at a flat run just as Hunter came running around the corner. Hunter threw two shots into the windscreen of the car; the driver's door opened and a man stepped out with his hands in the air. He was empty-handed.

'What do you want? Where is my sister?'

'In there,' said Hunter, nodding towards the building. 'Walk towards it.'

'No. I want to see my sister first.'

Hunter had been approaching the man. He was about 5ft 9ins tall, of slight build, with narrow shoulders and a long, narrow face. He had a straggly beard but a shaven upper lip. He stared straight at Hunter and kept his hands at shoulder height, with his palms open and outwards. He was wearing a dark grey business suit with a white shirt and maroon tie. He looked every inch a businessman but then he would need to if he were to reassure the woman from LFJ, even if only for a few seconds, that he was kosher. Just long enough to get her out of her car a task likely to be easier with his sister present.

Hunter stopped a pace short of the man and looked down at him. There was no hint of fear in the man's eyes, more a kind of indifference and insouciance that some people might find disconcerting. Hunter merely smiled.

'I want to see your warrant cards,' he said.

'What warrant cards?'

'Your ID. You are the police. I want to see them. I demand you arrest me and send for my lawyer.'

'Why do you think we are with the police?'

'I don't mean police. I mean MI6 or SO15.'

'MI6 don't operate in the UK. It's MI5 turf.'

'Whatever, I demand I be allowed to contact my lawyer.'

'You're making a lot of demands for someone who isn't in a position to ask so much as the time of day.'

'Where's my sister?'

'Jan? Where's his sister?'

'In that building, boss. I can take him to see her if he wishes.'

'Do you wish to see her?' Hunter asked reasonably. 'I am sure we can and will arrange for you two to spend a great deal of time together.'

Hunter held his gun in his right hand with it pointed at 45 degrees to the ground and to one side. He put his left hand out to grab the other man by his left arm and spin him around. He didn't get the chance.

The man kicked Hunter in the stomach with a move that took the TIFAT officer completely by surprise. Hunter managed half a pace back and to bend forwards while jerking his midriff backwards. If the kick had landed with its full force somewhere around his left upper abdomen or the left lower chest, Hunter's spleen could easily have been ruptured. Before he could recover the man stepped in and swept his right hand at Hunter's throat with the cutting edge foremost. Hunter got his left arm up in time to protect himself from what was another deadly blow. Before he could retaliate, Sameer was turning on his right foot and bringing his left foot back to kick Hunter in the left knee. If the blow landed accurately Hunter's knee would part like a rotten stick and he would go down. He would also be maimed for life.

Hunter threw himself backwards, landing on his back and hitting his head on the tarmac. Though he saw stars he continued the move and flipped backwards and onto his feet. He was seeing double when the man darted forward. Hunter did the only thing possible and that was to step into the attack.

His vision was clearing. He blocked a series of blows by the other man and then kicked him in the top of the thigh with all the weight he could muster. The man staggered but didn't go down. Instead he moved at Hunter with a dazzling display of arm and fist movements any of which would have done serious damage had they landed. But Hunter was no slouch when it came to hand-to-hand combat. He countered every move the other man made, blocking and attacking equally. They had been fighting less than two minutes with an intensity and level of concentration found in no other combat. The reason being whoever lost the fight would die. Hunter had a number of things going for him. He was taller and fitter than the other man who was already gasping for breath, the stench of cigarette smoke permeating the air between them. Hunter also had a longer reach but his other advantage was Badonovitch who could shoot the man if he had to.

The man was already weakening while Hunter wasn't even breathing hard. As the other man slowed so did Hunter. But he was now playing with the man. Teasing him almost as he cut and thrust with his arms and hands. The man was panting, his arms drooping until Hunter decided he'd had enough and kicked the man in the left upper abdomen. He put his weight behind the move and sent the man flying backwards. In his case with a ruptured spleen. The man's head hit the tarmac and unlike Hunter he made no move as unconsciousness claimed his senses.

Badonovitch pulled up alongside Hunter.

'Where were you?' Hunter gasped.

'I couldn't shoot from the angle I was at and then I could see you had the situation well in hand. You wouldn't have appreciated me interfering boss, you know that.'

Hunter nodded. 'You're right.'

'But I would have shot him if I thought you were going to lose.'

'You're all heart, Jan. Let's get this scumbag into the building.'

'I'll check his car.' Badonovitch put his head into the BMW and picked up a silenced pistol. 'A Sig 226 as used by the SEALS. Nice gun.'

Hunter picked up the unconscious man in a fireman's lift, bounced him up and down to a more comfortable position and headed towards the building.

'Jan, bring the car. We'll put it inside.'

'No point, boss. The door's electric and there's no power. I checked.'

'Okay, then we'll just leave it where it is.'

Hunter entered through the door and went into the big room. He dropped the inert form of Sameer alongside the body of his sister. The man was beginning to moan and wake up. His eyes blinked open and he stared straight into the eyes of his sister a mere couple of inches away. He jerked backwards, shock making his jaw drop open and his eyes squeezed tightly shut.

He turned his head and looked at Badonovitch. 'You killed my younger sister.'

'Yes, I did. But then, as you know, she deserved it. How many people has she killed?'

'She has only killed those who have deserved to die.' The man pushed himself up on his elbows.

'You mean like Abida? The young woman you are going to kidnap and hand over to Sabela Hamza later tonight? So she can ask her questions which if Abida doesn't answer to the lawyer's satisfaction she will be tortured?'

'That type of person deserves to die. I am fighting for holy jihad. My sister and I fight for Allah.'

'You killed people for money because you are greedy swine who should not be allowed to walk the earth,' replied Hunter.

'Who are you? What do you want?'

Hunter frowned. 'What makes you think we want anything?'

'Then why am I still alive? Are you arresting me?'

'We don't arrest people.'

'Then who are you.'

'Have you heard of TIFAT?'

The man's complexion drained as white as his swarthy skin would allow.

'I see you have.'

'You are enemies of my faith. Of my people. You are murderers of women and children.'

'No,' said Hunter, 'you're confusing us with Daesh. The filth who cut off people's heads, rape the women and children, put guns into the hands of nine and ten year olds and send them into gun battles.'

Hunter pointed his gun at the man's head and pulled the trigger. The bullet hit Sameer in the middle of the forehead and erupted out the back taking blood, brains and bone with it.

'We'll leave their car where it is,' said Hunter, 'but take their mobiles and guns. We don't want someone coming along and finding them. Guns are dangerous in the wrong hands,' he pontificated with a grin.

'Yep, boss, there's no doubt about that.'

They left the building and locked the door behind them. As they did Matt Dunston phoned.

'Nick? The girl is leaving carrying a briefcase. Presumably she's on her way to you.'

'Does the General know?'

'Not yet.'

'Okay, I'll tell him.' He called Macnair. 'Sir? Sameer and his sister are no more.'

'Good. Any difficulties?'

'Nothing we couldn't handle.' Hunter decided it was better not to tell his boss how close he had come to having his butt kicked.

'Okay, leave the bodies where they are and I'll get on to SO15 and tell them about the danger their officer is in and that she should be pulled immediately. I'll also tell them that we're dealing with LFJ. I'm sure with their budget cuts they'll be more than happy.'

'What about the bodies?'

'I'll explain we had a surveillance team on them and saw two people arrive and meet with them in the building. The two people left but you'd heard something and went to check it out. You then found the brother and sister dead and quit the scene. They can do the paperwork and not bother investigating too closely, as we have no way of identifying the perps.'

'Whoever you speak to probably won't believe a word of it,' said Hunter.

'Of course not. It's for the report and for political consumption if any inquiries are made.'

'Is that likely?'

'The way things are at present I wouldn't be surprised. Anyway, I'll deal with it.'

'Sir, it's 16.20. The woman Sabela Hamza will be here at 21.00. It would be a good idea if we just locked the doors for now and leave the bodies where they are. Just in case she appears and sees what's going on with a forensic and police team here.'

'What are you thinking, Commander?'

'These two killers vanish. She's unable to contact them. She'll want to know what's happening. She'll try and contact Abida. Panic is a powerful tool if we use it properly.'

'You're right. Panicked people make mistakes. I'll leave contacting the police until after Hamza has been.'

Hunter and Badonovitch left the building, locking the door behind them. They walked nonchalantly to where the car was parked and as they turned onto the main road they saw the SO15 officer arrive. They paused at the junction and saw her stop her car and use her mobile. Hunter drove away slowly, keeping a close eye on his mirror. He saw the officer's car pull out onto the road and race off in the other direction.

They were arriving back at the stakeout offices when one of the phones he had lifted from the killers began to ring. Badonovitch looked at the screen. The name Sabela was showing.

'Boss, this lot have no concept of real security.'

'It's their arrogance. Ignore it. That should have her going mental with a bit of luck.'

Hunter parked outside the offices and they went inside. Dunston greeted them with offers of tea or coffee. They settled on tea.

'Anything from across the way?' Hunter enquired, taking an appreciative sip of his brew.

'Yes,' Dunston smiled. 'They are really panicking about the money. Radwan has been raving about who they can and cannot trust.'

'Why don't we get Isobel to put some money into the accounts of some of their staff? She'll have all their account details from their employment files for salary payments. We can't make it too many people otherwise they might smell a rat but two or three should do the job. We'll then tell Sabela. Her response will be interesting.'

Hunter texted Isobel with the instruction to put £20,000 in three of the employees' accounts and to send details of their names and the banks to Hamza.

They didn't have long to wait for a response.

44

'Haatim I am very frightened.' There was no mistaking the stress and fear in her voice. 'What is happening? Who sent us the e-mail?'

'I don't know and can't tell. I don't believe Dawoud, Faris or Mutee would do such a thing.'

'That may be so but Dawoud is a highly accomplished hacker. We've used him often enough. So perhaps he's the one who hacked into the accounts and stole our money.'

'If he did he took millions so why keep only twenty thousand?'

'Because that's spending money. The bulk of the money could be anywhere.'

'Sabela, you're not thinking straight. You know millions have been taken and you're saying these three have taken some money to spend while the rest is hidden away? That's ludicrous! It makes no sense.'

The team heard a heavy sigh. 'You're right. I can't think straight. I don't know what it is but I feel as though I am thinking through a thick fog. It's peculiar. I have never had a problem like it before.'

'We've never been in a position like this before. Sabela, I am also very scared. We need to find the money. We need to get it back and we need to ensure the prince doesn't believe for one minute we had anything to do with what's happened.'

'How will we do all that?'

'We need to ensure that Tadeas al-Baghdadi gets blamed.'

'I repeat, how do we do that?'

'I don't know. I need to think about it. One thing we will do is record whatever he says to us tomorrow. He might let his guard down enough to be indiscreet.'

'Yes. I suppose it's possible. Let me try Sameer again.' There was silence for a full minute. 'Answering machine. I'll try Salma.' Another minute passed. 'The same.'

'Where are they?'

'How on earth do I know?'

Hunter knew from her tone that hysteria was welling up within her and her ability to think rationally would be further impaired.

'Oh God,' then she changed languages. 'Oh Allah, what's happening? Do they have Abida and if so where are they? Why don't they call? Why don't they answer their phones?'

Radwan ignored the rhetorical questions. 'Sabela, you must stay calm. We have to plan.'

'Plan what? What should we do? Tell me Haatim! Tell me how we get out of this mess.'

'We need to know who is doing this and right now there can only be one person and that is Tadeas. No one else could possibly have done this to us.'

'I said earlier what about the authorities?'

'Impossible in every way. They would not raid bank accounts and steal money. They would be breaking enough laws to end up in prison for a lot of years. Sabela you know this. We are going round and round in circles back to the same question. Who?'

They heard a door opening and a voice call out goodnight. There followed a plethora of similar farewells and then there were just the two of them.

'You just saw Mutee, Faris and Dawoud,' said Radwan, 'do they look as though they have stolen millions of pounds?'

'I don't know. I don't know what someone who steals millions looks like. Do you?'

'Of course not.' Radwan sighed. 'Sabela we have to stay focused. We need to hear from Sameer and we need to meet Tadeas. That is all we can do at this stage.'

'You're right.' Then she added, 'I need a drink.'

'I'll get it. Vodka and tonic?'

'Please. Light on the tonic.'

'So much for their Islamic beliefs,' said Dunston.

'As usual, hypocritical to a fault,' said Badonovitch.

They heard Radwan ask, 'Are you going to where Sameer is supposed to have Abida?'

'No. If we don't hear from Sameer or Salma then there's no point.'

'What should we do?'

'How the hell do I know?' There followed a string of expletives.

'Not very ladylike,' Dunston grinned.

'They are well and truly rattled,' said Hunter.

'Actually, I have an idea.' He phoned Macnair. 'Sir? What's the position with SO15?'

'I told them we had information that their officer Abida was in danger and that she should be pulled at once. I spoke to Danny Stockwell.'

Hunter knew Commander Stockwell from previous operations. A no-nonsense cop who didn't suffer fools gladly. He was also a rarity in the higher command structure of Britain's police force – he was not politically correct and didn't play the games necessary for higher office. But he'd made it clear to Macnair and Hunter over the odd drink or two that he was happy where he was. Catching terrorists and preventing attacks was his life's work, hobby and favourite pastime all rolled into one. He had never married and his work was his life. He was probably the most effective officer in Britain's police force at any level.

'Is he fully in the picture?'

'Not quite but near enough. He has a pretty shrewd idea of what's going on, can join the dots as well as anyone and knows there are some things it's better he doesn't know. Officially, that is.'

'Good. In that case I'd like Isobel to e-mail Hamza as though the message is from Sameer and tell her to meet them at the unit. Perhaps suggest it would be a good idea if Radwan accompanies her. There's nothing like the sight of a couple of dead bodies to scare the bejesus out of someone.'

Macnair was silent for a moment before he said, 'Yes, I like it. Keep them off balance even more. I'll get Isobel on to it right away.'

'Thanks sir. Tell Isobel to put in the e-mail unit 4b and to arrive at 20.30 and not before.'

'Any reason for the time?'

'No. It makes it all that bit more mysterious but we also need to get across there as well. I want to see their reaction. We'll also bug the place.'

After a few minutes Hamza said, 'There's an e-mail. It's from Sameer. No explanation only to go to the industrial estate unit 4b after half past eight.'

'Thank goodness,' said Sabela. 'Thank you. I need this.'

'I guess she's enjoying her vodka and tonic,' said Badonovitch.

'Matt, you stay and listen. Jan and I will go back and sort things out.'

When they arrived at the estate they hid the car in one of the units. They crossed to 4b, unlocked the door and entered. Everything was as they had left it. Sameer's blood had pooled and coagulated around Salma's face. They looked grotesque together.

Hunter placed a bug over the door and they left, leaving the door unlocked. Outside he placed another bug on the window facing the car park. They returned to the car and settled down expecting to have to wait at least an hour and a half. However, after forty minutes Dunston phoned.

'Nick, the Hamza woman can't wait any longer. She's leaving with Radwan now.'

'Good. This should be interesting if not fun.'

It wasn't long before a car nosed into the car park. Radwan was driving. He parked the car next to unit 4b and climbed out. Sabela Hamza quickly followed. It turned out she was an attractive woman who, they knew from her file, to be 35 years old with shoulder length hair and a voluptuous figure.

'Nice looking woman,' said Hunter. 'Her photograph doesn't do her justice.'

'I wouldn't kick her out of bed.'

'You'd never get the chance,' Hunter grinned.

The two men clearly heard her say in a nervous voice, 'It's spooky around here. Where are they?'

'I expect they're inside. Let's take a look.'

At the door Radwan called out, though none too loudly, 'Sameer, Salma, are you there?'

They both went in together. A few seconds later Hamza screamed and ran back out with Radwan on her heels. She leant against the car's bonnet, resting on her hands, her head hanging down. She dry heaved and then was as sick as a teenager after a binge drinking session. She began to moan while Radwan leant back against the wall, as pasty white as his swarthy skin would allow. He came to his senses first.

'We'd better get out of here. Whoever killed them may still be here or they may come back.'

She moaned and said, 'What's happening Haatim? Oh my God, what's happening?'

Radwan responded with a mouthful of expletives. 'I'm going. Either get in the car and come with me or stay and wait for the people who did this.'

He was as good as his word and climbed into the car. Hamza seemed to come to her senses because she straightened up and joined him. The car took off like a rocket, with its tyres squealing and the car fishtailing as it went round the bend.

'Nice one boss, that should discombobulate them for a while.'

Hunter grinned. He knew it wouldn't be long until Badonovitch had a new word to throw around. It was by way of being a hobby of his. The more obscure the word the better. But it was a good word in this case describing an enemy that was disconcerted and confused.

'So what's next?'

'I'll speak to Matt.'

He made the call and brought Dunston up to speed.

Dunston chuckled. 'Good. Their meeting with al-Baghdadi should be interesting. What are you going to do now?'

'We're wired into the offices so leave the gear to do the work. We'll drive to Paris via Eurostar.'

The two men returned to the stakeout. There were two cars in the car park and they belonged to Hamza and Radwan.

'They got back about ten minutes ago. She's in a pretty bad way, I am pleased to say. Care to listen?'

'What's happening Haatim? What's happening?'

'Stop asking me that! How in hell should I know? You've asked the same thing over and over again. Pull yourself together Sabela. We need to meet with Tadeas and speak to him. Perhaps he can shed some light on it.'

'Haatim, we have no money, we cannot pay our bills, we cannot pay wages and Sameer and Salma are dead. Murdered!'

There was silence for a few seconds and then Radwan said, 'What was to happen to Abida?' There was no reply. 'I'll tell you. She was going to be questioned, tortured if necessary and then killed. And you would have been there to see it.'

'I had to be there. I have the questions that need answering.'

'No, Sabela, you could have given a list to Sameer and they could have done the questioning. You wanted to be there because you enjoy it. You like inflicting pain. No, I'll correct that. You like watching others suffer but are afraid to do it yourself.'

'That's not true,' she gasped. 'I hate the sight of anyone or anything in pain.'

'Don't lie to me and more importantly don't lie to yourself. I've thought that over the last few years you have become more callous, harder in your attitude but that is not true.'

'It isn't?'

'No. I think you have always been like it.'

'So why have you stayed with me?'

'You know why.'

'I've told you I don't love you.'

'I know you have. But I can't help my feelings for you.'

'Even if I am a callous what? A bitch?'

'Yes, even if you are both those things.'

'Haatim, I told you a number of times. I will not leave my husband and I am only interested in one thing, which is the destruction of the west. Piece by piece I will make their soldiers pay for what they've done by attacking them in my way at every opportunity. It may take hundreds of years but I will be looking down on earth when the world is an Islamic Caliphate. Don't you want the same thing?'

There was silence for a few seconds. Then slowly Radwan said, 'I thought I did. But now I am not so sure. We are ruining the lives of very many people in our endeavours to sow hatred and distrust amongst the non-Islamic people of the west. The slavery and the drugs are against the teaching of Muhammad, peace be upon him.'

'It is all for the greater good. Sacrifices have to be made. We need the money to pay for what we are doing.'

'Notice,' said Dunston, 'that the sacrifices are always those made by other people.'

'Which reminds me,' said Hunter, 'I want to ask the General if he knows who committed the attack . . .' he paused. 'Listen!'

'Sabela we have the explosive vests arriving in two days at Grimsby. It's cash on delivery. We need thirty thousand pounds for the vests.'

'Listen to him,' said Hunter angrily, 'he's talking about explosive vests as though they were a consignment for Marks and Spencer.'

'I'd forgotten.'

'It's too late to cancel the shipment and you know what these people are like. Crossing them isn't a good idea.'

'That's the problem when you deal with Serbs,' said Sabela bitterly, 'they do not really believe.'

'My God but she's a hypocrite,' said Dunston. 'But then, people like her usually are.'

'We need to find out which ship and when,' said Hunter. 'They mentioned Serbs but is that as the suppliers back in Serbia or is it the ship's crew?'

'There's no way of telling,' replied Dunston.

Hunter phoned Macnair. 'Sir? Did you get the last transmission from the lawyers' office?'

'No. I'm at home.'

'There's a ship arriving in Grimsby in a few days carrying explosive vests.'

'How many?'

'They didn't say. What we do know is that they need thirty grand to pay for them. I don't know the going rate for such fashion accessories.'

'I don't either. So what do you suggest we do?'

'Get Isobel to send an e-mail as though it's from Haatim Radwan. Have them arrange a meeting for the delivery somewhere in the docks and to confirm the price is thirty thousand in cash. Also that we need confirmation of the day and time.'

'That should work. Okay, consider it done.'

'Right, sir. In the meantime we're take the Eurostar to France. If we hurry we should catch the twenty two hundred from Dover. The recordings will continue to be transmitted to you so you can keep us in the picture if anything of interest happens.'

'Is there anything you need?'

'Yes, sir. David Hughes and Don Masters would be a good start. Also Chris if he's available. I was also thinking of talking to Romain Goulart at the DGSE. Tell him what's happening and asking him for clearance to proceed.'

The General was quiet for a few seconds before he said, 'No. Leave it for now. I'll tell them if I think it's necessary.'

'Roger that, sir.'

'I'll send the other three. Do you need anything else?'

'Not that I can think of.'

'By the way, the recent explosions have all been suicide bombers,' said Macnair, 'and I guess we now know who supplied the vests.'

'And the money. Also, someone would have to go to Grimsby, collect the explosives, hand over the cash, take the gear somewhere and then arrange its distribution. I think Lawyers For Justice would be the right people with the right cover and organisational skills to do just that. Hang on sir, they're talking about the shipment again.'

'I can arrange an overdraft for the company account,' said Hamza, 'and get the thirty thousand we need. Faris and Dawoud can go and collect the vests. They've been before so they know what to do.'

'Are you sure the bank will give us the money?'

'Of course,' said Hamza. 'We've always had a very healthy account so I see no problem.'

'No, I mean giving it to us in cash. Will they do that?'

'Of course they will. It's paying in cash that can be a problem, not withdrawing it. Money laundering laws are pretty strict but won't affect us in this case. If the manager asks I will tell them it's to do with sharia banking laws. He'll nod, try and look as though he knows what I am talking about and hand over the money.'

'That should work.'

'If we fly to Paris at lunchtime we can be at the Luxembourg Gardens in time to meet Tadeas.' There was a quiver in her voice.

'Have you arranged a time?' Radwan asked.

'Yes. I suggested seven o'clock and he has agreed.'

'He won't be alone, you can be sure of that.'

'What does that matter? We need to resolve matters. And anyway, what if he isn't alone? What can they do in the middle of Paris?'

'Sabela, for such an intelligent woman you ask stupid questions. How about kill us?'

45

The team caught the train by the skin of their teeth. It wasn't busy. There had been too many explosions on both sides of the Channel. People were staying at home.

In Calais they found a hotel and crashed for the night. Breakfast was day old croissants, weak coffee and a bad attitude. They hit the road at 08.40 with a three hours' drive ahead of them. In fact, the roads weren't busy and they made good time. At the A26 and A1 junction they pulled off to find a service station to fill up with diesel and good coffee and to take a natural break. Hunter had been driving and he handed over to Badonovitch.

The General phoned. 'Hamza and Radwan are catching an afternoon flight to Paris. They've confirmed meeting with al-Baghdadi at 19.00 at the Luxembourg Gardens. They've been generous enough to tell us which bench they'll be on.'

'How did they decide that?' Hunter asked.

'From Google earth photographs.'

'In that case we'll bug it as well as a few more benches in case al-Baghdadi has enough security savvy to sit somewhere else. Also it's a popular venue. The bench they want can easily be in use.'

'They're planning to be there between 18.00 and 18.30. If anyone is using it they hope it'll become vacant before al-Baghdadi arrives. Two people and a couple of cases should be enough to stop anyone else sitting there. I assume you have the parabolic mics with you?'

'Yes, sir.'

'You may be able to set them up as well as plant a few bugs. The others will be with you around 17.00. If there's nothing else I'll just wish you good luck.'

They dumped the car in a twenty-four hour multi-storey car park and took a taxi to the Gardens. It was a beautiful summer's evening, the grounds were glorious and people were strolling around, enjoying the sunshine and warm breeze. Many were arm-in-arm, even the older folk, it was that sort of place. It reeked of romance of a bygone age.

They had knapsacks over their shoulders and walked around the grounds separately. Hunter was dressed in his light cream safari jacket and brown trousers. The loafers on his feet were ideal for running in.

He identified the bench that the lawyers planned to use but a family of mother, father and three children were already sitting there. The kids were beginning to fidget and Hunter figured it wouldn't be long before they left. He was right. A few minutes later he took possession along with Badonovitch and they both fixed bugs to the arms and back of the bench. Meantime, Dunston was sitting about 50 metres away with his back to the target bench. Alongside him was his knapsack out of the top of which poked the parabolic mic. Hunter phoned Dunston who didn't answer but put his hand to the back of his head.

'Well Jan, a nice day.'

'Yes Nick it is.'

Dunston made the same signal. They were being heard loud and clear. He signalled again. It meant the bugs were also active and recording. There would be no contact between them for the rest of the day. There was no telling who was watching the area.

Hunter and Badonovitch stood up, slung their bags over their shoulders and went for a stroll. Dunston stayed where he was, took out a paperback, plugged in earphones and settled down to await events.

The beauty of the place was lost on the two TIFAT men. They were looking for the enemy. Instead they found three friends, each one wandering in different directions, ignoring one another.

'Hi, Nick,' Bletchley said, his mobile phone to his ear. He wasn't using it, it was for show. The microphone behind his ear allowed him to transmit and hear the others simultaneously.

'Good trip?' Hunter also looked as though he was using a mobile.

'Painless. Anything happening?'

'No. But if I was al-Baghdadi I'd have plenty of security covering the place.'

'I concur but I can't see anyone.'

Don Masters jogged past wearing high visibility running gear. He sat down on a nearby seat, hung his head between his legs and pretended to be panting for breath. 'I haven't seen anyone either.'

'I'm going to walk out of the grounds,' said Hunter, 'and buy something to eat and drink at the store around the corner.'

When he returned he was lucky enough to find the bench next to the target bench was vacant. He sat there with his picnic of a prawn sandwich and fresh orange juice seeming to be enjoying himself. Around 18.00, the two lawyers entered the grounds and headed for the bench seat they had earmarked. They were unlucky. A young woman plus two children were sitting there.

Hamza and Radwan stopped and stared. They seemed not to know what to do next. Then he took hold of her arm and led her away, walking slowly, him looking around while she stared at her feet.

'Got them on the mic,' said Dunston. 'I'm patching you in.'

'We'll need to loiter,' said Radwan, 'and as soon as those people leave we can try to get to the seat before anyone else does.'

Hamza didn't reply for a few seconds and then she said, 'I'm scared Haatim. I don't know what we're letting ourselves in for. What if he does something to us?'

'Like what? Kill us in broad daylight in the middle of Paris? That's ludicrous. He needs us as much as we need him.'

'I wish I could believe that.'

'What do you want to do? Leave or stay here?'

'We have to stay,' she said slowly, 'we've no choice.'

They lapsed into silence. Suddenly the three on the bench stood up, the kids began to run away and the woman, hurrying after them, yelled at them to stop. The two lawyers hurried over to the seat and claimed it for themselves.

Hunter checked the time. It was 18.43.

'Heads up,' said Badonovitch, 'there are three targets coming in from the west and three from the south.'

'Clocked them,' said Masters who was leaning back on his bench with his face slightly angled to the sun. There were a couple of teenagers sitting next to him, a boy and a girl, holding hands. The girl looked at Masters who smiled back. She said something to the boy who also looked then they both stood up and walked away. Masters was relieved to see them go. There was no telling what was going to happen in the next minutes. He unzipped his bumbag and took a reassuring hold of his silenced Glock.

'There's another three coming in from the east,' said Hunter.

'Ditto from the north,' said Hughes.

'We've got company,' said Hunter who watched as two men in smart suits approached him. Both had grim looks on their faces.

Hunter held out his hand. 'Romain, Malcolm said you might be coming.'

The second-in-command of the DGSE shook Hunter warmly by the hand. 'Let me introduce Phillipe Thomas.'

The two men shook hands and at the same time took appraisal of each other. Hunter recognised a fellow warrior when he saw one.

'We'd better go for a walk,' said Hunter.

'We're going into the palace,' said Romain Goulart, 'all arranged by General Charney.'

The three fell into line and strolled nonchalantly towards the building. Hunter said, 'Dave, head for the palace.' The other two glanced enquiringly at him. 'One of my men. He may be useful. You'll understand when you meet him.'

'The palace is closed for renovation work,' said Goulart, 'and all the workmen have now gone home. However, I have a key.'

There was a temporary wire fence surrounding the front, a section of which was easily pulled to one side. Moments later they went through a side door with Hughes at their heels. Introductions were made.

Thomas nodded at the bag over Hughes' shoulder. 'Sniper?'

Hughes nodded. 'An A3.'

'Good gun. I've used one a few times myself.'

'Where?' Hughes asked out of professional courtesy. If it was only on a firing range that was one thing, if it was in combat that was something entirely different. Shooting inanimate targets did not compare to putting a bullet into somebody's head and watching as their brains, skull and blood erupted everywhere.

'Syria. An insertion against a Daesh commander.'

'Did you get him?'

Thomas grinned. He was in his middle forties; squat, wide shouldered with a healthy tan. He was bald but made up for it with a luxurious moustache. He had a round face, bushy eyebrows, piercing brown eyes and a wide mouth. His smile said it all.

'Him plus eight others in his entourage. There were two of us.'

'Nice one. When was that?'

'Eighteen months ago.'

'In Aleppo?'

Thomas nodded.

'I heard about it. Eleven hundred metres and some?'

'Twelve thirty.'

'Nice shooting.'

'I know who you are, of course,' said Thomas. 'Your reputation precedes you.'

Hughes looked surprised.

Hunter said, 'Okay you two, enough of the mutual admiration.'

Goulart said, 'General Macnair has briefed me. You know we cannot shoot people on French soil unless they are a threat to the lives of ourselves or innocent bystanders.'

'We know,' said Hunter. 'Hang on a sec. Yes, Don?'

Masters said, 'Nick, they are definitely armed. They all have a pistol under their jackets. We've identified twelve of them. They're sitting and standing anything from fifty to a hundred metres from the bench the lawyers are using.'

Dunston spoke. 'They're a real piece of work, Nick. They're brazen, it's the only word to use.'

'Maybe they've spent too long in Saudi where they are never questioned about what they're up to.'

'That would make sense if they are Mutawa. Nobody would dare question them,' said Dunston.

Hunter relayed what had been said to the two Frenchmen. 'You know what this means?'

'That they are rank amateurs,' said Thomas.

'Christ!' Goulart exclaimed. 'That's all we need.'

They knew that amateurs were prone to panic and react badly.

'If this lot are brainwashed into protecting al-Baghdadi without thinking about the consequences of their actions, they could easily start shooting before we can stop them,' said Goulart.

'We can only do one thing,' said Hunter, 'let the meeting take place and follow al-Baghdadi and pick him up somewhere else.'

'What about the lawyers?' Goulart asked.

'They're not going anywhere. We can get to them anytime,' said Hunter. 'Are you alone?'

Goulart shook his head. 'I have twenty men sitting out of sight ready to go.'

'Armed?'

Goulart's look said it all. They wouldn't be of much use if they weren't. The four men had made their way upstairs. From the first floor window they had a stunning view of the grounds. Hunter pointed out his team. The Saudis looked like a shoal of sharks circling their pray, dead eyes anticipating a feeding frenzy.

'People are leaving the park,' said Thomas.

'They are looking at those men and sensing trouble,' replied Hunter.

'Who do these swine think they are? They are acting as though they own the place. This is Paris. We don't tolerate this sort of behaviour,' said Thomas.

'What are you going to do?' Hunter enquired. 'We would like to hear what those two have to say to al-Baghdadi. However,' he shrugged, 'it's now your call. Actually, why did you come? Why didn't you just leave it to us?'

'What would you do? Arrest them?' Goulart asked.

'No. We were going to listen to whatever was said between al-Baghdadi and those two,' he nodded towards the grounds, 'and at the earliest possibility, up close and quiet, kill al-Baghdadi.'

'I appreciate your candour, Nick,' said Goulart. 'I don't like euphemisms at a time like this. One of the reasons we came was that General Macnair had information that at least ten or more people were coming here to protect al-Baghdadi.'

'Where did the info come from?'

'Mossad. It seems they have been monitoring the activities of al-Baghdadi for some time.'

The Israeli secret service was not only effective but it could be trusted by the west – at least up to a certain point. The point being as long as it was in Israel's interests.

Hunter checked the time. It was 19.28. 'He's late. So what do you want to do? Romain, it's your call.'

'I want Dave to set up here to cover the park. I see your men have already moved to cover those swine but tell them under no circumstances to shoot unless the Saudis open fire first.' Goulart broke off to listen to a message. 'Merci. Three cars have just pulled up. They are full of men. One is being treated with deference.'

'Al-Baghdadi?' Hunter suggested.

'We don't know. We don't know what he looks like.'

'No photo from Mossad?'

'No. Just the fact that he would be arriving with a lot of help.'

'Sounds more like a small army,' said the RN Commander. 'You all set, Dave?'

'Yes, Nick.' Hughes had placed the gun on an occasional table under the window. He had extended the tripod on which it rested and stood comfortably behind it, moving his aim from one target to the next. The window was open but the end of the barrel of the silenced rifle was inside the room so nobody would see it sticking out.

Another message was transmitted to the DGSE officers.

'The drivers are staying in the cars. Nine men are heading into the park. One is walking in the middle, surrounded by the others,' reported Goulart.

'Bloody hell,' said Hunter, 'you'd think they wanted to start a small war.'

'Who does he think he is,' Hughes asked, 'the President of the United States?'

'Romain, what do you want to do?'

'If we try and arrest them they look jittery enough to start shooting. Innocent people could get hurt.'

'That's almost inevitable,' said Hunter. 'And stopping them is not worth the life of a single bystander.'

'I agree. Let them have their meeting while we watch what happens. In the meantime I am going to call for more backup. I will not let armed men walk around my city as though they own the place. Present company excepted of course.'

Hunter grinned and nodded. He turned on the receiver so that it was broadcasting into the room.

Five of the nine men stopped a few metres from the seated lawyers and turned to look outwards. Two of the other four carried suitcases and one had an overcoat slung over his arm. The other two stepped around the bench and stood behind it.

'Who are you?' Hamza asked, looking up at the man who was standing in front of her looking down.

46

'I have come with a message,' said a heavily accented voice.

'Where's Tadeas?'

'Alas, he could not come. He has a deep-seated distrust of the west and does not feel comfortable being here. Even in such a beautiful city as Paris.' The man sat down beside her.

Hunter and the others exchanged glances.

'Now what, Nick?' Dunston murmured.

'We watch and listen.'

'I have another eighteen men just arrived,' said Goulart, he spoke into his phone, telling them to stay where they were but to be ready to move fast if they were needed.

'This is unacceptable,' they heard Hamza saying, 'totally unacceptable.'

'So is the loss of our money. I should tell you that the prince is very annoyed.'

'So are we,' hissed Hamza, 'and we want to know where it has gone. The only person apart from us who had access to the bank deposits and investments was Tadeas and you are telling us he is not available to account for what has happened?' There was no disguising the incredulity in her voice.

'Of course not. He cannot. He knows nothing about it.'

'We didn't do it. Why would we? We are fighting holy jihad and would never steal from our own.'

'The prince does not agree. He has reminded us that Tadeas had access only to the money he needed to disperse to our holy warriors.

You are the only people to know where all the accounts are and have access to all of it. The whole portfolio,' he added for good measure.

Hamza gasped. 'What are you saying?'

'The prince has decided that it is time to sever all connections with your firm. You will no longer be acting for the prince in either a legal capacity or in your other activities.'

'You can't do this!' There was desperation in the woman's voice.

'We have been ordered by the prince to sever all ties. He does not trust you any longer and he is also concerned that if it isn't you then it could be the western authorities. To protect himself he needs to end all connections.'

'But . . . But it cannot be the authorities. They wouldn't dare. They don't have the authority to steal our money.'

'You are wrong,' the man spoke softly, 'there is one organisation. Ruthless and working with the blessing of many of the world's governments and who will kill and steal to get what they want.'

'Who? Who are you talking about?' Hamza asked, her voice several octaves higher than normal.

'I know the answer,' said Radwan. 'Oh God, why didn't we think of it sooner?'

'What are you talking about?'

'Don't you see, Sabela? TIFAT. The so-called International Force Against Terrorism.'

'That is correct, Haatim. If they are on to you and follow any paper trail that might or might not exist then the consequences could be dire, especially for the prince.'

'But we have cut offs,' said Hamza. 'There is no way they can follow a trail back to the prince.'

'Can you guarantee that?'

'What? Guarantee it? Why . . . Why of course not. There is no such thing as a guarantee when it comes to computers.'

'So there is no choice but to draw a line under our activities and start again somewhere else. Tadeas has been given a second chance. He is to find another firm to do as you have done and if it takes a year, then *insha'Allah*. It is the will of God but at all times we must protect the prince. He and he alone is the real driving force behind our worldwide holy jihad against the infidels.'

'What is to happen to us?' Hamza whispered.

'You die,' was the harsh reply.

The two men behind their backs placed their hands on the lawyers' shoulders, holding them still while at the same time ensuring they sat up straight.

The man sitting with them rammed a silenced pistol into Radwan's side, under his arm and fired twice. The bullets went through Radwan's body and stopped in the middle of Hamza's. Shock registered on both faces. Radwan was lucky he died in a couple of seconds. Hamza wasn't so lucky. She opened her mouth to scream but the man behind roughly put his hand over her mouth. She convulsed for a few seconds before she died. Blood was coagulating on the ground under the bench. The two suitcases were arranged each side of the bench to try and hide the mess and an overcoat was also thrown under the bench. It wasn't that effective but would do for long enough for the Saudis to leave the park.

'Let us go,' said the man, standing up.

'What do you want to do?' Hunter asked. 'Arrest them? What if they resist?'

'Then we'll have one hell of a gun battle and we could end up with innocent people being killed or wounded,' answered Thomas.

'So we'll wait until they leave,' said Goulart. 'They have to disperse. We'll pick up as many as we can. We'll arrest them for being in possession of firearms and identified as terrorists.'

'And if they do resist?' Hughes asked.

'We'll cross that bridge when we come to it, as you English say,' said Thomas.

'I'm Welsh, but I'll let it go,' Hughes said, packing away his rifle.

The four men stood at the window and watched as the last nine men to arrive headed back the way they had come. The remainder, who had been scattered around the park, headed in different directions, walking quickly, obviously eager to get away.

'Let's go,' said Goulart. 'Jules? Follow them discreetly, we'll catch you up.' He was speaking as they hurried down the stairs. 'We have three unmarked cars close by, that should be sufficient.'

He issued more orders to his men. They would be arresting as many of the Saudis as possible, preferably without any shooting.

They climbed into the third car. Thomas drove. Goulart received directions from the other two cars and they quickly found themselves heading out of Paris and taking the A3, the Autoroute de Normandie.

'In ten minutes,' said the DGSE officer, 'we can pull the cars over and arrest them.'

'Three cars?' Hunter queried?

'Oui, you are correct. We need more men.'

'Or we reduce the opposition,' said Hunter.

'What do you mean?'

'They are in a hurry to get somewhere. Where? It would be useful to know. Maybe more members of a terrorist cell? Maybe jihadists who are living here who help the attackers without taking part themselves? Maybe nothing but that would be useful to know. So let's reduce the odds, just in case.'

'How?' Goulart asked.

'We stop the third car. If we get ahead we find a place for Dave to shoot out a back tyre. They'll probably think they've had a blowout. If we get one of the cars just behind they can move in quickly and arrest the men in the car.'

'It could work,' Thomas said, thoughtfully.

'I know just the place,' said Goulart. 'It's a half-hour away.' He gave his instructions to the other two cars while Thomas speeded up and hit 160kph in a few seconds.

They passed the two DGSE cars as well as the three targets. They arrived at the D113 turnoff a good five minutes ahead of the trailing cars. Both sides of the autoroute was thick with trees but at that point there was an added advantage. Roadworks on their side of the road brought the cars down to a single lane and a speed limit of 50kph.

Thomas parked in a lane running alongside the autoroute but out of sight of it. A two minutes walk brought them to the ideal ambush sight behind a felled tree; the angle to the target was less than twenty degrees.

'Wait a moment,' said Goulart and spoke to the drivers in the other cars. Then he said, 'My two cars are bracketing the third car. Dave, you shoot out the tyre and my men will take care of the rest. They can move in front and back. There shouldn't be anybody in the line of fire and I have told my men that if there is any sign of a weapon by the terrorists they are to shoot them. That they are not to hesitate.'

Moments later Goulart said, 'Here they come. They've just reached the roadworks.' He paused. A few more seconds passed and then he said, 'Here they are.'

'You okay, Dave?' Hunter asked.

'No problem, Boss.'

The target was less than 100 metres away and travelling at barely 30kph. The jihadists' cars in front were pulling away at 50kph.

The sniper was lying behind the tree, the barrel of his rifle resting on the trunk. He was breathing steadily, his heart rate was normal, his target large in his sights. He fired. The bullet took out the tyre on the rear passenger's side and the car was suddenly sliding left and right, making control difficult. The driver pulled over to the right but didn't manage to clear the road before the car stopped. Immediately cars queued up behind, and the French drivers, not known for their patience, hit their horns long and loud.

'Let's go,' said Goulart.

They were quickly back on the road and speeding to catch up with the two cars belonging to the terrorists. They were still in the roadworks and quickly closed up on the two cars that were still travelling at the speed limit. Goulart's mobile rang. He listened to the caller.

'That was one of my men at the car. The Saudis didn't have time to make a move.'

'Did they find anything?' Thomas asked.

'Four pistols plus spare ammo. We'll get them on terrorism charges and with the way things are in France right now we can expect them to receive lengthy sentences. And being done for terrorism probably means they won't serve their full term.'

'Why not?' Hunter asked.

'Even hardened prisoners don't like terrorists. The chances of them serving let's say a full ten years and living is highly remote.'

'Can you be sure?' Hughes asked.

Goulart's smile was wolfish when he looked over his shoulder at the two men behind him. 'I can guarantee it.'

He didn't need to say any more. His phone rang again. He listened, acknowledged the call and broke the connection.

'The front car is coming after us. They won't be long.'

The roadworks ended and the stream of traffic increased speed.

Thomas said, 'It looks like they are headed for Rouen or possibly Le Havre.'

'My bet is on Le Havre,' said Hunter. 'Romain, can you check what ships are in the harbour?'

'What are you thinking?'

'Check for a super yacht.'

'I see. This unknown prince we've heard so much about. Why do you think there could be such a ship?'

'It's a long shot. You know that the Saudi princes travel with large entourages just to show how important they are. That's how they managed to put so many men into Paris. It also explains their lack of professionalism. They're of a mind that a large number of armed men can substitute for trained officers. We see it all the time in the Middle East.'

The other three nodded.

'That's one reason al-Baghdadi didn't come. The prince decided to cut his losses and remove the two people who could identify him.' Hunter shrugged. 'Pure hypothesis of course but if a yacht is there then it makes sense. If there is, what do you want to do?'

'I have already said I don't like people coming to my country

421

carrying weapons, shooting people and thinking they can get away with it.' His mobile rang. He listened for a couple of moments, said, 'Bien joué,' and ended the call. 'That was a report from the other car. They've checked the men's mobiles and are certain no messages were sent and no calls made.'

'Good,' said Hunter, 'that'll have the others worried.'

Goulart's phone rang again. He listened, thanked the caller and broke the connection. 'It seems Nick, you were right. There is a super yacht berthed at Le Havre.'

'Whose is it?' Thomas asked.

'It's owned by an offshore company registered in Bahrain.'

'I'll get TIFAT onto it,' said Hunter. 'What's the name of the yacht and the name of the company?'

'Tell Malcolm to phone my office and ask for Julie Monart. She can give him the details.'

Hunter made the call and passed the information to Isobel. 'She'll put someone on to it.'

Headlights flashed behind them.

'That's my car,' said Goulart.

'What do you want to do about the men in the two cars?' Hunter asked.

'If they head for Le Havre once we get to the port I want to stop them,' said the DGSE officer. 'Whoever this prince is it'll put the frighteners on him.'

Goulart's phone indicated a text message. He read it. 'Merde!'

'What is it?' asked Thomas.

'It's incredible,' said Goulart, 'but the yacht has diplomatic immunity!'

'How the hell can that be?' Hunter asked.

'Ask the Ministry of the Interior, the Ministry of Foreign Affairs and anyone else you can think of,' said Goulart, making no attempt to hide his anger. 'It means we can't board the yacht.'

'We don't want to,' said Hunter.'

'We don't?' Goulart was surprised.

'What would be the point?' Hunter asked. 'There's nothing we can do. You couldn't arrest the prince without causing the biggest diplomatic row France has ever been embroiled in.'

After a few seconds Goulart nodded. 'You're right but it makes me so angry.'

'We'll focus ECHELON onto all transmissions from the yacht.'

'Thank God for the system,' said Goulart. 'Our politicians are morons. We'll continue to work together but I envy you.'

'You do?' Hunter was surprised.

'Yes. Britain will be a more secure country. You'll have better control over your borders, you'll be able to throw more criminals out of the country than you have in the past and as a result you will be a lot safer. You will be able to fulfil the first obligation of any government, which is to keep its citizens safe.'

'We think so,' said Hunter.

Goulart nodded morosely. 'We're jealous.'

Hunter smiled. 'Like you said, we'll work closely together in the fight against Islamic terrorism but it's an uphill battle.'

'It's a bloody steep hill and it's a real war,' said Hughes. 'And I don't mean bloody in the figurative sense but the real meaning of the word.'

'Amen to that,' said Thomas.

47

'They're heading for Le Havre,' said Goulart. 'Let's go Phillipe. We know where the yacht is berthed and I've just received photographs of the area. Here Nick, take a look.'

Hunter examined the photographs on the iPad closely. 'How do you want to play this? Like I said, it's your call.'

Shrugging, Goulart said, 'General Charney and I don't want any court trials if we can help it. We have enough to deal with as it is. We also want to send a message to the terrorists.'

'And that is?'

'We're not going to play at policeman while they murder our citizens. We will also be sending the same message through diplomatic channels, especially to Saudi Arabia but a few other countries as well.'

'Good. When do we reach Le Havre?' Hunter enquired.

Thomas replied, 'In about half an hour.'

'The yacht is berthed on the Quai Pierre Cellet,' Goulart said. 'It's berthed starboard side to so it can quickly put to sea. This whole area will be deserted at this time of night. You can see on the iPad that the road branches off from the Avenue Lucien Corbeaux along the quay. There are very few streetlights, many steel containers as well as two buildings.'

'Any details about the yacht? Hunter asked.

'Er yes, here's a text. She is one hundred and fifty metres long, has a beam of twenty metres, carries thirty six guests and has a crew of at least seventy. There's a helo on her stern. That's about all. If the so-called guests are bodyguards and with such a large crew it's no surprise they could send as many men as they did.'

Hunter said, 'As we're not intending anything subtle, Dave can just shoot the drivers. We'll then play it by ear.'

It sounded callous but none of them had any illusions about the sort of people they were going up against.

Thomas put his foot down.

'Pierre, I suggest you tell the second car to slow down,' said Hunter.

'Why?'

'We're going to ambush these men. No quarter. None of the politically correct claptrap of making an arrest and all that entails.'

'So?' Thomas frowned.

'So we don't want too many witnesses. Someone writes their memoirs in twenty years time and they tell the story of the ambush. The lawyers will leap on it and we could be in trouble. We see it all the time.'

The others nodded.

'I'll order the other car to stay outside the port.'

They arrived at Le Havre and quickly made their way to the area where the yacht was berthed. They parked the car and stood for a few minutes examining the place.

There were two lights casting an orange glow at the end of the road. Where they stood it was dark. Goulart used a flashlight looking for something suitable to partially block the road. Their luck was in. Outside the nearest building they found three industrial sized aluminium rubbish bins on wheels. They rolled them across the road and placed them from the corner of the building to a fence on the other side. The road was blocked but if any car smashed into the bins they would easily be thrown aside.

From where they stood they could see the yacht. The gangway was still in place but it was obvious she was ready to depart. Her engines were running and there was only a headrope and sternrope holding the large vessel in position.

'Can't be long now,' said Goulart.

The three men were 100 metres in front of the rubbish bins and heard the sound of racing car engines.

'Here they come,' said Hunter, 'Dave, you ready?'

Hughes was standing behind the farthest bin, which reached shoulder height, his sniper rifle at the ready. 'Yes, Boss. No problems.'

That was Hughes' normal reaction to any situation.

They saw the loom of lights and then two cars came rapidly into sight going faster than the roads warranted.

His angle to the vehicle was less than 15 degrees. At 100 metres Hughes opened fire. It was a turkey shoot. His first shot killed the driver in the lead car; his second shot took out the second driver. Both cars swerved to the left, towards the Bassin Théophile Ducrocq. The front car smashed into a steel goods container, the second missed and flew through the air and into the water.

Hughes stood up and began to collapse his silenced rifle while the other three ran towards the crashed car.

'Romain,' said Hunter, 'you and Phillipe take the car in the water. I'll deal with these three.'

The smash had badly crumpled the car. Hunter had his silenced Glock ready when he dragged open the rear door on the driver's side. The man's brains were splattered across the back of the car. The front seat passenger hadn't been wearing his seatbelt and had smashed into the windscreen. He was obviously dead.

The man behind the driver had been thrown forward and had smashed his head into the back of the driver's. He wasn't moving and didn't appear to be breathing. Hunter put a bullet in the man's head just in case he was still alive. The man sitting behind the passenger had been wearing his seat belt. He stirred and turned his head to look at Hunter. In Arabic he asked for help. Hunter obliged with a bullet in the forehead.

Hunter ran the few dozen metres to the water's edge. The other two men were standing looking down at the water. Goulart was moving his torch methodically back and forth but there was no sign of any of the passengers.

Thomas glanced to their right and said, 'Look.' He pointed.

The super yacht was moving majestically away from her berth. The three men watched her for a few seconds before turning their attention back to the water. They stayed there for a few more minutes.

Goulart said, 'I don't think anyone survived.'

'I can guarantee nobody's alive in the other car,' said Hunter.

The DGSE officer combined a Gallic shrug with a cynical smile before he said, 'Good. It's time we sent a message to the terrorists that, what's that saying in English?'

'Do you mean the gloves are off?'

'Yes, that's the one. The gloves are off. We need to hurt them and hurt them badly.'

'Romain even if your politicians agree there are far too many people who will scream about human rights and justice and fair trials and all the rest of the claptrap, which we all know will result in more deaths at some point. After a few weeks the politicians will wring their hands, also bleat about human rights, in public at least, and you'll have your efforts curtailed back to a point of virtual uselessness. We've all seen it time after time.'

'I know. There's another English saying and that is we should make hay while the sun is shining. Or in this case wipe the swine off the face of the earth before they can kill or hurt other innocent people.'

'We need to find out who owns that yacht. If it is someone close to the Saudi king then I don't . . .' Hunter paused.

They were still standing at the edge of the basin when they heard a noise coming from the surface of the water. It was the sound of splashing. They were standing a mere two metres above the water and Goulart flicked his torch back on. He shone it at the water straight into the face of the man who had killed the two lawyers. The man put a hand up to cover his eyes, sank beneath the surface and came up spluttering and gasping. He was suddenly moving frantically in a manner that showed he couldn't swim.

The four men watched him dispassionately.

He called out in Arabic and then English. 'Help me! Help me! I am drowning! Help me!'

His frantic thrashing had brought him closer to the jetty and he looked up, still splashing around. He sank beneath the surface and came up again, spitting water and gasping for breath.

'Help me! For the love of Allah, help me!'

Hunter said in Arabic, 'Like you've helped the poor souls who have been brought into Europe, into slavery and bondage? Like you've helped the people who have drowned as they try to escape the wars in Africa and the Middle East?'

'That's business,' gasped the man, 'that's all it is. Just business.'

For a second Hunter wasn't sure how to react. Disgust and hatred coursed through him in equal measure. He was too slow in pulling his Glock. Goulart beat him to it. He fired his gun as fast as he could pull the trigger, emptying the magazine into the body of the Saudi although the man was dead with the first shot.

Hunter understood how the older man was feeling. 'Better?'

'Yes. I just wish I could put a bullet into every bastard who is smuggling those poor people to whom they have promised safety and help.'

'Romain, we've rebelled against the politicians and the do-gooders in the past. Remember a couple of years ago?'

'I remember. It didn't last long. A lot of senior people in the security services were forced to take early retirement.' He sighed. 'You are about the only people who are not shackled.'

'I can tell you that's a battle General Macnair is fighting just about every day.'

'I don't want to know. If things continue like they are then we'll have even more problems in the future. I really worry for my children and soon to be grandchild.'

Hunter grinned. 'Congratulations granddad.'

'Yeah but Nick, what sort of world will he or she be coming into? The mess is ours and we seem incapable of fixing it.'

'This is the sort of conversation we should be having over a large scotch,' said Hughes, ever pragmatic. 'What are we going to do now?'

'I need to make a few calls,' said Goulart.

'I need to talk to the General.'

Hunter made the call and brought Macnair up to date with events then he asked, 'What about the yacht, sir?'

'We still don't know who owns her but we're getting there. Leo has identified two dummy companies so far. He said he'll know sometime tomorrow. Anyway, good work. You may as well come back.'

'Will do, sir.' He waited until Goulart finished on his phone. 'Romain, we're done. The General has told us to return home.'

'Then take the car. I've quite a few things I need to do here like fire a few rounds from the pistols of the dead men.'

He didn't need to elaborate. To shoot the terrorists the forces of law and order needed a reason to shoot. Being shot at was about the only one acceptable.

'I'll be busy for the rest of the night. There's only one ferry from here and that's to Portsmouth in the afternoon. Your best bet is to drive to Calais. Thomas, can you go with them?'

'I'll be happy to,' said Thomas. 'There's nothing you need me for.'

'Good. Then I'll see you back in Paris.' He and Hunter shook hands warmly. 'Thanks for all your help, Nick, it's much appreciated by those of us fighting on the ground.'

'My pleasure, Romain.'

Hughes and Goulart also shook hands and the three men returned to the car, leaving Goulart standing next to the basin, looking meditatively at the water and the corpse now floating on the surface.

It was an easy two hours and a few minutes drive along the motorways to Calais. Since the removal of the immigrant squatters' camp known as the Jungle, the area had become much more peaceful. It was 03.55 when Thomas stopped the car at the ferry terminal. They shook hands and he drove away. In the terminal they discovered that the first ferry was at 05.45, boarding at 05.00.

There was a café where they discovered the coffee to be lousy and the bacon rolls unappetising so they ditched them in a rubbish bin. Being the first ferry of the day access was actually at 04.45. They passed through a non-existent customs control, showed their passports and boarded the ship. This time the coffee was good and the full English breakfast better than adequate. By the time the ferry cast off they were relaxing in comfortable seats, Hughes with his eyes shut and gently snoring, Hunter fighting to stay alert. Trouble could come anytime, anywhere and if it did one of them needed to be ready for it.

They swapped poses an hour later. They arrived in Dover on time and disembarked at 07.00. They caught the 07.47 train to London St Pancras, a journey of 2hrs 10mins. Much to the surprise of the passengers, as evidenced by their open comments, the train was on time.

When they arrived the city was hot and humid. They walked to Kings Cross and caught the 10.30 for Edinburgh. An hour and forty-two minutes later Hunter's phone rang.

'Yes, sir?'

'Where are you?'

'Just approaching Doncaster.'

'Good. Get off there, hire a car and I'll phone back in half an hour.'

The train was pulling into Doncaster and Hunter stood up and nudged Hughes' foot with his own.

'Wake up, Dave.'

'What's up?'

'We've been ordered to get off.'

'Where are we?'

'Doncaster.'

Hughes groaned. 'I was enjoying my dream. What's going on?'

'No idea. The General said to get off and hire a car. Something's up. He'll phone back in half an hour.'

The train came to a halt and the two men alighted. They grabbed a taxi to a national car rental office and took possession of a Ford EcoSport. They parked a few hundred yards from the car depot and Hunter phoned Macnair.

'We've been working on the information we've gleaned from the lawyers' offices as well as monitoring their phones, e-mails and the rest of the social media they use. It seems the ship carrying the bomber vests arrives tonight. I've spoken to the Grimsby port authorities and they said the ship is due to dock at 22.30.'

48

'Anything else you can tell us, sir?' Hunter asked.

'The ship is twenty thousand tonnes. A rust bucket I gather but has all the sea worthiness certificates it needs to operate in European waters. Owned by a company registered in the Bahamas, so no surprise there. According to their declared manifest they are carrying spare parts for agricultural machinery, which I suspect will prove to be the case. There's a crew of ten. A tug will be on standby but not buttoned on.'

'That's pretty normal nowadays for a ship of that size. It saves some berthing fees. How long will the ship be in harbour?'

'Until the morning when they'll unload it. According to the crew list they are all European Union nationals and so once they are alongside they can go ashore.'

'Is that likely?'

'Grimsby is a busy port. Plenty of places to go for a late night drink or two and maybe something more.'

'I take your point, sir.'

'We don't know what you'll be facing so Chris, Don and Jan will meet you at the Premier Inn in Grimsby. It's in the Europa Park. Whatever you do, those explosive vests must not end up in the country.'

There was no need to tell Hunter what he had to do. No arrests, no trials, no paperwork, no future for the terrorists. Or in this case for the men who would make money out of terrorism.

They quickly drove to the M18 motorway, headed north to junction

5 then turned east. It was an easy journey with light traffic and Hughes slept all the way. The satnav guided them an hour later to the hotel. The other three were already there.

They met in Bletchley's room where the greetings were brief.

'Anything more?' Hunter asked.

'Yes, we've been sent a photograph of the ship, The Compass Rose, and it's pretty much what you'd expect a 20 years old coastal ship to look like.'

'Rust streaks and belching smoke?' Hughes suggested.

'That about sums it up. The ship will be berthing in Alexandra Dock, near Freshney Cargo Services.' Bletchley used his laptop to show photographs of the ship and the dock area.

'Any thoughts?' Hunter asked.

'We start with the obvious question,' said Badonovitch, 'and that is do we take them out on land or onboard?'

'The General made it clear that none of the vests can reach the shore.'

'In that case it's a shipboard attack,' said Bletchley.

'We could arrive dressed as customs officers,' suggested Masters.

Nodding, Hunter asked, 'Do we know anything about the handover?'

'Not yet. According to the General that detail will be exchanged just before the ship docks,' replied Bletchley.

'Why?' Hughes asked.

'Some notion of security?' Bletchley suggested.

'I want the recipients as well,' said Hunter. 'It's okay to stop this shipment but we also need to stop the terrorists. If we don't then all that will happen is in a few months, maybe less, they'll get their hands on more explosives and it starts all over again. So we have two jobs. We take out the ship's crew and we take out the terrorists.'

Masters said, 'I have a plan, boss.'

'A cunning plan by the look on your face,' said Bletchley, aping a well-known character from television.

Masters shrugged. 'I wouldn't go that far.'

When he'd finished the others nodded.

'Okay you guys, check the gear,' said Hunter. 'Dave and I need to do some shopping. We'll also visit the docks and recce the area.'

'What about access?' asked Bletchley. 'Don't we need some sort of pass?'

'All arranged. The General has spoken to the Port Authorities. We'll just use our usual ID cards.'

'Local police?' Masters asked.

'He's had a word with the Chief Constable.' Hunter grinned. 'He gave him the option to leave it to us or he can deal with it. Apparently it took the CC all of five seconds to agree not to touch it with a barge pole and to stay well clear.'

'What about customs officers' uniforms?' Badonovitch asked.

'That's a good point,' said Bletchley.

'Check the Internet,' said Hunter, 'there's bound to be a store around here that sells them.'

'The nearest is Hull,' said Masters a minute later.

'Okay. Don, you and Jan go there and pick up a uniform each. You two will be the customs officers. Dave, I want you covering the area as usual. Chris, you and I will be looking out for the terrorists.'

'How will they get in,' Masters asked, 'without the right ID?'

'Good point. What would we do?' Hunter asked.

'Use a boat,' said Bletchley.

Hunter nodded. 'I agree. Okay you guys, get going while we think this one through.'

The two men left while the other three looked closely at the Google Earth photographs of the docks. They found the inner harbour where the marina was situated and zoomed in on the Humber Cruising Association building.

Hunter phoned Macnair and told him what he wanted. The general was back ten minutes later.

'I spoke to the harbour master who tells me that a floating gin palace arrived yesterday.'

'Could be anybody's,' said Hunter. 'I guess we need to wait until the details of the handover are sent.'

'Maybe, maybe not. The boat is registered to a company in Guernsey. We've checked it out and found it in turn is owned by a trust in the Bahamas. It's the usual obfuscation.'

'So it looks like a good bet.'

'We'll take a wander over and see for ourselves,' said Hunter.

'I don't need to tell you to be careful, but also remember they could be innocent people enjoying a summer cruise.'

'There's one serious flaw in that argument.'

'Do tell, Commander.'

'Who in their right minds would come to Grimsby instead of one of dozens of beautiful ports all up and down this coast?'

'Yes, that is a good point. Only don't let the good burghers of Grimsby hear you say that.'

'I'll do my best, sir.'

Macnair broke the connection.

'Chris, you take a gander at the gin palace. Dave and I'll go shopping for a few things.'

Hunter drove to the marina a mere two miles away and dropped Bletchley off. He then headed for the Freshney Place Shopping Centre. They were there for the mundane purpose of purchasing toiletries and new clothes, which didn't take long. A decent cup of coffee was also very welcome in one of the numerous coffee shops in the centre.

They reconvened back at the hotel. Chris Bletchley opened the proceedings.

'Well, it's a gin palace all right. A forty foot Sunseeker.'

'Did you see anybody?' Hunter asked, taking a sip of instant coffee he had just made and trying hard not to grimace.

'Four people. Two women and two men. I would say of Middle Eastern origin but with pukka English accents. Real upper class stuff.'

'What age would you say?' Hunter asked.

'Late twenties, early thirties. The women are very attractive.'

'Were they friendly?'

'I'd say so. All smiles, said they were on a cruise for a couple of weeks, enjoying the weather. More or less what you'd expect.'

435

'They don't sound like terrorists,' said Hughes, frowning.

Bletchley said, 'I couldn't agree with you more. However, there was one awkward, or perhaps I should say interesting, moment.'

'What was that?' Hunter asked.

Grinning, Bletchley replied, 'I asked them why had they docked in Grimsby when there were so many more picturesque places.'

'What did they say?'

'It seemed to catch them out for a few moments then one of the women said they had called in to refuel as they had been running low on diesel and water. I nodded and wished them a safe and happy cruise and left.'

'Did they refuel?' Hughes asked.

'Nope and according to the harbour master they are scheduled to leave at zero six hundred.'

'A stupid lie,' observed Hunter.

'Nick, I'm telling you these are not the sort of people to strap on an explosive vest and kill themselves.'

'So they're part of the supply chain.'

'I think so.'

'Okay, I'll get Isobel . . .' the words were hardly out of his mouth when his phone rang. He saw it was Macnair and put it on speaker.

'Yes, sir?'

'We've received messages that are going back and forth from the ship to someone in the Grimsby area.'

'On the boat?'

'We think so. Wait a moment, Commander. Thank you, Isobel.' There was a few seconds of silence. 'According to the latest communication between the Compass Rose and whoever, they will meet at midnight. Ah, this makes sense. I'm pretty sure it's the boat. The message says that they will go alongside the ship and collect the packages. I've been looking at a chart of the port as well as photographs and they can easily move round to the other dock, collect the vests and get out to sea. There's nothing to stop them.'

'I agree. Sir, Chris doesn't think the people on the yacht are the type to commit suicide. That they are probably facilitators rather than participants.' Hunter explained their reasoning.

'I'd like to know who they are.'

'We can find out tonight. We'll ask them. Politely, of course.'

'Of course. Commander, I want the end users as well as these people.'

'I concur, sir.'

'Sir?'

'Yes, Chris.'

'Sir, I saw these people. They look to be the sort who enjoy the highlife. I think it won't take much of a chat to get them talking.'

'Good. Incidentally, Romain Goulart phoned. The other men at the Luxembourg Gardens were all picked up. They weren't off the ship. Some had French citizenship but half of them were illegals. The DGSE played it cannily. They followed the men, arrested some they thought were becoming spooked but traced some of them to their homes. Romain tells me that three of them are married with kids.'

'What will happen to them?'

'The families? Nothing. Though Romain did say that two of the older teenagers they picked up were seriously radicalised. They gave some trouble and had to be restrained.'

'So problems for the future,' said Hunter.

'Precisely that and there's nothing to be done until they commit an illegal act.'

'Such as killing innocent people.'

'More than likely.'

'The men picked up all carried guns. At the homes the DGSE raided they found more weapons as well as explosives.'

'Well thanks for that, sir. Some lives will have been saved at least.'

Badonovitch and Masters returned with the uniforms. The rest of the evening the team spent in their rooms getting some shut-eye. Like the trained warriors they were sleep came easily.

At 22.00 they assembled in the car park and departed the hotel in the two vehicles. It was only a couple of minutes to the entrance to the docks. When they stopped at the barrier they had a surprise.

Hunter showed his ID. 'I believe you've been told to expect us.'

'Yes, sir,' said the uniformed officer, 'there's someone here to see you.'

A man in police uniform came out and Hunter instinctively straightened up behind the wheel.

'I wasn't expecting to see you, sir.'

The Chief Constable of Humberside smiled and held out his hand. Hunter shook it, wondering what the man wanted.

'Don't worry, Commander, I'm just here to wish you good luck. This is my direct mobile number, if you need anything call me. Knowing Malcolm like I do I doubt there is anything you'll need but I'll be here with an armed response unit just in case.'

'I take it he's briefed you on what's going down.'

'Yes.' The CC was in his mid fifties, with a long, narrow, clean-shaven face. He was looking grim. 'I wish we had the authority to do what you're doing. But you know, as soon as so much as a shot is fired we have an inquiry and woe betide anyone who has broken the ludicrous rules under which we must operate.'

'Amen to that, sir.'

'If just one of those vests reaches shore a lot of people could be killed and many more badly hurt. If there really are ten of them then Christ alone knows how much damage could be done. Commander, take as many prisoners as you can but at no risk to yourselves.'

'Yes, sir. General Macnair said the same thing. He suggests some plea bargaining might result in us finding the suppliers of the vests. We'll certainly be able to tell where the PE comes from.'

'Pity it's plea bargaining and not water boarding,' said the CC.

'I like your style, sir, but that's a no-go unfortunately.'

The CC sighed and said, 'I know it is. We must be civilised at all costs even when dealing with amoral, vicious animals like these Serbs.'

There was nothing Hunter could say to that observation so he kept quiet.

'I've spoken to the General. I know you'll be on an open line to him so if anyone gets away and starts in this direction let him know and he'll contact me.'

'Will do, sir.'

The barrier was raised and the two cars entered the docks. They parked near to where the ship was due to berth and settled down to wait. A couple of men appeared and took up position at two of the bollards just as the Compass Rose hove into sight. It took 20 minutes until the ship was settled alongside and the gangway was put into place.

'Okay you two,' said Hunter, 'go and do your stuff.'

Masters and Badonovitch looked the essence of Customs and Excise officers. Under their arms they carried imitation leather document cases. Inside each of them was a silenced Glock.

'You see okay, Dave?' Hunter enquired.

Over their earpieces they all heard Hughes reply in the affirmative. He was flat on his stomach, legs apart, on the top of a third container on the other side of the basin. It meant he had a good view of the ship and the entrance to the basin and any boat that came their way. He had his rifle pointing at the bridge. The distance to the target was 195 metres. 'I can see three people. They're pacing around. They look nervous. One of them seems to be yelling something.'

Macnair came over the radio. 'Gentlemen, the ship has just sent a message to say that they have arrived. They received a reply that said they, whoever they are, will be arriving in the boat in about twenty minutes.'

Badonovitch and Masters arrived on the bridge.

Hughes transmitted, 'I can see one target on the stern and another on the bow. But that's all. Hang on. I don't know where they think they are but the one on the stern has a pistol in his hand. He's pacing back and forth. I'd say he's as nervous as a cat on the proverbial.'

'What's happening on the bridge?' Hunter asked.

'Don just pointed at the bow and the three men looked where he was pointing.' He paused. 'All three appear to be getting down on the deck.'

439

A couple of minutes later Badonovitch reported, 'They gave up without a fight. We've tie-wrapped them good and tight. The Master is demanding a lawyer and is cursing us in both English and Serbian.'

'I can hear him ranting.'

'Shut up,' Masters said. 'I said shut up or I'll kick your teeth in.'

The man continued ranting, suddenly groaned and stopped talking.

'He'll need a dentist at some point,' said Masters.

'Good. Dave, what's happening with the two lookouts?'

'I'm sure the man in the bows is also armed. Who the hell do these people think they are carrying guns so openly?'

'They're not expecting any trouble except possibly from the people bringing the money. After all, the Serbs hate Muslims, which was why they tried to annihilate them back in the early nineties. They don't trust them an inch and could be worried that they'll try and take the vests without paying for them,' said Hunter.

'Makes sense, I guess,' said the sniper.

'Boss,' said Badonovitch, 'the vests are here in a cupboard at the back of the bridge. In waterproof bags.'

'There are fifteen,' said Masters. 'The usual. PE and ball bearings. Velcro fasteners and a deadman's switch. The det is battery operated. Basic and easily made safe. We'll get to work on them.'

Hunter and Bletchley headed up the gangway. As they reached the deck a man suddenly appeared through a door in front of them and yelled something in Serbian. Hunter had his silenced Glock in his right hand down by his side. He pointed it at the man's head.

'Don't say a word and get down on your knees.'

The man swore and launched himself at Hunter. He was three paces away, took two and died with a bullet in his brain.

'Chris, you take the man in the bows, I'll go aft.'

Now they were on deck they could see the rust streaks and poor maintenance associated with an old tramp steamer.

Hunter made his way cautiously towards the stern. His pistol was held out at arms length in a two-fisted grip, precisely in the way depicted in every cop show on television.

He passed the end of the superstructure and was a few paces from the stern deck when there was a sudden commotion behind him.

49

Hunter whirled around to see a body thrown against the bulkhead, its head pretty much disintegrated.

'You need to be more careful, boss,' said Hughes.

'Thanks, Dave.' Hunter paused a few seconds while his pulse rate dropped back to normal. That had been a close call. He could see the weapon in the dead man's hand.

The lookout had suddenly turned to look Hunter's way. He called out in a language Hunter guessed to be Serbian. Hunter was five metres away and he took a pace forward and into the open.

'Drop your weapon.'

It never failed to surprise Hunter how stupid a person could be with a gun in their hand even if there's one pointed at them. The man began to raise his pistol and Hunter put a bullet into his chest. The man flew backwards, groaned and died.

Bletchley said, 'The lookout is tie-wrapped. No trouble. As good as gold.'

'Meet me back at the gangway,' Hunter ordered.

They stood in front of the watertight door next to the gangway. It was held closed with one solid iron bar, which Hunter pushed up, opening the door. He stood to one side and eased the door open. Bletchley was kneeling, clear of the door, his pistol held in a two-handed grip and pointing at the opening. There was nobody there. In front of them was a corridor. The linoleum on the deck was mostly worn through; the white bulkheads either side were grimy, the paint turning faintly yellow with age.

There were three brown, wooden doors either side of the corridor. At the first door on their right Hunter stood to one side, twisted the door handle and pushed it open. Bletchley stood on the other side, which meant they could cover both sides of the cabin. It held two unmade bunks, a wash hand basin and a couple of wardrobes. It was unoccupied. They repeated the performance at the door on the left with the same result.

The next door on the right had the legend 'Nered Soba' in white paint. They could hear noises from inside, either people talking or a programme of some sort being shown on TV.

Hunter opened the door and both men stepped into the room. It consisted of a series of Formica-topped tables and uncomfortable looking chairs. Three men were watching TV, surprisingly in English. Hunter guessed the sign on the door was Serbian for 'Mess Room'.

There was a metal-topped counter opposite the door and a galley behind. The air smelled of old cooking; a sort of mixture of boiled cabbage and burnt fat.

On the tables were three pistols and two AK74s. One man sat next to them, the other two were a table away.

'Don't move,' said Hunter.

The Serb next to the guns tried to snatch one up. Shooting a gun out of someone's hand as shown in fiction was precisely that – fiction. Even for marksmen as good as Hunter and the team who spent hours every week practicing. There was only one sure shot to take and Hunter took it. He put a bullet through the centre of the man's sternum.

The other two men jerked up in their seat as Hunter turned his gun on one of them while Bletchley covered the other.

'Do you want to die?' Hunter asked in a reasonable tone.

The men nervously shook their heads.

'Cover them, Chris. If one of them so much as twitches shoot him. Do you understand what I just told my colleague here?'

The two men exchanged glances and nodded. Hunter used plastic tie-wraps to secure the men tightly to their chairs.

'Who are you? What do you want?' asked one of the men in heavily accented English.

'We're the people who are here to stop you selling explosive vests to Muslims.'

'Huh, we would never do that. We hate Muslims.'

'You may hate them but you're burying that hatred for the sake of a sackful of euros,' Bletchley replied.

That shut the men up as they sat and glowered. Hunter and Bletchley quickly searched the remainder of the ship but didn't find anyone.

'Boss,' said Hughes, 'there's a boat entering the harbour.'

The two men hurried outside and watched as a luxury craft came slowly towards them.

'That's the boat from the marina,' said Bletchley. 'I'll stay here in the shadows, just in case one of them recognises me.'

Masters and Badonovitch appeared, each carrying a bag in their left hand. Their right hands were holding Glocks down by their side.

The two men and both women on the gin palace were on the deck. One of the women was at the helm, the men were fore and aft with ropes in their hands. The second woman stood amidships with three hefty looking bags at her feet.

Hunter knew that they were rapidly approaching the most critical moment of the operation. There was no trust on either side. So who handed what over first? In this case, if the exchange was for real, then the separate bags of money in exchange for a few bags of explosives each time made sense.

The heads of the people in the yacht were two metres below the coaster's deck. The team had stayed out of sight, apart from Hunter who was leaning on the guardrail and looking dispassionately at the four people on the yacht.

The man in the bow asked, 'Do you speak English?'

'Yes,' said Hunter, 'of course.'

'You are English,' was the surprised reply.

444

'Yes. My colleagues are Serbian and don't speak very good English. Pass up your bow rope.'

The rope was thrown, adroitly caught and its eye dropped over a bollard. Hunter went along the deck, caught the stern rope and tied it to the guardrail.

'Now pass up the money.'

'No. I want to see the vests.'

Hunter reached down, picked up a bag, attached it to a hook and lowered it to the boat. It dangled an arm's length from the woman with the money at her feet. She reached over, grabbed the bag and swung it towards her while Hunter lowered it down. She opened the bag and looked inside. Tentatively she reached inside and lifted out one of the two vests. She looked closely at it. There were strips of plastic explosives about half an inch thick and one inch wide running the length of the vest. The strips covered the whole of the vest. There was a simple switch attached to a small box containing two AA batteries. That was connected to a hand-held thumb release that fitted in the palm of the hand. When the thumb release was pressed the circuit was complete and the bomb went live. Once it was released the PE exploded. Hence the name, deadman's switch.

Hunter could see that Bletchley's assessment of their ages was fairly accurate. They looked to be in their late twenties, early thirties, they appeared well heeled and the man who had spoken sounded educated.

'How does it work?' asked the woman.

Hunter told her.

'How do we know it'll work?' asked the man at the stern.

'You can try it out of you like. Put the vest on, Velcro it closed, take out the battery holder from the pocket, slide the switch to on, take the deadman's switch, hold it tightly in either hand and press the button. You'll be ready to go. I suggest whoever tries it moves off the boat, probably easiest by jumping into the water and swimming to the far end of the basin. Then let go the button and you'll be no more. Totally painless of course but there'll be nothing lcft to bury.' Hunter paused. 'Actually, that may not be true. Maybe your legs will still be intact. So who wants to give it a try?'

The offer was greeted with silence.

'Good, none of you. So let's get the show on the road. Send up the first bag so we can check it.'

The holdall was placed on the hook and Hunter dragged it up the side of the ship. He upturned the bag and checked a couple of the bundles of notes by flicking through them.

'Seems okay. We'll send down two bags.'

That was the signal for Badonovitch and Masters to step forward with their pistols drawn and pointed at the four terrorists.

'Incidentally, you're under arrest,' said Hunter.

The scene became a frozen tableau and then the woman at the helm did something incredibly stupid. From nowhere she grabbed an automatic and pointed it at Hunter.

'I'll shoot you if I have to. And believe me, I know how to use this. I spent six months in Syria fighting the non-believers in the name of Allah.'

'You don't want to do that,' said Hunter.

'I'm not bluffing.'

'I'm sure you're not. Okay Dave.'

The woman's head exploded in brains, blood and splinters of bone.

The other woman began to scream, the man in the bows bent over and vomited, while the man in the stern yelled out in anguish and started to sob.

Badonovitch dropped a jumping ladder over the side and Bletchley and Hunter quickly climbed down onto the boat.

'You bastard,' said the man who had been sobbing. 'You killed her!'

Hunter stepped up to the man, grabbed him by his throat and hit him as hard as he could in the guts.

'You filth would have used these vests to kill and injure hundreds of people. You call me a bastard when people like you shouldn't exist.'

The man's legs were folding under him and Hunter let go. The man collapsed onto the deck and curled up in a ball.

In the meantime, Bletchley had passed the other bags of money up to the ship and returned all but two of the explosive vests. Masters had doctored these two.

The boat's engines were still running and Hunter stood at the controls. A quick glance told him all he needed to know.

'Let go Jan. We'll see you shortly.'

The ropes were released and thrown down onto the deck. Bletchley made the prisoners sit on the bench seat running across the stern of the boat.

'What are you going to do with us?' asked one of the men.

'That depends on you. I can assure you that you'll come out of this alive if you tell us what we want to know.'

'What . . . What do you mean?' The woman asked in a quavering voice. 'You can't kill us. You said we were under arrest.'

'That was then, this is now. She shouldn't have tried to shoot me. A silly mistake when all's said and done.'

'Do you know who her father is?' asked one of the men.

'Nope, and I don't care,' replied Bletchley.

'The Saudi ambassador. There'll be hell to pay for what you just did.'

'Are you kidding me?'

'No, of course not. Her father . . .'

'Never mind her sodding father. Are you kidding me there'll be hell to pay? If you're really saying you believe it then you don't live on the same planet as the rest of us. She was committing an act of terrorism by buying explosives and handing over a million euros.'

'She had diplomatic immunity,' said the women.

'It does not apply in these circumstances. Diplomatic immunity is waived where acts of terrorism and certain criminal acts are concerned.'

'Her father would never have waived those rights,' she said.

'It's academic, she's dead.'

447

'I will see you in jail for this,' said one of the men.

'What in hell is the matter with you people? I just told you if you're lucky you might just live. If you're not, you won't.'

The three exchanged nervous glances. 'I demand you take us back to the shore. That we are handed over to the police and properly processed.' The man who spoke looked at Bletchley defiantly.

The SBS Captain leant forward and casually backhanded the man across the mouth. The stinging blow and loud slap shocked the three of them. Bletchley sat back and smiled. 'Now be quiet. How we doing, Nick?'

'This'll do. Four miles offshore and no other vessel in sight.'

The sea was flat calm, there wasn't a cloud in the sky, the night was filled with stars and a half moon was just appearing over the horizon.

'Which one shall it be?' Hunter asked.

'Which one?' Bletchley asked the three prisoners.

'What do you mean, which one?' asked the woman.

'Which one is going to try out the vest so that we can prove it works?'

'What are you talking about?' she said. 'We don't want to try it out. There's no need.'

'In that case where were you taking them?'

'What do you mean?'

'Stop asking me what I mean. You speak perfectly good English. You had fifteen vests. You were taking them somewhere to be used by someone. Who and where?'

'I'll not tell you,' said the woman. The two men said the same thing.

'Okay,' said Bletchley. 'Eenie meenie miney mo, catch a terrorist by his, or in this case, her toe.'

'What are you doing?' asked one of the men.

'Deciding which one will be strapping on the vest and going for a swim. Oh, with your dead friend along for the ride, of course. Now where was I? You interrupted me. I'll have to start from the beginning.'

'No! Wait you can't,' said the man who had demanded due process.

'Why can't I?' Bletchley looking puzzled.

'It . . . It's illegal. It's murder. You can't.'

Bletchley stood up hit the man hard across the jaw with the butt of his automatic and put one of the vests on him. He dragged the man to the side of the boat, took hold of the dead body and, doing his best not to get bloodied, tied them together.

Next, he placed a lifebelt over the head of the man and secured it under his arms. He slid both bodies into the water. A few seconds later the man groaned and lifted his head. He put his hand to his wound, which was bleeding slightly and groaned again.

'Where am I? What's happening?' He looked around and suddenly seemed to realise where he was. 'Help me! Help me! Don't let me drown!'

'You won't drown,' said Bletchley. 'Okay you two, are you going to answer my questions?'

'Huh,' said the man glaring at Bletchley, 'you won't dare do anything to Abdul.'

'Hey, Abdul, how's the water?' Bletchley leaned over the side and grabbed hold of the lifebelt, pulling the inert form partly out of the sea. He reached down into the pocket where the battery holder was stored and moved the switch. He let go the belt and said, 'Okay, Nick. Let's go. It's thirty seconds and counting.' He turned to the other two. Keep looking back.'

Hunter gunned the engine. In seconds it was up on the plane and at a mile distance the belt exploded. The sound was muted; the explosion felt through the soles of their feet as it travelled through the water.

The girl screamed and began to sob, the man collapsed, ashen white.

'Who's next?' Bletchley asked in a conversational manner. 'How about you?'

The woman returned his stare in horror. Then she moaned and wet herself.

'You can do with a bath, so it had better be you.'

'No . . . No please. For the love of Allah, I don't want to die.'

'You'll kill innocent people in the name of Islam yet you don't want to die? What kind of swine are you?'

'It wasn't meant to be like this. It wasn't,' she said in desperation. 'We were told to take the vests to . . .'

'Shut up Barika. Say nothing!'

'No, you be quiet, Parvez. I never wanted to come. I told you that. You said it was for the good of Islam, for Allah and I believed you. And do you want to know why?'

It was Bletchley who asked the question. 'Why?'

'Because I wanted to believe. I wanted to think there was more to life than a failed, arranged and loveless marriage.' She moaned. 'I don't know what I thought. Holy jihad seems like a noble cause. Killing people, hurting people like . . . like it is on the TV and in films seems unreal somehow.' She appeared to rally her strength. 'Seeing Wafa die like that was obscene. It . . . It wasn't the way I thought of it.'

'What the hell is that supposed to mean?

She was silent for a few seconds. 'I can't explain it. Death . . . Death in the abstract is one thing. Seeing it for real is something else.'

'I've heard all that before,' said Hunter, 'and so has my friend here. I'll ask you one last time, where were you taking the explosives?'

Parvez screamed at her not to answer, but she did. Even for two cynical professionals like Hunter and Bletchley the answer shocked them.

'The Saudi Arabian Embassy.'

50

The problem arose what to do with their two prisoners.

The man let loose with a tirade of Arabic. Hunter listened with interest. He threatened the woman, swore by Allah he would kill her if they survived what was happening. She replied she didn't care. Her best friend and her brother were dead. She blamed Parvez for what had happened. She cursed him and called down the prophet Muhammad to send him to Jahannam where he would stay for eternity in the company of the devil.

The man raised his right fist above his head to strike the woman but wasn't quick enough. Bletchley grabbed the man's wrist and twisted it while at the same time bending it backward. The wrist went past ninety degrees and the back of his hand touched his arm. The snap was loud in the idling boat, where the engines were barely above a murmur. The man screamed and began to sob, holding his wrist in his lap, bent over in pain.

'What now, Nick?'

'Barika, what do you want to do?' Hunter asked.

'What . . . What do you mean?' Her voice was subdued. The horror of violence had penetrated her veneer of righteous holy jihad. Reality had set in.

'What do you want to do? Die? Go to prison for the rest of your life? Live a quiet life somewhere, away from these morons? Or maybe you'd like to go back to so-called holy jihad.'

'No, never! Never that!'

Her vehemence was plain to see.

'What is it you do?' Hunter asked.

'What?'

'What's your job?'

'I'm a nursery school teacher. In an inner-city school. Mainly deprived children and immigrants. I speak Arabic as well as Farsi.'

'Do you enjoy your job?'

'Oh yes, I love it.' Her face lit up with a brief smile. Hunter could see that she was very attractive with shoulder length black hair, big brown eyes and a wide smile. Then the smile faded. 'The children are so hungry to learn. If you ask them what do they want to be it is always a doctor, a teacher, an engineer.' She smiled in remembrance and said, 'Two young girls said they want to be famous but not for any reason. It's very funny.' Then she recollected her situation and placed her face in her hands and sobbed.

'Would you like to go back to your job?'

She removed her hands and looked up at Hunter. 'Yes, of course but it is too late now. I cannot believe I have been so stupid. So easily manipulated. Brainwashed to do what I did.'

'Was there an imam involved?'

'Yes. At the Wandsworth mosque. His name is Abdullah Abdullah. Very original. He's from Iran. He came here claiming political asylum about ten years ago but makes no secret of the fact that he hates the west and everything and everybody that's western.'

'Why am I not surprised?' asked Bletchley, not expecting an answer.

Hunter looked at his friend, nodded and jerked his head at the water. The RM Captain understood immediately. He used the butt of his pistol again to knock out the man known as Parvez.

He began to put the second vest on the inert form.

Barika watched in horror. 'What are you doing?' She looked at Bletchley and said, 'Please, I don't want to die.'

'You're not going to die,' said Hunter. 'But you heard this man. If we let him live what will happen to you? Suppose we hand you over to the police? You'll get twenty years to life. All the good you could do, should you choose to, will be wasted.'

452

She replied in a quiet voice, 'I know.' Her head hung down and her shoulders shook. It was obvious she was crying.

'Do you have children?'

She looked up and gulped before replying. 'No. I . . . I think of the children at my school as my own. I know it's stupid, but I can't have any.'

'So you decide. We take you back to shore and have you both arrested. You go to prison for a very long time. However, you told us about the Saudi Embassy. It will come out at your trial. It will be many months before you have a chance to testify so the likelihood of you living long enough to do so is pretty remote. The Saudis won't want any of this to come officially into the public domain. Neither will the British government come to that. Trade is far more important than the lives of a few citizens, believe me. So the probability is you'll be killed. Alternatively, we throw this scum overboard, he vanishes forever and you go about your life doing the good I suspect you are more than capable of doing.' Hunter's tone was friendly, supportive, giving her a way out. 'What do you want?'

'I want life to be like it was. I want my brother and friend here on this boat where we should be enjoying ourselves. I want . . .' she faltered.

'It's not going to happen. Now, time's-a-wasting, what do you want us to do with Parvez?'

She looked at her friend, lying on the deck, inert. 'I . . . I guess it had better be the police and prison. I don't want him to die.'

While they had been speaking Bletchley had finished dressing Parvez in the vest.

'Barika, you gave the right answer. However, it's not the one I have chosen. Over the side.'

Bletchley slid the body into the water just as Parvez was coming to. This time there was no lifebelt but Bletchley kept a firm grip on the terrorist's collar.

The man struggled, kicking his legs frantically. 'Don't let me drown,' he beseeched. 'Please, don't let me drown.'

'I won't. I'm going to blow you to Kingdom Come instead. You will be tiny pieces, some of which may be eaten by the fish idly patrolling the area looking for food.'

'You can't do this,' Parvez gasped. 'You can't! Barika, tell them to stop. Don't let them do this!'

Barika looked at the cold, frozen features of Bletchley who pulled the body further out of the water, reached into a pocket of the vest, slid the switch to operate and let go the man's coat. Parvez dropped beneath the surface and then popped up gasping for breath and spitting out seawater.

'Okay, Nick. Let's go.'

This time, instead of moving fast and far Hunter drove the boat more slowly. They knew how effective the explosive was so there was no need to put too much distance between it and them.

Parvez turned from pleading for his life to cursing them. He included Barika in his vitriol who stared at the man who had been her friend in abject horror.

'Any second now,' said Bletchley.

The words were barely out of his mouth when the explosion occurred. One second the terrorist was there, the next he no longer existed.

Barika put her face in her hands and sobbed bitterly.

'Shut up, Barika,' said Hunter, 'and count yourself lucky. You're going to live.'

'I don't understand what you are doing.'

'You're not going to prison,' said Hunter.

'What . . . What do you mean?'

'What I say.' The harshness was no longer in his voice. 'You've been stupid. You've been misled and you went along with it all. I think you're a good person who is in over her head. I think you shouldn't waste your life but continue doing what you have been. The kids need you and people like you. So I'm going to let you go free.'

Hunter turned the boat slightly to starboard and headed towards a jetty outside the port complex. 'Collect your gear and get ready to go ashore. I suggest you walk to the train station and go back from where you came. If anyone asks you what's happened to the others tell them you don't know. Tell them anything you like. Who in the embassy were you dealing with?'

'I don't know. I only knew the vests were to be delivered there.'

'Did you hear a name?' Bletchley enquired.

She was silent for a few seconds and then she said, 'Not a name but Parvez and my brother said something about the Military Attaché.'

'I might have guessed,' said Hunter.

'You know him?' Bletchley asked.

'I've never met him but I do know of him. Get your stuff Barika.'

She went below and returned in a few minutes carrying a small suitcase. She sat silently while Hunter manœuvred the boat alongside a dilapidated, wooden jetty.

The three of them stood in silence, then Hunter said, 'You'd better go. You've been given a chance I'm not sure you deserve. Try and enjoy the rest of your life and while you teach the children, try to steer them well away from fundamentalism and holy jihad. There's nothing holy about killing innocent people.'

'Thank you,' she replied in a small voice before clambering ashore. She stood and watched as the boat went astern from the jetty, turned and headed back towards the lights in the port. Hunter hoped the general agreed with the decision he'd taken.

'You did the right thing, Nick.'

'Yeah, I hope I don't come to regret it one day.'

The General called Hunter into his office. Hunter had just showered after a tough workout starting with a 5-mile run followed by a session in the gym with Matt Dunston and Chris Bletchley. Hunter had a couple of bruises to show how tough that had been. When they practiced unarmed combat there was no quarter given, just braking the attack at the last second. It wasn't always possible to get it exact, hence the occasional bruise.

'Nick, take a seat. Actually, coffee first?'

'Thanks, sir. I don't mind if I do. Do you want one?'

'I've just topped up, thanks.'

For a change the coffee was freshly brewed. Too often the General had stewed coffee on offer that Hunter had learned to replace knowing the General didn't feel offended.

With a mug of coffee in hand Hunter sat opposite his boss at the desk next to the window. The weather had finally turned and a light rain was falling and a cool wind blowing. It was typical for June in Scotland.

'I see in the news that an imam from the Wandsworth mosque was found floating in the Thames with four times the drink/driving limit of alcohol in his bloodstream.'

'Yes. Don and Jan did a good job there. Any word on the girl?'

'She seems to be okay. She's back at school on Monday. She's been telling everyone that she had a row with her brother and left the boat at Grimsby.'

'Anyone looking for the three dead?' Hunter asked.

'Yes. The parents of the man Parvez. The boat's been found abandoned in the North Sea, the blood has been identified as that of the girl Wafa and the whole thing is now a mystery on the same scale as the *Marie Celeste*. The file has been placed in the unsolved pile. Incidentally, Isobel has also been digging further into the Saudi Military Attaché.'

Hunter took a sip of his coffee and then said, 'Yes sir, so I understand. Isobel's filled me in.'

'He's a nasty piece of work. A fundamentalist, yet he's here in London.'

'Sir, he's here to cause trouble. We know that and so we need to do something about him.'

'I concur. Only we can't go around assassinating diplomats who we think are our enemies.'

Hunter grinned. 'That would cull a hell of a lot of diplomats from our streets.'

'That's for sure. Including a few Europeans.'

'So what do you propose we do about him sir?'

'I'm going to talk to their Ambassador and have a few words in his shell-like. See if that has any results.'

'Do you think it will?'

'Yes. Because we've identified the owner of the super yacht.'

'Oh? Who is it?'

'The first cousin to the Saudi king. His name is Ibn-Mohammed Saud. A fundamentalist to his fingertips. He apparently likes to beat his servants using a cane. In front of guests I might add.'

'Sounds charming.'

'MI6 has a dossier on him, which they've forwarded to us. I'll let you read it.'

'What do you intend doing about him?'

'Nothing. He's untouchable.'

Hunter's mouth turned down but he nodded. He was pragmatic enough to know that some you win and some you lose, he just hated it when the latter was the result. 'And what about our friend Tadeas?'

'I'm not sure. I'm still thinking about it.'

'We could call in a favour from our Jewish friends.'

'I don't like being in debt to anyone, and that includes the Israelis.'

'Okay, sir, so what about the MA?'

'He will be sent home. I will suggest to the ambassador that it's done quietly and soon, otherwise the information could leak, the papers could exaggerate the story beyond recognition and embarrassment will be heaped down on the House of Saud.'

'Think he'll go for it?'

'He won't have any choice. I've a file with recordings of conversations and photographs, text messages and e-mails between the Saudi Military Attaché and people we know to be fundamentalists in this country and across Europe. The man is up to his neck in the whole rotten jihadist programme and we can prove it.'

Hunter shrugged. 'You know what the Saudis are like, sir. Their pride will be hurt.'

'Tough. This is just between the ambassador and me. No other government officials involved and that's the way I'd like to keep it.'

'When are you delivering this message?'

'Tomorrow afternoon at a reception at Buckingham Palace.'

'Buckingham Palace? What on earth are you doing there? I mean, how did you get an invite to be there?'

'I've known Prince Charles for quite a few years. I called him and explained the situation and he dispatched a couple of invitations.'

'You have the prince's phone number?'

'No. Isobel got it for me.'

Hunter smiled. Why wasn't he surprised?

'But you said two tickets.'

'Yes, you're coming as well.'

'I look forward to it.'

'Good. Incidentally, the attacks across the EU seem to have dropped and fewer migrants are trying to cross the Med.'

'I saw that in the daily brief. I guess if the money supply is disrupted so is the business.'

'It seems that way. But it'll return to its old levels sooner rather than later.'

'I guess you're right, sir.

'By the way, I've been meaning to tell you. The CC at Grimsby phoned to say how delighted he was with the outcome.'

'Glad to be of service, sir, as always.' Hunter finished his coffee and placed the mug on the coaster in front of him.

'That's all for now. I've booked us into the Naval Club in Hill Street for tomorrow evening. There's a train tomorrow afternoon that will suit us. Is that okay with you?'

Hunter suppressed a grin. A suggestion from the general was on a par with a royal command. 'Of course, sir. I'm looking forward to it.'

51

Their journey south was pleasant. The first class carriage they occupied was virtually empty and the afternoon teas they ordered fair to middling, which was about all one could hope for on a Virgin train. They were approaching King's Cross when Macnair's phone rang.

His face became bleaker as he listened to the message. Hunter was watching him.

'What's happened?'

Macnair sighed. 'That woman, Barika.'

'What about her?'

'She's been murdered.'

'Damnation! How did it happen? When and where?'

'Last night. In her flat in Wandsworth. Her throat was slit. Right through to her windpipe.'

'Any clues as to who did it?'

'I'm calling the Commissioner.' He scrolled down his contact list and found the direct line. He pressed the right buttons.

'Alec? Malcolm. Do you know anything about the woman murdered in Wandsworth last night?' He paused. 'I guess I didn't really expect you would, you've too much on your plate. I don't know her surname but I can tell you her first name is Barika, she's an ethnic Saudi but a British citizen and has been killed by fundamentalists probably from Saudi.' He fell silent for a few seconds. Then, 'She was part of an on-going operation we are involved with. I'm sorry to tell you but the person you should look closely at is the Military Attaché at the Saudi Embassy.'

As there was nobody in earshot Macnair put the phone on speaker.

'Malcolm, my day started badly because of the bloody politicians I have to deal with and is ending worse because of what you're telling me.'

'I'm sorry, Alec, but I thought you should know.'

'Yes, well, thanks for that. The MA will have diplomatic immunity.'

'I know. But presumably you can declare him *persona non grata* and have him expelled.'

'Hardly a punishment if what you tell me is true.'

'I can't guarantee that it is the MA but if he didn't actually commit the crime he will have been involved. That you can be sure of.'

'Care to tell me how you know all this?'

Macnair paused for a second and then said, 'Yes. We intercepted the delivery of over a dozen explosive vests a couple of days ago.' Now he stretched the truth, 'This woman was involved but decided to help us at the eleventh hour. We stopped the vests being delivered although they were not going to the end users.'

'So where were they going?'

'Hang on to your hat, the Saudi Embassy, for the MA.'

'Anything else you'd like to tell me? You know, just to further inflame my ulcer.'

'We've checked the man out. It will come as no surprise to learn that he's a distant relative of the king.'

'They usually are,' was the Commissioner's dry reply.

'Alec, I appreciate you need proof before you can make wild accusations but you may find some surveillance cameras have footage of him in the area. One thing I can tell you, these people are really arrogant. They're security precautions are sloppy, to say the least.'

'That's encouraging to know. Okay, Malcolm, thanks for that. Leave it with me and I'll see what we can do.'

'I'll see you tomorrow.'

'Tomorrow? How? Where?'

'The garden party. I expect you're going.'

'Oh, yes. Okay, I'll brief you then.'

The connection was broken as the train pulled into King's Cross. Hunter was looking a mixture of glum and thunderous anger.

'Don't beat yourself up, Nick, there was nothing more you could have done for the woman.'

'Maybe I should have anticipated this happening.'

'How? Come on, that's ludicrous. You did what you could. The fact she chose the path that led to her death was all down to her.'

'I know that, sir, but what a waste.'

'There's plenty of that going on. Come on, a stroll to the club will help to clear our thoughts.'

They spent an agreeable evening in the club, loitering over an excellent steak dinner and not a bad red house wine. Over the port Isobel forwarded photographs of the Military Attaché. He appeared to be in his forties with black hair parted at the centre. His moustache was luxuriant with hints of grey while the rest of his thin face was clean-shaven. He had a pointed chin, narrow eyes and bushy eyebrows.

'An unappetising looking thug,' said Hunter. 'I wouldn't mind a few minutes alone with him.'

'I'm sure you wouldn't. However, we have other fish to fry.' His phone vibrated again. There was no loud ringing. Ring tones were forbidden in the bar and restaurant, though use of a phone was allowed. It was a compromise between the traditional peace of the club and the modern age. Some of the older members still made a fuss but as they were dying out, the objections to using the phone were waning by the day.

'Alec.'

'Hello Malcolm. We've done some face recognition work and there is no doubt the MA was in the vicinity of the woman's flat around the time she was killed. It doesn't mean he did it but in view of what you told me I figure he's involved.'

'You can be sure of it. So what are you going to do?'

'Pass the info to the Home Office. Expelling senior diplomats,

461

especially those who are lodged in the brackets known as friends of ours, is a serious business.'

'Good luck with that. Tell the Home Sec from me about the explosive vests though she should know all about it by now.'

'Where were they found?'

'In Grimsby.'

'Ah, that makes sense. Were you lot involved?'

Macnair chuckled. 'Only on the periphery.'

'Sure. In a pig's ear. Thanks for that.'

Macnair had angled the phone so that Hunter could hear what was being said on the other end.

'The system stinks,' was Hunter's pronouncement.

'It surely does but we've always known that. Incidentally, are you taking the leave owed?'

'Yes, thanks.'

The following day Macnair spent most of it on his phone while Hunter made arrangements for a holiday following a conversation he had with Leo back in Rosyth. He used a travel agent to book his flights along with a hotel.

They arrived at Buckingham Palace ten minutes after kick-off time of 16.00. There was a queue to enter the grounds, which was slowly but surely moving forward. Gone were the days of waving an invitation and proceeding through the famous gates. Now security was rightly top of the list and as a result the whole process took a lot longer than usual. The two of them had been in line for about 10 minutes with at least another 15 to go when they were approached by a police officer in the uniform of a Chief Inspector.

'General Macnair?'

'Yes.'

'Gentlemen if you come with me there's a side gate. The Commissioner asked us to keep an eye out for you and suggest you use another gate. It's the one the security detail uses.'

They followed the CI. 'That was thoughtful of the Commissioner,' said Macnair.

'Here we are.'

The two TIFAT officers were escorted into the grounds and left to wander amongst the burgeoning crowds.

'How many people are at these events?' Hunter asked in surprise.

'Usually a few thousands. In this case there's only about fourteen hundred, or so I've been told.'

'There's the Commissioner,' said Macnair and led the way over to where an imposing looking individual in police uniform was standing talking to a man in a dark grey suit.

Handshakes and introductions were brief. The man was a senior officer with SO15.

Alex Baldwin was in his early sixties, squat, with a baldhead and a round face. He looked tough and someone who had come up the hard way. In fact he was the son of a Scottish landowner of many acres, had gone to Eton and Oxford, left the army as a captain, joined the police and moved effortlessly through the ranks. If he was ever asked, which was rarely, he would say he had been born with a silver spoon in his mouth and had licked from it often. In fact he was highly intelligent, hard-working, ruthless when it came to criminals and didn't suffer fools gladly. This applied in particular to politicians who he disliked as a class but found one or two individuals acceptable. He and Macnair had known each other ever since Macnair joined the army a couple of years before Baldwin left it.

The SO 15 officer was named Jules Petrie. He was the sort of man who was lost in a crowd of two. Hunter had heard of him and knew him to be very good at his job. He was tall, rake thin with prematurely grey hair. He had a long face with blue eyes, an aquiline nose and thin lips.

'Do you see who's over there?' Baldwin nodded his head at a small group of people about ten metres away on the other side of a flowerbed.

'Ah, the Home Secretary, the Saudi Ambassador and two men who look like Saudi bodyguards,' said Macnair. 'Who are the other two?'

'Home office civil servants. Bad form really to bring your own bodyguards to events like this, shows a lack of respect for the way we do things. When I pointed this out to the Home Sec I was told to put up with it. That she didn't want to upset our close allies in the Middle East.'

'So what is she doing about their Military Attaché?' Hunter asked.

'Nothing. The incident is to be ignored,' said Petrie.

Hunter looked at the man in astonishment. 'Tell me you're kidding.'

'I'm afraid not, Nick. That comes down from on high. Which in this case probably means the Prime Minister herself. Talk of the devil, look who's just joined them,' said Baldwin.

'The Military Attaché,' said Hunter. He glowered at the man, his blood boiling to see him standing nonchalantly in the group. He made up his mind to do something about it. As far as Hunter was concerned the MA was a dead man walking.

For those who wanted it there were teas or coffees, soft drinks, petite sandwiches and cakes. Most people seemed happy merely to be there and didn't bother with the small eats and drinks.

'In view of what you've told us,' said Macnair, 'we're wasting our time being here.'

'Oh, I wouldn't say that. I think it's worth letting the Saudis know we know what they did. It may help them to curb their actions in the future,' said Baldwin.

'Look you guys,' said Hunter, 'begging your pardon, sir,' he addressed Macnair, 'but I don't get it. They were bringing in explosive vests to the country. If just one had gone off the devastation would have been horrendous.'

'The Government is saying that there is no proof. Which they are right about,' said Baldwin.

'What do they expect? Sworn affidavits, the Attaché holding the vests, or the dead woman at his feet with a bloody knife in his hand?' There was no disguising the frustration in Hunter's tone.

'Welcome to the world of international politics, a gutless government and a hamstrung police force,' said Petrie. 'Oh, and please do excuse my cynicism. It comes with the territory.'

'Yeah, I genuinely don't know how you guys manage,' said the RN Commander.

'A large scotch when I get home helps me,' said Baldwin, with a bleak smile.

'I'm more of a Chardonnay man myself,' said the SO15 officer. 'That and having two young teenage girls to listen to as they squabble over the Internet and argue about their friends.' He smiled. 'They're twins,' he added as if that explained everything.

'Good, the Home Secretary is moving away and there goes her minions. Quickly Malcolm, if you're going to have a word with the Ambassador it had better be now.'

Both Macnair and Hunter hurried across the lawn, the grass like the baize on a snooker table and intercepted the Ambassador just as he was walking away with the other three men in tow.

'Ambassador,' Macnair called out, 'a quick word if I may.'

The Ambassador stopped and turned to look at the two men approaching. His two guards planted themselves between him and Macnair. The General pushed past them and one put out his hand to grab hold of Macnair's shoulder.

Hunter was right there and grabbed the man's wrist in a vice-like grip. 'Don't. General Macnair wishes to speak to the Ambassador.' Hunter then leaned forward and said softly, 'If you put a hand on him I'll break your wrist.'

The bodyguard was about thirty years old, 5ft 6ins tall, swarthy with a drooping moustache. His overgrown belly suggested a sedentary life of little or no exercise. As a bodyguard, Hunter decided, the man was about as useful as a doorstop. Maybe that was it. Not a doorstop but a bullet stop. Taking a bullet for the protectee was about all the man would be able to do. The man dropped his arm and stood glowering at Hunter.

'Ambassador, my name is Malcolm Macnair.'

'I know who you are, General. You are the man who is in charge of TIFAT. The International Force Against Terrorism. Such a quaint title for your organisation.'

The Ambassador was immaculately dressed in a white thawb with a red and white checkered keffiyeh with a black headband. He was fat with a round, smooth face, bushy eyebrows and a large, hooked nose. Not, Hunter decided the most prepossessing of men.

'Good. In that case I would like a private word with you.'

'I don't think this is the time or the place. Why not make an appointment and come to the Embassy sometime next week.'

'Here and now,' said Macnair icily. 'It's for the best and will only take a few minutes.'

The Ambassador appeared to give the notion some thought before he nodded and said, 'Very well. I will give you two minutes. I wish my Military Attaché to listen to what you have to say. After all, if you are telling me something, or asking me something, then I will probably need his advice.' The man's smile showed nicotine-stained teeth.

Macnair shook his head. 'This is strictly private. My colleague here will also stay out of earshot.'

'Your colleague? You do him an injustice. I know who Commander Hunter is. He is well known in certain circles. His exploits have been brought to my attention on numerous occasions. However, so be it.'

52

Hunter stood a dozen paces away from the two men with his arms crossed. Although he appeared to be watching them his peripheral attention was on the Military Attaché a couple of yards away. There was something of the predator about him, though Hunter acknowledged to himself that could be more imagination than fact. Probably connected to the idea the man had killed a young woman.

The Ambassador suddenly looked at the MA and scowled. A few minutes later Macnair held out his hand, the two men shook and Macnair patted the Saudi on his shoulder with a smile. The tiny microphone he had just affixed to the Ambassador's shoulder was white and virtually impossible to notice unless a careful search for it was made.

Macnair walked away and nodded to Hunter to join him. They strolled along shoulder-to-shoulder for a minute or two while Hunter placed his earpiece behind his right ear. The small receiver was hidden under his hair. They stopped, faced each other and appeared to be speaking together.

The MA was talking to the Ambassador. Their voices were being transmitted loud and clear. With a listening range set at three metres the background and extraneous noises were filtered out.

From the corner of his eye Hunter saw the MA suddenly start and look in their direction. The man was too far away to be certain but Hunter thought he was scowling at them. Which, considering the information imparted by the General was more than likely.

The two Saudis were speaking Arabic, their language as intense as their postures. Hunter was translating for the benefit of the General.

467

'Are you mad?'

'What do you mean, sir?'

'Trying to bring explosive vests into the embassy?'

'But I thought you knew. I was told you knew all about it.'

'Of course I didn't you moron. Financing the jihadists is one thing, actively attacking the British is something entirely different.'

'It is all part of the same war.' The man's tone was truculent.

The Ambassador sighed. 'Does the prince know?'

'He directly authorised it. Otherwise we would never have done it.'

'I thought as much. And what about the woman? The school teacher?'

'What about her?'

'Did you have her killed?'

'No. I don't have others do my wet work. I did it myself.'

'That's what General Macnair just told me. Curse the man and his organisation. I would like nothing better than to see him and that buffoon Hunter have bullets in their heads.'

There was a few seconds silence and then the MA said, 'If that is what your Excellency wishes then I can arrange it.'

'How? Where? More importantly, when? Once they are back in Scotland they are virtually untouchable.'

'That means we have to strike while they are here, in London. It will be a simple matter. I'll leave and make suitable arrangements. They will have arrived using the tube, I suspect. Cars and taxis will be at a premium. I'll deal with them then. You can leave it to me, your Excellency, I won't fail you.'

'You had better not. If you do you will be sent home and to say you will do so under a cloud is one of the great understatements of the year. Do I make myself clear?'

'Yes, your Excellency.'

'Good. I will keep my eye on them. When they leave I will call but don't answer it. I shall hang up as soon as we're connected so stay alert.'

'Yes, your Excellency.'

They watched as the MA headed for the garden exit, already on his phone. Hunter and Macnair watched him go.'

'I wonder what he plans doing?' Hunter murmured.

'It will be interesting to find out. We'd better give him time to get organised. In the meantime I'll contact Isobel.' A few seconds later Macnair said, 'Isobel? I want you to put a ten minute continuous feed into the monitors around the St James's Park tube station as well as the route from Buckingham Palace to the tube. I'll let you know when I want you to implement it. Okay thanks. Also, you have the photos of the MA, see if you can find him in the area or at the St James's Park underground station. Both above and below ground.' He knew that with the face recognition software they used, if the Attaché was anywhere on camera, they would find him immediately. It would be helpful to have confirmation as to his whereabouts.'

'Care to tell me what's going on?' Isobel asked.

'As it is now on record that London is the city with the most surveillance cameras anywhere in the world it would be a good idea if we're not filmed doing what we're about to do.'

'Something criminal?'

Macnair was grinning. 'I'd hardly call it a crime. More like doing the world some good.'

They knew that one of Isobel's team would access the systems controlling both the surface cameras as well as the underground. They would take a ten minute recording and then plant it ready for use into the computer systems. That way, when the feed was broken, it wouldn't show as a blank screen but be replaced by the recording. The chances of anyone looking at a screen so closely as to recognise the same recording ten minutes later were virtually non-existent.

The two men parted and spent the next hour talking to several of the guests. Macnair spent time with His Royal Highness the Prince of Wales, mainly chatting about international terrorism but also about climate change. The Prince was passionate on the subject, Macnair more circumspect.

Finally they decided it was time to go. Just to make certain a welcoming committee was waiting for them, the General tracked down the Saudi Ambassador to say goodbye with completely false bonhomie on both sides.

As the two TIFAT officers strolled away, over his earphone Hunter heard the Ambassador say, 'They are coming. I asked them how they were travelling and Macnair, the fool, told me by Underground from St James's Park on the District Line to Upminster. Good. Make sure neither of them survives the journey. And don't forget they won't be armed. Nobody can bring a weapon into this place so have no fear.'

Hunter relayed the information to Macnair who grinned in anticipation. He phoned Isobel and told her to start the recordings.

'You know we are breaking all sorts of protocols don't you, Commander?'

Hunter grinned. 'If you mean leaving before the monarch then yes, sir, I do. We won't be invited back.'

'I suspect you're right.'

They were approaching the Underground when Hunter said, 'Our eleven o'clock. Two men, both looking our way.'

'I see them. Not very subtle are they?'

'Where's the Attaché?'

'I guess he's below waiting for us.'

'With back-up?'

'I'd think so.'

The rush hour was dying down. People were tired and irritable after a long day and were hurrying to get home. Many had long journeys in front of them, cooped up with other fractious individuals, many having to stand, most of them fed up to the back teeth with their daily grind.

'Let's go into the coffee shop,' said Hunter. He nodded at a Costa's next to a Timpson's dry cleaning and key-cutting establishment.

'Any reason why?' They changed direction and moved towards the door.

'Yes, sir. Puts them off their stride. There are too many people around and I don't want any innocent bystanders to get hurt. They're bound to be armed. And you know better than anyone, sir, that a bullet up close can easily pass into a second body and at the wrong angle a third person can be seriously injured.'

'You're right.' Macnair pushed open the door and they walked up to the counter. The place was empty, the caffeine junkies having fed their habit all day. Now most were looking forward to a glass or two of stronger stuff.

They took seats at a table farthest from the door. They sat shoulder to shoulder facing the door and with the exit to the toilets next to them. While Macnair had bought the drinks Hunter had checked out the back entrance. It was easily accessible and was normally held closed by a heavy metal bar. Due to the weather it was wide open.

'They haven't moved,' said the General.

'Their field craft is non-existent.'

'That makes our lives all the easier.'

'Your right, sir, but you know what gets me?'

Macnair smiled. 'Pray, do tell.'

'Their arrogance. The way they're behaving. It's as though they don't take it all seriously.'

'It's not that.'

'Then what is it?'

'In their own country they can do pretty much as they like. They make the rules and they break them. I suspect that adjusting to dealing with a real professional situation is something they can't comprehend.'

Hunter nodded slowly. 'That makes sense.'

'What are your plans for your leave? Do you have any?'

'Still deciding, sir. I can't make up my mind between a horse riding experience in Colorado along with some whitewater rafting, or diving in the Seychelles.'

Macnair nodded, keeping a straight face. 'Whatever you decide to do I am sure you'll have a good time.'

'I'm sure I will.'

The talk continued in a desultory fashion for the next twenty minutes. Finally, one of the Saudis walked away leaving just one man. He was standing on the corner of Broadway House, smoking, glancing continually across the street at the door to the coffee shop.

'Sir, you don't mind if I reduce the odds a little, do you?'

'I was going to suggest it. Also, we could do with a weapon or two.'

'That's what I was thinking.'

'What's your idea?'

Hunter told him, got a nod of approval and left the table. He went through the door marked toilets and out through the open rear door and into a short lane. He hurried down the lane, turned left and 50 yards later, took another left down a second lane and back to the main road. He crossed the road, entered a short lane, turned left again and went 50 yards to end up at the corner to the lane at the end of which stood his target. He speed dialled Macnair and broke the connection before he answered. The General walked out of the coffee shop and stood by the door where he looked at his watch impatiently tapping his foot.

Their attacker was suddenly alert and stood up straight, staring across the street. Hunter passed industrial waste skips for an internal building project that was going on as well as a large, wheeled, aluminium rubbish bin. He was a few paces behind the man who was still staring at Macnair when Hunter waved an arm in the air. The General stepped to the edge of the road.

'Hey,' he called out and gave the man the benefit of his middle finger.

At that moment Hunter stepped behind the man, slid his left arm around the man's neck and dragged him backwards. The man gurgled and grabbed Hunter's arm with both hands and tried to pry it loose. The man's heels dragged along the ground for the five paces it took to reach the first skip where Hunter bent the man's head over the edge. He shifted his grip, placed both his hands on either side of the man's head and rammed down hard. The noise of the man's neck breaking sounded like a rotten twig snapping. Hunter relieved the man of his wallet, passport, mobile phone and a Sig Sauer P320 one of the finest handguns made by the Swiss company. He slid the body into the half empty skip and dragged a few lengths of timber over the body to hide it.

He retreated to the coffee shop the way he had come. By this time the General had refreshed their coffees.

'Nice work.'

'Thanks for your help, sir. Giving him the bird was inspired. Now, where's the other one?'

'Speak of the devil, he's just turned up.'

Hunter stood and said, 'Back to work.'

The second target stood at the entrance to the lane and called out. Hunter crossed the road with his right hand under his coat, the Sig clasped in his fist. The man had taken a couple a paces into the lane and called out a name, louder this time. He must have sensed Hunter approaching because he jerked around, his mouth dropped open, he reached under his coat for his weapon and received two bullets for his trouble. One hit the man's chest and the other his stomach. The distance was less than four feet and the man flew backwards. He was now lying alongside the skip Hunter had already used.

He grabbed the man under his shoulders just as Macnair joined him. Dragging the body behind the skip the General removed the wallet, passport, mobile and a second Sig from the dead man. The man was about 5ft 10ins tall and weighed 210lbs at least. The General took the dead man's feet and they lifted the body into the skip on top of his colleague. They shifted more rubbish and hid the bodies from sight.

'Time to take the subway,' Macnair announced, taking out his mobile and speed dialing. 'Isobel? We're just going into the tube station.' He listened for a few seconds. 'Okay, thanks.'

'What did she say?'

'There are three of them. One either end of the platform we'll be using with the MA in the middle.'

'What are they doing?'

'Nothing, just sitting.

'Why hasn't the transport police asked them what they're up to?'

'Why? They're not harming anyone. They're waiting for a friend to join them on the same train. They are spread out so that they don't miss him.' Macnair shrugged, 'Besides, who's going to ask? The transport police are stretched thinly enough as it is without bothering about three men peacefully sitting in an underground station minding their own business.'

'How do you want to play this, sir?'

The General told him and Hunter nodded agreement.

53

They bought the necessary tickets and made their way to the platform. They appeared not to notice the sudden movement of the Military Attaché as they appeared. There were still a few dozen people around and the two TIFAT officers pretended to be in deep conversation while keeping a wary eye out for an attack. Now both men had silenced weapons courtesy of the enemy and were standing close to the wall, their right hands under their jackets, their fists holding the guns.

The MA stood and walked away towards the end of the platform where he stopped and spoke to the man standing there.

'These fools are beyond belief,' said Hunter. 'Amateur night isn't in it.'

They heard the rattle of a train approaching and the Upminster train coasted to a halt. They climbed onboard. The three men did likewise. Macnair and Hunter kept their heads bowed, so as not to be seen by the surveillance cameras recording events in the carriage.

Once the train was above ground Macnair called Isobel and told her what train they were on. A few minutes later she phoned back to tell them that the surveillance feed had been hacked and was now on a recording loop of a few minutes. It was more than enough for their purposes.

Although the carriage was half-full passengers came and went, the number gradually dwindling. Finally after Hornchurch the three Saudis and the two TIFAT officers were all that was left.

'Here we go,' said Hunter.

The two men were sitting sideways to the carriage, each with a hand under their jackets. The Attaché was approaching them with a grin on his face, his right hand down by his side, a gun clutched in his fist. Behind him came a second man while the third approached from the opposite direction. They also had silenced weapons in their hands. Continuing in their arrogant fashion the weapons were pointing at the floor.

'I am happy to see you again,' the MA began, now only a few metres away from his targets.

He didn't get any further. Hunter was taking the double shot, Macnair the single.

They both fired simultaneously. Macnair hit his target in the forehead and fired a second shot to make sure.

Hunter deliberately shot the MA in the stomach sending him backwards. His next two shots hit the second man in the head. Hunter didn't wait to see the results but stood up and stepped to the inert form of the MA who was curled up, his hands pressed against his belly, blood oozing between his fingers.

'You shouldn't have been talking,' said Hunter, conversationally, 'you should have been shooting. But then that would only have meant you dying a second or two earlier.'

The MA opened his eyes. 'You are a dead man.'

'You are so stupid. You shouldn't have killed the schoolteacher.'

'She,' he gasped, 'she was a traitor to Islam.'

'I was going to put you out of your agony, but I don't think I'll bother.' Hunter fired twice. He blew out the man's ankles just as the train pulled into Upminster Bridge.

Hunter and Macnair pocketed their weapons and exited the carriage. Nobody got on. Isobel had already doctored the surveillance cameras at both stations, Upminster Bridge as well as Upminster. The two men walked out of the station and strolled along the street. The white walled pub called The Windmill was ahead of them and they went inside. They settled on a pint of real ale each while waiting for a taxi to take them back to the city.

476

'Cheers, sir.' The words were barely out of Hunter's mouth when they heard and saw the twos and blues of police cars descending on the area. A couple of ambulances followed. At that moment their taxi drew up, they drained their glasses and left.

Back in central London they spent twenty minutes walking around the area where the club was situated ditching pieces of the guns they had acquired. They used drains as well as a number of skips they came across during their wandering. Thank goodness there was so much development going on in the area, was the way Hunter put it. In the club they stopped in the bar for a sandwich and a tot of whisky. For both of them it was doubles.

'We were talking about your leave earlier, if you're flying from London you may as well stay here. No point coming back to Scotland for a couple of days.'

'Thanks, sir. I will. It's much appreciated.'

'Enjoy it and don't get too lonely.'

The following morning they were having breakfast when Macnair's phone rang. A glance showed it was the Chief Commissioner of Police.

'Hello Alex, this is a pleasant surprise.'

'Malcolm, you won't believe what has happened.'

'Try me.'

'The Saudi Military Attaché has been murdered.'

'You don't say.'

'You don't sound surprised.'

'Nothing surprises me, Alex, you should know that by now.'

'I don't suppose you know anything about it?'

'You're right. You don't suppose correctly.'

'Hmmf. Let me just say that whoever was responsible is owed a bucketful of gratitude by the nation.'

'I'm pleased to hear it. Should I ever find out I'll pass on your thanks.'

'Do that. Oh, and thanks Malcolm.' The connection was broken.

'You heard that?'

'Yes. He's no fool.'

'Quite the reverse. You know, the breakfasts they serve here must be about the best in London.'

Two days later Hunter was at London Heathrow. He had checked in his luggage with Saudi Airlines and was in the first class lounge with a cup of excellent coffee in front of him. He was sitting in such a position as to be able to see the door. He watched as three men entered and made their way towards him. He watched them with an impassive face.

'Of all the first class lounges in all the airports in all the world and you three just happened to walk into the one I'm in.'

'Hello, Boss,' Badonovitch grinned.

'Hi, Nick,' said Masters.

'Good coffee, Nick?' Bletchley enquired.

Hunter couldn't help it. He chuckled. So much for Macnair's exposition not to be too lonely. 'So how come you three are here?'

'Taking a vacation, Nick,' said Bletchley, 'just like you are.'

'How in hell did the General find out where I'm going?'

'Isobel saw Leo working at something on the computer. She asked him what. He told her it was for you and that he was looking for the whereabouts of Tadeas al-Baghdadi. She mentioned it in passing to the General and here we are. Also, he sent a message. We're to go to the American Consulate when we get to Jeddah. There'll be someone there to help us.'

'Any idea who?'

'Nope,' said the SBS Captain, 'but whoever it is will supply us with whatever we need.'

They were flying first class. The food was excellent, none of them accepted a drink and they all slept most of the way as only trained military personnel are able to do. An hour out from Jeddah an announcement was made and the Saudi women, many of them exquisitely made-up and immaculately dressed, began to use the extra spacious and numerous toilets in the aircraft. The purpose was to remove all signs of cosmetics and to change from fashionable clothes into the burka. Hunter also observed that prior to changing their appearance, the women were talkative and smiling. Afterwards they were subdued with their heads bowed. It was like a switch had been flicked and the modern progressive women were catapulted back to the sixth century. All very insulting to womanhood thought Hunter.

Jeddah International Airport was a beacon to modernity and superb infrastructure and architecture. The older airports such as those in Europe were pathetically inadequate by comparison.

At border control they told the officers that they were there to see the historic sights dating back a couple of thousand years and also to visit the world famous grand mosque in Mecca.

Their passports were stamped without any hesitation and they were through and out into the searing heat of Saudi Arabia. The neon sign in the airport had announced that the temperature was 36° centigrade, almost hot enough to fry an egg on the sidewalk.

They took a couple of taxis to the Intercontinental Hotel, all of them happy to be in the air-conditioned cocoon of the Mercedes cars. At the hotel they booked in, each with their own luxurious room. Hunter upgraded to a suite. It would make any planning conference that much easier to conduct.

They had no need to go to the American Consulate. The Americans came to the hotel. Hunter opened the door to Hiram Walsh and Lizzie Montgomery.

'I might have guessed,' was Hunter's way of greeting them after shaking the Colonel's hand and kissing the Captain on her cheek.

'Malcolm thought you could use some help. Bugs?'

Hunter shrugged. Walsh removed a gizmo the size of a mobile phone, elongated it's aerial and began to slowly and methodically sweep it around the rooms. While he did so Lizzie did the talking.

'Nice place. Must cost a fortune.'

'You know what they say, Lizzie, if you've got it, flaunt it.'

'Is that what they say? I wouldn't know. I don't have any of it, whatever it is. Wow, fresh fruit on the sideboard, a fabulous view of the city, the sea in the distance, a dining table that seats eight and I suspect a large bedroom and a plush bathroom.'

Hunter smiled and nodded. 'I'll give you a tour later on.'

Lizzie shook her head. 'No thanks, Nick.' She lowered her voice. 'I'm afraid you are confined to the dustbin of history my friend and ex, emphasis on the ex, lover.'

Hunter grinned, turned the palms of his hands up and shrugged. 'The story of my life.'

'What is?' Walsh rejoined them.

'My luck with the opposite sex. Okay?'

'Yeah.' He took another, similar sized piece of kit from his briefcase and switched it on. 'That'll disrupt any signal to a parabolic mic aimed at the windows.'

'Thanks, Hiram.'

'What do you want to do about weapons?'

'I've been thinking about it and I guess the answer is nothing. The only ID we have with us is our passports. If we were arrested on the most spurious of reasons and they found our TIFAT ID we'd never get out of prison.'

'Never mind never getting out,' said Walsh, 'you'd not survive.'

'Yeah, that's a better prognosis of what would happen. We won't bother with weapons. We can use some surveillance gear and some trackers. I want al-Baghdadi on his own for a few minutes before I break his neck. Do you have any info on him?'

'Some good news, actually,' said Walsh.

'Oh? I'm always open to good news.'

'In three days time there is going to be a religious conference here in the hotel.'

'And al-Baghdadi will be here?'

Walsh nodded. 'He's been promoted to number two at the Mutawa.'

'Look, I know who they are but what about their powers?' Hunter asked. 'Do you know what they are?'

'Well,' said Walsh, 'you know they're the religious police. They exist in all Islamic states but with slightly different forms of authority.

Here in Saudi they are actually known as Mutaween. Their stated job is to enforce Sharia law as defined by the Committee for the Promotion of Virtue and the Prevention of Vice.'

'You're kidding!' Hunter couldn't help saying.

'Nope,' Lizzie said, smiling, 'when it comes to hypocrisy the Saudis are in a league of their own.'

Walsh continued. 'There are over three and a half thousand officers and many thousands more volunteers who spy on their fellow citizens and report them for the most minor of infractions. If unrelated men and women are caught socialising, or engaged in prostitution, or homosexuality, or shopkeepers don't close at prayer times, which let's not forget is five times a day they can be arrested. They enforce dietary laws, ensure alcohol isn't sold, made or drunk and will seize any product that they assess as anti-Islamic. Note that. It's what they assess and there's no comeback. They ensure no other religion is practiced in the Kingdom. In fact, in 2014 the Saudis passed a law calling on the death penalty for anyone bringing into the country a publication that supports any religion other than Islam.'

'Are you telling me that if I brought a bible into this country I can be arrested, tried and given the death penalty?'

'Yes,' was the stark reply.

'Good God but this country is barbaric,' said Hunter.

'A big problem is that a Mutaween officer can decide on an issue and there and then actually whip the individual they see as guilty,' said Lizzie. 'But here's the kicker. It's usually women they beat up on, not the men.'

'That figures. So what's the conference about?'

'The implementation of Sharia, the role of the Mutaween in its enforcement as well as what is deemed a suitable punishment for transgressors in a modern age.'

Hunter shook his head. 'Are these people for real?'

'I'm afraid so,' said Walsh, 'which makes them all the more scary. However, we have to put up with them.'

'Yeah, I know. The Saudis are the biggest purchasers of western armaments in the world and a hell of a lot of jobs depend on their goodwill.'

'Don't forget we also need a few wars to use up the ammunition,' said Lizzie, 'as well as lose aircraft that are shot down or equipment that's blown up.'

The two military officers nodded.

'How long does it last?'

'It's an all day event,' said Walsh, 'starting with the Fajr.'

'The morning prayer?'

'Correct. It has to be said between the beginning of dawn and sunrise.'

'Which makes it around four thirty to five,' said Lizzie.

'Early start,' Hunter commented.

'It shows how religious and faithful they all are,' replied Walsh.

'How long does this conference go on until?'

'The Maghrib,' said the Colonel.

'Just after sunset,' Hunter said musingly, 'which is about 18.45?'

'Spot on,' said Walsh. 'After that the conference will break up. By the way, I have good news. Malcolm texted me to say that they had been keeping an eye on the guest list for the hotel for the conference and that al-Baghdadi is booked to stay here the night before as well as the night of the conference. Which makes sense as he lives in Mecca. He's in room 1601.'

Hunter smiled. 'Next to Chris. Then I guess that's where we'll make our move.'

54

The team spent the next few days as tourists. They agreed the country was fascinating, steeped in wonderful historic fact mixed with fiction and dotted with historic buildings and monuments. The majesty and splendour of the Grand Mosque of Mecca was awesome, even to the cynics from TIFAT. One shocking statistic they learnt was that since 2004 over 1,600 people had been killed at the mosque due to stampedes caused by panic, accidents such as a crane collapsing and a fire. A few thousand more had been injured. Yet it was deemed a sacred duty for all Muslims, if they could afford it, to visit the mosque in their lifetime. The journey to Mecca was known as haj and people beggared themselves in order to make the journey.

They received a message from Rosyth telling them there would be 368 people at the conference, all men, with about half staying in the hotel.

On the morning of the conference, the faithful proved how devout they were by appearing in one of the conference rooms, which was stripped of chairs and tables, to recite the Fajr. After that they went into the dining room to gorge themselves on a superb buffet washed down with excellent coffee or numerous kinds of tea.

One thing that had been missing in their planning had been the identity of Tadeas al-Baghdadi. However, Lizzie had supplied the solution by being in the corridor at the time a Muslim man exited room 1601. She had been pretending to use her mobile and had stood a mere few feet from the door. The man had glowered at her and said something to her face that was Arabic and hence incomprehensible to her. Lizzie glowered back.He was dressed in traditional Arab garb, was about 5ft 6ins tall, thin, with a straggly beard and narrow face.

The man began to look uncomfortable for a few seconds before turning and walking away.

Lizzie went in the opposite direction. She had at least four photographs of him.

At a turn in the corridor Lizzie looked back in time to see al-Baghdadi step into a lift and the doors close. She phoned Hunter.

'He's on his way to the lobby. Here are the photographs I managed to take.' She sent them to Hunter.

'Good. Thanks. I can see a family resemblance with the other al-Baghdadis. Yes, here he is. He's heading for the dining room. See you shortly. Jan,' he turned to Badonovitch, 'go into the dining room and keep an eye on our friend. If he leaves let me know.'

Hunter used the phone in the lobby to call the front desk. Speaking Arabic he told one of the receptionists that he had locked himself out and wanted a key sent up immediately. He was asked his name and he told him al-Baghdadi and insisted on immediate service. It was promised and he saw the man gesture to a youngster in a maroon uniform with a rimless hat of the same colour. Hunter moved quickly across the foyer and stepped into a lift.

He was waiting outside the door to room 1601 when the boy arrived. He slipped him 10 riyals, which was £2 and took the cardkey. He let himself in and quickly searched the room. There was nothing unusual to be found. Like the rest of the hotel the room was luxuriantly furnished but consisted of a bedroom and bathroom only. Hunter planted a few bugs around the place as well as attaching a bug to al-Baghdadi's clothes. His phone rang.

'Boss, he's on the move. Heading to the elevators.'

'Thanks, Jan. I'm finished here.'

Hunter went next door and knocked 5 bells. It was immediately opened and he went inside.

'Okay?' Bletchley greeted him.

'Yeah, no problems.'

They heard the door open and what sounded like someone rummaging through drawers looking for something. A phone rang and al-Baghdadi answered it.

'Yes, my prince. You will be arriving tomorrow. I shall meet you in the port at five o'clock. Have no fear, I shall be there.'

Then seconds later the door opened and closed again. Hunter phoned Badonovitch and told him al-Baghdadi was on the move again.

'Hiram brought you something,' said Bletchley, handing over a pencil case size box. Hunter flipped open the lid. Nestled inside was a hypodermic needle.

'What is it?' Bletchley asked.

'Ever heard of tetrodotoxin?'

'Presumably it's some sort of poison.'

'Correct. Found in the blue-ringed octopus and the puffer fish. It paralyses the body and gradually kills you over about three minutes. Painless but frightening if you know what's going on. Al-Baghdadi will know exactly what's going on because I'll tell him.'

'What are you going to do?'

'After their conference I'll be waiting for al-Baghdadi in his room.'

'I'll help.'

'Are you sure?'

'Of course I am. What if he's not alone?'

Hunter nodded. 'Okay. Thanks, Chris.'

They waited until the devout were saying the Maghrib. Hunter and Bletchley let themselves into the room next door. They settled down to wait in the two armchairs they had moved to face the door.

Masters phoned. 'Al-Baghdadi is heading for the lifts.'

'Is he alone?'

'No. There are two others.'

'Okay, we can manage them.'

'No, hang on Nick. The two men are talking together and ignoring al-Baghdadi. I guess the Mutaween aren't very popular even with the devout.'

'Okay, thanks for the heads-up.' He broke the connection and said, 'He's on his way.'

Two minutes later they heard a noise at the door. It opened and a single man was silhouetted in the doorway. He stepped in and turned to the side with the door casting light into the room. He placed the keycard into the slot next to the door and the light in the bathroom came on. Bletchley and Hunter had switched off the remainder.

The man closed the door and turned around, fumbling for the light switch. As the light came on Hunter stood up and walked towards their target. Al-Baghdadi was suddenly aware of his presence and took a step backwards.

Bletchley was next to Hunter. Al-Baghdadi opened his mouth and looked as though he was about to scream when Bletchley hit him in the jaw. He flew backwards and hit his head on the wall, collapsing in a heap.

Hunter grabbed the man by the front of his clothing pulled him to his feet, shoved him across the floor and dumped him into a chair. Hunter tapped his face, bringing him back to full consciousness.

He began cursing in Arabic. Hunter let him. The man then tried to stand up but was easily pushed back into the chair.

Bletchley went behind the man, clamped a gloved hand over his mouth and held him down. Hunter picked up the hypodermic that was on a side table, jammed it into al-Baghdadi's thigh and pressed the plunger. The man's eyes were wide open and staring at the needle. He began to struggle but was unable to do more than wriggle slightly. His efforts began to subside and Bletchley let him go.

'Who . . . Who are you?' The voice was a faint croak.

Replying in Arabic Hunter said, 'We are from TIFAT in Scotland. We're the people who killed the other members of your family and stole all the money from your accounts as well as removing all your investments. You are vile filth and a traitor to your faith. You are now dying. I have injected you with a poison that is paralysing your muscles and shutting down your vital organs. You will be dead in about,' Hunter looked at his watch, 'two minutes. You will die alone. Let's go Chris.'

Al-Baghdadi tried to speak but all he managed was a gurgle and to dribble out of the corner of his mouth as his head drooped to one side.

The two men left the Saudi to his death.

'I think we'll leave in the morning,' said Hunter. 'There's an early BA flight that we can take.'

'Okay, I'll tell the others,' said Bletchley.

Peace and tranquility blanketed the hotel for the night. In the morning Walsh met with them and relieved them of their extra pieces of equipment. The team then took a couple of taxis to the airport and booked onto their flight.

While the rest went through to departures Hunter announced he had something to do and he'd catch them up.

He left the airport and met Walsh outside.

'Are you sure about this, Nick?'

'Positive.'

'Okay. Here's the Glock and here's another hypo of poison.'

'Thanks Hiram. Both are much appreciated.'

'The yacht was moved last night. She's no longer alongside but at anchor about half a mile offshore.'

'Any reason why?'

'Apparently the prince is leaving early in the morning and there's a lot less fuss if they leave from anchor and not from the port. He does it whenever he comes to Jeddah.'

'That makes sense.'

'By the way, does Malcolm know about this?'

'No. He'll be able to deny all knowledge with a clear conscience. Besides, I understood from a message I received that the target is off limits.'

'Says who?'

'Says our government.'

'Well I've got news for you, buddy, my government shifted him to the top three most wanted a couple of days ago.'

'Most wanted?'

'Yeah. Most wanted dead. There's no chance of an international arrest warrant, no chance of making him persona non grata in any of the western countries so his demise is the only solution.'

'The Saudi powers also need to know why he's been killed. Otherwise they won't stop interfering in jihadist terrorism because they believe themselves to be untouchable.'

'We know that at one level that's the case. Armament sales are so huge what does a few bombs here and there matter? After all it's usually only the little people who die.'

'Such cynicism even for an old Colonel in Special Ops.'

'Less of the old. But yeah, I'm a cynic. Aren't you?'

'Of course I am. Cynicism is the engine that keeps us going. It leads us not to trust certain people.'

'You mean like politicians?'

'Exactly like them. Along with bankers, the pharmaceutical companies, the oil industry, the armaments industry as we've already mentioned as well as the overseas aid industry which is about as corrupt as the rest of them.'

'I couldn't agree more,' said Walsh. 'Nick, as soon as you've finished what are you doing?'

'I've made all the necessary arrangements.'

'Are you going to tell me?'

'Sure.' He gave Walsh the information and ended by saying, 'That's why I want you to drop me at the marina. The purchase should have gone through by now and I want to check her over.'

'I like it. Hopefully it'll be the last place they'll look for you. Assuming anybody comes looking that is.'

'If they know he's dead then they will. He's the cousin of the king. They'll close the country down. There'll be no aircraft in or out, the borders will be shut and the only way out will be an early exit by sea. Are you sure the prince has an audience with the king?'

'Like I told you, it's a family celebration of some sort or another. About a hundred of the nearest and dearest in attendance. If it follows the usual timeline then it'll finish at midnight and that means the prince will be back at the port thirty minutes later.'

'Ideal.'Hunter's phone rang. He saw it was Bletchley, thought about whether or not to answer it and then decided it was the least he could do.

'Yes, Chris?'

'Nick? Where are you? We're boarding right now.'

'Good. You'd better get going. Something's come up. I'll phone you when you get to the UK.'

'What do you mean something's come up? What . . .' he stopped speaking. 'Nick, you bloody idiot. We should be there with you.'

'No, it's better this way. Seriously, I have a plan and none of you could have helped.'

'What am I going to tell the General? Hell Nick, more to the point what am I going to tell your sister if anything happens to you?'

'It won't so don't worry.'

'Where's Jan? Is he with you?'

'No. He's with you. I saw him going through to departures.' He paused. 'Actually, I saw him approach departures. The stupid bloody idiot. Hiram, is there a taxi behind us? Been with us since we left the airport?'

'Yes. I was going to take a few corners to see if he's following.'

'He is,' Hunter sighed.

'Who's in it?'

'The idiot Russian I have on my team.'

Walsh laughed out loud. He couldn't help himself.

55

The car pulled up at the marina with the taxi right behind it.

'I should have you court-martialled,' Hunter greeted Badonovitch.

'You're right boss. When we get back do that and I can get into the private sector and make some real money.'

Hunter grinned. 'Stupid Russian.'

'I know boss. My mother always told me I didn't have the sense I was born with.'

'Funnily enough my mother says the same about me. Thanks, Jan. I appreciate you being here.'

'That's okay, Nick. I take it we're going on a sea voyage?'

'Something like that.'

'Jan, I've got something here for you,' said Walsh.

'Yes, sir. Thanks whatever it is.'

Walsh handed over a bumbag. 'Glock plus silencer. Nick, I've got a long gun in a bag in the trunk. You'd better take it with you. Also a couple of vests. The new ones with the shoulder pads. You never know, they may save your worthless hides at some point.'

Hunter nodded and grinned. 'You may be right, and more thanks.'

'Is there anything else I can help with?'

'No, that's okay Hiram, you've done enough.'

They shook hands and the two TIFAT men watched as Walsh drove away with a cheery wave.

Hunter led the way to the sales office of a boat broker where they were welcomed with smiles and offers of coffee. They smiled back but refused the drink. Hunter signed ownership papers, refused insurance and thanked the broker for his help. Next door was a chandlers that sold just about every nautical item known to man including a hand held sat-nav. As a back up Hunter bought charts covering the area from Jeddah to Port Sudan. He knew the direct distance was the best part of 220 miles, which he figured would take about 36 hours, if the wind was from the right direction, at the right speed and held steady. The weather forecast was about as perfect as he could have hoped for - north-northeast at a steady 15 knots. Port Sudan was south-southwest and that meant a simple running before the wind on a steady bearing. Of course, that was all being well. However, the laws of the sea meant something would probably go wrong. It was the way of things.

The small supermarket in the complex sold fresh fruit and vegetables, every soft drink imaginable as well as cooking and eating utensils. They stocked up on two of everything in galley utensils and bought plenty of food. They also bought bottled water, tea and coffee. There was an efficient though small fridge onboard big enough to hold fresh milk, packets of lamb chops, the fruit juices, tomatoes and lettuce.

She was named *The Adventuress*. She was 32ft 7ins length overall and at the waterline she was 26ft 3ins. Her beam was 7ft 11ins and her draft 5ft 5ins. She had a fin keel with a spade rudder and her rig type was known as a fractional sloop. Inside she had two midships berths with the galley just aft of them. The sink was to starboard and the cooker to port. The companionway step-down was just aft of the galley while the head and shower were all the way forward. She was a sleek craft, easily manageable by one person, never mind two such highly experienced sailors.

Hunter had already checked the inventory of sails and rigging although he hadn't taken her on any sea-trials. There hadn't been time, which wasn't the best way to buy a yacht. They turned on the pumps to empty the fresh water tank and flashed up the engine. By the time they moved to the fuelling point the water tank was empty. They had the attendant at the fuelling berth flush out the diesel tank and fill it again. Water finding its way into diesel tanks wasn't an unknown phenomenon if the boat hadn't been used for a while and could cause the engine to cut out. They also refilled the water tank, the water to be used for washing, while their drinking water came from the bottles.

According to the engine's instruction booklet there was now enough fuel to last 48 hours of continuous use while pushing the yacht along at 6 knots. This meant they should reach their destination with a margin of 12 hours to spare.

'What now?' Badonovitch asked.

'Now we put her through her paces by circumnavigating the prince's ship and then we'll come back. However, before we go, how about I make a cheese and tomato roll?'

'Sounds good, Nick. Thanks.'

'Coffee or a cold drink?'

Badonovitch wiped the sweat from his brow. It was 34C and although there was a steady breeze from the north it did little to cool the air around them. 'An ice cold lager would go down a treat but I'll settle on an orange juice.'

'Coming right up.'

They ate and drank in minutes and then prepped for sea. They threaded the mainsail and jib while they allowed the engine to warm through. They cast off, Hunter engaged the gears and they set out sedately for the Red Sea. Outside the port they hoisted the jib and mainsail and cut the engine. The wind billowed out the red nylon sails; the bows lifted up a few inches and the boat picked up speed. She ran sweetly through the water, heeled over about 10 degrees to port, the sea burbling along her hull. The super yacht loomed ahead and they passed close to the yacht's stern. Hunter steered in a straight line to ensure the wind wasn't taken out of her sails by the hull of the yacht.

'See the guard on the stern?' Hunter asked.

'Yeah, as well as the one in the bow. They looked to be carrying AK74s over their shoulders.'

'At least they didn't point them at us.'

Once clear they turned to starboard, ran for a mile and then turned another 45 degrees. Ten minutes later they turned again and were now headed directly for the marina's entrance. They went in using the jib without the engine running. Hunter took her alongside with a gentle touch and Badonovitch leapt ashore with the bow rope. They tied up using the bow and stern ropes only, not bothering with breast or spring ropes.

'I'm going to the chandlers for a pair of binoculars,' said Hunter, 'they might come in useful.'

'Okay, boss. I'm going to sit on the waterfront and watch the prince's yacht.'

'I'll see you in a while.'

They took it in turns to wander around the seafront and to keep an eye on the super yacht. Boats came and went all afternoon, most carrying passengers back and forth, some with what appeared to be provisions. Later a fuel barge chugged alongside and spent an hour obviously filling up the yacht's diesel and fresh water tanks. Though the latter would also be kept filled using onboard desalination pumps.

Around 20.00 one of the yacht's sleek boats was lowered into the water and taken alongside the midships gangway platform. The prince appeared and walked down the wide steps and onto the platform. There he stepped gingerly onto the boat, which rocked a fair degree. Hunter was watching at the time and focussed the binoculars on the spectacle. The prince was fat to the point of obese and looked distinctly uncomfortable sitting in the stern of the boat as it cast off and headed for the shore.

Hunter put away the glasses and appeared to ignore the approaching vessel. He noted there was a helmsman standing in the bows, a man in the stern with a boathook and two men with automatics strapped to their waists sitting amidships either side of the boat. They didn't appear to be taking much notice of what was around them and didn't even look towards Hunter who was a mere 20 metres away. The boat was entering the marina and it was obvious which steps the prince would land at.

Hunter recognised the ennui that had the two men in its grip. The job was boring without a scintilla of challenge. The men were poorly trained, probably spent no time at all honing their skills and on top of all that they were in familiar territory. Nobody in his or her right mind would do anything to a prince in Saudi Arabia. If they did it would mean a very painful death.

A Rolls Royce was already waiting for the prince. He climbed out of the boat with one of the bodyguards taking his hand to help him. Now he was onshore Hunter could see that he was about 5ft 5ins tall and about the same around. He had two chins that wobbled as he waddled. He was dressed in traditional Arabic garb, which did nothing to hide his obesity.

He was escorted to the car and deferentially helped in. One of the bodyguards climbed into the front passenger seat while the other sat next to the prince.

The evening dragged but finally Hunter decided it was time to move. The first idea he'd had was to take out the prince and his men while alongside but there were a number of people still out for a stroll even at that time of night. That left plan B. The two men cast off and headed across the marina and as far as the entrance to the port. They edged alongside the wall and waited in the solitude and peace of the shadow of the harbour wall. They had timed it well. They didn't have long to wait.

Badonovitch was using the binoculars and announced, 'Here they come.' He pushed *The Adventuress* away from the wall; Hunter engaged the gears and the yacht moved slowly across the entrance. He was watching the other boat as it came nearer. He changed direction to starboard and then port as the two boats closed on a steady bearing.

The helmsman on the boat suddenly woke up to the fact that the yacht was less than 10 metres away and closing. He called at them to alter course away and that the prince was onboard. Hunter waved and yelled out an apology. Now they were about six metres away and the two bodyguards suddenly sat up to take notice.

One reached for his gun. He didn't make it. Badonovitch's bullet entered the man's forehead and blew out the back of his skull. Hunter's first shot hit the helmsman in the chest and knocked him overboard and his second killed the second bodyguard. Badonovitch fired twice in quick succession now barely a boat's length away and killed the two boatmen. The prince was looking at the two TIFAT men in abject horror. As the boats touched he began to shake.

'Please, don't hurt me,' he spoke Arabic having heard Hunter use the same language seconds earlier. 'I will give you whatever you want. Dollars, euros, pounds. Millions of them.'

'Give back the lives of the people who died trying to cross to Europe,' said Hunter in English. 'Or arrange to free all those sold into slavery not only in the west but the rest of the world. Or those who have been sold to the sex trade. Can you do that?'

The prince's jaw dropped open and he stared at Hunter as the automatic was pointed at his head and the gun spat two rounds. Quickly Hunter climbed into the sleek boat and took the yacht's bow rope from Badonovitch. He tied it to the cleat on the stern on the boat, took the helm of the motorboat, engaged the gears and headed out to sea. He turned the boat to port and hugged alongside the outer wall until they reached the end. He turned to starboard and gradually increased speed, moving away from the shore and the super yacht that was now at least half-a-mile astern.

'You okay, Jan?' He spoke over his shoulder.

'Fine. You can take her up a notch or two.' A quick glance at the speedometer showed they were travelling at 15 knots and Hunter eased the throttle forward. At 20 knots he was satisfied. He had identified the autopilot, which he now engaged. He stood watching the compass for a few seconds pointing steadily at 205 degrees and nodded in satisfaction. He checked the fuel tanks. They were half full. He had no idea of fuel consumption but he did know that if he lightened the boat it would go that bit further. He told Badonovitch what he intended doing.

'Do you want a hand? I've tied the wheel so we're not veering off anywhere.'

'No, you're okay.' Tying the end of the anchor chain around the feet of the prince, Hunter tried to shove the body into the water. He pushed it as far as the gunwale and bent the torso over the side. He placed the anchor on the back of the body, took hold of its feet and lifted and shoved at the same time. The prince slid over the side and out of sight.

Now that they were about five miles from land the sea was picking up slightly. Long, undulating waves with the odd white cap was soporific and the wind was as it had been all day, a steady 15 knots from the north-northeast.

The radio on the console came to life asking for the boat's whereabouts. Hunter was tempted to reply but decided it was better not to. He switched it off. The voice was a distraction. He continued sliding the other bodies into the water. He had nothing to sink them with and so hoped the blood would attract the sharks in double quick time.

He checked the fuel. A quick calculation suggested there was enough petrol for another three hours. They ploughed on, no lights showing, the satnav in the yacht showing a steady reduction in the distance to go to Port Sudan.

Dawn was breaking when the engine coughed. It coughed again and then quit. The two boats drifted to a halt.

'Time to abandon ship,' said Hunter. He used the guards' automatics to punch holes into the bottom of the hull and the boat quickly began to settle.

Stepping back onboard the yacht the two men watched as the water lapped over the side of the hull. Seconds later it was on its way to a watery end.

They hoisted sail, adjusted their course slightly and ran before the wind, the mainsail out to starboard and the jib out to port. The bows lifted a few degrees and she settled down to a steady 8 knots. Distance to go was 118 miles according to the satnav. The prince's boat had towed them halfway to their destination. Time to Port Sudan was 15 hours as near as dammit, all being well, with calm seas and a steady wind. Estimated time of arrival at the port was 20.00.

Hunter got his head down and slept the sleep of the just and the good until 11.45. He and Badonovitch changed places and soon the Spetsnaz's gentle snores wafted up from below deck. According to the satnav they had 74 miles to go so he was still expecting an ETA of 20.00.

Unfortunately the peace and tranquility didn't last very long.

Two fast moving speedboats suddenly loomed on the horizon and headed directly for them.

56

'Jan, look lively, we've got what looks like unwelcome company.'

Badonovitch popped out of the saloon like a jackrabbit. He had his Glock in his right hand dangling down by his side, out of sight. Hunter's was next to him on the console in front of him while the rifle was lying along the seat next to his right hand.

'How do you want to play this, Nick?'

'I was about to say let's see who they are.' He had his eyes glued to the binoculars, 'but I can see. The boats are the same colour as the one the prince was using.' The boats accelerated and headed directly at them. In keeping with their sloppiness when it came to close quarter protection the two boats were relatively close together.

Standing in the cockpit of both boats was a man holding an AK74, the banana shape of the magazine unmistakable. Alongside him sat a man at the helm while near the stern was a second gunman holding an automatic rifle.

'Six to two, Nick. What do you want to do?'

'Let's see how this plays out. If . . .'

The words were barely out of his mouth when the man in the nearest boat raised his weapon and opened fire. The boat was 80 metres away and luckily as he pulled the trigger a larger than normal wave caused the bows of the boat to rise up a few degrees. The hail of bullets he fired passed overhead but tore through the jib.

Hunter and Badonovitch didn't hesitate. They both raised their Glocks and opened fire on the nearest boat, shooting as quickly as they could pull the trigger. Aiming accurately wasn't an option. One of their bullets hit the helmsman causing the boat to veer hard to starboard where it rammed the second boat.

Hunter replaced his handgun on the console, snatched up the rifle, aimed and fired. He missed the second gunman who pushed his colleague off the seat and away from the helm, grabbed the wheel, rammed the throttle open and took off like a bat out of hell. Hunter didn't bother wasting a second bullet.

He shifted aim while Badonovitch reloaded his magazine, which took him about two seconds.

The second target boat was turning sharply and out of effective range of an aimed Glock but well within the effective range of the rifle. Hunter fired and the bullet hit the gunman who was standing at the stern in his stomach. He staggered, the boat heeled again and the man tipped over into the sea. The second gunman sprayed bullets in the direction of the yacht and both men dropped to the deck.

Be prepared was a rule with them and they both had on their Kevlar vests. Which was just as well. A bullet passed through the yacht's hull and hit Hunter. He was lucky. The bullet scraped his left bicep muscle and hit his side. He grunted in pain but a quick feel showed there was little blood apart from a trickle down his arm.

Badonovitch held his fire while Hunter suddenly knelt, aimed the rifle and fired. He hit the second gunman who went flying over the side. The boat began to turn sharply to starboard while at the same time it was increasing speed. It headed away from the yacht as fast as it would go.

'You okay?' Badonovitch asked.

'Yeah. Just a scratch. How the hell did they get here so quickly?'

'Who knows? More importantly why did they open fire on us like that? They didn't bother to find out who we are. Let me check your arm.'

Badonovitch ripped Hunter's shirtsleeve up to the shoulder. You'll live, boss.' In a cupboard under the console he took out a first aid box, wiped the blood away and placed a plaster over the wound. Hunter winced and the Spetsnaz added, 'Were you hit anywhere else?'

'The bullet hit my side.' Hunter removed the Kevlar vest and lifted his shirt. The bruise was already beginning to form. He wriggled his torso, felt around the area where the bullet had hit and then pressed down more firmly. 'It's okay. I don't think any real damage has been done.' Reaching into the first aid kit he found a bottle of painkillers and swallowed a few.

'I'll get something to drink.'

While Badonovitch was below Hunter changed the jib for the spare. Like any modern yacht they carried a complete second set of sails.

Badonovitch returned a few minutes later with cold juice and mugs of tea. He also had a couple of energy bars with him.

Hunter took the bottle of juice, said thanks, and drained it in one long swallow.

They set the sails, adjusted their course and headed towards Port Sudan. It was 13.35.

Sipping his tea, the Russian said, 'They'll be back.'

'Probably. More men and more guns I would think.'

'Any ideas?'

'Change course and head south. Maybe they won't find us.'

'How do you figure they got here so fast?'

'They must have raised the alarm as soon as the prince didn't return and when they didn't get an answer on the radio. They could have covered a lot of sea looking for us in their super yacht with boats deployed.'

'How did they know it was us?'

'God knows. Maybe they're shooting up everything they see. Maybe somebody saw us.' Hunter shrugged. 'Whatever happened we need to prep for the worst.'

The wind backed and there was a sudden gust from the west causing the yacht to rock a few degrees. Hunter looked to starboard and saw clouds building up. They weren't much at that stage but he commented, 'Nice bit of cloud coming our way. With luck it could mean a storm's brewing. We'll be able to weather it far better than the speed boats.'

They adjusted the sails. With the wind no longer behind them their SOG – speed over the ground – was barely five knots in the direction they wanted to go.

They took it in turns to work between decks while the other kept watch. They took apart cupboards, lifted the decking, removed the bunks and doors and used every scrap of wood they could find to create a wall on each side and across the stern of the cockpit area. The wooden walls were 6ins thick and would stop a bullet or two. A magazine full, fired from close-up was a different thing altogether.

Hunter was sure there was a cold front on the way. The wind continued to back to the west and the temperature dropped a few degrees centigrade.

The longer they sailed the more they were being pushed eastwards and so they started the engine and again aimed directly towards Port Sudan. They were maintaining speed and course but now would not be arriving until the early hours of the morning.

The sea had picked up and there were short sharp waves about half a metre high coming in from the west. The yacht took them in her stride, thanks to the steadying influence of the sails. Hunter didn't envy anyone in the speedboats coming after them.

It was 18.36 which meant sunset was 30 minutes away when Hunter announced, 'There are two, no three, fast approaching boats. There are three men in each boat. Yep. They're from the super yacht. Standby to repel boarders.'

The three boats were spread out, at least three cables apart. The one in the centre was coming in the fastest and was the point of a V formation. Each boat had a helmsman and two armed men. The gunners were hiding behind the hulls; the helmsmen were literally sitting targets.

Hunter settled down behind the rifle and took aim. He relaxed his breathing, his heart rate slowed; he took careful aim through the telescopic sight at the nearest helmsman. The sight moved up and down as the small yacht and the speedboat moved with the waves. It was a shot that David Hughes could take with a 99.9% chance of a hit. Hunter was a realist and figured his odds were closer to 75%. At about 700 yards Hunter figured it was time to shoot. The speedboat was rocking with the sea while the yacht was relatively steady. The man's torso and head were showing through the windscreen and Hunter pulled the trigger when the telescopic sight centred on the target's chest.

The bullet hit the man in the sternum killing him and sending the boat careering off to starboard. He changed aim before either of the other two helmsmen could react and fired at a second target. He hit the man in the shoulder, sending him sprawling onto the deck. The third helmsman turned his wheel violently to port. The boat heeled over at a steep angle, half her hull out of the water, before she dropped back down and rocketed off at high speed. The other two boats were now back under control and they also turned away.

Now there was one boat with three men and two boats with two men each. Still uncomfortable odds but at least they were already turning in favour of the two warriors from TIFAT.

They watched as the boats split up and moved to come in from three directions, surrounding the yacht. There was another gust of wind and the yacht rocked. The three speedboats rocked more but then settled down to a stable enough platform from which to fire automatic weapons with an expectation of hitting their target.

One of the boats was closing faster than the others. Hunter scanned the sea and said, 'Jan, take the boat at six o'clock. I'll take the one at two o'clock. Ready?'

'As ever, boss.' Badonovitch held both Glocks. His chances of hitting the target with a single shot weren't good. A fusillade of bullets however could either score a hit or put off their attackers.

The figures went through Hunter's mind. The effective range of an AK 47 was 400 metres, for an AK 74 it was 500 metres while the effective range of a Glock was 50 metres. The effective range of the L115A3 was as near as dammit 2,500 metres. That meant the kinetic energy of the bullet was five times that of the AK. This meant that at a range under 1,000 metres there wasn't a pleasure boat in the world with a hull that could stop a round.

There were no helmsmen in sight. They had lined-up the boats and were ducked down out of sight. Not that there was any protection from a high velocity round fired from a sniper's rifle.

Hunter fired and worked the bolt to reload. He fired a second shot. The first round penetrated the stem of the target boat about six inches above the waterline. It travelled as far as the engine block ricocheted off the solid iron and turned down through the bottom of the hull. The second bullet flew about six inches higher and took out the stomach of the man at the helm.

The boat continued to come straight at the yacht and the two gunmen onboard stood at the windscreen and opened fire with their weapons on fully automatic. In spite of the twisting and bouncing of the boat the wooden wall took half a dozen rounds before the shooting stopped.

Hunter hadn't bothered to even look to see what was happening to his target, as his attention was needed elsewhere. The second boat that Badonovitch had emptied the Glocks at was closing fast. Not surprisingly it didn't appear as though a single one of the Russian's rounds had hit their target.

Hunter was aiming straight over the stern. There was a sudden strong gust of wind and just as the gunmen opened fire their boat rolled hard to port. Most of the rounds flying in their direction missed except one that hit Badonovitch on the back of his left arm and furrowed a line of blood up to his elbow where it chipped the bone. The Glock fell from his hand and hit the deck.

'You okay?' Hunter asked as he opened fire at the boat that was now less than 300 metres away.

'I'll live.' Badonovitch changed the magazine in the Glock he was holding in his right hand and aimed at the other vessel coming in fast on the port side. He ducked just in time as round after round hit the wooden wall they had built causing it to fall in at an angle of about 30 degrees. The speedboat was now within about 100 metres.

Hunter's first shot at the new target ploughed through the hull and into the helmsman but that did nothing to stop the boat or the gunmen changing their magazines and start firing again. Working the bolt, Hunter fired twice in quick succession. His first shot hit one of the gunners in the lower face and blew it apart. His second shot hit the other gunman in the shoulder and flung him to one side. The problem they now faced was that the boat was on a collision course with the stern of the yacht and moving at about 20kts faster. Hunter figured the boat would hit them in about ten seconds.

He flung himself at the console, flipped the autopilot switch and turned the wheel to starboard and into the wind. The speedboat missed their stern by centimetres.

Badonovitch opened fire at the third boat, which was now at 8 o'clock to the yacht and paralleling their course. It was 50 metres astern and about 30 metres to port having slowed down for some reason.

Badonovitch changed his magazine and took aim. There were two men holding rifles and a third at the helm. One was shouting at the helmsman and pointing at the yacht. The speedboat was rocking dangerously as the wind and waves picked up. Hunter diagnosed the problem.

'They've either run out of fuel or you hit something that's ruptured the feed.'

Suddenly the two gunmen on the other vessel realised the yacht was moving away and turned to shoot at them. Hunter was ready and took out the man on the right. Before he could change aim Badonovitch hit the other man with two bullets to the torso. The helmsman lifted his hands in the air as though surrendering. That wasn't an option. The last thing they needed was for the super yacht to appear, rescue the man and for him to give a description of them and the yacht. The king of Saudi's reach went easily as far as Sudan.

Without a shred of remorse Hunter fired and blew the man into the water.

'We'd better sink the boats,' said Badonovitch.

'I think that might be a good idea.'

The first boat Hunter had shot up had sunk without a trace. The second one was still heading south at a rate of knots and would be out of sight shortly while the third was wallowing close by.

Hunter put the yacht alongside the speedboat and pointed the rifle at the deck. He fired twice. The holes were large enough that the boat would sink in the next thirty minutes or so.

'That'll do. Let's go.'

57

The weather had been kind to them. The increase in the wind and the waves had given them an edge. That plus the sniper's rifle had made all the difference. However, the weather was continuing to deteriorate and in military parlance beginning to blow a hoolie.

'Oh hell,' Hunter yelled. 'Jan, take a look below. How much water are we taking on?'

Badonovitch put his head through the hatch and looked up. 'It's sloshing across the deck.'

'Figures.' He flicked two switches and a couple of bilge pumps started. A quick glance over the sides showed the water spewing clear.

Hunter turned the yacht to starboard so that she was headed directly towards Port Sudan, still 54 miles away on a bearing of 198 degrees. Due to the wind and waves being on their starboard bow Hunter had the sails close-hauled. The bows were oscillating around 220 degrees to make good their designated track over the ground. Their SOA was now a mere 3.5kts and would take them most of the night.

'Jan, I'm going to ditch overboard everything we don't need. You check below to see how much damage has been done.'

He threw the wooden walls they'd built over the side. He put on a lifejacket and harness before rigging safety lines fore and aft. He attached his harness to them. Next he made it for'ard and ditched the anchor.

Badonovitch appeared.

'What's it like?' Hunter yelled out. Speaking in normal tones was becoming more problematic as the wind was now whistling through the rigging.

Badonovitch shrugged. 'The pumps are holding their own. That's about as good as we can hope for.'

'You're right. I'll go and take a look and make some tea.'

'That's something you Brits and us Russians have in common.'

'What's that?'

'The notion that tea solves all problems. Except we make a decent cup while you use teabags.'

Hunter grinned. 'I wouldn't say it solves problems but it does alleviate a good deal of pain and stress. Talking of which, how's your arm?'

'Sore. I just popped a couple of painkillers. That'll do me.'

Hunter knew his friend to be one of the toughest men alive. He wouldn't admit being in pain even if his arm was hanging off. It occurred to Hunter that if Badonovitch hadn't come along he would never have survived. He also knew better than to say thanks. Badonovitch didn't do gratitude very well.

'I've loosened the fridge and two of the cupboards,' said Badonovitch, 'I can pass them up.'

'Okay, let's do it. We'll strip her bare. Maybe we'll get a knot or two more out of her.'

They spent the next half an hour ditching the insides of the yacht until all that was left was the cooker and a gas canister. The tea when Hunter made it was very welcome.

They pitched and rolled all night but gradually they drew closer to the coast with Port Sudan visible directly ahead.

They were wet and cold but it was nothing to what they had been through in past operations nor, more significantly, when they had been training in their respective military specialisations.

Dawn was late. The sky was black with cloud and the rain was belting down. Visibility was a few cables and now, five miles from the harbour entrance a new problem was raising its head. Shipping was beginning to appear all headed in the same direction – Port Sudan.

Large ships were anchored in the roads, waiting for customs approval as well as tugs to help them dock alongside. They also needed the pilots who would navigate the ships into the port. Hunter knew there was an irony when it came to pilots. They navigated the ships yet the master was still responsible for the ship's safety and safe passage. Stories of incompetent pilots and stressed out masters were legion.

The wind was abating and the clouds thinning when the sun appeared on the horizon. They were now four miles away from the entrance and beginning to pick up speed slightly as the wind veered clockwise and began to push from the starboard quarter. The yacht's speed crept up to five knots and they were looking good to reach the harbour entrance when Badonovitch looked astern.

'Derr'mo,' he said in Russian.

Hunter looked over his shoulder. 'Yeah, you're right. We're up to our necks in it.'

The super yacht was about five miles astern and heading down on them at a rate of knots.

'If they don't run us over they'll machine gun us to death,' said Badonovitch phlegmatically.

'Quick Jan, close haul the mainsail while I take care of the jib.'

They took seconds to do both and then Hunter changed course 30 degrees to starboard and headed straight for a large cargo vessel about three cables away.

The super yacht looked to be about ten minutes out while the yacht was four minutes from the hull of the cargo vessel.

Hunter looked back just as a helicopter lifted off the decks of the super yacht, dipped its nose and came straight at them. The helo would be on top of them in less than two minutes.

In fact it took 105 seconds before it was hovering 200 metres away with a side door open and a man with a machine gun sitting in the middle.

'Standby to go over the side, Jan' Hunter yelled. 'Try for under the keel.'

'Roger that, Nick.'

They heard the sound of a machine gun above the sound of the helicopter rotors but as they were about to throw themselves into the water both men hesitated. No bullets were coming their way.

'Look!' Hunter pointed to starboard.

A second helicopter came into sight hovering just off the nose of the first helo. They could see the open door and a man in a flying suit cradling a machine gun shooting into the landing gear of the super yacht's helo. The helo wavered and then the gunner aimed the gun straight into the face of the pilot and pointed at him to leave. The pilot hesitated and the gunner fired three shots into the windscreen alongside the pilot blowing it out.

The yacht's helo dipped away and raced back towards the super yacht. The second helo moved above *The Adventuress* and lowered a double harness lift. Hunter and Badonovitch slipped into it and they were whisked away.

'Who are these guys?' Badonovitch yelled.

'If I didn't know better I'd say Griffiths Offshore. You see the logo on the side? It's been painted over but you can just make it out,' Hunter yelled into Badonovitch's ear.

The helicopter was already moving rapidly towards the shore as they reached the door. Another surprise awaited them.

'Hello sir,' yelled Hunter.

'Nick, Jan, glad to see you both alive,' General Macnair yelled back. 'Enjoy your little escapade?'

'Yes, thanks very much,' Hunter replied, briefly wondering what was going to come next.

Another crewmember slid the door shut and the wind noise immediately dropped to a manageable level.

'Good job,' said Macnair, 'so well done to you both.'

'What are you doing here, sir?' Hunter asked. 'And how did you get hold of the helo?'

'I phoned your father. He fixed it.'

Just then the pilot turned and lifted his thumb, smiling.

'Burg?' Hunter and Badonovitch spoke in unison.

Burghard Schwarzkopf had been with TIFAT at the very beginning. He was a highly talented pilot with a license to fly rotary and fixed wing aircraft. After 12 months he had left the organisation due to family pressure as well as being tempted by a large hike in salary. Hunter wondered how Schwarzkopf had become involved. But then, knowing the General, somehow he wasn't surprised.

The helo flew at max speed and minutes later landed at Port Sudan airport. It touched gently down and the rotors immediately started to wind down. The three men climbed down and waited until Schwarzkopf joined them.

'Let's go,' said the General, handing the machinegun to Badonovitch. 'Thanks Jan.'

'My pleasure sir.'

The three men followed Macnair to a Gulfstream G550 parked to one side of a hangar. The new international airport was already looking slightly bedraggled and at that time in the morning was practically deserted.

They climbed into the plane; Schwarzkopf took the left-hand seat and Hunter the right. Engines were flashed up; they were taxiing in minutes and lifting off in less than ten.

Schwarzkopf ignored the demands by the air traffic control officer not to taxi, not to takeoff and to return immediately. He ignored the orders and shoved the throttle to the stops while aiming for height. Max speed 588mph, range 6,700 miles, distance to Prestwick 3,300 miles as near as dammit. Flying time at 500mph approximately 6hrs 40mins.

'Care to bring me up to speed?' Hunter enquired of Schwarzkopf.

'You'd better ask the General.'

'No. I mean how come you're here?'

'You know how it is, Nick. I thought I was in love. Left you lot and went offshore and was bored out of my skull within six months. I stuck it out but changed jobs from flying Aberdeen to the rigs to flying Port Harcourt to the rigs.'

'A bit of a difference.'

'You can say that again. You know that country is best described with the sentence if God was to give the world an enema it's where he'd shove the tube.'

'Yep. That's how I remember Nigeria.'

'We stuck it for four months . . .'

'Hang on a second. Who's we?'

'Francesca. My wife for all of nine months before she found a capitalist banker to go off with. The divorce papers came through last week. I phoned the General twenty-four hours ago, give or take a couple of hours, and here I am. Back in harness so to speak.'

'That still doesn't explain how you came to be here.'

'That I can't tell you. You'd better ask General Macnair.'

'I think I'd better.' Undoing his seatbelt, Hunter stood up and made his way back into the main cabin. 'You okay, Jan?'

'Yes thanks. I've cleaned the wound, it's only a scratch. A couple of painkillers and I'll get some sleep. You?'

'Fine. The bruise is fading and the scratch is healing. The usual.' Hunter sat next to his boss. 'Care to tell me what's going on, sir?'

Macnair's smile reminded Hunter of a shark. 'Before I start were you two shot?'

'Hardly that. Jan took a round along his arm while I had a round ricocheted into my side and across the top of my arm. Or rather, the other way around. Nothing to write home about.'

'Okay as long as you're sure.'

'I'm sure. So how come you're here in Sudan? What's going on?'

'Chris phoned me that you weren't on the plane. Then he told me Jan was missing as well. I guessed immediately what you were up to. Knowing you like I do I didn't think you'd be happy about letting the prince get away with it. Also Jan wouldn't let you go on your own.' He looked across the aisle and a few rows behind where the Russian was sleeping soundly, smiled and looked back at Hunter. 'He considers himself your guardian angel.'

Hunter looked uncomfortable for a moment before nodding.

'I contacted Hiram who confirmed what I thought and how you planned to get away. Not a bad idea on the whole. As soon as the prince's death was discovered, which was about fifteen minutes after you'd committed the deed, the king literally closed Saudi. Nothing in or out by air, ship or vehicles. Only a totalitarian state like Saudi can do something like that. The international community is screaming blue murder but the Saudis put so many resources into finding out who did it that they very soon knew about the yacht.'

'How did you know?'

'We were listening in on just about every phone call, text and e-mail in and out of Saudi.'

'So then what did you do?'

'Burg tell you about his situation?'

'Yeah. Briefly.'

'He phoned me yesterday. I'd already made up my mind what I was going to do but needed a pilot I could trust one hundred percent and he popped up on the radar, so to speak.'

'Okay sir. But the Griffiths helo?'

'Ah, that was a bit more difficult. I phoned your father and he contacted your cousin Richard. Griffiths Offshore is drilling for oil about eight hundred miles south. He arranged for the helo to be brought to Port Sudan and placed there for our use. It'll be on its way back south already.'

'They covered the company logo.'

Macnair nodded. 'It's better that way. You know the old adage, if you're going to lie make it a good one and don't stop.'

Hunter grinned. It was something the General said regularly. 'Well, thanks, sir. I'm not sure how we'd have managed. It was a close call.'

'You would have managed, of that I have no doubt. Only don't go off radar like that again.' Which was about as close to a rebuke he was ever likely to get from his boss.

Hunter nodded. He didn't mean it and Macnair didn't believe it. And both men knew it.

'Oh, some good news.'

'What's that sir?'

'We've been collating info from as many resources as we have.

ECHELON has been working overtime in Europe and our European partners are delighted with the info we've passed them. It seems the flow of immigrants has eased and there appears to be less trafficking.'

'Seems? Appears? Sounds like political speak.'

'It is. The problem is the bosses of the security services all across Europe aren't allowed to speak to the press. They have to go through their political masters.'

'Sir, mind if I get a coffee? I'm in urgent need of a caffeine fix.'

'No, go ahead. I'll take one as well.'

Hunter busied himself with the coffee machine for a few minutes, checked Badonovitch was still asleep and then rejoined the General.

'Good coffee,' Hunter took an appreciative sip. 'Sorry sir. I'm all ears. You were saying?'

'Illegal immigration is well down, criminals across Europe have been arrested and many people who have been living in slavery have been identified and rescued.'

'What's going to happen to them?'

Macnair sighed. 'I don't know. It's a problem for our political masters who are behaving like rabbits caught in headlights.'

'That's the Europeans,' Hunter said scornfully. 'They haven't a clue what to do about the problem.'

'It's worse than you think. Did you know that Saudi Arabia has offered to build one mosque for every one hundred Muslim immigrants that come to Europe?'

'Where did that come from?'

'That's according to the Lebanese newspaper *Al Diyar*, which is usually a reliable source of information.'

Hunter nodded. It was one of the many rags produced in the Middle East that the analysts of the western security services examined carefully. A nugget here and a nugget there sometimes added up to a rich seam of information.

'And are we going to take them up on their kind offer?'

'Probably. Unless there's enough local resistance to stop it happening.'

'Sir, you know as well as I do that the Saudis will spend millions on mobilising public opinion screaming xenophobia, islamophobia and all the rest of the phobia alphabet soup.'

'We know that. Which is another good reason why being out of the EU makes us safer.'

'I take it you've spoken to Europol?'

Macnair shrugged. 'What can I say? You've read their website. It's all talk and little achievement.'

'But good on paper and good when it comes to sound bites about the cooperation we enjoy thanks to the EU.'

'Such cynicism in one so young, Nick, but true.'

'Not so young, sir but more cynical than ever.'

'We're cooperating as much as ever at operational levels but we're still getting too much political interference. And that's across the board in all countries.'

'What's happened to that shower of swine Lawyers for Justice?'

'Closed down. Isobel has done a very good job blackening the names of every one of them. The last we heard was that they can't get jobs for love or money.'

'Good. I hope they end up begging in the streets.'

'We'll keep the pressure up. Their names are red-flagged. As soon as one appears looking for a reference of any description we'll blacken his or her name totally. It's a side issue but I'll be damned if any one of them gets a job on my watch.'

'Good one sir. Your idea?'

'No. Actually it was Leo's.'

'Good for him. A nice bit of lateral thinking.'

'There's one more job I want you to do.'

'Yes sir?'

'I want you to meet with King Abdullah of Saudi Arabia.'

'Where, when and most importantly, why?'

'London in two days to tell him what happened to his cousin. I want him to get the message very loud and very clear. No diplomatic grovelling speak but clear and harsh.'

514

58

'I'm sure you have a good reason sir, mind sharing it with me?'

'How many princes are there?'

'No idea. A lot. I doubt even the Saudi king knows for sure.'

Macnair nodded. 'You're probably right. Look up the history of the House of Saud and see how many kings and princes have been murdered by their own family since the establishment of the dynasty in 1818. There are 15,000 members of the family but the wealth is in the hands of a mere 2,000. The in-fighting makes the Borgias look like boy scouts and girl guides all rolled into one.'

'So what am I saying to the king?'

'We've put together a complete dossier on everything that's happened. Names, dates and places. Not ours of course, theirs. I want you to give it to the king. I want you to make him understand that he had better use his considerable influence and control over his family to stop what they are doing. No more smuggling people and drugs. No more smuggling weapons, explosives and selling slaves.'

Hunter shook his head. 'It won't happen.'

'Oh it will. It'll last a few months, maybe a year then it'll start all over again and we'll have to go back in and try and stop it. And after we do . . .'

'Round and round in a circle we continue to go.'

'Correct. Probably going faster each time.'

'How so?'

'The enemy will become more sophisticated, better trained, armed and financed. And you know the sad thing about it all Nick?'

'No, sir.'

'We can't stop it.'

'Was that the conclusion you all arrived at when you attended the western powers world terrorism summit meeting in Washington?'

Macnair sighed. 'I'm afraid it was.'

'Hence the news blackout.'

'Not quite that but as near as dammit. We couldn't tell the full story to the public. They'd freak.'

'How have you managed to keep it so quiet?'

'The presentations given by the NSA, CIA, TIFAT, MI6 and about another dozen Security Services bosses frightened the bejesus out of the politicians who were there. It was made clear the dangers we faced if the information about dirty bombs was released. Panic wouldn't be close to what we could face. Anti-Muslim sentiment is running high as it is. Think about what could happen if it was broadcast that jihadists were going to get their hands on weapons of mass destruction and if they did they would use them.'

'A lot of innocent people will be killed, hurt and blamed. Mind if I get another coffee?'

'No. Go ahead.'

'Do you want one?'

'No, thanks. I'm fine.'

While Hunter made himself another coffee Macnair continued.

'It was part of the scenario we went through at the summit. No matter how we tried to spin it, it doesn't look good. There's an inevitability to it that's mind numbingly frightening.'

'And the Saudis are right in the middle of it all.'

'At one level that's correct, I'm afraid to say. Which is why I want you to pass a message personally to the Saudi king in no uncertain terms.'

'His Arab pride may get in the way of his rational thinking.'

'Tough. But it's one of the reasons we are doing it this way. Nice and private, no fanfare and no so-called advisors listening to what you are going to say to him.'

'In other words nobody whispering in his ears about the sacred duty of the faithful to continue holy jihad against the infidels. He's between a rock and a hard place, no matter what he decides.'

'Which is why I want to keep it private. Allow the king time to digest what we have to tell him.'

'And that is?'

'Nick, you must impress on him that underneath the velvet cloves, honeyed words and promises of eternal friendship there beats a heart of solid steel. That he and his kingdom will be wiped off the face of the earth if a dirty bomb does go off anywhere in the world.'

'Is that likely?'

'No. It's an empty threat. It's one of the reasons you are to speak to him alone. We need him to believe it. He isn't the brightest spark in the universe and so getting him to believe the threat may be possible. The advisors he has around him are, on the whole, intransigent bigots who hate the west and believe in an Islam based in the sixth century. The king is more progressive but only if he relies on his own council.'

'They'll eventually get to him. Persuade him that they are right in all that is meaningful in their religion.'

'Inevitably. But it's a delaying tactic while we continue to look for a better and more permanent solution.'

'So where am I going to meet him?'

'It's all in this dossier.' He handed his top officer a buff folder. 'Read it and tell me what you think.'

Hunter opened the folder. It didn't take him long to read through it. He looked up and said, 'You've got to be kidding me.'

'Nope. His entourage takes over the arcade and he does his own shopping for a couple of hours.'

'On his own?'

'Apparently. He does it twice a year.'

'What do other customers think of the arrangement? Also, what do the shop owners think?'

'There are eight shops, boutiques really. Very expensive merchandise for the super rich. I've checked the Internet. The cheapest watch

I could find in the specialist shop was $2,000. Diamond earrings start at about $5,000. The tailor's sell suits at ten grand a pop.'

'Dollars, pounds or euros?'

'Does it matter?'

'I guess not. All top prices?'

'Well over the top. Things nobody needs and don't really want but every item just about costing more than I earn in a month.' He paused. 'It's obscene.'

'I still don't see how he gets the place all to himself.'

'He pays for it. Twenty thousand euros for each boutique whether he buys something or not. He usually does, mind you.'

'Sir, where did all this come from?'

'Pierre Charney told me.'

'Is this general knowledge?'

'No. I suppose it's an indication of their sloppy protection work but each time the king goes to France he has an evening of so-called rest. In fact it's to allow him time for his shopping spree. This will be his sixth visit in three years and the last five times he has done the same thing.'

'There's no guarantee he'll do it this time.'

'True. If he doesn't we'll have to resort to plan B.'

'Which is?'

'I don't know yet. I'm still working on it.'

Hunter nodded as though this was a fair enough answer.

'By the way, Nick, there was an interesting sub-plot at the conference.'

'Oh?'

Macnair nodded and smiled. 'It seems the EU commissioners plus some of the left wing politicians in Europe wants us shut down but wiser heads are prevailing.'

'How?'

'The Americans laid it on the line. We stay operational in Europe or relocate to the USA. Their Secretary of State did the honours with the presentation.'

'Using info supplied by us?'

'In a nutshell. He also pointed out the value of using ECHELON and the idiocy of the Europeans insisting all recorded messages, e-mails etcetera should be automatically wiped away after thirty-six hours.'

'That's the EU Court of Justice ruling.'

'Correct. Our cousins have told the leaders of the free world that they had better shape up and take real responsibility for the protection of its citizens. That includes spending two percent of a country's GDP on defence.'

Hunter nodded. He knew it had been a bone of contention with the Americans for a long time and justified at that. 'What about the EU Court of Justice ruling?'

Macnair chuckled. 'He told them to get it changed.'

'There will have been a lot of people there who won't like that.'

'There were and they screamed blue murder. In private of course. None of them has the guts to stand up and try and argue against what is eminently reasonable.'

'And TIFAT?'

'It was agreed that our best location for operational purposes is Scotland. Interestingly, the Polish Prime Minister said we could relocate to his country if we wished.'

'I bet that went down well.'

'Like a lead balloon. Still, it should mean we'll be left alone to carry on with our job for a while yet.'

'A while?'

'Of course. The inmates are ruling the asylum. The issue will raise its ugly head again.'

Hunter smiled. 'You're right. But that's good news. If you don't mind, sir, I'm going to get my head down.'

'Please do. We've another four hours at least to go.'

They landed at Prestwick Airport, and taxied to an area of the field that was privately owned by TIFAT through a series of shell companies. Customs and immigration were a formality. The General was well known as the boss of TIFAT. Hunter knew that officialdom as applied to their comings and goings were more honoured in the breach than in the observance, quoting Hamlet. They transferred to a helicopter that Schwarzkopf also piloted. They arrived at Rosyth in time for afternoon tea but scrubbed round it and went straight to the bar. Badonovitch opened it and Hunter put the drinks on his tab. The rest of the team appeared shortly after the bar opened. It was a knack almost exclusively known to military personnel. The bar opened and the information spread like wildfire. This was particularly the case if someone else was buying.

They spent three days examining the details of the area and the shopping arcade. Romain Goulart was their liaison though he made it clear there was nobody apart from himself and General Charney who knew about the operation. Secrecy was paramount. There were too many leaks at the DGSE. Goulart had supplied detailed drawings as well as photographs of the boutiques and area.

'Direct action is the best,' said Bletchley. 'We place canisters in all the shops as well as the arcade. Electronic release or timer knocks them all out and we borrow the king for an hour. We explain the facts of life and return him to the arcade.'

The others nodded. Nothing sophisticated so less chance of a cock-up. They all knew not to underestimate sod's law. They had discussed clever and complex ideas, but had found reasons to discard each until they arrived back where they had started.

Both Macnair and General Charney approved the plan. What made it particularly appealing to the DGSE was that the Service de la Protection or SDLP whose task it was to protect foreign dignitaries amongst others would not need to know what was going on. They had never liked the fact that the king went into the arcade with just a couple of bodyguards but they now accepted it as the norm. Charney had told Hunter that the first time they had tried to insist on close quarter protection using the SDLP there was nearly a political rift between the Saudis and the French. In the end the French backed down but only after expressing their displeasure in the most strenuous of terms. Charney had then smiled and said that expressing their displeasure in strenuous terms at diplomatic level was a characteristic of the French that made them world leaders in the art.

Word came through that the king was due to visit the arcade the following evening at 20.00.

'Time to rock 'n' roll,' said Masters.

In the team were Hunter, Bletchley, Masters, and Dunston. Jan Badonovitch was spitting blood at not being there and had protested vehemently that he was fit to go. However, the General made it clear he was to rest until his arm healed properly. The bone in his elbow had been chipped and needed fixing.

Their gear consisted of Glocks with silencers and 12 round flat cylinders about the size and shape of a woman's powder puff. They were small enough to fit into the palm of the hand, were activated when pressed against a solid surface, had instant sticking glue and discharged gas without the hissing noise normally associated with high pressure gas escaping through a valve. The gas knocked someone out in about five seconds and was effective for up to ten maybe 15 minutes. If an oxygen mask was placed over the recipient's face then they would recover in minutes.

Schwarzkopf piloted them in the Gulfstream. They landed at Charles de Gaulle airport where Romain Goulart, second in command at GDSE met them.

They took taxis into the city. They had rooms at the same hotel the king would be using – the luxurious Le Royal Monceau, Raffles Paris.

The king had the whole of the top floor while the team was spread out in different rooms. The arcade they would be visiting was a couple of hundred metres along the prestigious Avenue Hoche.

Hunter and Bletchley met General Pierre Charney and Romain Goulart in Hunter's room. It was large enough to hold a double bed as well as a sitting area with a coffee table plus four armchairs. Hunter ordered coffees from room service.

They spoke in general terms until the coffees arrived and they got down to business.

'It's a delicate situation,' said the head of the DGSE. 'We have massive arms trades with Saudi Arabia, as do the British. We have to tread very carefully.'

'We agree,' said Hunter. 'But we can't just let the Saudis continue what they're doing. We have to make a stand somewhere.'

Charney waved his hand in front of his face, as though swatting a pesky fly, or in this case, a pesky truth. 'Oh, we're agreed on that. Malcolm and I have discussed the situation at length. Did you know he has spoken to Britain's Prime Minister?'

'No I didn't,' replied Hunter. 'That's not the sort of thing he does normally. Speak to our PM that is.'

'Yes, well he also spoke to my President who in turn sent for me to ask me my opinion. Both leaders agree that as long as your true identity is kept hidden from the Saudis then there is nothing to lose.'

'It should be. I'll be the one doing all the talking and will only use Arabic.'

'Are your language skills good enough?' Goulart asked.

'He'll know I'm not a native Arabic speaker but that doesn't matter. I'll let him think I'm an American. After all, the USA and Saudi do hardly any business together especially now that America is self sufficient in energy.'

'I like it,' smiled Charney. 'When in doubt blame the Americans.'

Hunter nodded though it wasn't an attitude he harboured. 'What about his bodyguards?'

'He has three with him at all times. We also supply three close protection officers whenever he leaves his hotel.'

'Are they armed?' Bletchley asked.

'Ah,' said Goulart, 'that's something of an issue. Officially our men are armed, his bodyguards shouldn't be.'

'Shouldn't be?' Hunter queried, sipping his coffee.

Goulart nodded. 'They are armed though they shouldn't be.'

'Why are they carrying then?' Hunter asked.

Charney blew out his cheeks and exhaled slowly. 'Politics. Again. Leave them armed and they're happy. Demand they give up their guns and we could create a diplomatic problem nobody wants. So it's the lesser of two evils.'

'What if one of them shoots the wrong person?' Bletchley asked.

'The Saudis will scream diplomatic immunity and whoever commits the crime will be whisked out of the country.'

'Are they trigger happy?' Bletchley asked.

Charney shook his head. 'We don't know. They've never been tested. From what I know of them they're sloppy and not very professional.'

'That makes them dangerous,' said Hunter, 'as we know all too well. Amateurs panic and are more likely to shoot first and ask questions afterwards.'

'You are right, Commander,' said General Charney, 'which is why you need to be extra careful.'

'We will be,' said Hunter.

59

They arrived at the shopping arcade at 16.45. They came separately to avoid drawing attention to themselves. It was also a busy time of the day and there were plenty of customers to mingle with.

Hunter walked into a boutique selling handbags. Some of them were the price of a car, albeit a small one. The room was about 10 square metres with rows of display cases. If you wanted to touch the merchandise you needed an assistant to open the case and hand over the item. Hunter took his time, surreptitiously checking the layout, looking for exits and other rooms. At the rear of the shop was a toilet for the use of customers. Hunter guessed that if someone was browsing and needed to use the facilities it was better they did so in the shop. A weak or full bladder could easily curtail a person from spending money.

There were four other people in the shop, all women, all idly looking at the bags. Each one had a handbag over her arm, which as far as Hunter was concerned didn't look anything special. What the bags had in common was a name and logo displayed prominently in one of the corners. It was an ostentatious display screaming look how rich I am. As far as Hunter was concerned it was more a display of inadequate people saying look how pathetic I am. Shopping is all I have in the world. From listening to what the women were saying he realised two were Russian and two were Arabic.

He stood at one of the display cabinets and spoke to a sales assistant hovering nearby. He pointed at the item he was interested in and even managed not to wince when she told him the handbag with a famous motif on its side was for sale at 4,500 euros.

While he stood at the counter he slid his left hand underneath the overhang. He pressed his fingers firmly onto the wood and stuck the gas dispenser in place. The timer was already set to operate at 20.30. If the entourage was late then Masters had an override transmitter that added 10 minutes to the timer each time.

He thanked the assistant for showing him the bag, shook his head to indicate no, and left the shop. He crossed the five metre wide passage and entered the watch shop opposite. It sold Rolexes, Cartiers, Emporio Armanis and a dozen other makes most of which Hunter had never heard of. Each watch cost in the thousands. Some were diamond encrusted, pure gold, and had enough features to confuse a space scientist.

He left without buying anything but did deposit his powder puff. He wandered outside and headed back to the hotel. The others arrived over the next fifteen minutes. Each shop as well as the arcade was heavily burglar-alarmed. Luckily no alarm would be set. However, CCTV cameras covered the shops, the arcade and the approaches. Leo had hacked into the system and had already made recordings of the area. At the right time he would superimpose them into the system.

At 19.30 they left the hotel. The evening was warm and muggy with the threat of a thunderstorm in the air. Hunter wasn't sure whether a storm would be good or bad. Good for the operation, bad if the king changed his mind about visiting the arcade.

They strolled along, Hunter with Bletchley, Masters with Dunston. They each wore lightweight jackets underneath which they carried their silenced Glocks. However, it would need an extreme emergency before any of them drew a weapon.

At 18.00 the arcade had been closed. It was still shut with no indication it was going to open again that evening. On the other side of the street were benches and they took two, sitting nonchalantly, talking the kind of inconsequential nonsense people resorted to when it was necessary to fill a silence. In Hunter's and Bletchley's case they talked about Susan and the nuptials she and her mother were planning. Both women were in their element. Hunter joked the event would be bigger than a royal wedding to which Bletchley nodded gloomily.

At 20.00 to the minute a Rolls and a Citroën drew up outside the arcade. At that moment the roller shutters slid upwards and out of sight. Lights were on and the shops and arcade were well lit.

They watched as the king climbed out of his Rolls Royce. Two of his personal bodyguards stood close by looking to helping him rather than looking for trouble. The third bodyguard was also the driver. He exited the car and followed the other three men.

The French close protection officers were of an entirely different calibre. The three men stood at the entrance to the arcade, their heads turning continuously, their eyes not still for a moment. Apparently satisfied they entered the arcade and the roller shutters closed behind them. Hunter phoned Leo who hacked into the CCTV system. The recording had been doctored to reflect the lower lighting as the evening wore on and the storm clouds continued to grow. It was a delicate art that Hunter hoped wouldn't be tested. In spite of their precautions an expert could easily tell that what was being shown wasn't in real time.

At precisely 20.33 Hunter stood up. 'Let's go.'

They walked down a side alley and around to the back. Hunter's picklock gun made short work of the lock. Before pulling open the door all four of them pulled black ski masks over their faces. They then slipped on a gas mask that covered their mouths and noses and turned on the small oxygen canisters they had attached to their belts.

The back door led into a small foyer where a second door led into the arcade proper. It was gratifying to see the bodies lying on the floor, inert but breathing.

A quick search showed that all the men plus the shop staff were unconscious. Because the gas was only good for a short period each person was given an injection in their thigh guaranteed to put them under for at least 30 minutes. While the others administered the drug Hunter placed an oxygen mask over the king's face. After a few minutes the king groaned and moved his head. Hunter tapped the man's face a few times and he groaned louder. Then his eyes opened, he took one look at the black masked face staring down at him and began to shake.

In Arabic Hunter said, 'Take it easy, your majesty. We're not going to hurt you. But we have taken this unusual step to reinforce what I am about to tell you. Do you understand?'

There was no reply.

Hunter tapped the royal face on each cheek and repeated, 'Do you?'

The king nodded his head and croaked, 'Yes.'

Checking a small meter he held in his hand Hunter ensured the gas had dissipated before removing his facemask. He held up a memory stick. 'On here are details about one of your cousins plus senior officers in the Mutaween who are involved with people smuggling into Europe, transporting slaves and drugs as well as armaments and explosives. Your cousin is or was, I should say, Ibn-Mohammed Saud. I killed him. I'm telling you this so that there is no misunderstanding of where you and I stand. The names you find on here are of people in your kingdom as well as Europe. I am giving you a month to purge Saudi Arabia as well as Europe of these people. What you do with them I leave to you. But please be assured we will know whether or not you have carried out my instructions and if you haven't, I will visit you and ensure your reign as monarch will be a short lived one. Do you understand?'

The king nodded, cleared his throat and said, 'Who are you? You speak Arabic but you are not an Arab.'

'Never mind who I am. Just rest assured that I have a very long reach. Our investigations into the activities of Saudis in the trade will continue. I will kill those you don't deal with but like I have already said, your name will appear on my list. You will never know where, when or how but I will ensure your death or you spend your life in seclusion in Saudi Arabia.'

'Are you an American? CIA?'

Hunter shrugged, neither admitting nor denying it. The king could think what he liked. He placed the memory stick in the king's pocket.

'Your majesty, I will treat you with the deference you are entitled to but you must do as I say. Although I am here carrying out the operation the decision to act is taken at the very highest level. Please believe that. Do you understand?'

'Yes,' the king croaked. He cleared his throat and repeated, 'Yes,' this time in a stronger voice.

'The staff and your bodyguards will recover in about twenty or thirty minutes. I suggest when they come to you continue shopping as though nothing has happened but that's up to you. And what you tell the others I also leave to you.'

The team left the building the way they had arrived locking the door behind them. They removed their ski masks before appearing on the pavement outside the arcade and then strolled towards their hotel. Hunter phoned Macnair and brought him up to date on events.

'Bravo Zulu, Nick and tell the others well done. I'll see you back here tomorrow.'

'Yes sir.'

The other three were strung out behind him and they didn't meet up until they arrived separately in Hunter's room. There the whisky, soda, ice and cold beer was already awaiting them.

'Bravo Zulu from the General. Now, who wants what to drink?'

It was whiskies and soda all round. Hunter had barely taken a sip of his when his phone rang. He glanced at the screen.

'Hang on you guys, this doesn't augur well. It's the General. Sir?'

'Ah, Commander, sorry to break up your little celebration but you're needed. Burg is prepping the Gulfstream even as we speak.'

'Where are we going?'

'Cardiff. Six armed men have taken over the National Assembly building for Wales. They've also taken hostage about two dozen people. As far as we can tell the men appear to be Middle Eastern or North African. A spokesman for them speaks heavily accented English.'

'When did this happen?'

'Just after 17.00 today. The Welsh police thought they could deal with it,' Macnair sighed, 'but they couldn't.'

'What happened?'

'The terrorists shot one of the AMs and dropped his body out of a window. From what I can gather the Chief Constable is way out of his depth and finally asked for help. The request passed up the line to us.'

'I have control and authority and it's gloves off?'

'Correct. You know what to do.'

It was Hunter's turn to sigh. 'I guess I do.'

'Incidentally, on a lighter note new figures are coming in with regards to illegal immigrants crossing into Europe. They've dropped significantly.'

'It won't last.'

'We know that. Keep me in the picture.'

'Will do, sir. We'd better get going.'

'Good luck.'